PRAISE FOR
Nightmasters

"Author Loran Holt is sure to wow readers from 16 to 96 with her beautifully written NIGHTMASTERS. Untested mage Kelgan—along with a startling array of unique characters— faces life and death tests in this unparalleled fantasy journey. The author's world-building skills are evident from the get-go. Equally important, Holt's grasp of good versus evil, honor versus dishonor, and the fine line between triumph and tragedy provides the underpinning of her creative efforts. Delighted readers will savor this five star treat!"

—LAURA TAYLOR
6-Time "Romantic Times" Award Winner

NIGHTMASTERS

BOOK ONE ··· DOUBLES TALK

LORAN HOLT

ACORN PUBLISHING

FROM THE TINY ACORN...
GROWS THE MIGHTY OAK

Nightmasters, Book One: Doubles Talk

First Edition
Copyright © 2020 Loran Holt
All rights reserved. No part of this book may be used or reproduced in any manner whatsoever, including Internet usage, without written permission from the author.

Book cover by Damonza.

Book interior design and digital formatting by Debra Cranfield Kennedy.

www.acornpublishingllc.com

ISBN—Hardcover 978-1-947392-96-0
ISBN—Paperback 978-1-947392-89-2
Library of Congress Control Number: 9781947392892

NIGHTMASTERS

BOOK ONE

...

DOUBLES TALK

The Summons (which begins it all)

T he voices came, night after night. *"Too much." "Too little."* *"Too soon." "Too late." "Too few." "Too many."* Then came the laughter, one high and mocking, one low and scornful.

The voices faded with the dawn. An hour of blessed sleep ensued before he rose to begin another round of the day's obligations. This day, unable to keep his eyelids from drooping shut during his late afternoon tutoring session, he cut short a surprised pupil in the middle of an illusion. Muttering a feeble excuse, he hastened back to his room for an illicit nap. The sleepy chirping of birds settling in for the night startled him awake. He realized the lateness of the evening hour. For a moment he hated them, then he felt ashamed. They happily twittered, glad of every day. *So should I be. Am I not doing what I have always wished for?* So, *should* he be, but, of late, was not.

With a groan he rolled over the side of his cot and staggered to the small washstand with its apologetic mirror, Kelgan Defthand, Senior Apprentice Mage. Jokes about "SAMs" abounded among the lower classmen. He surveyed his hollow-eyed reflection with disfavor. It soberly regarded him—a snub nose, a wiry crop of sandy curls, indeterminate hazel eyes. *Not exactly impressive.* Only his lanky height set him apart from the crowd.

Kelgan had shown so much promise at the beginning. A dangerous promise. It had been so easy. As a latecomer to formal training at the Academy, he was already five years past the usual admission age of fourteen. His talent manifested itself during his toddler stage, but the death of his father kept him, the eldest of five, close to home. Only his mother's remarriage had freed him.

His step-father, a miller and a kindly man, had insisted that Kelgan follow his heart and talent. He caught up with ease, quickly outstripping the other apprentices. He sailed through the basics of sorcery, cutting his apprenticeship from ten years to six as he rapidly earned the sobriquet of Defthand. Now he was a senior apprentice, just short months from graduation and only a bit older than his peers. During their recent lesson periods, his master, Sargal Wishworker, had begun to notice Kelgan's slowed reflexes, wandering attention, and lackluster performances at even the simplest spell-casts. Sargal's comments remained neutral, but his curiosity was obvious. The sudden inability of a senior star-pupil invited further scrutiny.

Kelgan acknowledged that his ego swelled with his ability, pride in his accomplishments earning him many a sour and resentful look from his less able fellows. Was that what was behind this? Could a disgruntled junior have concocted an oh-so-clever and spiteful retribution? *No.* This was sorcery far too sophisticated for a mere apprentice, even himself. The voices, more than just disembodied whispers, possessed distinct personalities. One, rash, impulsive and malicious, the other older, patient but infinitely cruel. He didn't doubt that both represented pure evil.

A peremptory knocking at his door brought him back to reality with a start. He strode to the door and threw it open, giving no hint of the unease he felt at the unusual interruption.

"You are summoned to Magister Wishworker's study," announced one of the juniors with a smug smile.

A summons of this sort generally meant a dressing-down, and the junior made no effort to conceal his malice. Concealing his emotions, Kelgan acknowledged the summons with a curt nod, threw his cloak around his shoulders and followed the junior.

He paused to lock his door, remembering a past carelessness. The incident began innocently with a request from another junior.

"Senior Apprentice Defthand, can you help me?"

"Of course, Second Year Apprentice Notready," he had replied, emphasizing the other's title as he stared down his nose at the junior.

"It's the increase spell, s-s-sir," stammered the junior, "I just can't seem to increase anything more than the tiniest bit."

His mind gave an almost physical wince, as he recalled what happened next. The junior showed him the desiccated orange pip he wished to turn into a half-grown tree. Kelgan repeated the words of the basic increase mantra *at least* three times for the seeming dolt of an underclassman, who forgot *at least* three words every time, until at last Kelgan shouted the words himself. To his horror, the single orange pip became a small orchard, knocking the windows out of the dormitory and punching several nice holes in the ceiling.

Peals of laughter accompanied his performance. Three of his fellow year-mates, hidden in the closet, recited an echo spell every time he repeated the increase cantrip, thus tripling the effect of the spell. Pushing the memory from his mind with effort, he resumed his pose of superiority. Deliberately blocking any glimpse of his room from the curious junior, he stepped out and fastened the door behind him.

A blustery wind assailed them as they left the dormitory. The sky appeared leaden and the clouds hung low, obliterating any trace of the Manlost Mountains, which rose in jagged splendor from the Academy's perch in the foothills. Below the school, Kelgan glimpsed his home town of Belleran. Beyond that sprawled the Bellerwald Forest and, almost farther than the eye could see, the autarchy of Bellermond. The Academy, itself, possessed no name. None was needed.

The first fat drops began to splash angrily on the pavement by the time they reached the Sorcerers' lodge. Drawing his own dun-colored cloak more tightly around him, the junior smirked, said, "Here you are," and turned on his heel.

Kelgan swallowed the sudden lump of apprehension in his throat. The inquiry had come even sooner than he expected; before he could prepare a convincing excuse. He was dark-frakking sure no one was going to know about the voices! Not yet, at any rate. Did he hear a faint whisper of scornful laughter? Forcing himself to calm for a second time, he rapped at Sargal's study door. A surprisingly thin voice for one so powerful bade him enter.

Kelgan stepped through the doorway into the low-ceilinged room; then halted abruptly, blinking in surprise. The room contained not only the Master Sorcerer, but a good half-dozen others as well, including two women. *How could so many fit in here?* The room overflowed with the collection of a lifetime of magical research—books on every surface, mysterious vessels of even more mysterious contents, alembics for the distilling of who-knows-what (mostly for show, since Sargon rarely used them for anything but the creation of a rather heady aperitif), and a scattering of various bones. Unused to anyone but himself and Sargal, Kelgan marveled at the throng.

His eyes, of course, went first to the women. One, an obvious aristocrat, was heart-stoppingly lovely. Her pitch-black hair, which seemed to absorb rather than reflect light, swirled in unceasing rhythm around her head as though she remained outside in the storm rather than sheltered within the walls of the study. Her skin appeared to be a uniform ivory—no tinge of rose to either cheeks or lips, and her eyes the same well-deep ebony of her hair. Kelgan felt his chest constrict painfully when he looked at her. Whether attraction or repulsion, he could not say.

Brown was the first impression he received from the other woman, brown hair, eyes, tanned skin, brown riding dress. *Almost certainly a lady's maid,* he dismissed her. A closer look proved her to be attractive in her own way. However, she seemed unaccountably nervous, plucking at the waistband of her skirt.

A man, whose kinship with the black-haired woman could not be gainsaid, either in coloring or in beauty, stood at the fireplace with his back half-turned to the room. The richness of his clothing proclaimed him a person of importance, as did his indifferent stance. The other three men were armed retainers, shocking inside the Academy, where no arms were allowed.

"Come in, come in. Don't stand like a first-year novice," ordered Sargal.

Feeling a fool, and at a disadvantage before the women, Kelgan did as instructed.

Sargal announced, "I have a commission for you, my son."

Feeling more foolish than ever; Kelgan just gaped. This was so far from the reprimand he had anticipated, he could find nothing intelligent to say.

Sargal ignored his seeming idiocy and hurried on. "My Lord, may I present Under-Mage Kelgan Defthand the most advanced, as well as most able, of the Academy's pupils." Kelgan noted that Sargal took care not to call him a Senior Apprentice. "Kelgan, this is Lord Nevander di Nerrill, of Nerrill's Keep."

As he bowed, Kelgan eyed the young lord with curiosity. Everyone had heard of the di Nerrills, although few had actually encountered them. A group of armed men, sometimes, in the town, an occasional coach and entourage—that was all anyone saw or knew. Rumors were plentiful, but how close they came to truth was anybody's guess.

"Lord di Nerrill has need of a wizard to perform rather simple, routine, spells for him," Sargal added, "and I thought a change of scene would do you some good."

So! What Sargal didn't say was obvious. This was a rebuke, and Kelgan would be expected to return with a better attitude or else!

Kelgan bowed again.

"I shall do my best to please Lord di Nerrill, Magister," he said through gritted teeth. He felt the sting of Sargal's emphasis on "simple" and "routine." This "commission" was merely a ruse in lieu of an outright dressing-down, and Kelgan felt his face burn in shame.

Lord di Nerrill, who continued to gaze into the fire, ignored the introduction. He whirled at Kelgan's words and fixed him with an unblinking stare. Kelgan winced at the appearance of hostility patent in the gaze.

"I should think you would, Under-Mage." The Lord bared his teeth in a wolfish smile, as though the words were but a jest.

In spite of Lord di Nerrill's almost unearthly beauty, Kelgan felt it must overlay something far darker, and harder, than could be perceived by the non-magical. Did Sargal not feel it as well? The Magister was old, but his behavior had never given Kelgan the slightest hint of the encroaching feebleness of age. Despite his voice,

Sargal exuded power. Kelgan always felt Sargal could read his soul with one sharp glance. Why then did he seem oblivious to the menace radiating from Lord di Nerrill, but so apparent to Kelgan? A second's reflection told him Sargal was just as aware, else there would be no oddness in the Master's behavior. Kelgan felt the jaws of a large trap close around him—he was being cast into the hands of a Black Warlock!

Shaking his head at this ridiculous idea—of course Sargal would never consider such an action—he gathered himself and attempted to at least look like a competent Under-Mage.

He had just glanced at Sargal with unease when, in a bewildering about face, Lord di Nerrill suddenly exuded charm and charisma. "Forgive my ill-humor, Under-Mage," he cried, "it has been a long ride through beastly weather, and I have let it upset me. There is no reason you should be included in my bad mood." He smiled gaily and waved his hand at the two women. "Let me present you properly to my sister, Neroma, and her companion, Terencia."

Kelgan bowed yet a third time, in the direction of the women. The companion, Terencia, dropped a hasty curtsy, while Neroma di Nerrill merely stared. The agitation of her hair increased, but she made no other acknowledgment.

"My sister is badly affected by inclement weather," commented Lord di Nerrill, by way of explanation.

Kelgan, who suspected consciousness of superior position, rather than response to the weather, at the heart of Neroma's seeming rudeness, muttered something noncommittal. Clearing his throat, he ventured to question Lord di Nerrill, "Can you tell me something of my duties, milord?"

"Duties!" cried Lord di Nerrill, "nay, nay! Rather foolish trifles, insignificant bagatelles, for one so talented." His sidelong glance at Kelgan combined malice with derision, thus turning his ostensible praise into insult. "Once you are settled comfortably at my estate, then it will be time to speak of your 'duties.'"

Kelgan turned once again to Magister Sargal with a look of inquiry. "You will be a guest in Lord di Nerrill's household as long as he has need of you," affirmed Sargal.

Was it only imagination, Kelgan thought, or did Sargal's voice stumble over the word guest? The commission would have been an unwelcome one, no matter who the commissioner, but coming from Lord di Nerrill it was doubly so. Kelgan would not have wished to leave the familiarity of the Academy until he had solved the problem of the whispers. To follow Nevander di Nerrill, whom Kelgan could not help comparing to an unusually beautiful spider, into his web made his stomach churn.

"When do you have need of me, milord," he asked.

"Lord di Nerrill plans to return with you tonight."

There! No mistaking the quaver in the elder Mage's thin voice that time.

How could this be? Sargal's mastery of power always seemed virtually unlimited, his wisdom profound. What threat could turn him from a sorcerer of unparalleled confidence to a trembling old man?

Nevander di Nerrill shrewdly eyed Kelgan. "Can you be ready within the hour?"

Kelgan swallowed a denial and whispered, "Yes, milord."

"We will meet again here, then, in one hour," Nevander's voice rose on an inquiring note, once more as though he easily read Kelgan's reluctance and urge to flee.

Kelgan merely said, "At your pleasure, milord," and turned on his heel.

Once through the door and back in the hall, Kelgan felt the sweat break out on his forehead and also trickle down his armpits. That there was more to this commission than the "mere bagatelles" Lord di Nerrill had so dismissively cited, he had no doubt. A "mere" that could shake even Sargal's poise was not a "mere" Kelgan wished to have revealed to him. What use could there be for an Under-Mage? Moreover, why an Under-Mage in the first place?

Back in his room, Kelgan packed swiftly. He had few enough belongings, anyway. His kit of herbs and philtres always stood ready at hand. He smiled as he tucked the kit in his pack. Laypeople always expected a Mage to use magic powders or charms to cast a spell, when every sorcerer knew magic sprang directly from the mind. The kit proved useful for parlor tricks, however, and the herbs for healing simple ailments where magic would have been intrusive.

Glancing around the room, a tingle of panic assailed him. Bare though it was, it now took on the aspect of a refuge, familiar as a glove, and as snugly fitted to his personality. Shaking his head to dispel such thoughts, he swung his gray cloak around him, shouldered his pack and left the room. He had a moment of sour amusement as he left the door standing wide. They wanted to know what lay within—well so be it. Grimacing, he strode across the courtyard once more through the now driving rain.

··· 2 ···

Another World (where they eat better)

Lord di Nerrill and his small entourage plodded almost silently through the dark. The horses' hooves were muffled by the mud of the roadway, and no one seemed to feel either the need or the energy to speak. They had passed quickly through the town and plunged deep into the forest. The only light came from a shaded lantern carried by one of di Nerrill's men-of-arms, who led the procession.

To Kelgan's surprise, the women rode pillion behind the other two men-at-arms; the fourth horse was waiting for him, leaving no doubt that his submission to their "request" was expected. An inexperienced rider, he had assumed (or hoped for) a coach at least, especially if Lord di Nerrill's assertion were true—that his sister fared badly in storms. Certainly, she seemed no worse off than he, himself, wet to the skin and barely able to keep his teeth from chattering. Her uncovered hair, which by all rights should have been plastered to her skull, still moved in that unearthly rhythm, apparently lifted by a Zephyr particular to herself. No stranger to peculiarity, still he found that pulsing dance unsettling.

He found Neroma di Nerrill unsettling, as well. She had uttered not a word even to her companion, Terencia, as they prepared to depart, yet she and her brother seemed in constant communication. Now and again she would turn her great eyes on Kelgan as though she would impart some dire knowledge, but not a sound escaped her.

In the odd haste of their departure, she had stood still and aloof, watching the preparations closely, but taking no part in them. When all was ready, she mounted without assistance and with no offer of any, Kelgan noted. Then they were away into the night, beginning their miserable trek to Nerrill's Keep.

Kelgan lost track of the passage of time. It could have been days since they'd quitted the Academy. On and on, chilled by more than the rain, Kelgan's head began to nod. He was recalled quickly to himself by a familiar voice, which whispered in his ear. *"Too, too much!" "Too, too many."*

The tone sounded petulant, no laughter this time. He gave a great start, eyes wild, convulsively grasping the reins to keep from pitching headlong. Nevander di Nerrill dropped back to his side to inquire in a low voice, but with that tinge of derisiveness that was starting to rasp Kelgan's nerves, "Are you all right? Not much farther now."

"Sorry, milord, just a little drowsy," he replied.

"What an amazing fellow you are," taunted di Nerrill, "able to sleep through anything, I warrant." He spoke still in the same low voice, but the derisiveness increased.

He grasped the reins again, this time to avoid aiming a punch at his Lordship's nose. "I guess so," he agreed, outwardly mild.

Di Nerrill gave a small snort of amusement and regained his place behind the lantern-holder.

They seemed to be nearing the Keep. The horses had begun to pick up the pace without prodding, perhaps in anticipation of oats and a warm, dry stall. He envied them. A warm dry stall would have been just fine with him—he would even settle for oats—a cold, stone Keep, the last place he wanted to be. Dimly yet, some wavering lights could be seen, punctuating the otherwise blank page of night with bright periods.

At least the infernal rain will be off my head, he growled to himself.

The word "infernal" caused a crawling sensation at the base of his neck. Infernal! Like the whispers? Were those demons besetting him; creatures from an unimaginable dimension of evil? Is that why they only came at night, the hours when evil could easily broach the barriers which sunlight erected?

Shrugging his shoulders, he murmured "Superstitious rot" and forced a humorless laugh at his own folly. *So easily does one become a craven.*

"Something amuses you, Mage?" inquired Lord di Nerrill.

"No, no, milord. I was just hoping to get out of this pea soup, and obtain some real pea soup," Kelgan temporized.

Lord di Nerrill gave another snort at this feeble jest, and spurred his horse. The others followed suit. They racketed downhill, making what Kelgan thought an unwarranted amount of noise after the claustrophobic silence of the forest journey.

Either the watchers on the walls had remarkably keen eyesight, or some mysterious signal had alerted them to the source of the racket, because the drawbridge rattled down at the same instant as the portcullis rose. The small band galloped through as though the devil chased them, followed, to Kelgan's baffled amazement, by four stout bearers carrying a recently slain boar.

More like the devils ride with us. Keeping his seat with difficulty, he felt bruised by that final explosive rush.

What was that in aid of? Kelgan wondered. The sudden inexplicable rush, after the plodding silence of the journey, not to mention the almost ludicrous appearance of the hunters, further jangled his already uneasy state. The clang of the portcullis behind him made him feel cut off from the world, and simply added an exclamation point to his gathering anxiety.

He felt Neroma di Nerrill's great eyes on him again before she slid, unaided as before, from the back of the horse.

"Come, Mage," urged Lord di Nerrill, "quickly to my study."

He noticed that somewhere during the trip he had been promoted. Lord di Nerrill seemed to have dispensed with the "under" portion of Kelgan's title. He followed the Lord into the Keep.

Astonished, he stared upwards. Rather than the gloomy dungeon of his imagination, the great hall was gay with fluttering pennons, like colorful butterflies darting near the ceiling, and well-lit with torches. Heavy tapestries covered the walls and a fire roared (the only word for it) in a fireplace taller than a man.

Lord di Nerrill glanced around impatiently. "You can gawk later, Mage."

Stung by the implication that he was an unsophisticated bumpkin, Kelgan hastened after his host.

Di Nerrill's study was another surprise. By some miracle of hydraulics, a fountain played chattily in the center of the room. A small brook cut a swath from the fountain, flowed to an opening in one wall, and plunged in a miniature waterfall to the moat below. Torches again filled the room with their yellow glow, and small strategically placed braziers warded off the chill emanating from the damp stone walls. No tapestries here to hide a man, but high-backed, bonneted chairs with soft cushions foiled the best efforts of the drafts.

"Come, let me show you my waterworks." Lord di Nerrill's voice rang unnaturally loud and false to Kelgan's ears, and His Lordship's smile more resembled the baring of a predator's teeth.

Does he never perform a natural action? Is he always a strutting player even in his nightrobe? Aloud, he said, "It is a most charming and clever toy, milord, and soothing to the ear." To himself he added, *and could be constructed by a first-year apprentice.*

"Approach the water closely, Mage, you will find it delightfully scented."

Kelgan did as he was bade, standing at the very rim of the fountain. "Indeed, milord, it is a most delicate and refreshing scent."

What nonsense is this? Why are we babbling as inanely as the brook? Scented fountains were not exactly a novelty. The fashion of the moment, they were toys for most of the aristocracy. *Am I supposed to applaud? Gush like the fountain? Does he think I'm such a country dolt, that I would be impressed?* Resentment caused him to silently grind his teeth.

His host stood shoulder to shoulder with him and gazed into the water for some moments without speaking. Then he turned toward him with a face as unlike that which Kelgan had come to expect as Kelgan's from Sargal. "Now, *now,*" he repeated, "we cannot be overheard—either physically or *psychically.*"

"What?" exclaimed Kelgan.

"It was necessary to get you here on a foolish pretext," asserted Lord di Nerrill. "Now I am going to tell you a story, and I will apprise you of your *real* duties." The predator rictus returned briefly to his face and then was wiped away.

"What did you mean when you said we could not be overheard psychically?" Kelgan inquired. "Is the room warded?"

He was already familiar with the use of water to blot out voices, although he had not seen it used in such a spectacular manner. However, he had felt no warning tingle, which usually alerted him to the presence of another's magic. He had, however, attempted a few abortive experiments of his own with various wardings not in the book, many of which eluded him entirely. Nonetheless, he refused to admit that to His Lordship.

"As you must know, the delightful scent serves another purpose than delectation," replied di Nerrill. "It is, itself, the ward."

Kelgan's eyebrows shot upwards—a ward of scent! Sargal had spoken contemptuously of such-like, and was scornful of all physical aids. His own failed experiments prompted him to assume Sargal's scorn, which, in turn, influenced his own attitude toward herbs and philtres.

"But those are not *real* magic," he burst out.

Lord di Nerrill's eyebrows now imitated Kelgan's, although he displayed the first real amusement of their acquaintance. Yet again, he seemed to pick Kelgan's thoughts from his brain. "You are thinking of potions and unguents, my friend. Are you not? This, ah, effect is somewhat different. But now to my story."

··· 3 ···

Other Voices (other ears)

"Several months ago," related the Lord of Nerrill's Keep, "I began to have what I thought at first were dreams. It seemed that voices were whispering to me in my sleep. They asked meaningless questions." Breaking off, he noticed Kelgan's wild stare and ashen visage. "What...?"

"Milord, was one voice high and petulant, the other low and self-confident?"

"Yes, that is exactly how they seemed," affirmed Lord Nerrill, a knowing smile creeping across his face.

"Milord, I, too, have heard these whisperers, heard them till I fear to close my eyes lest they assail me. Mine ask no questions, however, only taunt me with statements I don't understand," Kelgan exclaimed excitedly.

After he blurted out this admission, Kelgan silently berated himself. *Curse me for a fool! I really am a bumpkin. Has he bewitched my brains? Why tell him anything until I have heard all?*

All his earlier suspicions came flooding back. Was this some ruse to gain his confidence? To what end? If di Nerrill was responsible for the voices, this elaborate hoax was totally superfluous. He already had Kelgan where he wanted him. Wanted him for what? Why? Kelgan was nobody, a clever Under-Mage, still some months from graduation. Talented, yes, he could say that, but lacking either experience or maturity. Try as he might, Kelgan could understand none of it.

As Kelgan fumed inwardly, Lord Nerrill continued to stare at him with a quizzical expression. "Please call me Nevander," he said, was his anticlimactic comment.

Kelgan began to laugh at the utter absurdity of this bland request, soon whooping helplessly in nervous reaction. Di Nerrill clapped him several times on the back with more than just friendly force as Kelgan struggled for control.

"I'm s-s-sorry, milord, uh, Nevander," he gasped. "You caught me off guard."

"Do you not appreciate the seriousness of my tale, Mage?" Di Nerrill spoke with hauteur, but a slight smile quirked the corners of his mouth.

Kelgan sobered quickly. "I haven't heard much of it yet, mil—Nevander. But, yes, if *anyone* can, I do appreciate the seriousness."

"Let me continue." Nevander's brow veed with concentration as he resumed his narrative. "At first, I disregarded the voices, attributing them to the Lord of Night-mare. However, they grew ever more insistent, till finally they intruded on my waking hours."

Kelgan started. "They come in the daylight?" The idea filled him with dread.

"No, never till the sun has flown and the night has closed in. But come with darkness, they do. Nevertheless, the continual anticipation of their presence fast began to affect my every action, were it day or night."

"You said they asked meaningless questions. In what way were they so?"

"Ah," replied Nevander, "I should better have said the questions held no meaning for me. They asked me *'When, Nevander?' 'Why, Nevander?' 'How soon, Nevander?'* How could I understand such questions? I only know that, as the months went by, I began to feel a sense of some impending catastrophe. That is when I felt I must turn to the Academy."

Kelgan felt a faint prick of his earlier suspicion.

Seeing his face darken, Nevander demanded, "Out with it."

"You do not need us. Either you, yourself, are a sorcerer, or you have one already in your employ," stated Kelgan, while thinking, *one of the Black persuasion, it's obvious.*

"Oh." Nevander's eyebrows rose. "And why say you that?"

"The scent warding is enough to tell me," replied Kelgan in the same flat tone.

"Hmmm, well, I'll admit to knowing a few simple spells, but nothing of consequence," demurred Nevander.

"Simple!" Kelgan took a step back in amazement.

"Surely, this is but a first-level exercise for you Academicians," retorted Nevander in patent disbelief.

Kelgan hesitated. Should he dissemble? Should he admit ignorance to one whom he did not trust? He had already betrayed himself with regard to the voices. Again, he reminded himself that it mattered little; Nevander di Nerrill had had the advantage of him from the start.

Deciding to be candid, he confessed, "The psychic scent warding is not within my repertoire, milord."

Di Nerrill looked both astonished and suspicious. "I have stated my preference for my first name," he reminded Kelgan.

"Sorry, Nevander," Kelgan sighed, "but until a few short years ago I was just the stepson of a miller. I haven't rubbed elbows with too many lords."

Nevander acknowledged, "We will indeed be 'rubbing elbows' for some time, I imagine. But, tell me, is this the whole truth when you disclaim knowledge of the scent ward?"

Even though he did not fully trust di Nerrill, Kelgan felt hurt when his own word was doubted. "I would have no reason to lie in this regard mi... Nevander. Why would I want to appear less competent than I am?"

"You didn't ask for this commission, and you do not trust me even now. Perhaps you hope to be sent home in disgrace," replied di Nerrill.

Kelgan ruefully acknowledged the justice of di Nerrill's accusation. "You're right, I didn't want the commission. Besides, you've given me no reason to trust you."

"How have I given you cause to distrust me?" di Nerrill inquired frostily.

Answers crowded to Kelgan's tongue—all sounding equally

feeble. Finally, Kelgan chose the simplest, "I don't know you."

Di Nerrill threw his hands in the air in a gesture of frustration. "And so, because you do not know me, I automatically become your enemy?"

Kelgan's frustration was equal. "No, no, not my enemy, just not my friend."

Di Nerrill smiled with genuine warmth. "You have the right of it, my reluctant Mage. But, please, afford me the benefit of the doubt, especially since we seem to be in the same boat. I will tender you the same."

"So," he continued, "you are nearly a full-fledged sorcerer but the scent ward is unknown to you. This is not a pleasant surprise, Under-Mage."

Kelgan took notice of the fact that he had been demoted again.

"Nor to me, Nevander," Kelgan stated. "I did not understand why you wanted an Under-Mage in the first place. Is it possible you thought us more powerful than we are?"

"More powerful than I, certainly," affirmed di Nerrill, his dismay evident.

At that moment, the study door opened. Framed in the doorway stood Neroma di Nerrill, haloed by the hall light. She posed there for some seconds before stepping into the room.

Kelgan was positive the dramatic effect was well-calculated in advance. *Another play-actor*, he thought with annoyance, *more studied even than her brother.*

"Nevander...," she began.

For the first time Kelgan heard her voice—if velvet could speak, it would have that exact sound—low, husky, somehow furred. Di Nerrill beckoned her to the fountain.

Once more Kelgan was subjected to the plaintive scrutiny of Neroma's eyes. *What does she want of me? Why do I feel she implores, although she has asked nothing?*

Her hair, in its blind search, brushed across his face. Another *frisson* chilled him, the same mixture of attraction and repulsion sweeping over him.

"Nevander," she began again, "you have stayed here too long. You must come down."

"I have not yet made the situation clear to the Mage," replied di Nerrill.

"It will become clear," she retorted. "You *must* come down."

Di Nerrill sighed, "My sister is correct, Mage, the flower of suspicion grows quickly in such a fertile pot. We must go down to the hall. You need sustenance, anyway, some of that pea soup perhaps?"

Kelgan smiled weakly and followed them out the door.

Once more in the gaily decorated hall, Kelgan couldn't decide if he felt relief or discomfort. There was a respectable number of people milling there, which was unexpected. Somehow because of their rare appearances (or more accurately nonappearances) in the town, Kelgan had seen Nevander and Neroma di Nerrill as melancholy hermits, not ordinary nobles with active social lives. Although their extraordinary looks certainly set them apart from the run-of-the-mill.

Nevander di Nerrill greeted a few bystanders and introduced Kelgan. "General Cordain, meet our latest entertainer, fresh from the court of Aldera." Di Nerrill's firm grip on Kelgan's arm warned him to silence.

"What does he do?" General Cordain favored Kelgan with a somewhat unfriendly glance.

"Sleight-of-hand and spectacular effects," replied di Nerrill gaily.

Cordain's expression became even less friendly. "A Magician!"

"An entertainer, General, here to give us pleasure. But first a late repast, then just one or two illusions before we retire."

Kelgan groaned silently. Parlor tricks!

"Say nothing," whispered di Nerrill, under the guise of passing Kelgan a glass of wine.

Kelgan attempted to assess the situation. It seemed that no one trusted anyone else. Kelgan did not trust di Nerrill, at least as yet. Di Nerrill obviously found his own court untrustworthy. They just as obviously regarded his Lordship with suspicion, since di Nerrill deemed it necessary to conceal Kelgan's true identity.

Kelgan gave up the effort; he simply possessed too little information. The only fact he could be certain of was that *he* heard the voices. He could not even be sure that di Nerrill did. He was sure di Nerrill needed him for some purpose as yet unrevealed; less certain was whether that purpose would be in Kelgan's own best interest. The food was good, however; so was the wine. For the moment, Kelgan allowed himself a bit of relaxation. Then he caught Neroma's gaze and his muscles tightened.

He saw that the assembled throng gave her a wide berth. To a man, or woman, they turned nervously aside as she floated among them—a raven at a gathering of macaws. She, in turn, either did not notice or did not care.

As she captured his eye, her head made the slightest of nods, and for a moment, the ebony tendrils of her hair seemed to reach toward him. *No rest for the weary,* he thought. Kelgan pushed his plate away and gained Neroma's side.

"Time," was her only comment. Kelgan grimaced and prepared to make a fool of himself.

Di Nerrill was already drawing the attention of the assembly. "My friends, a rare treat—a master of sleight-of-hand has agreed to perform for us."

The almost imperceptible emphasis on 'friends' did not escape Kelgan. Eyes turned his way and a curious murmur ran around the room.

These people must be starved for diversion, if I'm considered a 'rare treat.' He suspected his host's self-deprecated talents were not common knowledge to the group present.

He moved to the dais, where all could see him clearly. Quickly he ran through a few simple exercises of prestidigitation, which drew a few chuckles from the crowd. He produced an egg from one lady's elaborate hairdo, caused coins to appear and disappear, and other small feats. When he saw that his audience grew restless, he proceeded to one or two more complex illusions, aided by just a touch of real power. As he did so, he felt the unmistakable warning tingle which announced the presence of another's magic. At the same time, he felt a light touch as though someone unseen had brushed by him. For a moment his control faltered and the illusion threatened to collapse. Regaining control, he quickly brought the performance to an end. Scattered applause and a few mutters of disappointment rewarded him, but most were already turning away.

Kelgan's shirt, scarcely dry from the long, wet ride, clung damply to him again—this time from nervous perspiration. There was another trained sorcerer here beside himself (and possibly) Nevander. Not only was there an unknown Mage present, the unknown was well aware of Kelgan. That light touch had been a probe. How much had been learned was impossible to ascertain. His concentration had been focused on his silly illusion, and he had had no reason to think he should keep his guard up. *Why did I not think so, more and more I am a fool. I should wish to shield myself from Nevander, if no one else— certainly until I learn more. How is it I have become so careless?*

On and on he berated himself as the assembly dispersed. What time was it? Kelgan felt as weary as an old man. It must be well into the early morning hours; sleep seemed weeks ago.

"Now for bed," said Nevander at his ear. "I will show you the way myself."

Kelgan thankfully followed di Nerrill up the stairs to the bedchambers. When he had been shown to his room, he threw himself on the bed fully dressed and sank instantly into slumber.

"Too good." "Too bad." "Too smart." "Too stupid." Obscene giggles with each comment.

Kelgan sat up with a gasp, his heart pounding. Light seeped through the cracks in the shutters. He had no idea of the time, but there was stirring in the courtyard, and raised voices floated up to him. Feeling heavy-eyed and fuzzy-headed, he rolled out of the bed.

A basin of water had appeared on a chest near the bed. A suit of clothes in brilliant colors, utterly unlike the gray of his robes, was thrown over a chair with a note attached. "Try these," the note suggested tersely.

Kelgan had heard no one enter, but since he had not bothered to bar the door, anyone could have, and presumably had, come in. Because it had been so late, or rather so early, he corrected himself, the voices had not had their usual shot at disturbing his sleep.

Too close to dawn, then with a chill—*but if it was not they that woke me?* He reassured himself, *it must have been a servant with the basin and clothes.*

He washed as best he could, and donned the new outfit. The shirtsleeves were a bit too short, the hose a bit too long, the tunic a bit too tight, but all in all not a bad fit. Since Kelgan stood a good four inches over six feet, and his host a good five inches under, he knew the clothes were not from Nevander's personal wardrobe.

Whose, then?

Pirouetting in front of a small mirror he laughed at the vivid colors. The tunic was a rich russet with a curious design in turquoise and gold worked on the front, the shirt a lighter shade of the same turquoise and the hose striped turquoise and russet. He glanced at his discarded clothing and laughed again. The contrast appeared almost ludicrous.

"So I am to join the ravens, as a stork in borrowed plumage," he muttered. Sobering quickly, he pondered the motive behind the gift. Camouflage? Protective coloration?

He cast his mind back to the events of the previous day and their many contradictions, especially the oddness of their return to the Keep and what followed. He would have sworn di Nerrill wanted to keep his visit to the Academy a secret, yet they had entered the Keep in a thunderous rush, which should have alerted the curious for miles around.

Moreover, although he and di Nerrill had been, at most, half an hour closeted in Nevander's den, Neroma had deemed it too long, asserting that his host would be "missed." If he hadn't been missed during the nearly twenty-four previous hours of his absence, why would half an hour make a difference? Why was it necessary to keep Kelgan's identity hidden?

Kelgan felt as though he had entered a play to which he had not received a script. What was his role, what were his lines? And what role would his Lordship play today? The haughty noble? The earnest confider? The concerned brother? Faugh! Kelgan wished himself back in his cramped cell at the Academy. Together, he and Sargal could have puzzled out the solution to the whisperers.

The unpleasant recollection of Sargal's quavering voice and indecisive manner returned to him; perhaps it would not have been quite that simple. Unease settled around his shoulders like his own gray cloak; it felt equally familiar. Scrubbing at the nape of his neck with his hand, he stepped into the corridor.

His hair rose. Neroma stood silently outside the door. Her unexpected appearance made his heart thud. *Darkness to my nerves! I'm starting to jump at shadows. Almost literally,* he observed, *I know no better shadow, dark and silent as she is.*

Neroma took him in with what seemed to be her usual wordless fashion. Her eyes flickered momentarily in an expression he could not read, but somehow he sensed she was entertained at his expense.

She turned and walked away; then glanced backward at him, surprised that he did not follow. He hastened awkwardly after her.

She expects me to perceive her thoughts, he realized with astonishment, *and I can't. But Nevander can,* his thoughts ran on, *that's obvious from the way they react to one another. That's why she so seldom speaks, she has no need with him. I must mystify her by my lack of response; I imagine she thinks everyone with talent communicates mind-to-mind just as she and her brother.*

He pondered this interesting revelation as she led him back to Nevander's study. Mindseers were rare. The Academy had one or two a generation; moreover, that was their only talent. If Nevander di Nerrill was adept at other magic... discomfited, Kelgan sought to banish the return of his becoming-too-familiar unease. No, surely the scent ward must be inferior magic, similar to the granny spells which 'everyone knew' were all the magic women had; for that reason, women were not admitted to the Academy, since 'everyone knew' they could not be trained. Feeling more confident, Kelgan squared his shoulders and loped after Neroma. Neroma, in turn, continued to glance back at him with a somewhat frustrated expression.

"Good morrow, my Mage," di Nerrill greeted, bursting with good spirits.

Kelgan eyed him with a slight scowl. His thorough wetting of the night before, not to mention the lack of sleep, would bring on a cold; he felt sure of it. Nevander needn't be so confoundedly cheerful.

"Feeling a bit under it this morning?" inquired di Nerrill, "a good breakfast by the fountain will set you to rights." Nevander waved his hand at a small table drawn close to the plashing waters. "Sit, sit," he commanded, suiting his action to the words.

Kelgan sat. A steaming cup of something that smelled inviting, but totally unfamiliar, was placed in front of him. He looked up; Terencia, Neroma's companion of the night before, stared back, unsmiling. She added a dish of several appetizing fruits and some warm bread to the table. Making a peculiar moue, she turned away.

Tired of trying to puzzle out the meaning behind the odd behavior of everyone at the Keep, Kelgan began to eat without comment, the food good. The tisane, or whatever was in the cup, must have contained a mild stimulant, because he felt his fatigue wash away, along with the feeling of cotton wool in his head.

"To continue my story," said di Nerrill as he broke the silence as though there had been no interruption. "I was saying that, as the months went on, I felt a sense of impending catastrophe. What I did not say is that it has already begun."

Kelgan's mouth dried instantly. Unable to swallow the morsel of bread he chewed, he spat it out onto the plate. "Already begun," he whispered.

Nevander's face was suddenly old, "Our world is vanishing, little by little," he announced.

Kelgan gaped in incredulity. Certain now that his host was insane, he debated whether to run out the door, jump out the window into the moat, or simply scream for help.

"You *must* listen," Neroma's furred alto sounded by his ear.

Kelgan leapt, wall-eyed, like a gaffed pike. He had not heard, nor even sensed, her approach.

For a moment a twinkle gleamed in Nevander's eye. Fully aware of the effect his words had made, even in this dire circumstance he could not restrain his flair for drama. The gleam vanished; the old sickly look returned.

"You think me mad," he affirmed. "You, who hear even as I."

Kelgan had the grace to blush.

"The voices we share, I admit. Nevertheless, the world is still here, as far as I can tell."

"When the time is right," Nevander stated soberly, "we will undertake a journey to prove the truth of my words."

··· 4 ···

Come and Gone

Kelgan's mind whirled in confusion. The world vanishing! What world? From the Academy's aerie, he could see nearly to the autarchy of Finermond on one side and that of Lower Bellermond on the other. The heavy hand of the Autarch, Orengnor the Angry, still lay over his village, just as it had as long as he could remember.

From what the itinerant tinkers said, the same held true for the rest of Bellermond, not to mention those towns and hamlets claimed by Autarch Hieronymous the Hearty. Hieronymous was widely supposed to be hearty for food, drink, and pretty, young—very young—boys, according to the tinker tales. Known as the 'belly-cozy' ruler of Finermond, the pun on bellicose never failed to elicit chuckles from the tinkers whenever the corpulent Autarch's name arose.

All the world he knew was still there and operating normally, as far as he could tell.

Nevander's eyes expressed contempt. He seemed to read Kelgan's mind, or at least his face. "This is not the world, Under-Mage."

Again, the presumption that he was a bumpkin. Of course, this wasn't the whole world. He knew that! There was lots more world he had never seen—consciousness of his ignorance brought a rush of crimson to Kelgan's cheeks. He had never been farther from his village than the Academy; he hadn't even been to Finermond. And, he had never even seen either Orengnor or Hieronymous for himself.

Tinker-tales were all he had to go on, all he knew of what lay beyond.

The world could disappear right up to my bedroom, he thought peevishly, *and I probably wouldn't even know it was gone.*

Aloud he inquired crossly, "How do you know it's gone? And what am *I* supposed to do about that? I'm not even a graduate."

Nevander gravely regarded him.

"You are something of a disappointment," he acknowledged.

As usual, when criticized by anyone but himself, Kelgan was unwarrantedly injured. "What did you expect?" he pouted.

"The Academy has a, um, reputation; its graduates are welcomed—and feared—everywhere," retorted di Nerrill. "I assumed one so close to his final test would be more than adequate. Furthermore, I wished to allay any suspicion which might arise, did I hire a Master Mage."

"Whose suspicions?" Kelgan wanted to know.

"Would that I had an answer," was Nevander's gloomy response.

Suddenly Kelgan felt cold. His mind had recalled the tentative brush of the unknown other felt at the previous night's gathering.

Nevander di Nerrill's acute perceptions didn't miss Kelgan's distress or the color draining from his face.

"Tell," was his command.

"Last night, while I played the jester, did you attempt to communicate with me?" Discomfort made Kelgan's tone sterner than he had meant.

"Communicate? You mean...?"

"Yes. Mind-to-mind."

Silently, Nevander and Neroma stared at him. Again, he was bemused by how identical their ebony gazes were, like a walnut struck down the center.

He felt an icicle drip down his spine as the silence grew. Then, Neroma whispered, "You felt...?"

"Yes, I felt. How about an explanation?" demanded Kelgan.

"I can't explain," demurred Nevander, "I, uh, we *are* mind-seers, but it was not I, last night."

"Nor I," frowned Neroma.

"*Someone* tried to probe me. I was using just a little bit of power to boost my illusion"

"Stupid," hissed Neroma in a surprising display of temper.

He stopped, taken aback.

"I'm afraid my sister is right, Kelgan," said Nevander, worriedly addressing him by name for the first time. "We cannot put a face to the enemy, thus it could be anyone."

"Tell us all," Neroma urged, resuming her usual demeanor.

"Well, as I was saying" Kelgan continued, feeling as self-conscious and awkward as a newly-admitted apprentice, "I was using a bit of power in that last illusion, when I felt a touch in my mind, light as a feather, but I got the same tingly feeling I get whenever anyone else uses magic. Anyone trained, that is," he added.

A flicker of amusement passed over Neroma's face so quickly Kelgan could not be sure he really saw it.

"That's it?" queried Nevander.

"Yes, just that one light touch."

Both di Nerrills silently absorbed this information, leaving him to his thoughts for a time.

He was disturbed by Nevander's reference to the 'enemy.' Remembering the aura of evil that manifested itself from the voices, he admitted the justice of the term. They *were* the enemy. But who were *they*?

Nevander broke into his troubled musings. "Do you realize what you have said? Mage's *train* only at the Academy! You would have recognized anyone from there, and you *did not.*"

Kelgan stiffened in shock. He had ignored the implications of his statement. Unless the unknown magician was *very* old and traveled little, he would have met the other at some time during his apprenticeship. After all, there weren't that many Academy Mages in the world. And most of them, yielding to nostalgia, came back at one time or another.

Kelgan strained to recall the names and faces of the previous eve. No use! In his resentment at being treated as a performing animal, he had paid little enough attention.

"All were strangers, as far as I can determine," he offered uncertainly.

"No one—not a soul—struck a chord of recognition?" demanded Nevander.

"They strike no chord at all," he cried in frustration. "They are but blurs in my mind. And... it gives me an aching head to think of them."

Neroma looked grim. "A spell of overlook," she asserted.

"Nonsense," Kelgan began and stuttered to a halt.

Of course! He hadn't been *that* inattentive. *Some* faces would have returned to memory, as well as many details of the evening, which were also mysteriously irretrievable. Someone at the gathering had wished to remain anonymous. Someone Kelgan would have known perhaps, at least by sight?

"It would appear that the secret of my presence lacks a bit in the secrecy department," he observed ironically.

A grimace from Neroma; a bitter laugh from Nevander.

"My precautions do seem both naive and inadequate," agreed Nevander. "I fear I am an amateur at intrigue." He smiled wolfishly.

Kelgan had his doubts about that. On reflection, however, his arrival appeared a combination of stealth, clumsy ruse, and downright idiotic attention-drawing. None of the above accorded with his estimation of his host's character. As was becoming usual, none of it made sense. Nothing had made sense since he had stepped into Sargal's study—was it really less than twenty-four hours before? It felt to him as though he had been playing this fool's game for a lifetime. And it *was* a fool's game. Of that he felt sure. Furthermore, he possessed no illusions as to the identity of the fool.

With one of her bewildering shifts from indifference to compassion, Neroma came to his side. Slipping her hand in his, she gripped it hard.

"Nevander, you must *tell* him. He has been honest, can we be less?"

Di Nerrill looked as though he would disagree, then, with bad grace, he acquiesced.

"Neroma is right, as always. I have wrongly used you and your ignorance of us."

"Tell me what I do not know," snorted Kelgan.

"What you do not know," Nevander interposed gently, "is the extent—and the implication—of that use."

··· 5 ···

Other Places (Other ears)

"Now?" "Later." "Faster?" "Slower." "Secretly?" "Openly." "Too young?" "Oh, no, never too young." A malevolent giggle ensued.

Without knowing quite why, Baroness Daliane Bervaine found herself standing on the cold tiles beside her bed, the sound of her own shriek echoing around her.

Her husband, T'Jules Bervaine, Baron of the line Wysach, sat up in some concern.

"Daliane, Daliane, what is it?"

Daliane fought to recall. There was something; some terror just on the edge of memory.

She sank down on the bed.

"I... I guess it was a dream."

"That's a bit of an understatement, my dear," observed her husband. "Must have been one helldark of a dream. Shouldn't be surprised if the whole place knew about it."

As he spoke, a frenzied knocking began at the door.

"Baron? Baroness? Are you well?"

"Let us in."

Sweeping a sheet elegantly around his scarred and muscular body, the Baron strode to the door and flung it wide. A small crowd of distressed retainers stood outside.

"Yes, gentlemen... and ladies," catching sight of Daliane's worried handmaiden, "we are well. A bat was nesting in the rafters and startled Her Ladyship, that is all."

Expressing relief, the group disbanded. T'Jules shut the door with a smirk and rebarred it.

"Tee Jee, you know I'm not afraid of bats." Daliane's mouth turned down in disapproval.

"I know, my dear, but if I had told them it was a nightmare, they would have been sure I was beating you. Or worse," he added with a leer.

Smiling, Daliane snuggled back in her husband's arms. Thus reassured, she fell quickly into a doze.

"Too pretty." "Too happy." "Too sad." "Too bad." Mocking laughter.

Daliane's eyes snapped open. She lay motionless and staring into the darkness until dawn pinked the east windows with only too welcome light.

Regarding her heavy-lidded and dark-circled countenance over the breakfast tray, some days later, T'Jules experienced a pang. The one thing constant in his universe was his wife's equable disposition. Daliane faced life, ever with both easy optimism and realistic courage. She never fretted or brooded, just plowed into living with all the strength her small body could command. This languor was totally outside his experience. He was frightened. Was she ill? Was it serious? He couldn't imagine life without her.

"Daliane, you've got to tell me what's wrong!"

She reluctantly raised her eyes to him, and regarded him with a stranger's face. His throat contracted, and he seized both her hands frantically.

"Daliane!"

She collapsed into his arms, weeping. T'Jules scarcely knew what to do. To his knowledge, she had never shed a tear before.

"Tee Jee, darling, I'm afraid I'm going mad."

Dumbstruck, he held her until the storm of weeping showed signs of abating. Then, he held her away from him, to look in her eyes.

"Dally, you're the sanest person I know. You're what keeps me sane. How could you possibly think otherwise?"

"Tee Jee, I've been hearing voices."

"Voices?"

"Every night for the last two weeks, as soon as I fall asleep, I hear them." She shuddered.

"You've been having bad dreams, dear," T'Jules stated firmly. "They're disturbing your sleep, and you are exhausted."

"No!" Daliane almost shouted. "No," she went on in a calmer tone, "they're not dreams. I thought they were at first, but I *hear them*. I hear them, and they are evil... evil." She began to sob again.

Deeply disturbed now, T'Jules lifted his weeping wife in his arms and carried her to the bed.

"I'm calling for P'Relna, the healing-woman," he said in a carefully cheerful voice. "She can give you something to make you sleep without those troublesome nightmares."

"T'Jules, they are not dreams. Whatever they are. They're. Not. Dreams." Daliane's voice rose to a near scream at the end.

The Baron took his wife's face in his hands and stared long and hard into her eyes. In spite of her obvious distress, what he saw there seemed to reassure him.

"All right, Dally, let's talk about it."

"You remember the night I screamed?"

He nodded.

"That was the first time. I thought it was a nightmare, only so frightening, and I couldn't quite remember...." Her voice trailed off for a moment. "But when I shut my eyes they started again, and I wasn't even asleep!"

"You've heard them *every night*, since then?"

"Yes, sometimes they let me sleep for an hour or two. But they never go entirely away, until the dawn. When the sun rises, they fade away; I get a little sleep after that."

"What do they say? Do they talk to you?"

"No. They seem to speak only to each other. One sounds the elder... the other..." She broke off, biting her lip, then resumed. "They say strange things... and they laugh. Oh, Tee Jee, that's the worst. Their laughter is horrible, horrible and cruel."

"Try to remember exactly what they say."

"It isn't always the same, but they say things like 'too rich,' 'too poor,' 'too young,' 'too old.' It doesn't make any sense. I don't know what they mean." She wrung her hands, her agony evident.

The Baron captured them in his big ones. He noted, as he never failed to, how small hers were. How frail she seemed, with a soul far too large for its tiny shell. He well knew, however, that the frail shell was actually tough, wiry, and skilled as a man with a sword. To see her helpless and tear-stained made his heart ache.

"Last night," she admitted, slowly, as though the words gave pain, "I heard them with my eyes open."

He grunted with shock. Madness? Or evil? The thought of evil directed at *her* made anger burn, red-hot and dangerous, within him.

"You are certain you did not merely dream you were awake?"

"I was not in bed," she answered simply.

··· 6 ···

Fool's Choice

"I mplication? What implication beyond that you play me for a fool?" Kelgan's temper threatened his judgment.

Neroma squeezed his hand harder as her hair wrapped his shoulder. Kelgan was surprised to realize she still held it, and even more surprised at the whisper of feeling her tresses provided.

"The implication, my delightful Mage.... You'd better sit down, by the way, this will take a while and may have an effect on your knees.

Releasing his hand, Neroma motioned to the chair. Kelgan complied, resuming the seat he had abandoned.

"Your presence here was neither accident nor chance," Nevander continued. "We, my sister and I, have been watching you for some time."

"Watching! Watching me! How? Why? How could you have...?"

"Known about you?" Nevander finished for him. "That is a story in itself."

"I *saw* you," interjected Neroma. "I was scrying the Academy...."

"You... *you* were scrying the Academy?" interrupted Kelgan, his voice vibrating with amazement and disbelief. A look of amusement passed between sister and brother.

"Unused to the idea as we understand you to be, know this," intoned Nevander. "Neroma is a powerful sorceress, far superior to myself. And you, I guess," he added as an afterthought.

"A wild talent, I assume," Kelgan's tone sounded contemptuous, though he strove to conceal it.

"On the contrary." Icicles dripped from Nevander's words. "Controlled, channeled, and powerful."

"Be easy with him, my brother. The idea of a woman-mage is yet new."

Neroma's contralto pulsed with laughter at his expense, yet a tendril of her hair wrapped around his neck with affection. He felt ashamed of himself, as well as angry with his patrons; they always contrived to put him at a disadvantage. Well, in all fairness, perhaps contrived was not the right of it. Although he had not been aware of it previously, he really *was* at a disadvantage, knowing nothing but his village and the Academy. Of course, the Academy was scarcely a backwater; all the world's news was gathered there by the Mages, and many of the world's most important people were drawn there. And yet....

Neroma and Nevander waited with tolerance while he went through yet another of his mental struggles. Becoming aware of their silent expectancy, he flushed.

"I am continually playing catch-up."

"It's not your fault, my friend, my yet-to-be-it-is-hoped-friend," amended Nevander with a twinkle. "The Academy guards *some* secrets."

"And you guard others, it would appear," accused Kelgan. "The scrying, for example. How was that accomplished? The Academy, we are all told, is scry-proof."

"That is *almost* true," responded Neroma. "At certain times, and under certain conditions, the defenses weaken. These times are rare, for they depend on a combination of variables which rarely occur. I happened upon them only by accident, and it took months—two years, in fact—before I understood the combination of just the right vessel—only the purest crystal and the purest quicksilver to fill it. It was even longer before I could manage to repeat my original probing in just the right combination of weather patterns. Then, however, I continued at every opportunity and happened on *you*."

It was Neroma's longest speech. Kelgan loved the sound of her voice, its essence like dark wine pouring over him. He was conscious, however, that she must regard him as a sort of cripple, unable to hear her in his mind as did Nevander.

Does she think my magic crippled as well? he wondered, the thought giving him a strange pang.

"Let me finish my story of why you are here, my Mage, with no further interruptions. Then, you may ask everything further you wish to know."

Nevander began anew.

"As I had begun to explain, Neroma's scrying revealed you to us. Your quickness, your enthusiasm, and obviously superior talent drew our attention. We could see that you had a special ability."

"Special," Kelgan burst out. Nevander held up a hand for silence.

"Since our seeing opportunities were few and far between, we were astonished at the rapidity of your advancement every time we saw you again."

"Then we became aware that something was wrong. You appeared tired and distracted, your abilities blunted. We could see your master eyeing you with disapproval. At the same time, as I have already told you, the 'disturbances' had begun here. Again, it was Neroma who realized the truth."

Nevander paused, staring into the distance for some moments before he continued.

"We decided, between us, that we had to have you here, even before your graduation. We wanted to observe you."

Nevander stopped, somewhat discomfited.

"I have made it sound as though you were an alchemical experiment. We actually wished to get to know you, before entrusting you with our secret and suggesting an alliance. We concocted a pretext for Sargal's benefit, which only seems to have made him suspicious. Although I do believe his suspicions are more that I am a Black Warlock and wished to suborn you for evil purposes."

Nevander chuckled, as though at a good jest. Kelgan joined in, albeit somewhat uneasily. That had been his first thought, as well, and even now, he was less than sure. Few of the Academy's graduates turned to the Dark Side, but those who had were notorious. Stories of their evil deeds passed from generation to generation. Would an aura of portentous infamy surround his host? Could it be hidden behind Nevander's depthless black eyes? He knew he was being melodramatic, but he could not suppress his wondering.

Nevander's glance was shrewd as he continued. "The night ride, the peculiar arrival, all were designed to keep you slightly off balance. Neroma and I wished to see how you behaved in mysterious circumstances. Forgive us for our foolish plot." He bit his lower lip in chagrin. "It looks even more foolish, in light of what you have told us. We wished to conceal our purpose from more than just you. Unfortunately, our secret seems to be no secret at all, if only to at least one other."

"How is it you, or Neroma, did not feel the presence of the other?" he queried.

"We have said that you were a special case, Kelgan," Neroma interposed. "Were you not aware that few mages are able to sense one another? They are too accomplished at shielding."

"Was shielding not a part of your training, Under-Mage?" demanded Nevander.

Demoted again! "Of course," he answered defensively, "but we only use our shields while casting."

"Exactly," said Nevander triumphantly, "and yet you had no trouble sensing the probe." His face clouded as the realization came to him. "If you always use your shields while casting, why were they so easily penetrated?"

Blushing furiously, Kelgan wished himself anywhere else. "I didn't think it was necessary to raise *my* shields." That was not *exactly* the truth. He had been careless, not something he wished to admit.

He wilted inwardly as he reluctantly met the stony stares of brother and sister.

"Didn't think it was necessary?"

"I... I... didn't think there were any wizards here."

"Kelgan, do you always do so little thinking?"

He felt a surge of temper.

"Well, you didn't tell me anything, how was I to know...." To his horror, Kelgan heard the whine in his voice.

Tendrils of Neroma's hair again gently patted his shoulder.

"While it is true you knew naught of our intrigues, you should know to be always on your guard. You should have realized, as well, when *we* concealed your identity, that *you* should also have concealed it."

Kelgan didn't feel he could say, "I didn't think," another time. His slight lie had trapped him and made him appear even more foolish and careless. Instead, he forced a weak smile and acknowledged, "I have much to learn."

"Nay, our dear Mage, "contradicted Nevander generously, "the fault is ours. These are things I am sure you would have apprehended in your last months of apprenticeship, had we not interrupted your progress."

Kelgan was grateful for the mercurial changes of mood which seemed to afflict both his employers. Once more a Mage and in their good graces!

Nevander continued, "That does not alter the fact that we must supply the lack. A few lessons with us...."

Lessons, he groaned inwardly, *am I to begin again?*

"I was close to graduation," he protested, "Sargal assured me I had learned nearly everything I needed to know. It was only a matter of refinement."

"Ha!" snorted Neroma. "The Academy has become so inbred and parochial it cannot see what is under its very nose. Besides," she added waspishly, "they ignore women."

"But women...."

"Have no magic? What about me? Haven't you learned anything?"

"But you...."

"Are an exception? Nonsense! We are many."

"I don't...."

"Believe it? Of course, not. You're a man." Neroma folded her arms; her hair stood straight up, begging for an argument.

Kelgan was growing quite tired of having his sentences finished for him.

"What I was *trying* to say was that you and Terencia are the only women I've met in a long time. Furthermore, I don't really know any women very well outside of my mother... and my sisters," he added reflectively, recalling a puzzling incident, or two, involving his sister, Serin.

For a moment, he was blinded by a pang of home-sickness—the warmth of his mother's kitchen, the giggles of his smallest siblings as they rolled around with their old sheepdog, Dantig, and especially his sisters, Serin and Elgina, who were blossoming into lovely young womanhood. They'd already begun to treat him with the superior airs only fifteen and sixteen-year-old girls can assume with brothers. The room swam for a moment before his eyes.

Nevander brought him back to himself.

"Perhaps I would better term them exchanges, rather than lessons," twinkled Nevander. "We are, as yet, unaware of the scope of your powers, as are you of ours. I am a mere dabbler. Neroma, however, possesses power to match the best."

Attempting to choke back any disbelief, Kelgan murmured, "Indeed!"

Neroma startled him with a full-blown laugh. Her laughter was almost a tangible object; warm, deep, and lilting, it surrounded him like Joseph's coat of many colors.

"I look forward to our exchanges, Kelgan." Still chuckling, she left the room; her hair fluttering like suppressed giggles. The room became a chilly expanse with her disappearance.

A new thought struck him. "How is it that I can sense neither you nor Neroma? If my talent is such a fair gift, how am I blind to the two of you?"

Nevander directed a sober gaze at him.

"Neroma and I never lower our shields while awake. When we sleep, we never fail to employ the scent ward which renders us invisible to psychic spies."

Kelgan was staggered. Constantly vigilant! Perpetually shielded! Never relaxing for a moment! Against whom? How long?

He must have spoken the last aloud, for Nevander answered, "From the first we knew to fashion shields. From childhood, that is."

"But why? What threatened?"

"Our mother was a powerful prophetess," answered Nevander. "It is from her that we received our talent. She foresaw a terrible occurrence, which could destroy us all, but she could not tell when, or from whence, it came. Thus, all our lives she had us prepare so that when it befell, our defenses would be as a second skin."

"If you have been practicing all your lives, and you keep your shields raised at all times, how then do the voices assail you?"

Shamefacedly, Nevander gave a slight cough. "My father was the most ordinary of mortals, albeit a noble one. My sister inherited all our mother's talent; I, being male and a half-breed, received only a portion. At the moments between waking and sleeping, or just when I step from the protection of the wards, I am vulnerable. I cannot maintain the wards as successfully as my twin. She sets it up for me."

Sensing Kelgan's unwillingness to believe, coupled with his inability to disbelieve, Nevander kindly dismissed him. "We will discuss this in more detail when we meet for our lessons."

Kelgan felt as though he had slipped beneath the wheels of a tinker's cart, events moving too swiftly for him to assimilate the barrage of completely new ideas being thrown at him.

What did Nevander mean, "being male? He had always assumed that was the proper gender—after all, he had talent neither of his parents possessed. Especially his mother, dear as she was to him. Everyone *knew* women had but little talent (and that mainly worthless). Everyone *knew* any mage worth *his* salt could only be trained at the Academy. Everyone *knew* the world was permanent and couldn't just "disappear."

Everyone knew voices didn't come whispering out of the night, saying things of unreason. Voices from the land of the mad....

He drew his knees to his chest and hugged them. As though alone, he rested his head on his knees like a disconsolate child.

He felt Nevander's hand on his shoulder. "Kelgan, give us but a few days, and some of what troubles you will be resolved."

Kelgan managed to nod without raising his head. He wasn't sure what really troubled him could be resolved so easily. *That* was the blow to his self-confidence. He had been so sure of himself, so swaggeringly arrogant when he had easily surpassed the other young men, many of them older than himself. Now, in less than twenty-four hours, two strangers had reduced him to the level of the naive adolescent he had been when he entered the Academy.

Another troubling thought assailed him. How many unauthorized magicians like the di Nerrill's were there? He had thought last night's unknown prober was concealing his identity from himself, but was it from the di Nerrill's instead? Could it be a woman? The voices sounded undeniably male... Kelgan's thoughts trailed off.

The next thing he knew, he was being shaken vigorously.

"Kelgan, wake up."

It was Terencia who pummeled him, and not gently. Wincing, Kelgan straightened. He had fallen asleep in the chair, still in his doubled-up posture, head still resting on his knees.

"Ow, Darkness," he swore as he unbent his cramped limbs.

Terencia snorted unkindly, but sobered at the scowl on his face.

"Really, Kelgan, I am sorry, but you look like a stork somebody sat on. How could you have fallen asleep all bent up like that?"

"Well, I got precious little last night," Kelgan rasped. He could see the humor, at least from Terencia's standpoint.

"What time is it?"

"It's late afternoon. You missed lunch."

"Why didn't anyone wake me?"

"Neroma said to leave you alone, you needed your rest."

"Rest won't help if I'm crippled in the bargain."

Terencia snorted again, "Don't worry, Neroma will take care of your aches and pains with one of her potions."

A slight tinge of... what... colored Terencia's voice.

Kelgan took a closer look at Neroma's companion, the overall brown impression persisted. She was dressed today in a gown which showed off the admirable curve of her breasts and which was girt low to accentuate a small waist. It was, nevertheless, in the same unrelieved woodsy color of last night's riding costume. Nearly matching her hair and eyes, it gave her the look of a tiny oak sapling which had sprung to life. There was a sparkle in those eyes, however, he found uncommonly appealing. His interest did not go unnoticed by Terencia, who swept her lashes down and up with an unmistakable flutter.

What would have happened next remained a mystery. Neroma made one of her soundless entrances, appearing as though conjured from smoke over Terencia's shoulder.

"Ah, Kelgan, awake at last."

Terencia gave a start, then her mouth turned down in a pout. Muttering an excuse, she hastened from the room. Neroma's eyes followed her with an enigmatic gaze.

"I trust your nap left you improved."

"I feel like I'd been ground between my step-father's mill wheels."

Neroma "humphed." "I think that can be dealt with," she assured him briskly. Wisps of hair crooked like so many hands on hips.

"Neroma," Kelgan paused, unsure what to say next.

"The tisanes are not addictive, Kelgan."

"That's not... not what I...." Floundering, he sputtered to a halt.

Neroma took pity on him; hair caressed his cheek with an almost loving manner.

"I know, I understand."

More than I do, was his melancholy thought.

··· 7 ···

Again, the Others

T'Jules, Baron Wysach, stared down at his sleeping wife. How thin she was! Wrenching himself away, he moved silently to the window. He stood morosely, unseeing eyes turned toward the setting sun. The Vindark Sea glittered in the distance as the last sun rays grasped futilely at the wave caps. Soon their grip would loosen entirely, as the shining ball which furnished their arms plunged below the rim of the world. Soon, too, when the room dimmed, Daliane would rise from her uneasy slumber to begin her "day."

"Like bats," he murmured, "the very bats we joked about."

Rumors of the Baroness' peculiar 'indisposition' abounded. T'Jules had tried to confound them by making periodic announcements through her life-long physician, P'Relna. P'Relna had hinted vaguely at a 'brain fever,' complicated by some unspecified 'liver involvement.' Nevertheless, Daliane's continued absence from all official engagements spawned an amazingly vicious variety of baseless guesses. Among them, and the cruelest, that Her Grace had committed suicide and now wandered the halls of the castle as one of the undead, seeking victims to join her in her lonely plight. The truth, that Daliane now slept by day and wandered by night, proved almost as unpalatable.

She had suggested the arrangement to him, after weeks of torture from her 'voices.' Weeks where naught availed, neither nostrums concocted by P'Relna, nor warding spells cast by the court magician (admittedly not one of the Academy's brighter scholars).

Unwilling at first, T'Jules had consented to her plan as he watched her slip further and further from health and farther and farther from him.

Now, though far from ideal, her topsy-turvy hours at least allowed her some snatches of rest. She was eating almost normally again and had regained a bit of weight. Although still pale, her skin had lost the wan translucency which had so frightened him.

They were together from dusk to midnight. He was not entirely certain how she spent the rest of the hours until dawn, but he knew she paced the castle corridors, adding fuel to the rumors of the undead Baroness.

He heard a rustle behind him. Daliane was awake. Her skin seemed to have become light-sensitive. She could tell, almost to the second, when the sun would disappear below the horizon. She was up and instantly alert just before its farewell.

"Tee Jee, darling," she said, "what a beautiful evening."

The forced cheer in his wife's voice gave T'Jules a pang. Her former happy lilt was now entirely submerged in a brittleness and artificiality that pained him almost past bearing. He found himself answering with the same strained heartiness.

"Indeed it is, beloved. Come and look."

She came to stand by his side. Even though she had regained some weight, she looked somehow diminished. He realized that her sturdy personality had always made her appear larger and stronger than she really was. Now, with that vitality stripped from her, the truth of her fragility was revealed.

She had volunteered nothing about the voices since they had begun their unconventional arrangement. She had not volunteered, and he had not asked. By tacit agreement, they avoided the subject entirely. He could no longer abide the silence, not when the voices stood between them like a gray fog, obscuring their real sight of each other. He needed to know.

Grasping her shoulders, he demanded, "Dally, look at me."

Her eyes met his for a heartbeat, and then slid guiltily away. She had been this way for weeks; never really looking at him—always around him, or beyond him, or beside him—everywhere but into his eyes. Seeing her reluctance, he seized her chin in both his hands and held it firmly. She tried to twist away, reminding him of a trapped sparrow. Finally, she wilted visibly; surrendering, she looked fully at him.

Feeling a brute, he continued, "Dally, do you still hear the voices? I haven't asked, because I didn't want to distress you further, but now I must know. We cannot go on like this."

She did not question or protest. Her eyes swam with tears, but with a semblance of her old courage, she answered, "Yes, Tee Jee, I hear them nearly every night. Some nights they leave me almost entirely alone, other nights, they are almost constant. Most of the time, they come at random, just when I think it's going to be all right, just when I start to relax and read or.... That's why I walk. For some reason, movement seems to hold them at bay."

"What do they say? The same things...."

She moved uneasily under his hands. "No, not... not exactly."

"Well?"

"They...," She choked, and then started over. "They tell me to wait, because they are coming."

··· 8 ···

Keeping Up with the di Nerrills

In the many weeks he had been at Nerrill's Keep, Kelgan had learned much. So too, he felt to his satisfaction, had his hosts. Neroma's power had stunned him with its depth and its alien quality; she was mistress of spells hitherto uncontemplated. He, however, regained stature in their eyes, due to the breadth of his competence. Nevander, as he admitted, dabbled at spellcasting, while being a powerful mindseer.

As was Neroma, a fact which rocked Kelgan's previous assumptions to their foundation. Most particularly since she displayed knowledge of magic that he had not yet learned. She had generously shared the casting of the scent ward with him; a generosity which kept him awake that night in a solitary pout for some hours—the reason being that he still had not mastered it.

Another blow to his previous feelings of male superiority concerned the scrying. Yes, he could perform what he now knew to be an amateur version of that action; but Neroma's facility astounded him (and made him so jealous, he took it out on his bed pillow). In his defense—he felt—was the fact that he followed Academy procedures exactly. It wasn't his fault if they were slightly outdated, was it?

He now realized the importance of seeking out the proper vessel for each occasion. The Academy simply used iron basins polished to a high sheen. These worked very well for certain 'peerings,' but were well-nigh worthless for others. Kelgan assumed that difficulty would be solved by practice; and perhaps he was right, nevertheless, the time wasted on repeated attempts now appalled him. All in all, his ego felt pretty deflated. Feeling discretion was the better part of valor, he kept it to himself. He comforted himself with the knowledge that he was better than Nevander at all but mindseeing, and neither of the twins was at all adept at healing.

Volunteers from the household staff, which astounded Kelgan with their number, had been provided for him to minister to. At the behest of the di Nerrills, he concealed his true ability and prescribed harmless nostrums, while at the same time using his powers to truly rid them of their ailments. He felt both pleased and touched for their gratitude. This proof of some superiority earned him more than a modicum of praise from both the twins.

They had taken to sleeping together in Nevander's study so that Neroma's wards could protect them all. Well, not exactly together. Kelgan and Nevander occupied cots on one side of the fountain, and Neroma, behind a screen, slept on the other. Lumen, may His light protect them, only knew what Terencia thought of this arrangement. Even though they all retired to their separate rooms at dawn, it was obvious to anyone with half an eye that they had been absent all night, and Terencia had two perfectly good and observant ones.

She spoke infrequently to him, and then only most coolly and formally, calling him Master Defthand. Kelgan, both amused and annoyed, felt uncertain about how to set things right.

She had just knocked, entering his room with a pitcher of wash water on his invitation to come in.

"Good morrow, Master Defthand, did you sleep well?"

He wanted to shake her for the sly innuendo in her voice. Did she think they were having an orgy every night, a *ménage à trois* with a little incest thrown in?

What do I care for the opinion of a lady's maid? he thought, realizing that opinions had come to mean a great deal to him. At the Academy, the regard of his peers mattered little. He knew he was better than they, and if they disliked him for it, so what? Even this limited glimpse of the outside had taught him something new, however.

Namely, he wasn't as good as thought, even though the potential existed. Furthermore, he still had a long way to go toward realizing that potential. This unfamiliar perspective occasioned a change of attitude. He *cared* what others thought. Knowing that Terencia suspected him of carrying on shamefully with one or the other, or both, di Nerrills grated unbearably. How to fit that subject into a conversation was something else again.

He confined himself to assuring her that, yes, he had indeed slept well, and thanking her for the water.

She tossed him a scornful glance, then left him alone.

Kelgan washed and donned the new set of clothes draped over his chair. Once a week, with undeviating punctuality, a new outfit had appeared while he slept and the old one removed. The fit improved each time, until now they slid over his body as thought he had grown a second skin.

As from the first, the colors were the same rust and turquoise, however the patterns varied. The same device always appeared on the tunic, as well. He wondered at their significance. At the Academy, the youngest apprentices wore green, symbolizing their newness and potential for growth. When they graduated to junior status, they exchanged their sprig-like garments for ones of an all-over dun shade, which mimicked the pale earth of Bellermond's rolling foothills. Once advanced to seniors, unrelieved gray announced their nearness to genuine magehood, when they would at last wear white, banded at hem and sleeve with red, black and gray—red on the inner band nearest the heart, gray next, and black on the outside band, the color of anathema.

He wondered, as well, whether Sargal had been shocked to see the di Nerrills clothed entirely in that despised hue. Remembering Nevander's reference to Sargal's 'nervousness,' he decided Sargal was probably horrified, and yet he had not refused di Nerrill's request; sending Kelgan off to Lumen knew what. Had Sargal been operating out of fear? Guile? Certainly not Kelgan's guile, he had been as a lamb to the butcher.

Contemplating himself critically in the mirror, he was more than a little pleased with himself. A month of regular meals, and excellent food it was, rather than the Spartan and boring regimen of the Academy had filled him out some.

Not such a stork, he told himself gleefully. How would Sargal take to seeing him gotten up like a popinjay? Another cause for horror was a good bet. He slapped his thigh, then felt ashamed of himself at the pleasure the idea of shocking his old mentor gave him. Sargal had been good to him, their relationship, while not one of father and son, had been one of real affection.

What made him think of it in the past? Why "had been?" Surely *is* was the proper word. *Of course,* he would soon return to the Academy to finish his last six months of training and graduate. *Of course!*

He thrust away the thought that he was far beyond those studies now. He refused to think that the Academy was no longer necessary or important to him.

He and the di Nerrills prepared—but for what? After they finished—when?—he would definitely leave—but why? He would resume his old life, even if he didn't know how. Pushing aside those uncomfortable reflections, he bethought himself of the day's coming experiments.

Neroma and Nevander had been attempting to teach him the skill of mindseeing, by focusing the combined force of their thoughts on him as he lay on a couch, relaxed and receptive. So far, he had proved to be depressingly head-blind. Neither relaxed nor receptive, come to think of it. Try though he might to employ the techniques learned at the Academy to clear his head, slow his heart, etc., the moment they bent their concentrated efforts in his direction he became tense as a watch spring and his brain felt like a wooden block.

Trotting down the stairs to Nevander's lair, he braced himself for another disappointing round of failed attempts. He knocked and entered at the same time. Nevander and Neroma, who had their heads close together, sprang apart, looking guilty.

"You might as well know," said Nevander with an embarrassed laugh, "we have been talking of you."

"We have come to a decision," Neroma added, her hair emphatically punctuating her remarks. "You will never see mind-to-mind."

Kelgan's spirits sank. Not that he had held out much hope, mindseers were generally born, not made, but even so....

"No," put in Nevander, "you're definitely not a mindseer. We think you're something much more interesting.

Kelgan stared at di Nerrill. How could the head-blind be interesting? Unless it was simply because there were so many—at least at the Academy.

"Everyone we have known of, anyone with any kind of talent, even though unable to speak to other minds, can *hear* those minds if enough effort is expended," said Neroma.

Kelgan was intrigued in spite of his dismay. His assumption had been that the others were the same as he, unable to communicate or to receive communication.

"You, we don't know why, are different," Neroma went on.

Nevander chimed in. "You are completely opaque. We cannot reach into your mind with our thoughts, nor can we apprehend yours."

"Even when you are not shielding; even when you are trying desperately to cooperate with our efforts," Neroma added.

"If that's the case, why haven't I been able to shut out the voices before now?"

"We think they are many times more powerful than we," said Nevander. "Only Neroma's particular talent with perfumes keeps them from us. Nevertheless, we think you can develop *your* ability until even *they* cannot penetrate."

"It is only in deepest sleep that you are vulnerable," agreed Neroma, "and then only at the lowest point of the night."

"We have devised some mental exercises for you to perform," said Nevander. "You can practice them on the way."

"On the way? On the way, where?" Kelgan looked from one dark-eyed face to the other in bewilderment.

"You had not forgotten our journey, Mage Defthand?" asked Nevander. "It begins tonight."

··· 9 ···

One for the Road

Pellerin tossed feverishly on his cot. His mother's tears fell steadily on the hand she gripped tightly. She hoped the surety of her presence would calm him. His father stood behind her, limp in his despair. A tall, rugged, rawboned fellow, helplessness sat badly on him.

"Stop them. Stop! Stop!" Pellerin's anguished raving died away.

A sob burst from his mother. "He don't know me, Ezrael."

"Now, Bethne."

"He don't know me, Ezrael, and he don't know you neither. He ant gettin' better, an' that damn fool healer ant helpin' him."

Ezrael acknowledged the truth of her words with a shrug. "He be all we got, Bethne."

"All we gots no better than nothin'!"

"Voices, bad... bad. Stop... don't let." The sufferer's voice sounded hoarse and cracked.

His mother wet a cloth and wiped Pellerin's face, then tried to squeeze a trickle of water down his throat. Her effort sent the boy into a choking fit. After it passed, exhaustion quieted him.

"He caln't last, Ezrael," Bethne stated hopelessly.

With a groan, Ezrael dropped to a rough bench and covered his face.

"You've got to dig, Ez," Bethne went on mercilessly, "we've got to be ready. I'm gettin' his good clothes washed up, so's he kin look his best."

Dropping his hands, Ezrael stared at her in horror. "Dig, why you cain't mean... I won't believe it. I won't believe it. I won't dig, either."

"You have to, Ez. I see it comin! It won't be much past mornin'. It's in his face. I want him to go right, with everythin' ready."

"It's dark, Bethie."

"Take the lantern."

"Where?"

"We wants him close. Just by my roses is best."

After Ezrael left the hut, the mother once more resumed her post, clasping Pellerin's hand again in her own. Sleep overcame her, as it had to in spite of her grief. She lay across the boy, until their one aged cockerel announced the arrival of day.

Ezrael had just finished his melancholy task as the sun rose in golden mockery. Shouldering the shovel, he turned back toward the hut just as his wife's terrified scream reached him.

"*It's happened,*" he muttered, breaking into a run. Pushing in the door, he stopped in his tracks, realizing the reason for his wife's terror.

Pellerin stood calmly by his cot, donning the good clothes his mother had washed. Glancing up at his father with a chillingly unfocused gaze, he said, "Good morrow, Father. I trust you are well."

Slipping into his boots, Pellerin moved with the jerky hesitations of a stringed marionette to the door. Pushing past his father without another word, he headed for the small structure behind the hut which served as barn, silo, and stable. His mother and father followed wordlessly after him. Pellerin bridled their less-than-proud mare, Melba, and mounted awkwardly on her bare back. White showed all around Melba's eyes as she frantically rolled them back at him, her ears plastered to her skull. Nevertheless, she allowed Pellerin to stay on her back.

"Good-bye, Mother, Father," Pellerin said pleasantly and distantly.

Digging his heels into Melba's ribs, he set off toward the highway which ran across the Collett Valley. His mother whimpered faintly and slumped unconscious to the ground.

··· 10 ···

One More for the Road

O nce again, Kelgan packed his few belongings. Although they had not increased in number, they had improved vastly in quality. A new suit of clothing had been waiting for him after dinner. Instead of the rust and turquoise he had come to expect, these garments were entirely of the dove gray he had worn as an apprentice. No apprentice, not even the sons of the aristocracy, however, had anything half so fine. The shirt was of linen so soft, it felt like a maiden's skin. The hose and tunic were of equally soft and fine-spun wool. On the tunic, he could just make out the device he had come to think of as his own, worked in gray silk. The cloak matched, save it was oiled to inhibit the elements. Boots of suede like a kitten's whisper completed the outfit.

No longer a macaw, it's just possible I am to become a pigeon.

He was tempted to leave his little kit of philtres behind, but remembering his need with the castle staff prompted him to tuck it in his knapsack for possible future use. Pirouetting gracefully, in a sarcastic mime of a courtier, he seized the cloak from the chair and halted with a gasp. Beneath the cloak lay a polished leather scabbard with what looked suspiciously like a glittering sword-hilt protruding from it. Another terse message dangled from it. "Take me," it advised, "I will be your arm."

He dropped both cloak and knapsack, scarcely aware that he did so. Lifting the sword, he drew it gingerly from the scabbard. It felt heavy and deadly. In the hilt were set two cabochon gems, one amber, one turquoise, and along the gleaming length, his signature device was etched in the metal.

He felt the blood gel in his veins. Of what benefit was a sword to him? He was a magician, not a fighter, not even skilled with a quarterstaff. That should have been patently obvious to the di Nerrills. The fact that he was sure it *was* obvious, frightened him more than anything had till then.

He fell heavily into the chair, mesmerized by the weapon. Its gems coruscated in the half-light, pulling him in to their brilliance. *Why* a sword? Why a *sword?* Spellbound, he sat, rapt in the glow and wrapped by the glow.

His name, sharply spoken, broke the spell. "Kelgan," repeated the voice, "what are you doing?" The voice dropped almost to a hiss. "What is *that?*"

Dazedly, he looked up to meet Nevander's wide-eyed stare. "It's the sword you gave me with the clothes," was his puzzled response.

"We gave you no sword," insisted Nevander, "and what clothes?"

Kelgan sputtered like a failed petard. "But... but...." Gathering his wits, he produced a coherent sentence.

"Every week since I arrived, a complete set of clothes has been placed in my room, usually in this chair." He indicated the one he occupied. "There is always a note that says 'wear this' on top. The clothes from the previous week are always gone when I wake up, and the new ones are there. I thought... I assumed...."

"You thought we were providing you with a wardrobe that suited us."

"Exactly."

"*We,* on the other hand, thought you were a frustrated popinjay, welcoming the chance to air your fancies."

"Where did you think all those different outfits came from? You saw my baggage."

"A little clever sorcery; after all, they were always the same colors, with very little style variation."

"Until now," Kelgan reminded him.

"Until now," agreed Nevander with a grimace.

"What does it mean?" Kelgan asked grimly. "If not you, then who? I never felt a tingle. The things were just there."

"It means we have even more to fear than we knew."

He snorted. "More than *you* knew, perhaps. I don't know anything, and I'm afraid of everything."

Nevander also snorted. "I acknowledge the correctness of your position." Gravity settled around him again. "Do you think this is connected with your experience of the first night?"

"I cannot say. I *felt* something then... I was aware of the probe attempt. No presence announced itself with the arrival of the clothing. They just... arrived."

"Always the same two words?"

"Always, until now."

"And this time?"

Wordlessly, Kelgan proffered the note.

Nevander's face, already the same unrelieved ivory of his sister's, paled to bleached bone.

"The handwriting," he breathed, "it is mine!"

"Wha... ," Kelgan sprang to his feet, the sword clanging to the floor. He hastily bent to retrieve it, almost slicing off his hand in the bargain.

"Let me see the sword more closely," demanded Nevander.

He held it out, hilt-first. At Nevander's first attempt to close on it, a pale-blue flame ran the length of the blade, and spewed forth from the hilt with the crackle of heavenly electricity. Nevander tumbled backwards, swearing and clutching his hand. The sword dropped from Kelgan's nerveless fingers, striking the floor with a ringing suggestive of the knell of doom.

"Nevander, your hand!"

"It's nothing." di Nerrill waved him away.

"Let me see." He seized Nevander by the wrist, giving a shocked gasp at the sight. The fingers appeared puffed like pan-fried sausage, blisters already starting to break and ooze.

"T'would seem that is *your* sword," Nevander jested flatly through gritted teeth.

Kelgan made no answer, just rummaged in his knapsack for his medicinal kit. Selecting a salve, he applied it to di Nerrill's burnt fingers, muttering a few words to enhance the healing properties.

Nevander's fingers shrank back to a more normal size, much to their owner's relief, and he ruefully flexed them a few times. "We must adjust our attitudes toward you, my Mage—magician *and* warrior, in one."

Kelgan again resisted the urge to test the "warrior" appellation by applying a little force to his Lordship's teeth; gritting his own, he merely said, "You know better."

Retrieving the sword hastily from the floor where it had fallen, he managed, in his haste, to fetch Nevander a good thwack on the shins. His Lordship gave a high-pitched "Yow" and danced around on one leg, saying words he was astonished to hear from the seemingly aloof di Nerrills. Stammering an apology, Kelgan nevertheless felt a slight glow of pleasure he found impossible to squelch. *Warrior, indeed.*

··· 11 ···

Ready or Not

D aliane was preparing.

By day, she had T'Jules putting the guards through such continual drills and rigorous maneuvers, their battle-scarred captain refused to follow another order until he received an explanation.

"Damme, Your Grace, if you're expecting an invasion; I'd like to know about it."

T'Jules had fobbed him off with a lame excuse. "There have been disturbing, uh, rumors, B'Ress."

"Rumors. Rumors!" Captain B'Ress Ogard sputtered. But the captain returned to drilling his men like a faithful old warrior, despite grave doubts about the Baron's sanity.

Daliane also insisted that T'Jules hire two of the Mel'hachim to spar with her and with him, in secrecy. Taciturn and barbaric, these mercenaries from the far south—some said from hell—were known to give little quarter, even in practice. The gender of their opponents mattered not. Daliane fell into bed bruised and aching every sunup. One possible bright side to this torture was that she slept the sleep of the peaceful dead. Since the voices did not trouble her when she fought, all in all, there was something to be said for serious masochism. Life was looking up!

Also, on the plus side, her dogged persistence earned the grudging respect of the Mel'hachim. Although known for their absolute loyalty—once they accepted a contract, only death or mutual agreement could cancel it—they did not necessarily regard their employers with enthusiasm. Acknowledged the best warriors in the world, their self-confidence was not arrogance, merely assurance. They held no one in awe. Sincere and diligent effort, however, softened them.

Daliane's stoic acceptance of her bruises and cuts won their good-will, as well. She never uttered more than an occasional, "oof," during their not-so-mock battles. Each rough buffet seemed to prompt her to fiercer response. On this day, she even succeeded in forcing her partner back a few steps before her concentrated rush.

"She is one to reckon with."

T'Jules started as the deep voice of the second Mel'hach sounded at his shoulder.

The Mel'hach continued with a hint of amusement, "At least for some."

T'Jules rounded on him, then caught the twinkle in the usually flinty eyes of the mercenary. Realizing he was seeing the Mel'hach for the first time out of practice gear, the Baron studied the warrior for a moment before replying.

And what a study he was! Hair bound around the forehead with a beaded band, which fell in a cascade of multi-colored strands down his back nearly to his waist, sleeveless jerkin of red leather, beaded likewise, full leather trousers tucked into gaudily figured boots, and a crossed sword belt bearing the two short swords the Mel'hachim favored—the very epitome of barbaric splendor. Nonetheless, no one made the mistake of thinking the Mel'hachim overdressed fops, or at least no one made that error twice. Handsome, dark, and quick to take offense in their dealings, even their employers walked on the wary side.

Before his stare could be considered rude, T'Jules acknowledged, "Her courage shames even me."

The Mel'hach twinkled again at the "even," but made no comment. His thoughts were plain, however. T'Jules grinned suddenly, to be rewarded with an answering grin. Chancing a rebuff, T'Jules ventured a question. "You have been with us for five weeks, now, and the Baroness and I have only addressed the two of you as "Warrior." Do you have a name? And, if so, may we use it?

A mixed expression crossed the Mel'hach's face. After a moment of inner debate, he came to a decision. "I am Jorgo. My partner is Nadi, we are mated."

T'Jules sucked in his breath as he ascertained the meaning behind the words. "A woman... Nadi is a...."

The grin reappeared on Jorgo's face. "I have heard we all look alike to *klentah*."

T'Jules began to laugh. To his surprise and pleasure, Jorgo joined him in an infectious booming basso. Finished for the night, Daliane and Nadi met them.

"Has there been a humorous event?" queried the Mel'hachim woman.

"It is so, my wife," answered Jorgo.

Looking from Daliane to T'Jules, Nadi comprehended instantly. The sound of her laughter spilled over them in a husky imitation of her husband.

Daliane stood, baffled and silent until T'Jules explained. "Let me introduce Jorgo and Nadi, they are husband and wife.

Amazement and understanding strove for dominance on Daliane's countenance.

"But, why didn't we know?" she demurred.

"We always dress alike, and I am tall and slim," Nadi smiled, "in my padded practice vest, who could tell?"

"We alternated sparring with each of you, so that you would not grow used to just one of us," added Jorgo. "Our fighting styles are similar, but there are subtle differences."

"We had the same teacher," Nadi supplied, "my father."

"That was how we came together. She was the best opponent I had ever encountered," said Jorgo with pride. "It was safer to be on the same side."

Having experienced the banked ferocity of both the Mel'hachim, Daliane and T'Jules agreed fervently.

Daliane frowned. "Why did you not tell us you were husband and wife? We had no idea that Nadi..."

"Exactly," affirmed Nadi with a superior smile.

"We wish our employers to have no other expectations, save we are warriors," Jorgo explained.

"What we do not give, we do not ask." Nadi placed an arm around Daliane's shoulders. "With you, little one, there is no need." Her beaming smile was that of a proud mother.

Daliane flushed with pleasure at the implied compliment. T'Jules remained curious. "Why did you choose to reveal yourselves now?" Their deliberate choice seemed obvious to him.

"We like you," was Nadi's simple response.

"You have heart," said Jorgo, "and you do not give up."

"We have been pressing you, little by little, harder and harder," added Nadi, "you just keep working, harder and harder."

"You've been pressing us *harder*," Daliane was unbelieving, "harder than when we started?"

"Your skills have improved, my Baroness," chuckled Jorgo. "You didn't realize how much."

"I didn't realize at all!" corrected Daliane. "I was beginning to be very depressed about never getting any better."

"You and the Baron have been outstanding students," Jorgo reassured her. "You, in particular."

T'Jules was a bit ruffled by the Mel'hach's obvious admiration for his wife, until he realized how much Daliane needed encouragement. Besides, he acknowledged to himself, she was as good as a man, any day.

Jorgo interrupted his thoughts. "Might we ask a question in return?"

T'Jules was sure he knew what was coming. He exchanged a glance with Daliane, who gave a slight nod in confirmation. She answered for him.

"Please feel free to ask. Of course, we may not answer...." Her laugh was edged.

The Mel'hachim did not join in. Both regarded her so soberly, she felt the blood rising to her cheeks.

"Please... ask," she reiterated uncomfortably.

Nadi began gently. "We have noticed your schedule is irregular."

T'Jules "humph" interrupted her.

Nadi continued with a faint smile. "We have also noticed that there is a certain... desperation... evident in your practice."

"Nadi and I believe there is a danger which presses you. Not a sometime soon danger, but a *now*," rumbled Jorgo.

"Now and dire," interposed Nadi, "you are driven far beyond the need to protect yourselves."

Daliane chewed on a finger. The need to unburden herself warred with her fear of being thought insane. T'Jules stayed silent, leaving it to Daliane to make the choice. Nadi interpreted his silence correctly.

"Baroness?"

"C-come inside," Daliane turned abruptly away and marched toward the huge, oak double-doors, which opened into the castle's kitchens from the practice-yard.

Threading her way through the bustling kitchen staff without a backward look, she took the stairs to the floor above, two at a time.

The Mel'hachim merited many a long stare from the kitchen workers, who were cleaning up the remains of dinner and preparing for the morning breakfast. Since the warriors had previously repaired to the barracks to bunk with the soldiers, they had been seldom seen by the household staff, and then only from a distance. The air was thick with mingled awe and curiosity; responding to it, the Mel'hachim donned their haughtiest airs, striding as regally as lions, much to T'Jules' amusement. Out of sight of the kitchen, grins spread across their faces as they nudged each other jocularly. They exchanged a few words in Mel'hachi, in which *klentah* figured prominently.

T'Jules, who now knew what the word meant, found himself more than a little irritated at being grouped with "foreigners." He swallowed his irritation, however, thinking that course to be the better part of valor. True, while for the moment, they had found favor with the Mel'hachim, the unpredictability of the Mel'hachim temper was a well-founded rumor. It was always better to have willing employees, especially when those employees had long memories reaching far beyond the termination of the contract.

They arrived at the door of Daliane's and T'Jules bedroom. Daliane threw open the door. T'Jules was surprised that Daliane would invite the Mel'hachim there, and even Nadi and Jorgo looked dubious.

"Come in here," Daliane ordered. "I think it's safe until midnight."

A quick glance shot between Jorgo and Nadi, but they followed her in with no objection. Daliane slammed the door shut and barred it after the four of them. The Mel'hachim looked a bit nervous at this, but once again made no objection.

"I hoped I wouldn't have to tell this tale," Daliane began. "However, I should have foreseen that our unconventional living arrangement would raise questions."

Jorgo muttered something under his breath. At Daliane's look of inquiry, he said, with a touch of embarrassment, "At first, we thought you did not like each other."

Realizing he was referring to their separate sleeping habits, Daliane gave a tiny gasp of laughter and blushed.

Her warm voice reflecting her enjoyment of their discomfiture, Nadi added, "We saw, very shortly, that was not the case."

T'Jules loudly cleared his throat. "Yes, well...."

"Forgive my thoughtless interruption," rumbled Jorgo. "I am an insensitive fool."

Nadi patted his hand, "The very subject of many of our 'discussions.' Please tell us the rest of your tale, Baroness, and I will hold his tongue for you."

Daliane smiled, feeling she had at least one sympathetic ear.

"One night, I was awakened...."

At the conclusion of her story, the Mel'hachim sat stunned. Jorgo's knuckles were white where he clutched his short swords. "This is a terrible evil," he said, the first to speak. "One we have never met before."

"You... you believe me?"

"Of course, Baroness, you could not lie. We have seen this." Jorgo assured her. Nadi affirmed this assurance with a nod.

Tears filled Daliane's eyes. Impulsively she embraced both of them.

"Thank you. Thank you," she whispered.

And Two to Go

E zrael deposited Bethne on the now empty cot. Placing a wet cloth on her forehead, he chaffed her hands until her eyes fluttered open. They rested on him blankly for a moment, then memory returned, and with it panic. She jerked to a sitting position, screaming, "Pelly, Pelly." Ezrael forced her back on the cot, saying soothingly, "Now, now, Bethie, now, now."

She burst into a storm of tears. Through the tears, she choked out, "He died, Ez. He died. I saw him."

Ezrael made no answer, only held her as tightly as he could, without crushing her altogether. Superstitious fear froze his voice, but his thoughts ran wild. *Dead, yes, he were dead, all right.*

Bethne's sobs subsided, to be supplanted by a strange fatalistic calm.

"Somthin' called him, Ez, and he got up. T'warn't nothin' natural. T'were somthin' bad. He didn't rise joyful—an' did you hear him talk? That warn't our Pelly. He din't never call us but Ma and Pa."

Ezrael was still unable to force out a syllable. Not fear for himself constricted his larynx, but the virtually unthinkable idea of Pellerin in the clutches of an evil doer—power great enough to raise the dead. Never for a moment did he doubt Bethne. Pellerin had died, and then he had ridden away on their horse at the bidding of something too horrible to contemplate.

Bethne recalled Ezrael to himself. "We got to go to the city, Ez.

We got to go to the temple. We got to ask Lumen to either get him back, or take him to the Light."

Ezrael winced. He was not a religious man, although he gave lip service to the belief in Lumen, the powerful god of Light and Life. Moreover, he had the rural man's natural suspicion of cities. The Callett faire was big and populous enough for him, the faire attendees all solid men and women of the soil, like himself. Most had never set foot in the distant temple, and laughed at the idea that supernaturals had any impact or influence in their lives. The idea of asking a god directly for anything sat ill with him.

Ordinarily Bethne shared his views. Witnessing the death and resurrection of her only son had profoundly altered her outlook. That naked demonstration of godlike power had awakened her childhood faith. To balance Darkness, *there had to be Light.*

"Ez?"

"Yes, yes, Bethie, you're right. That's what we got to do." For her sake, he would do anything.

"Help me up, Ezrael, I want to go now."

"But... Bethie, we can't...."

"Yes, we can. We're going to pack what we need, and we're gonna go. Now!"

Ezrael helped Bethne to her feet with a sigh. She immediately began to bustle in her normal fashion. He could almost believe it *was* normal as long as he kept his eyes away from the empty cot.

"Don't stand gawkin', Ezrael. Help me."

He moved reluctantly to gather up a few things. He envied Bethne her ability to sublimate her grief and shock into practical action. Not that he thought in those words, he only experienced a vague yearning not to feel so old and muddled. Bethne always seemed to know what to do, or anyway she acted like she did. He wasn't very good at pretending. If he didn't know what to do, he couldn't act like he did.

"Bethie."

She rounded on him with hands on hips; then softened when she saw his face. "I know, Ez. But I got to do somthin'. If I don't, I'll have one of them fits like our old sow when we took her piglets. This is the only thing I kin think to do."

"You was allus a better thinker than me, Bethie."

"No Ez, I just thought about different things."

Different—like how, and why, and where. Driven by endless curiosity and boundless energy, she always needed to know. The boundless energy had waned a bit after the birth of Pellerin. They had waited a long time for a child. When one finally came along, it had proved both a chancy pregnancy and a difficult and protracted birth, which had left Bethne spent and weak—a weakness that had never fully retreated. She resumed her usual bustling manner; but when she thought he wasn't looking she would droop, her shoulders sagging, and put out her hand to support herself. Then she would heave a sigh, square her shoulders and continue as though aught had happened.

Those moments of weakness came more and more frequently as Pellerin grew to his teens. Bethne had been visibly weakening for some months now, and Ezrael had begun to prepare himself for the time it would be just him and Pellerin. He grimaced as the twist fate had taken struck him afresh. He deliberately drew his mind away from the thought that Pelly had been dead. Dead! And then he went for a horseback ride.

Ezrael felt himself approaching as close to hysteria as he had ever been. Thinkin'. That's what thinkin' would do for you. With an effort, he blanked his mind.

"We don't have no horse, Bethie. You'll have to walk all the way."

"We'll jes' have to hitch up the goat, Ez."

"The goat?"

"Course, Ez. We'll put our stuff in the goat cart. We'll still have to walk but we won't have to carry nothin'"

Embarrassed that he hadn't thought about that, Ezrael muttered his agreement. He marched out to bridle Capriola, the goat, stumbling over the doorstep as he went. Twice as embarrassed, he kicked the feed bucket at though it had tripped him, earning himself a stubbed toe.

Bethne chuckled in spite of herself, and shook her head in feigned disgust. Ezrael threw a sheepish smile over his shoulder and disappeared into the shed. As soon as he dashed from view, Bethne's pretense of strength fell away from her. She clutched her chair with both hands to hold herself up.

"Oh, Lumen," she whispered, "whatever shall we do."

··· 13 ···

The Obsidian Ophidian

As Nevander rubbed his shin, muttering imprecations under his breath, Kelgan once more gathered his belongings under Neroma's critical gaze.

"Well," she said finally. "You *look* useful, at any rate."

The floating locks of her hair pointed sharply in his direction, adding their own little sarcastic punctuation to her words. Although he knew Neroma to be more than forthright, speaking her mind without a qualm, Kelgan lost a few moments wondering what happened to her hair should Neroma tell a lie. Did those searching tendrils cross themselves like tiny fingers, hiding behind her head?

A buffet on the shoulder from the object of his attention woke him up. "Oh, sorry," he lied, "just making sure I hadn't forgotten anything necessary."

As he spoke, he felt the barest of tingles. Before he could focus on it, it died away, leaving him uncertain whether he had actually felt anything.

He swung nervously around at another rap at the door. "Terencia," commented Neroma, admitting her maid.

Terencia was dressed for travel. Still in unrelieved brown; but now she resembled a forester, woolen tunic, leather jerkin, hose and high leather boots. A workman-like dagger was thrust through her belt along with a pair of heavy gauntlets.

"Very pretty disguise," chuckled Kelgan, "I hope you don't run into anyone who proves dangerous."

"Terencia is actually a member of the Autarch's guard." Neroma remarked casually. "However, the Autarch has graciously loaned her to me more or less permanently."

Terencia bestowed a smirk of satisfaction at Kelgan's gape. "It's a long story," she said dismissively, "you look ready for a costume ball, yourself." She eyed the sword with raised brows.

"That's another long story," Kelgan retorted, feeling remarkably like a four-year-old (my costume can beat your costume—nyah, nyah, nyah).

Nevander and Neroma grinned as the other two exchanged glares.

"There's nothing like starting a trip in cheerful company," was Nevander's guileless comment. He rolled his eyes with an expression of exaggerated innocence.

Kelgan and Terencia looked abashed. "Truce," suggested Terencia, and offered her hand. "I'll save my comments on your swordsmanship until the time comes."

Kelgan accepted her hand with rather bad grace. "Truce," he agreed sulkily. It would have been nice if she had left the last sentence unsaid.

Sensing his thought, Terencia added, "You do look very handsome in that gray outfit, I must say."

Kelgan stammered a thank you, squelching the urge to tread on her instep.

"Midnight approaches," warned Neroma.

"We are ready," answered an instantly somber Nevander.

Kelgan was relieved to find he felt nearly clearheaded, almost prepared, and even a little bit brave. He had feared that at the last moment his knees would turn to water, along with his bowels. He started for the door, only to be restrained by di Nerrill.

"Not that way, my Mage." Moving swiftly to Kelgan's bed, he pressed one of the grinning gargoyles that decorated the headboard, revealing the tiled floor beneath.

Dropping to his knees, Nevander counted the tiles carefully backwards to where the middle of Kelgan's bed would have been. Pressing the corner of one tile, he muttered under his breath. A click, and a section of the floor slid down and under the rest of the floor. Cold, stale air flowed up; cold stone steps flowed down.

"Th-that was there all the time?" Kelgan squeaked.

"Yes, my Mage," affirmed Nevander. "But there was no need for concern, one can only go down...."

"Only down!" Gulping, Kelgan tried not to think of the dire reasons which might necessitate a one-way passage.

"I will go first, to light the way." Nevander continued, "Neroma next, then Terencia, and you, my swordsman, will be the last."

Once again, Terencia favored Kelgan with her superior smirk. As she bent to descend the staircase, the smirk changed to a shriek. Somehow, the hilt of Kelgan's sword managed to contact her presented posterior with a firm "thuck!" She whirled on the step, in fury.

"Damn knapsack," muttered Kelgan, stumbling a bit as he adjusted his various burdens, carefully keeping his eyes off Terencia.

With an unladylike oath, she disappeared from sight. Feeling an oppressive sense of finality, Kelgan followed. With the slightest of sighs, the floor slid back into place above him. Nevander's witch light was faint and somehow forlorn in the otherwise smothering blackness. Kelgan needed to stoop to avoid grazing his head, in a passageway obviously built for his much shorter companions.

"Ouch!" A projection from the ceiling caught him smartly on the crown of his pate.

Nevander's voice floated back to him, "I suggest lighting your end of the procession, my Mage."

What a lackwit, I am, cursed Kelgan; calling his light into being, he ducked just in time to avoid another smart rap.

"That's better," whispered Terencia, a trace of strain in her voice.

Kelgan was sympathetic; the damp frigid walls seemed to press in on them. *Lumen knows the ceiling presses down.* Kelgan ducked again. He began to hear the persistent murmur of water—fast moving from the sound of it.

"We approach," was Nevander's far from comforting remark.

Sweat trickled down Kelgan's side, making his teeth chatter in the icy air. To his surprise, Terencia reached behind her and gave his hand a squeeze of empathy. She had donned her gauntlets; the rasp against his skin was reassuring rather than otherwise.

The tunnel discharged them abruptly into a quay. Swift, black, water rushed passed them like spilled lamp oil. Sparks from the witch fire woke answering sparks from the greasy surface.

Terencia gave an involuntary, "Ugh!"

Nevander's ebony eyes displayed matching gleams as he informed them, "We will be following the river now."

"You mean... on it?"

Nevander nodded. "The boat is waiting."

Kelgan, who had never encountered a body of water bigger than the hip deep stream which chuckled behind his stepfather's mill, felt his stomach lurch sickly.

"Where...."

"Does it go?" Nevander anticipated him. "Underground for two hundred miles, then into the Magnus Aurea."

Kelgan sat on the quay; spots danced before his eyes. Underground for two hundred miles! This great ebony snake wound beneath their feet, had done so all along, and he had been totally unaware. *Snake. An obsidian ophidian.* He gave an hysterical chortle, which bubbled from his lips more like a sob.

Nevander stooped in concern. "Kelgan, what ails you?"

"I'm all right, I'm just... I'm just blind and deaf, is all. I'm a sorcerer! I didn't know there were stairs under my bed. I didn't know there was an enormous river under us. I didn't...." Kelgan choked on his next words.

Nevander shook him with some force. "Kelgan, Kelgan, there were wards, and you had no reason to suspect."

"There were wards," said Kelgan furiously. "I didn't even feel *them.*"

Neroma knelt beside him. "You must have noticed the scent in your room."

Kelgan stared at Neroma, a foolish expression breaking over his face. "A scent ward, one of your scent wards, I just thought it was the flowers from the garden below." *So that was why I had asthma every morning, they might have told me.*

Neroma answered him with a grin, and batted her eyelashes at him in a pretense of coy flirtation.

Kelgan got to his feet. A scent ward... of course! Even after their lessons, he had not yet really come to understand the principal behind Neroma's talent, nor had he been completely able to penetrate one of them no matter what counterforce he had brought to bear. He felt a little happier with himself, realizing it wasn't his complete incompetence, although a glance at the dark water made him queasy again.

Nevander gave him a shrewd look. "Do not be uneasy, my Mage, the river knows us well."

"Knows you, maybe," said Kelgan under his breath.

Nevertheless, he followed Nevander without hesitation to the tied-up boat. It looked no more than a walnut shell to Kelgan.

Terencia sidled up beside him. "I get seasick," she offered.

Kelgan smiled, grateful for her attempt to put him at ease. "I don't know whether I do or not, I've never done anything but wade," he responded. There was general laughter at that, puny jest that it was, but it gave them a sense of comradeship.

"You will be doing many things you have never done before, my Mage, and seeing sights you've never beheld." Nevander gestured extravagantly with both hands. "Never say I've not provided you with opportunity."

More laughter, but with a slightly uncomfortable edge.

Nevander untied the small craft and tossed the rope to Kelgan.

"Do push us off, my Mage, then jump with alacrity."

Nevander sprang gratefully into the skiff, leaving Kelgan to think, *posing again.* Nevander then helped Neroma and Terencia to board. "Now," he directed Kelgan.

Kelgan pushed the hull away from the dock, then attempted to emulate Nevander's graceful leap. He landed in an awkward sprawl of arms, legs, and rope, athwart one of the seats. With much pretense of care, the women helped him upright, untangling the rope from his limbs and ostentatiously brushing him off. He fumed inwardly, but did his best to present a nonchalant facade.

"Well away, my Mage," said Nevander, smothering a laugh behind his hands.

The boat lunged forward, neither hand at the tiller, nor at the oars. Peering over the side cautiously, Kelgan discovered that the boat rode entirely out of the water, barely touching the surface.

"A gift from our Mother."

Kelgan waited for further explanation, but Neroma sat brooding, her eyes directed at her shoes. He shrugged and looked away. Terencia shifted restlessly on the hard seat.

"It's cold."

It was cold. Their breath steamed in the air. Kelgan drew his cloak tightly around him, thanking his unknown benefactor for its warmth. The others followed suit. They sat in silence, wrapped in their own thoughts.

··· 14 ···

Une Petite Armée

"What will you do now?" queried Jorgo. "We are prepared for an invasion, what if it does not come?"

"The voices... they said they were coming," whispered Daliane.

"But what if they are not bringing an army?" Jorgo persisted.

"I... don't understand." Daliane paled.

"They are evil, but they are enemies of the mind. Will a sword hold them at bay?"

Daliane grew whiter, if possible. "What else can I do?" she asked in despair. "Pray that Lumina, our Mother, sends a miracle!"

"We in Mel'hachi, as you may not know, worship the Two, Foton and Fosfeen," explained Nadi, "but yes, a little prayer might help. We will be glad to add ours to yours." She affectionately patted Daliane's arm.

"Thank you, again," murmured Daliane.

T'Jules eyed Jorgo speculatively. "There was more behind that question than prayer, I think."

Jorgo acknowledged the truth of it with a nod.

"You might want to take an army to them."

"Take...." Daliane gasped.

Jorgo scraped his feet uneasily on the tile. His expression looked troubled, and he glanced at Nadi before he spoke. She gestured for him to continue.

"When you hear the voices, do you feel anything?"

"Anything?"

"A sense of homeland, personality, direction... *anything?*"

Daliane strained to remember. "I—I can't recall, exactly. One is younger, one older... one seems more impetuous. I—I don't know...." She broke off, biting her lip as panic bloomed inside.

Jorgo looked even more uncomfortable, and even more reluctant to speak.

"Would you let them come, and try to learn more?"

The room whirled. Daliane lowered her head to her knees. She breathed in short gasps. T'Jules gathered her in his embrace. After a moment she pushed away from him, saying, "Yes."

One word only.

Jorgo reached behind him to the cascade of beads falling down his back. Detaching a strand, he solemnly tied it in Daliane's hair.

"You are a true Mel'hach, my sister."

Nadi gently kissed her on one cheek, and Jorgo on the other.

"The Two keep you always in their glow," Nadi said.

T'Jules forced a smile. "Congratulations, newest of the Mel'hachim."

Jorgo winked. "*Klentah* become Mel'hachim through their wives. You are now an honorary member."

Nadi twinkled, and gave T'Jules a kiss directly on the mouth.

"The Two keep you as well, my brother."

T'Jules wished for a little less transparency. Used to being lauded as something of a champion, his nose was only a bit bent at being bested at the game by his small wife, but bent it was. Unfortunately, everyone seemed to notice. Well, maybe not everyone; that same small wife, in her own unflagging generosity, would never attribute less than generous feelings to him.

Thinking that, he laughed aloud, kissed Nadi resoundingly in return, and exclaimed brightly, "I am indirectly honored."

Jorgo and Nadi bent double; Daliane, joined in uncertainly. Lost as she had been in the dread of welcoming the voices deliberately, the by-play had passed over her.

Jorgo fetched T'Jules a friendly slap on the back, which took his breath away. When he could speak again, he suggested dinner.

Jorgo and Nadi hesitated. "It has not been the custom of the

Mel'hachim to mingle socially with their employers," demurred Nadi.

Daliane looked at her with appeal.

"But, then, you are our friends and now members of our family," affirmed Jorgo, jovially.

"And we would be honored," added Nadi.

White teeth flashed in their swarthy faces.

Daliane let her breath out in relief. "Oh, I am so glad. We need friends so badly."

T'Jules rang for a retainer. When old S'Mar arrived, the Baron ordered a meal, "A fine repast, S'Mar. We are... er... celebrating."

S'Mar eyed the Mel'hachim uncertainly. "For... four, Your Grace?"

"Of course, for four, we are entertaining friends."

"Friends," whispered the old man. "Certainly, Your Grace." Bobbing and edging backwards, the old retainer vanished through the doorway.

Feral grins shone in the dim light as T'Jules turned back to the waiting group.

"And now, my friends," he stressed the last word, "let us have as much light as the torches will provide."

"For a while," added Daliane. Her skin seemed stretched so tightly across her cheekbones, they gleamed as whitely as though the flesh had melted from them.

"We are with you, my sister," was Nadi's quick acknowledgment of Daliane's distress.

Daliane threw off her apprehensions with a visible effort. Forcing a smile, she demanded, "Nadi, Jorgo, tell us of Mel'hach."

Again, white teeth gleamed in response. "Our favorite subject," Jorgo stated gleefully.

With a snort, Nadi corrected him, "His *second* favorite subject, his number one favorite is how he never loses a fight."

"Well," challenged Jorgo, "do I?"

"How about that drifter from Mel'Hachdubin? I seem to remember some difficulty...."

"He tripped me," countered Jorgo.

They were interrupted by the return of S'Mar, followed by a good dozen kitchen servants bearing steaming bowls and platters.

"We're going to eat all that?" Nadi looked incredulous. "I will need a practice suit that stretches."

T'Jules gave an evil grin. "I think S'Mar felt it was better to sate the tigers' appetites before they started on the servants."

Jorgo and Nadi looked self-satisfied; and then fell to heaping their plates with gusto. Some dishes they exclaimed over with enthusiasm; others made them blink and grimace with surprise.

Surfeited at last, they fell back in their chairs with groans. "We will have to give up fighting and become *blutte*," sighed Jorgo.

"What on earth are *blutte*," wondered Daliane.

Nadi explained that they were fat, sea-going, little animals, whose thick layer of blubbery insulation gave them the appearance of floating rubber balls.

"But isn't Mel'hach a desert?" protested T'Jules.

"Much of Mel'hach, yes," replied Jorgo, "but we have nevertheless, a long sea-coast."

T'Jules and Daliane strained to imagine a desert that ran down to the sea, but failed; their moist, and timbered barony was the complete antithesis of such a land.

"We have never been seafarers, however," Jorgo continued, "the Mel'hach have historically looked inward—to the dunes, rather than the waves."

"It has been a struggle," sighed Nadi.

"That is why so many of us became warriors," Jorgo agreed. "We learn to fight in the cradle—the land, the snakes, the scavengers...." His voice trailed away as he gazed at some inward vision which sobered him.

"It is not all fighting," Nadi protested, striving to re-lighten the mood. "Remember the clan feast when we were betrothed?"

Jorgo gave a bark of laughter. "What do you mean, not all fighting? I gave your cousin bruises he'll never forget."

Nadi giggled girlishly. "And his wife took a bite out of your arm."

Jorgo ruefully displayed the scar. "That woman had *teeth!* And the heart of a lion."

"And the temper of a wounded she-kor," said Nadi from the side of her mouth.

Daliane laughed heartily, for a moment forgetting her coming ordeal.

They laughed and chattered through the night; the men swapping improbable stories of their many female conquests to the accompaniment of jeers and boos from the women. To Daliane's surprise, the first pale rays of dawn began to scratch at the shutters for admittance and still they sat, regaling each other with ever wilder tales. These had distracted her—almost—so that the voices remained just hissing whispers at the edge of her mind. *"Toooo," "Yesss," "Nooo."*

"I have kept you up all night," she gasped.

Jorgo leered and winked. "Nadi and I have been up many a night, before this."

Nadi fetched him a sharp kick in the shins, but smiled in remembrance.

"We will go, now," she said, rising to her feet and dragging Jorgo with her. "You will need to rest... for tonight."

Daliane's good humor evaporated and her fragile confidence crumpled like eggshells. The taut white look returned to her face as she clutched at T'Jules arm.

"Tonight," she whispered.

"We will all be here, my sister." Jorgo and Nadi spoke as one.

Daliane reached up to them as they towered over her with another of her impulsive embraces. Lifting her from her feet, both kissed her heartily; setting her gently down, they drifted away as silently as smoke.

Daliane stood for a moment in silence. Turning to T'Jules, she smiled almost naturally, overcome with her love for his never-failing support and understanding.

"Let's *both* go to bed, Tee Jee."

T'Jules swept her up in his arms and rushed her to the mattress.

··· 15 ···

Obscenely Obsidian

With a cry, Kelgan jerked awake. Impossible though it seemed to him, he had dozed, lulled by the hypnotic sameness of their progress. With the thinning of his wards, the voices quickly filled the silence. *"Too stupid!" "Too young!" "Too dull!" "Too tall!"*

"Are you suffering from cramps, my Mage?" inquired Nevander with a humorous quirk of his lips.

"I—I was dreaming... I think." Kelgan carefully straightened his right leg, which *was* cramped, come to think of it.

Terencia snorted. However, Neroma shot him a piercing glance; she had not missed the sudden ashen cast of his face. "Of what?" Her voice thrilled in its velvet bell tones.

Kelgan widened his eyes. "It was just a..." His voice faltered as he was struck with recall.

"Pray entertain us, Magister Defthand," Nevander spoke jocularly, but his gaze was keen.

"Voices," stuttered Kelgan, "it was the voices." He had everyone's attention now, including Terencia's.

"Too near." "Too far." "Too low." "Too slow." They had mocked with their obscene titters. When he told the others, Neroma's hand went to her throat. *"Here!"*

Kelgan jerked in shock. Her voice had *rasped!* He turned to Nevander, who sat slumped as though in despair.

"We had thought they could not follow The River." Nevander spoke with emphasis. He straightened then, and actually winked at Kelgan.

"Well, it's time for more, er, definitive measures!"

As he spoke, a faint fog began to rise around them, accompanied by a distinct floral perfume. It grew stronger, until Kelgan was dizzied from the sweetness, struggling to keep his wards warded against their wards. Terencia coughed and unobtrusively drew a handkerchief from her sleeve, applying it delicately to her nose. Neroma looked apologetic but the fog deepened and dampened. Beads of condensation began to form on everything and everyone, rendering the boat's occupants miserable and dripping.

Kelgan thought back to the first night of their acquaintance and the long, damp, forest ride. Now, as then, only Neroma's hair retained its separate and peculiar existence, each strand straining in concentration, ending in a tightly curled rosebud.

Half suffocated from the cloying fragrance and shivering wet, Kelgan thought, *I'm doomed to die of mildew with these people.* He carefully kept away from the thought of other, more dreadful ways to perish.

The boat suddenly lunged forward, more than doubling its already unnatural rate of speed. Taken unawares, Kelgan's chin hit Nevander's shoulder, forcing his jaws together with a snap and his teeth painfully into his tongue. His aggrieved yowl brought a curse from Nevander, and it reduced the women to helpless giggles.

"You could ub ward be," he huffed, causing yet another round of hilarity, joined this time by Nevander. After an indignant moment, Kelgan surrendered and added weak laughter to theirs.

The slight moment of humor, brief though it was, eased some of the tension which had gripped them since Kelgan's recital of his dream.

"We are sorry, Kelgan," apologized Nevander, "'tis best we not linger underground. I did not think to say 'hold on',"

"But, two hundred miles, we will be days," protested Kelgan.

"Not so, my Mage, for we skim and skip as the wind."

"And we are now invisible to probes," added Neroma.

"Will they not guess our direction?" queried Terencia. "After all, the current flows but one way."

"We are traveling far faster than before, little brown wren," winked Nevander. "Once we reach the bay, our direction is unguessable."

"I see," Terencia retorted repressively. Stung by the 'wren' she turned a withering eye on Nevander, then sniffed at the comical moue she received in return.

Kelgan became aware of a change in the rhythm of their motion—a rise in pitch of the wind whistling past them, an almost infinitesimal vibration that found a sympathetic rattle in his teeth, making his jaws ache. He grasped the seat beneath him firmly with both hands before peering warily over the gunwale. Although almost unsurprised at the sight that greeted this cautious glance, he failed to smother a horrified exclamation. Small pale faces with dismayingly pointed teeth set in slash-like mouths grinned up at him. Their heads punctuating the water like so many white periods, they appeared to be flowing the boat along, keeping it speeding forward at least a foot out of the water. His head spun and his stomach did an acrobatic maneuver worthy of a seasoned saltimbanque. Dropping his head quickly between his knees, he breathed slowly and carefully, suffering Terencia's rude snigger in silence. Indeed, Kelgan was afraid to open his mouth at all, certain that his hastily gobbled lunch would follow.

Conquering his nausea after a brief struggle, Kelgan raised his head to glance at Terencia. He realized, after a moment, that her face was as pale as his own and the pupils of her eyes had nearly swallowed the irises, making her look eerily like Neroma.

That thought made him glance in the direction of the di Nerrill twins, who had remained oddly silent in the face of Kelgan's malaise. They sat as though turned to marble, paying not the slightest heed to the by-play in the boat.

Kelgan felt a splitting of his psyche. He also noted that familiar ice-water crawl in his veins.

Finding Terencia's gaze again, he found her hand, as well. She said nothing, nor did he, but their fingers entwined convulsively. He carefully avoided speaking of what he had seen below them.

The boat surged on—so fast the tunnel walls blurred and wavered. Colder, colder, Kelgan did not remember putting his arms around Terencia, but realized she was huddled against him, teeth chattering. The wind stung his eyes although the fog and scent did not dissipate, and tore at his cloak.

··· 16 ···

A Happy Wanderer

The neatly dressed young man on the somewhat cantankerous and sway-backed old mare was polite—excessively so, *and* innocent, *and* fresh-faced, *and* harmless looking. Why then did the dogs back away spraddle-legged, hair standing stiffly erect on their spines? Why did the cats yowl and slink off on their bellies? Why did every infant shrink in howling terror?

This was not the first time the young man had stopped and asked, "Which way to Rivermouth?"

The tinkers had brought news of the strange youngster and his persistent query from other villages. The boy seemed to be zigging and zagging across the valley as though to hit every village possible.

When answered, he would bow stiffly in the saddle and tender profuse thanks, albeit his eyes never rested on the object of his gratitude. Then a flap of the reins, and the old mare would away in a shambling trot, ludicrous to behold, and one would have thought mighty uncomfortable to endure.

The tale of the mysterious youngster grew wilder with the telling. There were those who swore they had seen horse and rider disappear between one step and the next. And those who swore all the village cows went dry simultaneously with the first words from the young man's mouth. And then there were those who claimed to have heard strange voices echoing the question, *"Which way?" "This way." "That way." "No way."* But there are always folks who want to grab center stage by claiming the impossible.

The irregular course would, in the end, take the boy closer and closer to the destination he purported to seek, Rivermouth, where the underground river, Ebonspear, foamed out of the cliff face and dropped a screaming 500 feet into the Magnus Aurea, its dark, mineral-rich flow mingling with the turquoise marine waters and streaking them a mile out to sea. There, close to the confluence, the town had sprung up, as towns would wherever water brought a chance of trade, and with trade, a chance of prosperity. It was very like its counterparts worldwide, boasting a colorful diversity of lowlife—pimps, prostitutes, cutpurses, assassins, spies, vendors of all it took to dull your senses, cloud your resolve, or undermine your good intentions. A healthy slum, teeming with misery, disease and despair, jostled the docks where the incomparable wealth from the four corners elbowed back. The proximity added not one legitimate peni to the hungry coffers of the poor. *Legitimate,* that is.

From the noisome slum, the town rose, marking with its ascension a corresponding rise in affluence. Crowned by an architecturally mundane Great House; occupied by a fat, sly and mundanely criminal minor lordling. Only an unwillingly acknowledged Wysach connection kept T'Billi where he was, that and a fervid willingness to sell the lowest vices to the highest bidder. T'Billi showed an amazing incompetence for governance, but an equally amazing genius for overseer-ship. From the steam of the stews to the cool calculation of the assassin's guild, his fat, dimpled hands kept their fingers stirring in every pie.

T'Jules, his distant and not-at-all-kissing cousin, looked on T'Billi as a necessary evil given the overt nature of that evil. T'Jules usually kept *his* hands off unless T'Billi's abuses threatened to career out of control. Then, he administered a sharp reprimand just to show T'Billi he was really paying attention. T'Billi would assure T'Jules it was just a 'little' mistake, and T'Jules would pretend to be reassured, after which things would slide back to the status quo until the next time.

··· 17 ···

Confrontation

T'Jules gazed down at his sleeping wife, love catching in his throat and threatening to choke him. He gently stroked the hair back from her face and whispered her name. Her eyes fluttered open. She smiled drowsily up at him until realization struck her. "It's time," she stated flatly.

He nodded. "It's just a few minutes to midnight. Nadi and Jorgo are waiting outside."

"Let them in."

"Dally, are you sure?"

"Oh, Tee Jee, of course I'm not sure. I'll never be *sure*. I just have to do it anyway."

He knew her better than to offer her false reassurance. Taking her hand, he squeezed it tightly, and called out, "Come in, we're ready," knowing what a foolish thing he said.

Jorgo and Nadi entered, also hand in hand, their dark, handsome faces set in identical expressions of resolution. A startled T'Jules noted they wore fighting gear and were fully armed.

"We will be here, my sister," Nadi solemnly informed Daliane. Daliane nodded. Beads of perspiration gathered and ran down here forehead. Her hand was sticky in T'Jules'.

"Should I try to go back to sleep?" she queried. "Should I just shut my eyes?"

Daliane felt a sudden sympathy for netted fish she had seen in the past. Their gasping struggles came vividly back to her. She felt all the oxygen had been sucked from the room; she could never fill her lungs again.

Nadi, concern in her eyes, laid a commanding hand on Daliane's chest, "Slowly," she ordered.

Conscious of the vital, reassuring warmth of Nadi's palm, Daliane fought for calm. Her breathing slowed, and those distressing twinkly spots disappeared from in front of her eyes. Seeing improvement, Nadi removed her hand and Daliane nodded her thanks.

She repeated her earlier question, pleased to note that her voice had stopped squeaking. "What do you think? Should I really try to sleep or just lie here with my eyes shut?"

"Just lie back and shut your eyes, Dally," instructed T'Jules. "I won't ask you to relax." His feeble jest evoked an equally feeble set of chuckles. *Better than nothing,* he thought. Aloud, he continued, "If you fall asleep... well...." Fear wrenched his gut.

Nadi shot him a look of understanding. "We will be here," she reiterated.

Daliane lay back on the bed, straining to keep her breath regular and slow. She shut her eyes, attempting to swallow the lump of terror in her throat.

T'Jules reclined on the bed beside her, clinging to her hand as to a lifeline. Jorgo and Nadi sat one on each side of the bed, hands on sword pommels.

Long minutes ticked away. T'Jules found himself nodding, Jorgo gave him a half-smile. He and Nadi had not relaxed their vigilance for a moment. T'Jules experienced an arrow of shame, which passed through his body and left him preternaturally alert.

Daliane's hand clenched his painfully. He could see the fluttering of her heart at the front of her nightgown, and she was making small gasps. Her eyes rolled wildly back and forth although her lids remained clamped shut. Jorgo had risen. T'Jules heard the soft snick of a withdrawn sword.

Feeling himself utterly helpless, he placed a warning hand across Jorgo's chest. His lips barely parted as he hissed, "Don't!"

He could feel a bit of tension go out of Jorgo's body. However, the warrior made no move to replace the sword; nor did he resume his seat. The exotic planes of Nadi's face stood out in bold relief, reflected harshly in the flickering torchlight. Daliane had paled to a sickly gray, her gown soaked by the sweat of her silent terror.

T'Jules could not tear his eyes from her face, feeling that he shared her agony. Rapt as T'Jules was, it was Jorgo who first noticed that her breathing grew shallower and shallower, the pauses between breaths longer.

"Wake her," he said softly, then a shouted, "WAKE HER!"

Jerked from his empathic trance T'Jules frantically began to shake her. When that failed to rouse her, he slapped Daliane with sharp snaps. He neared hysteria when Nadi laid the flat of her sword, glowing red-hot from the fireplace against Daliane's limp forearm.

With a shriek, Daliane sat up, eyes unfocused and dark with madness. For a few seconds, all sat rigid and motionless. Then the clouds parted, and she knew them.

"Tee Jee," she threw herself at him with sobs strangling her. "Ow?" was her second exclamation, so prosaic and ordinary her onlookers appeared dumbfounded.

Jorgo's rumbling laugh drove some of the shadows, which had seemed to gather around the bed, back into the corners. "Her arm hurts," he observed.

"Yes, it does," agreed Daliane, baffled. She gasped aloud at the sight of the reddened blister running from wrist to elbow.

"What happened to me?"

His voice trembling from strain and fear, T'Jules explained, "We couldn't wake you, my love. Nadi...."

Daliane's gaze shifted to Nadi, whose dark cheeks shone with the tears slowly spilling down them.

"My dearest friend," said Daliane as she gathered Nadi into her arms.

"May I join you?" inquired Jorgo with a softness that fooled no one. And the four huddled together till light showed itself between the shutter chinks.

··· 18 ···

Snaking on the Edge

T he boat flew on. *Flew is the operative word!* thought Kelgan grimly.
Skimming above the oily surface—the twins frozen at the helm—Kelgan and Terencia sat as unwilling passengers in every sense of the word.

Without ceremony, Kelgan slipped his arm around Terencia's shoulders in an attempt to again still both her chattering teeth and his own. She stiffened at his touch, shooting him a glance of suspicion. Her years in the Autarch's guard had made her painfully wary of men. Was he taking advantage of the situation? Noting that his eyes were fixed on the backs of the unmoving pair in front of them, she relaxed, welcoming the warmth. Perversely, after some minutes passed without returning his attention to her, she began to feel resentful of his continued absorption. Kicking him sharply in the ankle seemed to remedy the problem.

"What was that in aid of?" he inquired through gritted teeth, rubbing his ankle furiously.

"What do you think is the matter with them?" she responded disingenuously, eyes wide and lashes fluttering.

"Come off it," he grated, "you're no *femme fatale.*"

The next moment found him sprawled between the bench seats, lights flashing before his eyes.

'What the...?" observing the look on Terencia's face, he subsided, drawing to the far end of the seat.

I seem to come up a bit short where women are concerned, and so far, I've been a bit short as a wizard, as well.

Glumly, he stared at his hands, vaguely aware of the renewed chattering of Terencia's teeth.

Lost in his thoughts, he began to toy idly with the sword at his hip. "Well, someone has faith in me." He didn't realize he had spoken aloud until he heard Terencia's snort of derision.

"Look," he began, in as conciliatory a tone as he could muster, "I don't know where I got off on the wrong foot, but whatever I did, I'm sorry."

Terencia snorted again, and then relented grudgingly. 'No, it's nothing you did. I'm just touchy; nothing has been right for a long time now."

"How long?"

"Since well before you arrived," she responded. "However, things worsened after that. I'm afraid I didn't trust you."

"Or like me, or give me a chance," he retorted, forgetting his identical response to the di Nerrills.

"Yesssss," Terencia admitted, drawing out the word. She thought, chin in hand for some minutes regarding him for a long moment. Then, she seemed to decide something. "You know, of course, that I am a member of the guard?"

He nodded silently

"But no one has told you the whole story?"

It was his turn to snort derisively. "Since when did I get the 'whole story' about anything?"

Terencia gave a rueful smile. "I told them it would be better if you knew it all... but then you *were* sure that you did."

Kelgan stared blankly before he understood the joke.

"I guess I was pretty proud of my Academy training."

"Mmmmmm," she assented.

"But if you didn't trust me, why would you want me to know everything?"

"I was sure you would betray yourself in some way when they told you. Some word, some gesture would have given you away. It would have been obvious to one of my training that you knew more than you should."

"Then why keep me mainly in the dark?"

"The di Nerrills did not agree with me, neither my assessment of you, nor my reasoning as a result. And, I have to admit, your act seemed perfect."

"My act?"

Terencia grinned wickedly. "Bumbling idiot." Then, for the first time since their initial meeting, she burst into genuine laughter.

After a beat, he joined her, although he found laughing at himself somewhat difficult under their circumstances. But then, he had to admit that his months with the di Nerrills had changed him. He felt he had become another person, living another life—no longer a naïve almost-wizard, narrowly focused and narrowly trained. Still....

A glance over her shoulder cut Terencia's laughter off like the silver flash of a knife. "For a minute..."

Kelgan sobered as quickly; he, too, had briefly forgotten their situation.

No change, no movement from the twins. Kelgan assumed his seat next to Terencia. He became conscious of a new vibration, which hovered on the edge of sound.

Terencia looked up at him in horror. "The Nightfall!"

··· 19 ···

Just a Wearyin' for Two

"**B**ethne, I've got to rest, and so does you," Ezrael tugged her down under a tree. Capriola, the goat, pleased at the respite, cropped the roadside grass enthusiastically.

"Jes' for a minute, Ez," Bethne protested, "We gots a ways to go 'afore sunset."

"Bethie, where aire we goin' in such an all-fired hurry?" Ezrael stared gravely into her eyes.

"You knows, Ez, you knows where we're goin'."

"An' what aire we goin' to do when we gets there, Bethie?"

"Why, why we're goin' to tell them...."

"Tell 'em what, Bethie? That our boy stole our only horse jes' after he died? That we're out lookin' for him so's he kin have a proper buryin'? That's after we git's him to give back the horse."

Bethne sagged into Ezrael's arms. Hopeless sobs welling up from deep in her chest shook her frame.

Ezrael patted her back in despair. "I'm sorry, Bethie, ah didn't mean to make you cry agin."

"I knows, Ez, an' you're right—I been so set on gettin' *somewhere*—I jes' din't think what I was gonna do when I got there."

"I knows, Bethie, I wants to do somethin' too. I jes' don't rightly know what. I dint never see nobody git up after bein' dead... 'specially my own boy." Ezrael's voice broke in the lost words, and tears of his own trickled into the crevasses of his weathered face.

They sat for a while in silence, hugging each other and their own individual pain. After a while Bethne ventured, "It'd be bad enough, if he was just dead... but he wasn't, Ez... he was and he wasn't."

Ez didn't bother to answer the unanswerable, just hugged her tighter.

"Let's go home, Bethie," he finally said.

She pulled away from him and glared into his eyes. "No sir, Ez. Don't know 'zactly where we're goin', but I knows I wants to be someplace—anyplace else but home."

Ezrael sighed in resignation. He had known what she would say—knowing her as well as he did. He sympathized with her need for any action, even though he preferred to be in familiar surroundings, waiting to see if Pellerin would somehow be impelled to return home just as mysteriously as he had been impelled to leave. He didn't understand any of it; the hair on the back of his neck stood up just thinking about it. He longed fiercely for the familiar, but he knew his Bethie. She always needed to take action to confront life, and he knew she needed to confront death in the same way.

"Let's go, Ez." Bethie stirred. "Let's find an inn and maybe have some dinner, maybe spend the night." She knew her husband as well as he knew her. They were almost one heart in two bodies, so she knew that, although she felt compelled to push on, *now,* hard as it was, she needed to comfort him.

Ezrael nearly choked with his love for her. She was doing this for him, throttling back her own necessity to be on the move for his sake.

She noticed his hesitation, his doubt. "I means it, Ez."

He kissed her forehead and rose to fetch the goat. Maaing its disapproval at being deprived of fresh greens, the goat dug in its heels. "Consarn, you stubborn old hunk of shoe-leather...." Ez began. A laugh from Bethne stopped him. It wasn't much of a laugh, but it was better than the despair that had gripped her for the past three days.

"By the Lights, Ez, I thought you meant me."

Ez gave a slight snort of laughter in response. "Well, Bethie, there is a resemblance."

··· 20 ···

All Souls Mayday

T'Jules smoothed Daliane's hair back from her damp forehead. "Dally, can you tell us what happened?

Daliane shuddered with a force that shook the bed. "Oh, Tee Jee, it was horrible. They said things...." She gulped.

"Water," said Nadi, holding a glass under Daliane's chin.

Daliane sipped gratefully; the slight respite seemed to strengthen her.

"They said terrible things," she went on. "They want... all of us. As many as they can...." Her voice faltered. "It's our souls, Tee Jee, they want our souls."

Aghast at this revelation, all fell silent for a time. T'Jules finally ventured a question. "What do you think they meant, Dally?"

"It—it keeps them alive, Tee Jee. I didn't understand it all, but they're not really either one."

T'Jules was confused. "Either one *what*, Dally?"

"Alive *or* dead." Three blank stares followed her flat statement; Daliane continued, "The worst thing is... they're not here."

Jorgo sought to express what all were thinking. "They're not alive, they're not dead, and they're not *here*?" His voice rose on the end to what would have been a comical squeak at any other time.

Daliane squirmed uncomfortably. "I know how it sounds."

"No, my sister, I do not doubt you," rumbled Jorgo in his natural voice. "We have known from the beginning that you say only the truth. We have also known, from your telling, that this is an evil like none other. Nadi and I have met and fought many bad men; they were only that—bad men. This is something far beyond our ken."

Daliane managed an almost-smile. "Far beyond my ken, too," she asserted.

"Dally, when you say they are 'not here', can you make that a little clearer."

"It's as though they are reaching through.... It's like...." Daliane helplessly shook her head. "They seem to be so far away and yet so close." She kicked the mattress in frustration with her small foot.

The immensity of his thought created a lump in T'Jules' throat. Clearing it with difficulty, he suggested, "Another universe?"

Heads swung toward him in disbelief.

"But that's impossible, Tee Jee," protested Daliane. "Anyhow, Lumina says we are her only children."

"No, the *priests* say we are her only children," countered T'Jules.

"We in Mel'hach do not recognize Lumina, as you know, my brother," started Nadi. "We save our devotion for Foton and Fosfeen, but we, too, believe this to be the only world, the stars our only universe."

"But we've never heard voices come out of the night, out of the air, out of...." T'Jules shook his head

"You have the right of it, my brother," intoned Jorgo. "The priests would not admit this possibility, either."

"How can we stop them if they can reach through the fabric of eternity itself?" asked Daliane with a note of hysteria.

"We don't know that there isn't a perfectly natural law that allows it," T'Jules said, attempting to comfort her. We just haven't found it yet, ourselves. Anyway, I never did believe we were Lumina's 'only children.' Just the fact that Jorgo and Nadi worship two completely different names proves to me there is a lot of room for doubt."

"A wise man," agreed Jorgo.

Nadi shot him a reproving glance then softened. "Neither of us is a true believer," she confessed, "we pay our respects to the Two just in case."

Daliane and T'Jules grinned.

"I don't even think the priests are 'true believers,'" snorted T'Jules.

"They just use the Goddess as a way to extort money and keep us in line."

The others rolled their eyes in mock horror at T'Jules' heresy.

"It's fortunate Vater M'Tilus is safely tucked in his bed," remonstrated Daliane.

"He is a good, kind man," admitted T'Jules, somewhat shamefaced, "and I would not hurt him with my careless talk."

"Nadi and I have a question, if you would not think us ill-mannered or ignorant."

"Never," chorused Daliane and T'Jules.

Jorgo made a slight grimace. "We do not understand your names."

T'Jules stared for a moment; then threw back his head in merriment; Daliane joined him with slightly more restrained amusement.

"How could you?" T'Jules finally gasped. "*We* wouldn't either if we hadn't been drilled."

"It's a bit complicated," added Daliane.

"First off, may I ask a question, in return?" T'Jules looked at the Mel'hachim.

Jorgo and Nadi nodded.

"Are you known only by the one name you have given us?"

Nadi spoke first. "As children we are known by our mother's names. I was 'Tomachild'."

Jorgo broke in. "I was 'Magdaboy'."

"Boys are specified?"

"Yes."

Nadi continued. "When we reach the Age of Passage, we are given the names we will carry throughout our lives, but we also bear the name of our clans."

Jorgo took up the thread. "When we mated, I gave up the clan of my birth, the Mishwa...."

"That is bear," contributed Nadi.

"To enter the clan of my wife—the Corva, or raven."

Daliane was interested. "Is this always the way it's done?"

"Yes, we are matrilineal."

"That is why we call a boy, a boy; he does not inherit and joins another clan at mating." Nadi gave a little snigger.

"But you seem so equal," protested Daliane.

The Mel'hachim flashed their white teeth.

"We are, my sister, however we always know the mother of a child. Sometimes knowing the father is not so easy." Jorgo's booming laugh engulfed them.

Bemused, T'Jules muttered, "I see."

It was Dally's turn to snigger.

T'Jules shook his head, "All right, my name, to reciprocate. To begin with, Bervaine, where we are now, is a baronetcy, not an autocracy. Nevertheless, I am purportedly an absolute ruler," he smiled deprecatingly, "and the 'T' in my name stands for *Tyrannus.*"

"Humphs," were heard.

"It's not as bad as it sounds," demurred T'Jules. "In reality, I'm held in check by several scores of minor nobles, many of them members of my own family, or clan, actually."

"And that is...?"

"Wysach."

"Tee Jee, you're not really clearing it up."

"Very well, from the beginning, once more. The name of my clan is Wysach, and we are the ruling house at the moment. However, males are known by their given names plus an indication of rank or occupation. Thus, I and members of my family who hold office are designated with a "T" before our names. I am, as well, a baron, so I am Baron T'Jules Bervaine of the clan Wysach. The Bervaines are all the same original family, but different clans."

Jorgo shook his head. "It seems the wrong way 'round."

T'Jules grinned, but said nothing.

Nadi looked inquiringly at Daliane.

Daliane winked at her. "Well, *I'm* from Finermond."

Jorgo and Nadi banged elbows trying to nudge each other.

Dally snorted. "I see you've heard of *our* autarch."

"The shadow of Hieronymus falls long," Jorgo affirmed.

"And wide," from Nadi.

"My father is Hieronymus' court astrologer. I have a brother to take his place, so father had to marry me off."

The shining dark heads bobbed as one.

Daliane went on, seeing they understood. "I was offered around...." Her voice cut off with a squeak, as T'Jules' big forefinger poked the ticklish spot on her ribs.

Ignoring him, she resumed as though uninterrupted. "Tee Jee was one of three who asked for my hand. His offer clearly impressed my father. For that reason, I was *determined* to hate him."

T'Jules interrupted again, explaining, "Except that from the first moment, there was no else for either of us."

"Tee Jee's right. I don't even remember what the others looked like."

"But your name..." Nadi recalled their original point.

"Oh, I'm simply Baroness Bervaine. Women don't have occupations, or clans, actually, they're wives of the baronetcy."

Jorgo and Nadi rolled their eyes in real horror this time.

Nadi echoed Daliane, "You seem so equal."

Daliane sighed. "My father was an enlightened man, in his way. He felt that I should be prepared for more than one eventuality. I have not only as much education as my brother, but a great deal more, er, practical training than he."

The Mel'hachim exchanged glances. "So, it would seem, my sister," acknowledged Nadi gravely.

Jorgo returned to puzzling out the various occupational appellations. "Vater M'Troilas?"

"The 'M' stands for Matis—of the Mother—indicating his complete subservience to Lumina."

"And Captain B'Ress?"

"Bellus."

"But...?"

"But you wonder why he's Captain B'Ress only, and I don't use a whole list of formal titles."

"Exactly so, my brother."

"Well, it's because he's an old family friend who served my father, as well. As I am of the clan Wysach, so he is clan Dortraine. Well, formally he's Captain B'Ress Bervaine (we all share that one) Dortraine. Some of those minor nobles I spoke of, Vater M'Troilas, for example, is from clan Consobol."

"And a Bervaine, as well," guessed Nadi.

T'Jules grimaced. "I'm afraid so."

Nadi grinned at his expression, seeming to lose the years and gravity of a warrior and return, for a moment, to girlhood. T'Jules wondered, as he watched appreciatively, what her childhood might have been.

"Nadi...." He hesitated, knowing the pride of the Mel'hachim.

"My brother?" She seemed to know his thoughts since her eyes held amusement, although her facial expression appeared solemn.

T'Jules settled on the indirect approach. "Are all Mel'hachi women warriors?"

Again, that startling flash of white. "We are all trained, yes, my brother. But that is not what you ask of me, is it?"

T'Jules reluctantly conceded.

Jorgo placed his great combatant's hand on T'Jules' arm. "We are now as of one mother, T'Jules. Ask of us anything without fear of insult."

Somewhat startled at Jorgo's use of his name for the first time, T'Jules sat silent for a moment. "I did not want to appear too intrusive," he began, "or too curious...."

"Or too rude, or too informal, or too...." Another poke in the ribs from T'Jules ended Daliane's interruption in another squeak.

A glance out the window sobered Daliane. "The day...."

"Is fast advancing, my sister, you must rest." A rumble of assent from Jorgo and the two rose, bowing strangely formal farewells, and took their leave, the rest of the story untold.

Daliane watched them leave with fondness, then turned to her spouse. "Tee Jee!" If there was more it was smothered in kisses. Breathless, they tumbled on the bed, danger, misery and fear annihilated, at least briefly, in the sensual violence of their passion.

··· 21 ···

We're Off to See... The Sea

A three-day rest at the inn, with regular meals and a soft bed, restored some color to Bethne's cheeks.

When she fretted about the expense, Ezrael soothed her.

"Now, Bethie, we bin savin' for our old age. I reckin we've just about arrived."

He was rewarded with a small smile and a slight poke. Not exactly vintage Bethne, but he was glad of anything besides the frantic, purposeless sorrow that had gripped her.

At breakfast on the morning of the fourth day, however, his heart took up its previous place in his boots when she announced it was time to get on the road again.

"Bethie, I thought...." he sputtered his frustration.

"We're still goin' to the city, Ez," she stated firmly. "I've been thinkin' they've got necromancers there."

Ezrael's eyes bugged in horror.

"No, Bethie, you cain't.... Besides, it's too expensive."

"You were right about the money, Ez. We might as well use it."

Ezrael slammed down his fist, flattening his hat in the process. He knew if he threatened to leave her, take the goat, she would only go on without him. Foreboding rose like bile in his throat, but he swallowed it along with any argument he might have offered.

"You're the boss, Bethie." It came out as a groan he couldn't suppress.

Bethne threw her arms around his neck. "You're a good man, Ez. Better'n I deserve, I reckon."

"I love you, Bethie," he croaked. "Allus did, allus will."

"Me, too, Ez," she replied. "But I has to know about Pell."

"Yeah, I guess I do, too, Bethie," Ezrael conceded. "I cain't jes go home and wonder. But I got a bad feelin' about it."

"I don't have a bad feelin', Ez," she responded. "I got a bad knowin'."

Ez shuddered and went to fetch the goat.

··· 22 ···

Oh, Shute!

The air whistled around the sides of the small craft as it raced toward its unseen destination. Unseen, but no longer unheard. At first a faint rumble, even now attaining the pitch and volume of a roaring forest fire, reached them. Terencia clenched her fists on her knees, shooting Kelgan a parchment-pale glance. He, for his part, could barely restrain himself from leaping over the side into the water. Only the thought of those little sharp-toothed faces held him fast in his seat.

"Get down," he shouted, "between the seats."

"What good do you think that will do us?" she shouted back.

"I don't know," he admitted helplessly, "but at least we'll have something around us."

She nodded curtly. Both crouched amidships, directly behind the unheeding twins.

"What about them?" Terencia put her mouth against his ear to be heard above the mounting clamor.

He shrugged. He had no idea whether they would risk even greater disaster if they attempted to pull the siblings down with them, or.... Panic rose again in him, convulsing his chest and stifling his breath.

Terencia saw. Mustering courage from some deep reservoir, she took both his hands and forced a grimace that was not quite a smile.

"See you in another life," she said.

Kelgan, although admiring her brave front, wasn't sure he cared for the sentiment expressed with it.

Light grew around them. Risking a quick reconnoiter, he poked his head around Nevander's frozen back and hurriedly withdrew it in terror.

"Water... water... waterfall!" he gasped. "We're going over."

He had not previously understood her reference to nightfall. Now it became only too clear.

Panic overwhelmed him. Never a sailor, the thought of that precipice of ebon wetness blinded his eyes and deafened his ears. He neither saw, heard, nor thought. Held fast by unreason, he tried to struggle to his feet; a stunning pain in his jaw cleared his head with dramatic suddenness.

Holding his jaw, which felt as though all his teeth had cracked off, he saw Terencia clutching the hilt of dagger which she had employed most effectively.

"What the Darkness do you think you're doing?" he screeched.

"What the Darkness did you think *you* were doing?" she mocked him in return.

"Uh, I guess I forgot myself, a little."

"Forgot yourself? A little?" Then she relented, "My father was a seaman, Kelgan. I've never shot a waterfall before, but I grew up around boats. I don't always remember that others didn't have my childhood. Nevertheless," her expression turned stern, "you don't stand up blindly in a boat."

Then her color drained. "How long?"

His teeth wanted to knock together like spoons in a tinker band. Clenching them firmly (and trying to ignore the ache this caused him), he gulped. "Two minutes, maybe less!" He desperately tried to summon up a protection spell, forcing the words out between clenched teeth, he was *almost* sure he had it right, no time left to worry about it.

Caught by natural impulse, they turned as one to look at the unmoving, unseeing di Nerrills. The same impulse sent them into each other's arms as the sound became a hungry throat and swallowed them.

··· 23 ···

Here

alvin groggily raised his head, fumbling for the snooze button. "Never," he muttered, "never, never, never."

Cracking one eye, he realized from the time that he must have hit the snooze at least twice before with no memory of it. Wide awake now, he threw back the comforter and leapt to his feet in one smooth moment. Once achieving the vertical, however, he just as swiftly dropped back on the bed, clutching his head.

"Never," he repeated, "no more boilermakers."

Putting his head between his knees, he breathed slowly and deeply until he thought he might venture once again into the upright.

"That's it, Cal, old buddy," he told himself, "easy does it."

Regaining his feet, he lurched for the bathroom. After sticking his head under the faucet and running cold water on it for several minutes, the clouds in his brain parted and a feeble ray of thought shone.

"Man, those dreams," he announced to his mirror image, "voices, made no sense at all." Deeply disturbing, however, and frighteningly real.

"Drink's bad for you, old buddy. Not a kid anymore. No dares."

His reflection regarded him unforgivingly. "*Not* a kid, *definitely*," it seemed to tell him.

Calvin Parker, 35, divorced, no children, middle-level lawyer and bar habitué, he was practically a cliché.

I'm a cliché, he thought, self-pityingly.

He could have sworn his mirror image nodded in contemptuous agreement.

"Okay, old buddy, I'll make you a deal." They winked at each other.

"I'm on the wagon. Yes, I mean it," he told himself. "I can see you have doubts...."

I've got doubts, all right, he thought as he turned from his self-accusing stare and turned on the shower. Stepping in, he blasted himself with cold water at full volume for some seconds before granting himself the dispensation of a little warmth.

His headache began to diminish, his stomach to settle. He was going to be good and late.

"Stopped to see Hartnell before I came in," he rehearsed his excuse. If he was lucky, he could catch his client briefly on some pretext and make his story somewhat true.

Feeling ashamed, he started to whistle *There'll Be Some Changes Made.*

"I mean it," he told himself again.

You're in trouble, buddy boy, when the only voice you hear is your own, he thought with a grin. The grin slowly faded. Voices... he heard other voices.

"Too much booze, old buddy. Pretty soon you'll be pointing at stuff that isn't there and screaming."

He shook his head, sending spray in all directions.

Rinsed, he shut off the shower; then froze as he reached for his towel. Something about water in his nightmare... water cascading down, water a strange color.

"*Too dry.*" "*Too wet.*" "*Too little.*" "*Too late.*" "*Too far.*" "*Too fast.*" Ugly obscene giggles.

"*Really* on the wagon, buddy boy."

He scrubbed at himself with the towel.

··· 24 ···

There

The boat burst forth from the tunnel. Kelgan, eyes screwed shut, clutched Terencia. He heard her gasp as she returned the pressure.

They plunged, impossibly riding the fall like a child's toboggan over snow.

Kelgan, sneaking a one-eyed peek above them, thought he saw tiny faces grinning down from where the torrent sprang. Once more forced to swallow bile, he clamped his eyes shut again and waited for the impact. He wondered if he would feel anything, or just wake in the realm of Lumen *May His Light Really Protect Us.*

Endless.... Slow....

The boat leveled off. Nevander's voice inquired cheerily, "Why are you sitting at the bottom of the boat, My Mage? And embracing Terencia, too. Is there something you haven't told us?"

Terencia was out of Kelgan's arms and up on the seat between one breath and the next. He remained where he was, ears buzzing, strange, sparkly dots dancing before his eyes.

"Dost thou need assistance, my Mage?" Nevander continued, in a parody of courtliness.

Both he and Neroma extended their arms and hauled him up between them. Identical expressions of sympathetic inquiry wreathed their faces. For some reason, he could think of nothing to say, but, "*I'm* supposed to be a mage."

To his surprise, Neroma leaned forward and dropped a kiss on his cheek. Ebony strands held his head for a moment, and her ebony gaze made him breathless.

"Indeed, thou art," affirmed Nevander.

"But not a sorcerer," came in Neroma's sable tones.

"I think I see," he shuddered.

"It is not *really* the black art, Kelgan." Neroma hastened to assure him, "just a little *grayer* than your own." A cheeky grin from Nevander.

"I don't care *what* color it is...." was the petulant response.

Again, identical expressions—this time of raised eyebrows.

"... *I* can't do it," his breath exploded furiously. His audience, all three of them, stared in identical expressions which he found difficult to read; but self-consciously felt were inward smiles at his expense.

Nevander enveloped him in a warm embrace, which, considering the disparity in their heights, took some doing.

Checking what seemed amusement in the face of his Mage's anger and self-reproach, Nevander said with utmost seriousness, "Kelgan, you don't understand, even yet. Ours has been a far different path which we have trodden since childhood. We, Neroma and I, are far closer to the elementals than you, and to certain, er, aspects of their realms with which you are not familiar. Howbeit, we cannot heal, as do you, nor can we sense the feelings or needs of others as you do. Ours is neither a craft of compassion, nor of empathy."

"I can't sense *anything* about you and Neroma," he protested.

"Ah, but we have explained before," retorted Nevander.

"We are constantly, and carefully, warded."

"I can't sense anything about Terencia, either," responded Kelgan, shaking his head is despair. "As a matter of fact, it feels like she isn't even there."

Terencia "humphed."

"Of course not, my Mage, do you never listen?" Nevander smiled with an edge. "We extend our protection to her, and we bolster your own, as well."

He threw back his head, nearly propelling himself over the side. The twins made hasty grabs.

"Another apology, I must be the sorriest mage in the Academy."

"Thou art a bit tedious," was the bland response.

"Oh, for Lumen's sake!" exclaimed Terencia. "Don't give him any reason to feel even sorrier."

Kelgan managed an only slightly shamefaced grin. "All right, from now on I'm going to tell you what a fine fellow I am—at every opportunity."

Terencia groaned dramatically, smiting her forehead with an exaggerated gesture. The twins chortled.

"Best to keep still," suggested Neroma wickedly.

She clasped his arm. "Seriously, dearest friend, your abilities complement ours. Your training is what we lack. We are like three legs of a stool, points of a triangle—without each of the others, all will fall."

He gaped. He didn't recall being her 'dearest friend' at any time in the past several weeks. Terencia reached out and gently tapped his jaw shut.

"We must go on," said Nevander. "The oars are now essential."

"The, um, oars?" he looked around wildly. "We have oars?"

"Surely, we will?" Nevander cocked his head quizzically.

After a beat, he understood. Neroma handed him four wooden spoons with what could only be called an exasperated expression. He spoke the spell of increase with definite misgivings. For that reason, it seemed more important than ever to concentrate on the most exact pronunciation of the words, the perfect tilt of the head, the most graceful and economic gesture of the hands. Not that he had ever been sloppy, he recalled with a wince.

"*Longitudus cocleare, existus tons!*" he virtually sang the few last words. Gesturing triumphantly, he surveyed the results proudly.

"Very nice, my Mage," was Nevander's dry comment. "Decorative, too."

Kelgan choked, as a closer look revealed a familiar pattern running the length of the now highly polished (surely mahogany) oars. The same pattern emblazoned on his very own chest, the same which had appeared each time on the changes of his clothing.

Raising an ashen face to Nevander, he guilted out, "I didn't...."

Nevander regarded the oars at some length, transferring his quizzical gaze at last to Kelgan's now flushed countenance.

"It would appear...." he began.

"I know how it appears," blurted Kelgan. "I just don't know how it appeared!"

"Mayhaps you have a soupçon of wit, after all, my Mage."

Kelgan looked confused.

Nevander sighed, "Perhaps not." He continued, "It appears you are unaware of certain, er, effects."

Kelgan bristled. "I may not be the best Mage around, (a snigger from Terencia) but I know what *I'm* doing when *I* do it (a slight twinge assailed him, *maybe not always*). Increase spells are for second-year apprentices. I've been doing them for four years."

Nevander leaned back, hand on chest, as though awestruck. "Four years," he repeated.

Goaded beyond endurance, and feeling that old familiar aura of bumpkin settling on his shoulders, Kelgan's fist shot out and caught His Lordship squarely on the nose. The resultant gasps of astonishment included his own.

"Oh Darkness, Nevander, I'm sorry. Let me see...."

Nevander submitted, with surprisingly good grace, to the ministrations of his wizard. Kelgan staunched the flow of blood from the Lord's nose and reduced the swelling that threatened to mar the up-until-then perfect features.

"You deserved that," came the even more surprising pronouncement in Neroma's alto bell tones.

"I admit it," said Nevander humbly. "Kelgan has been of the utmost forbearance."

Kelgan stared at him suspiciously. "It isn't like you to be humble."

"I admit that, too," countered Nevander cheerfully.

Kelgan found himself grinning. *Darkness, I really do like him.*

"However, my Mage, a little discussion on the matter at hand."

Kelgan remembered the oars.

"I can't explain how it happened, any more than I can explain the clothes, or the sword or...." He trailed off as he bethought himself of that first night, the feather light touch of another.

Nevander seemed to pick up his thought even though he claimed to be unable to reach Kelgan's mind. "Yes," he said, "we are not the only mages unknown to the Academy and to us as well."

"You don't think it was an Academy graduate?" finished Kelgan.

"I think the answer is in the device, which is surely not of Academy origin."

Kelgan concurred. "I've been afraid of that ever since I found out it wasn't you... but friend or foe?" He spread his hands in a gesture of helplessness.

"I think we may assume friend, or at least neutral," said Nevander. "If foe, you would be, well, I'm not sure, but you would have met with an accident."

Kelgan hardly turned a hair. "You're right. I must think."

"Think while pulling at the oars, my Mage, we are drifting out to sea. You and I will take the first turn."

Kelgan willingly seized oars. Unfortunately, he was far less sailor than wizard, nearly succeeding in snapping either the oars or the thole pins before getting them into the water.

"I seem to be closer to graduating from the Commedia than the Academy," he offered ruefully while splinters flew.

"Never mind, my friend, you will be an expert soon enough."

Turning the boat crosswise to the current, Nevander began to pull. Along the now rather distant shore, a horse and rider matched their pace.

··· 25 ···

What Dreams Are These

Bethne sat up with a cry.

"Bethie, what's wrong?"

Feeling foolish, she sank back into Ezrael's arms, "T'was only a dream, Ez. I thought I saw Pelly plain as day, but it couldn't 'a bin. He were by the sea."

"The sea, Bethie? Pelly dint never want to go to sea."

"I dint say he were goin to sea, Ez. He were by the sea—and he was still on our ole horse, too."

She was silent a while. "I don't know, Ez. It were so real."

"Dreams aire like that, Bethie. Yores allus were."

"I know, Ez. But this was so clear. An' the sea was strange, Ez. It were two colors—part of it wuz real black, like lookin' down a well—the biggest part wuz jest like ordin'ry ole water, blue like the sky."

Ezrael gave this interesting tidbit some thought. He'd never seen water like that, but then he'd never seen a dead boy get up and ride off on a horse before, either.

"Waal, Bethie, I ant never seed anythin' similar, but yore dreams has a way of seeing what's real, so I cain't say as you wuz only dreamin' an, there's no such thing."

"We gots to forget about the temple, Ez, and find that sea."

Ezrael was already sure that was what Bethne was going to decide. Nevertheless, he found he had been hoping she would carry on to their original destination. The temple, even if not where he had ever wanted to go, was at least familiar. Where this sea might be, what the meaning of the dark water, whether Pelly was there... he gave it up, knowing there was no dissuading Bethne. If he objected, she just might try to saddle up Capriola and ride there.

··· 26 ···

Ill Met By Daylight

After some breathless moments of rowing, Kelgan gasped, "Where are we going, anyway?"

"Do you but pull with a will, my Mage," answered Nevander repressively, "all will be revealed.

He swallowed a bubble of anger, and pointed out, "Well, if we're heading for shore, we have a welcoming committee."

Nevander, who had been straining at the oars with bowed head, glanced up and let the oars fall from his suddenly slack hands.

The boat slowed before Kelgan realized he oared alone.

"What...." he began, but choked it off as he took in Nevander's ashen, gaping visage.

Looking himself toward the small, motionless figure which awaited them, he felt tiny tiptoes of dread run up his spine.

Terencia drew her sword and laid it across her lap. Feeling exceedingly foolish, he mirrored her action.

Nevander waved a dismissive hand at both of them. "Nay, put up thy arms," he ordered formally. "Thou'll find them of little effect." He took up the forward oars again. "Pull on, my Mage. Fate stands before."

Kelgan, torn between annoyance at Nevander's persistent posturing, and fear of the unnaturally still horseman, bent again to his task.

They rowed on in silence, Neroma had spoken not a word since they had seen the figure on the shore. Her usual unrelieved ivory held the same sickly gray undertones as her twin.

The figure grew as they approached. He felt a wave of relief wash over him as the enigmatic duo revealed themselves to be a young man scarcely past adolescence and a sway-backed, spavined old nag carrying him. The boy's russet hair hung to his shoulders from his hatless head. He was dressed in festive clothing—a soft turquoise shirt, and his russet tunic matched the color of his hair. Kelgan's unease returned as he took in that familiar combination; particularly when he glanced at his companions, whose faces remained unchanged. Terencia grasped the hilt of her sword with white knuckles, just as Nevander did his oars.

He glanced obliquely at Terencia. She leaned slightly forward on her seat, with what he would sense was an air of anticipation. She still fingered the hilt of her unsheathed sword, evidently not believing Nevander's dismissal of the efficacy of arms.

Kelgan devoted a brief moment to reflecting on the many odd and seemingly diametrically opposed facets of her personality. Many times at the keep he had thought her behavior downright seductive. *Although, I know less of seduction than our old billy goat.* Since appearing in her grand uniform at the beginning of their journey, however, she had been by turns remote, hostile, sarcastic, and oddly awkward as though ill-acquainted with the male sex. Shaking his head, he bent his attention to the oars again.

The boat entered the shallows. Nevander shipped his oars, prompting Kelgan to do the same. Their craft, carried forward by the low waves, ground to a halt on the stony beach.

"My dear, dear friends, I bid you welcome. I have sought you long."

Kelgan was struck by the toneless nature of the boy's voice and by the awkward stiffness of his movements. A dreadful certainty filled him; nausea, a constant companion since his involvement with the di Nerrills, threatened once again. Swallowing hard, he jumped out of the boat and attempted to anchor it more securely on the beach. Nevander imitated his action with a rueful smile. Together, they managed to muscle the boat out of the wash. The boy dismounted with the same disturbing awkwardness. Stiff and disjointed, he set his feet on the ground as though they belonged to someone else.

Nevander, with a visible shudder, greeted the boy in a voice somewhat higher than his usual. The boy answered him tonelessly but politely.

"You have sought us, my boy, and you have found us," stated Nevander, staunchly treating the conversation as perfectly natural.

"The voices have called," nodded the boy, gravely, "and we have answered."

A powerful call, indeed, thought Kelgan, if what he guessed was true.

As though he had heard the thought, the boy retorted, "To be sure, my Lord, to be sure." Was there humor under those flat tones? Certainly, no twinkle in the vacant unfocused stare—was it mere parroting of Nevander's fake cheer? He narrowed his eyes, squinting at the boy, trying to bring him into focus. The dreadful surmise only grew. The boy remained strangely blurred, not to Kelgan's sight, but in his mind.

"I am ready, My Lords, and eager for our mission."

Nevander's voice faltered only a little. "Ah, yes, my boy, our mission." There he seemed to run out of steam.

An awkward silence fell; unfelt by the lad, it would seem. Neroma advanced to the side of her twin, and took his hand. Nodding to some unspoken directive of hers, he once again addressed the boy.

"We must all procure mounts as stalwart as yours, my lad." The swaybacked old nag rolled her eyes and snorted at this feeble sally as though understanding every word.

"Firstly, however," Nevander continued, ignoring comments from a draft horse, "we must undertake to conceal our sturdy craft well. It may be necessary to take to the sea again."

Not if I can grow wings, thought Kelgan.

"There is a near town, My Lord," contributed the boy through his motionless lips, "full of most-polite folk, I attest."

Without a doubt they were. I, too, am prepared to be most polite.

"We will hie thither with good speed, my boy," Nevander assented.

Hie thither. Even under these doubtful circumstances, Kelgan found suppressing a grin at Nevander's posturing very difficult.

The horse snorted again and stamped in agreement.

"I forget myself. The boy bowed shakily and nearly toppled over. Righting himself jerkily, he went on, "I am Pellerin, Ezrael's son, late of Beth-Ez Farm."

An excellent choice of words, Kelgan thought sickly. Again, suspicion of humor flashed through him, immediately discarded. *No, it could not be—not if this were...* he could not finish the thought.

The boy relapsed into his motionless, unfocused former pose. He neither waited nor anticipated—he was simply *there*.

"My Mage!" Kelgan jumped as Nevander addressed him. "Do you assist me to hide our transport."

"Can we not repeat the spell of appearing... in reverse, of course?"

"I fear not," rejoined Nevander. "We know aught of, er, the neighbors."

Kelgan sighed, but understood Nevander had the right of it... ordinary labor it must be, for ordinary people. He couldn't help wishing for a pair of ordinary seamen to make the task easier, however. He doubted the boy would be of much assistance, remembering the difficulty of a simple bow.

To his amazement, the boy herky-jerkied to his side to grasp the bow of the boat. He yanked in tandem with him, aided by Nevander and the women at the stern. Pellerin's nearness made ripples run up Kelgan's arms and converge at his spine but he shut his mind and gave all to their task.

"*No trouble with* that *bow.*" He felt that little bubble of hysteria rise again at his pun. With much heaving and hauling, they inched the boat over the sand and nested it in the scraggly bush grass.

"We will need to o'erturn it and cover it with sand," Nevander declared.

Kelgan groaned. The women directed poisonous glances at Nevander, who shrugged in reply.

For some reason unfathomable to Kelgan, the boy stepped backward, putting some distance between himself and the others. Nevander eyed him and then shrugged again. The other three joined him in a row, putting their shoulders to the task of tipping the boat. When they had finally succeeded in flipping the craft hull up, they set about turning it into a sand dune.

Winded and sweaty, when they had at last covered the boat to Nevander's satisfaction, Kelgan experienced a flash of understanding. *It looks like a grave, that's Pellerin's problem, too much like home.*

At this thought, he began to laugh. Wilder and wilder grew his whoops, until a stinging blow from Nevander's clenched fist brought him up short.

"Really, my Mage, control is the essence of a gentleman." The words were delivered with a simper that nevertheless failed to conceal real anxiety. Nevander searched Kelgan's face with a scrutiny that betrayed his fear.

"I'm sorry, once again, Nevander." He tried to pass off his fit. "I'm afraid fatigue gained the mastery of me."

"Of course, my Mage." Nevander sat back on his heels, a little, but only a little, satisfied.

To the astonishment of all, and nearly to Kelgan's repeat undoing, Pellerin dropped to his knees beside him and laid a cool cloth on his forehead.

"So does my lady mother," Pellerin intoned.

Kelgan could not speak.

Nevander came to his rescue with a mild, "You are goodness itself, my boy."

There was a pause, and then, "If you say it, My Lord."

Kelgan stared into the dead (yes, he knew it) eyes, unable to look away. Something, he knew not what, looked back at him from the turquoise depths, and he felt once more the feather light touch he recalled from the first night at Nerrills' Keep.

His next memory was of one of his own philtres waved under his nose and three anxious faces peering down at him. The boy had retreated into his out-of-focus self, the eyes were blank and opaque now, nothing winked from within.

Imagined, I imagined.... Aloud he said, "Forgive me again, everyone. When was the last time we ate?"

Nevander was all remorse. "A thousand pardons to you, my Mage, and to the brave Terencia, as well." Terencia gave him a long stare. He continued, with a small bow in her direction. "Neroma and I are trained to long fasts, but I have been working the two of you like slaves with nary a mouthful of sustenance. We depart immediately for the town to procure the same."

"And horses," added Terencia, her first words for not a little while. Her silence had held so long; Kelgan had almost forgotten she could speak.

"First things first," Nevander gestured airily, "food, for now, then provisioning for later."

"I shall remain here, at our meeting place," Pellerin droned in his uninflected style.

Nevander eyed him narrowly. "Perhaps, that would be best," he affirmed.

"Until you return," continued the boy, seeming to ignore Nevander.

Kelgan thought he detected a faint edge to the relentless monotone. Warning? Threat? Fear?

"I shall stay with Pellerin," Terencia declared unexpectedly.

Surprise confounded them all. Even, Kelgan could swear, the boy himself.

"I am conspicuous in my uniform," she offered.

The others nodded; a guardsman could stand out in any crowd.

Kelgan's stomach roiled uneasily, however, at the thought of leaving her with... what? Nothing of nature, he was sure. Strangely, Terencia seemed the least affected of them all by the boy's otherness. Her attitude again suggested anticipation to him, when he felt fear. Fear? Is that what he felt? No, no, by Darkness! He wasn't afraid, just... uneasy. Yes, uneasy, surely not more.

He gave up trying to bolster his psyche and admitted to himself his mental state during the last three months could best be described as abject terror. Terencia, he recalled, had shown flashes of the same emotion. What about the present situation could possibly have been interpreted as reassuring?

··· 27 ···

Getting While the Getting's Good

Daliane braced herself against the wall and shook her head in denial.

"Dally, I think we should wait. You're not up to another session tonight. We... nearly lost you, last time." T'Jules ran his hand down her hair and cupped her chin, pulling her face up to look at him.

"I've got to, Tee Jee, if I stop, I'll never start again. I've got to keep going and you've got to keep pulling me back. We have to see if I can find out anything that might tell us who, or what, or why...." She trailed off, frustrated by her previous failures.

T'Jules shook his head "Dally, this was a bad idea."

Daliane agreed with his assessment. "It *was* a bad idea, Tee Jee, but we *had* to do it. We agreed about that—and we have to keep on, and I'm the only one who hears them, and...."

T'Jules covered her mouth with a kiss—uncaring that the Mel'hachim looked on. She answered with a burst of passion. For a moment, the horror of those insidious, ugly voices of darkness faded from their awareness; then Daliane pulled away. She cast an oblique look at the Mel'hachim, who were studiously examining the architecture of the room as though they planned a palace of their own.

Dally blushed, then grinned. "All right, so I like him."

Matching grins answered her. "Tigers like meat," observed Jorgo.

Daliane flushed in embarrassment but was unable to stifle a little gasp of pleasure.

Nadi booted Jorgo in the ankle with a grimace. "The night

before a wedding, the men of a tribe force the bridegroom to sit up all night while they make... uh, well, suggestions. By the morning," giggled Nadi, "the bridegroom is nearly frantic with—I think you would say anticipation."

Daliane and T'Jules joined the laughter. Daliane, however, sobered first and asked, "What about the bride?"

"She beats him," was Nadi's complacent answer.

"What?" chorused the Bervaines.

Jorgo and Nadi exchanged amused looks.

Nadi explained. "She is given a ceremonial whip...."

"Used by every bride of the tribe," broke in Jorgo.

"For as long as anyone can remember," continued Nadi.

"If the groom becomes too...."

"Enthusiastic."

"She is permitted to give him a lash."

"However, the women of the tribe are usually warriors as well, so...."

"That's why we have had the whip so long."

"It's never been used!"

The four collapsed in laughter. Even though the story would have been only mildly amusing under normal circumstances, their shared fear caused them to clutch at any straw to take the edge off their near hysteria.

The dull chiming of midnight sliced through their laughter as sharply as a sword. Three sets of eyes turned toward Daliane. Gently, she took T'Jules' hand, knowing what it was costing them both, but trying, however poorly, to ease his agony. The pain in his chest reached an unbearable threshold. The fact that she would offer *him* reassurance nearly unmanned him. He forced what he hoped was an expression of calm on his face and returned the soft pressure of her hand.

Nadi drew her sword and moved to stand by the fire. Remembering Nadi's drastic action of the night before made Daliane's breathing become erratic. She gulped in mouthfuls of air, willing herself to calm. Gradually her breathing slowed. She lay back on the bed and closed her eyes.

T'Jules thought his own breathing would stop. Terror assailed him and to his surprise, he found himself shaking as though with an ague. His teeth rattled in his skull and silvery spots danced before his eyes. A man known for his berserker rage on the battlefield, as his scarred body would affirm, he was unused to helplessness and even more a stranger to fear.

"Baron," Jorgo repeated in a voice, which although not loud, held an edge T'Jules had not previously heard directed at him.

Cursing himself, T'Jules mentally grasped the reins of his runaway nerves. Clamping his jaws together, he forced his teeth to be still, blinking his eyes until they focused in surrender.

"I'm fine," he managed to hiss through his gritted teeth.

A frown of disapproval crossed Jorgo's face, but he held his tongue.

Mortification did what nothing else could. T'Jules clamped iron control on his emotions. Straightening his back, he again took possession of Daliane's hand. Its icy feel almost broke him again, but he managed a relative calm. "I think she's sleeping quietly. She doesn't seem to be hearing anything."

Jorgo's frown dissolved as he gently touched Daliane's head, "Perhaps they do not come every night."

"No, no, she said they never stopped—night after night...." T'Jules' voice broke. Jorgo frowned again. Before he could speak, Nadi stepped in.

"Baron, I think you should stand here by the fire," her tone, though sympathetic, brooked no argument.

T'Jules started to protest, but he realized he could not help Dally by becoming hysterical himself.

As he started to move away from the bed, a faint sound somewhere between a gasp and a moan came from Daliane. The next sound was a scream. Her eyelids snapped open, obviously focused on a reality unseen by the paralyzed occupants of the room.

"I won't go there. I won't go there," she repeated in a shrill monotone that punished their eardrums. Then Nadi's fist connected forcefully with Daliane's jaw. Her head snapped back, and she dropped with an audible thud onto the mattress.

Jorgo's knife was beneath T'Jules' chin before T'Jules even

realized he had his hands out, ready to encircle Nadi's throat.

Daliane moaned and stirred behind them. Her eyelids opened with a visible effort, and her eyes focused slowly. She pulled herself up to a sitting position; then, to the surprise of those watchers frozen in their murderous tableau, spoke almost impishly.

"Why do I always have to ask *what happened?*" she queried, gingerly feeling her jaw. "And why am I the only one who needs a healer? Although," she continued, "it looks like we might have needed more than one healer."

Hands dropped quickly to sides, and feet shuffled sheepishly.

Jorgo's teeth flashed their brilliant white. "We were just... or I should say, I was just demonstrating to the Baron...."

T'Jules finished for him, "The move he would employ should any attacker get past me and approach you."

"It seems one already did," Daliane observed dryly.

"It was I again, little sister," admitted Nadi. "We feared."

"I understand," Daliane assured her. "However, I think from now on, I'm going to enter these sessions fully armed, so that I can defend myself better while I'm being saved."

She fell back against the pillows, dissolved in laughter. "If you could have seen yourselves!" she gasped, "Ow! That hurts!"

She sobered. "I saw something this time."

Her audience dropped, as one, on the bed beside her.

"I'm not sure it'll be of any help, however," she went on.

"Tell us, little sister, and we will see," was Jorgo's gentle suggestion.

"It was... it was like a... a hole...." Daliane shook her head in frustration. "It's like trying to describe a dream. You can feel it, but you can't *say* it."

"Go on," urged T'Jules.

"It was like looking into a kitchen funnel; darkness that stretched away for... for, forever, I guess."

She bit her lips. "I was here, but not *here*. I mean, it was this world, but it wasn't."

"Dally," intruded T'Jules, "was it up, down, north, south? Anything?"

"I don't know, Tee Jee. I'm trying."

"I know, love. No one could try harder." He imprisoned her hands, which were clenched into fists of frustration.

"Just keep describing your impressions, and we'll try to make something out of them."

"I kept thinking about the Gobbler."

"The Gobbler?" Nadi raised her eyebrows.

T'Jules answered her. "A *very* old story, told to children. My nanny used to scare the curls out of my hair with it, to make me behave. If you were bad in this life, the Gobbler would catch you on your journey to the Light, then devour your soul so that you spent eternity in total darkness—inside the Gobbler."

"Ugh," chorused the Mel'hachim.

Here

T he day had degenerated from bad to worse. Calvin's ex had
called to hit him up for more money. Why didn't somebody
marry her, for chrissake, and take her off his hands. Okay, she *was*
disabled. And yes, he *had* been driving. Did that mean he had to
suffer for it forever? He never drank and drove anymore. Well, he
did drive himself home last night... he guessed. He got home
somehow. And anyway, it was only a couple of blocks.

His thoughts became more coherent. *How did I get home, anyway?*
What was in those drinks? Am I starting to blackout?

He grabbed the edge of his desk convulsively, as though for support.

Am I starting to get DT's? Hearing things. Those voices!

He laid his head on his arms. His headache, contrary to the usual
pattern, hadn't abated as the day progressed, but had only become
more ferocious. The pounding had begun to blur his vision.

Maybe it's something serious, was his panicky thought.

"Yo, Cal. Bad night, huh?"

Cal snapped to attention; smirking in his doorway stood the
stereotype of stereotypes.

Balding, paunchy, pens tucked carefully into a pocket protector,
hornrims perched askew on nose, Philip (privately tagged Pip the
Drip by Cal) Kirkwright looked gleeful at the thought that he might
be able to give Cal some trouble.

"I don't like to say anything mean—you know I hate gossip—but I
think he drinks on the job!"

"Oh, hey, Phil; I think maybe a touch of stomach flu. Although I did have fish for dinner—maybe it's food poisoning. Come to think of it, that snapper tasted a little funny." Cal gritted his teeth in a travesty of a smile, *Go away, you fat fool—go away!*

"Gee, Cal, that's too bad. Maybe you ought to go home. Of course, I know the Ballard settlement is about to close. I'll be happy to make the final pitch for you."

Of course, you would, you oversized midget, Cal kept his distaste from showing on his face. Aloud he thanked Philip insincerely, "I think an Alka-Seltzer will fix me right up."

Pip the Drip's eyes narrowed in suspicion or disappointment—Cal wasn't sure. Giving another ghastly grin, he caroled, "Well, back to work," and turned his back on the Drip.

The Drip continued to stand silently behind Cal for another moment or two, then "Humphed."

"Let me know if you feel worse Cal, old Pal." Snickering, he moved off at last.

Cal held his hands in front of him; they quivered like aspen leaves.

"Never again," he promised himself.

··· 29 ···

And Back Again

Kelgan and the twins set out for the town. Kelgan had dared to work a small spell of increase on all their bodies, and an even smaller spell of decrease on the twin's faces, so that anyone they met would see only three portly, unremarkable burghers out for a stroll. Travelers were fortunately few on the road, however, until they came within smelling distance of the docks.

"Faugh!" coughed Nevander, "can't miss the place."

Kelgan, whose years had been spent well inland, rather enjoyed the exotic mix of scents that wafted their way—the salt tang of the sea (the more insistent tang of rotting fish parts), perfumes, spices, unwashed bodies. He remembered, how long ago it seemed, that the air of the Academy never smelled of anything at all. Even the kitchen never leaked a molecule of cooking odor into the courtyards. That was one of the first things the newbies learned after their arrival at the Academy, how to cover up the malodorous results of their first spell failures (beginners used natural elements until they could cast unaided).

Revelation smote him! How could he have been so stupid? Of course, he couldn't manage a scent ward. It went against all of his training.

"Ah, hah!" he exclaimed aloud.

The twins eyed him from comically plump faces, but they said nothing.

Terencia sat casually on a rock. Casually, that is, with the exception of the drawn sword on her lap. Pellerin stood unmoving by his sullen mare, apparently seeing nothing, although he directed his gaze fixedly at the Autarch's Guard.

"I know what you are," observed Terencia, "and I know my sword won't make any difference. It makes me feel better, nevertheless."

The boy neither moved nor spoke.

"I know you know what I'm saying," she continued with a slight edge.

The mare rolled her eyes in Terencia's direction and whickered.

"Oh, not you, you spavined old bag of glue-fodder."

The mare snorted and showed her teeth as though understanding.

Pellerin spoke suddenly. "And *we... we* know what *you* are."

Terencia sprang to her feet; sword aimed at the boy's throat. He, however, had retreated into himself—immobile, eyes once more on the ground, seeming never to have moved.

··· 30 ···

Somewhere in Between

Bethne and Ezrael struggled on, increasingly footsore and heart weary. Their inquiries, concerning a young man and an old horse, were met with silence or outright hostility. Making signs to ward off the Darkness, folks hurriedly entered their homes or shops, slamming the doors emphatically behind them.

"He must'a come this way, EZ. Else why is they so skeered?"

"Yer right, as allus, Bethie. They knowed what he were, jes' as we know."

"I don' know *what* we know, Ez. We ain't never had no dead son afore this, 'specially not one ridin' a horse."

Ez gave Bethie a measuring look. Was that humor? Could Bethie actually make a joke about Pelly's death? Seeing the lines in her face, deeper every day, Ez decided Bethie simply spoke the truth. How could they know anything of what Pelly had become? The dead didn't walk—except in old folk tales—but Pelly *was*... Ez gave up. Blanking his mind, he yanked fiercely at the goat, which was veering off to the succulent verge.

"C'mon, you old pot-roast."

··· 31 ···

No Country for Weak Women

D aliane's sword glistened in a windmill blur. She pressed her attack with such ferocity, Nadi fell back in comic surrender and burst into laughter.

"Steady, my sister, you will dislocate something!"

Grimacing ruefully, Dally lowered her sword and struggled to regain her breath.

"I'm sorry, Nadi, I forgot where I was."

"Do not apologize for vigor, little sister, only for carelessness."

"Care...."

"You had forgotten, as you say, where you were, but also what you have learned. You swung with no heed and left a wide path to your vitals."

Dismayed, and still not a little winded, Daliane sank to the floor of the hall where she and Nadi had been sparring.

"Tee Jee would kill me," she opined.

Nadi gave another gust of laughter, "Better he than I."

Dally chuckled with her. "I guess that didn't sound too logical."

Nadi threw a sinewy arm around Daliane's slight shoulders. Serious now, she said, "This is not necessarily a time for logic, my Baroness, however it is definitely a time for reason."

"I have to think every step of the way, you mean. Even though...."

"The situation is unthinkable," Nadi finished.

"Unthinkable, illogical, irrational, undreamed of...." Daliane was working up another head of steam.

Nadi punched her lightly on the arm. "Back to the practice. When I approach so, you must parry so. No, step *this* way." Dally realized she had been manipulated into calm very cleverly.

They were joined shortly by T'Jules and Jorgo. T'Jules scrubbed at his face with a towel; his hair hung in damp ringlets and his padded vest bore dark splotches of sweat and mud.

"Phew," said Dally, wrinkling her nose. "What have you been rolling in?"

"He tried to fight a horse," Jorgo roared.

"It smells like the horse won."

Gathering his dignity, T'Jules explained, "Actually, I slipped while executing a difficult maneuver."

"Keeping his *nose* out of the maneuver was the difficult part," was Jorgo's gleeful contribution.

The women fell about in the hall, particularly at the sight of T'Jules crimson face. With bad grace at first, he joined them. Then with increasing amusement at his own clumsiness, he abandoned himself to laughter just for that moment.

They departed on that cheerful note for separate baths and joint dinner. After the meal, the four tensely awaited the strikes of the midnight bells.

"I do not think tonight is auspicious, my sister," rumbled Jorgo. "Nadi and I have looked, oof!" He broke off with a grunt as Nadi put her fist in his solar plexus.

"Looked? At what?" inquired T'Jules.

"He means outside," Nadi replied, her remark delivered with a peculiar expression.

"The weather... a storm is coming." Jorgo sounded a bit breathless as a result of his wife's tender attention.

"Why would that matter?"

"Actually, my sister, we do not know that it would, but we would be easier to forgo a night."

"Nadi speaks wisdom, Baroness, and you would be fresher with a breathing space," mumbled Jorgo, his eyes avoiding her.

For the first time, Daliane felt evasion emanate from her usually forthright friends.

"You're not telling me everything," it was not a question.

Jorgo and Nadi locked glances; the silence lengthened into discomfort. Jorgo put out his hand and laid it alongside Nadi's cheek; he gave a slight nod which she echoed.

"We have not told all, it is true, my sister," Nadi grimaced an apology. "However, we were uncertain...." Her voice died away as she contemplated the air in front of her.

"Straight out, that is best," counseled Jorgo.

To Market, to Market, to Buy?

K elgan, for the first time in months—he winced inwardly at how long it had been—thoroughly enjoyed himself. He had not been to a market since beginning his mage apprenticeship. A moment's sadness assailed him at the realization of his isolation.

In the thrill of learning how to control and direct his burgeoning abilities, he hadn't missed the hustle-bustle of town life. Later, with Nevander and Neroma, again the thrill of discovering previously unexplored territory had distracted him. Now—now, he reveled in the colors, the smells, the pushing crowds, the persistent hawkers as though he had awakened in a foreign country.

He came to himself suddenly, and realized Nevander was regarding him with some amusement.

He growled at Nevander, "I know, I'm just a bumpkin; always was, always will be."

Nevander's chubby mask changed comically.

"Ah, Kelgan, you mistake me." He threw an arm, or rather tried to, around Kelgan's shoulders, "I am vastly pleased to see *your* pleasure, albeit somewhat resentful; you never seemed to enjoy yourself nearly as much with us." In a slightly different tone, he said, "You really should do something about that inferiority complex."

Kelgan laughed until he could scarcely stand. Hoisting Nevander from the ground, he swung him around like a child, much to His Lordship's consternation.

Set on his feet once more, Nevander tried to look every direction at once to apprehend if anyone had seen. His discomposure was not aided by the sight of his generally solemn twin, seated in the dirt, clasping her sides while rolling in helpless merriment.

"Well, yes," he said feebly, adjusting his clothing.

"Don't worry, Nev (Nevander's eyebrows shot up), you've bolstered my self-esteem immensely." He lowered his voice. "Besides, no one knows you, if you take my meaning."

Nevander smote his forehead as he realized he had forgotten his plump merchant guise. "Ah, I feel much relieved."

His obvious sincerity sent the others off into a fresh gale, although they sobered quickly as they became aware that they were attracting notice.

Neroma picked herself out of the dirt, straightened her skirts, and said clearly, "Indeed, cousin, that was a most amusing story; you certainly got the better of that arrangement."

Kelgan was taken briefly aback. Neroma had seemed to him to be so aloof and remote from ordinary life, that he had actually not thought her capable of reality. He made a show of squinting at the sun's position.

"Indeed, the day is hastening on."

Nevander picked up the cue. "Yes, let us see who else is prepared to give us the better arrangement."

There were chuckles from some of the onlookers, who hastily turned their backs after receiving a glare from what appeared to be an inoffensive little fat man.

Nevander spoke *sotto voce*. "We must get what we need, and quickly, we know not what transpires by the shore."

Kelgan had nearly forgotten Terencia, and the strange boy they had left behind. Brought up short by guilty recollection, he nodded in agreement.

"Uh, but Nevander, we can't look like we're in a hurry."

"I pray thee, tell me why," demanded His Lordship at his haughtiest.

"We have to look like we don't care all that much; and we have to haggle," Kelgan remembered shopping trips with his mother.

"Haggle!"

Kelgan smothered a grin at Nevander's horrified visage.

"You're a merchant, remember? Haggling is the way it's done. You'll attract everyone's attention if you rush in, grab the merchandise and accept the first price."

Nevander uttered a low groan. "I bow to your infinitely superior wisdom."

Kelgan knew he had been insulted, but could think of no appropriate retort. On giving the matter a second thought, he decided action might seem better than words.

Striding to a nearby stall, which dispensed leather water jugs, he examined one or two with a desultory air. Sniffing, he began to turn away. The proprietor, apparently stung by the purported disdain, grasped Kelgan's arm and thrust another container under his nose.

"The finest calfskin...."

"Goat," interjected Kelgan.

"The finest *calf*skin," repeated the vendor. "Waterproofed by maidens no older than fourteen, using the same wax intended for candles in the holy Temple of Lights, itself."

"Meaning your old wife uses boat caulking."

The merchant's voice took on a wheedling tone, "Four scutti, master, a tiny price for such workmanship. You could journey to the Hall of Darkness without losing a precious drop of liquid."

Kelgan repressed a shudder; as far as he knew, he *was* going to the Hall of Darkness.

For the vendor's benefit, he snorted scornfully, "Journey! I couldn't get out of the market without leaving a river of ale behind me. Four scutti! I wouldn't waste one."

"For you, master, I just might—because of your honest face, mind you—I just might be able to say three."

"One and a half."

"Two and a half."

"Two."

"Done."

"How about three jugs for five scutti?"

"A robber! Did I say you had an honest face? I lied! Five and a half."

"Done."

After counting out the coins, Kelgan filled his arms with jugs and turned back to the twins, who watched in stupefaction.

They walked silently beside him for a few yards. Then, "I tender my apologies, my Mage; your wisdom is, indeed, superior. You have depths we are only beginning to plumb."

Guiltily glad to have scored even such a petty victory over the di Nerrills, Kelgan bowed with a slight swagger.

They purchased a quantity of dried fruits, dried meats ("It's better if you don't ask from what animal," he warned.), filled their jugs with ale, and bargained hotly for four warmer cloaks than they had brought. ("Methinks the lad has no need," was Nevander's observation.)

Neroma, who had been silent the entire time, suddenly announced, "I need boots."

Betaking herself to a cobbler's booth, she demonstrated that she had been listening and learning. She returned wearing a smart pair of black boots, as well as an expression which on anyone else Kelgan would have called a smirk. Besides the boots, she had acquired a rather ingenious little purse with a false bottom, which made it look empty to the overly curious.

"Congratulations," crowed Nevander, "thou will make a blacksmith's wife yet."

A dainty kick in the ankle from one smart boot cut short His Lordship's humor.

"I'm afraid it's now for the hard part."

"How so, my Mage?"

"We need mules, at least two of them. We can't carry everything in our arms for miles."

"We are carrying it now, my Mage."

"This is only a little food... what about blankets? A pan or two...."

Nevander looked uneasy. "I feel we must return, Kelgan."

Kelgan saw he was serious. "Do you think...?"

"I know not. Mayhap I am foolishly apprehensive, but dread assails me all at once."

"You and Neroma go back; I will get the mules and join you as fast as possible. We can use the cloaks for blankets and eat cold food for a while." Kelgan began to take the bundles from Neroma's arms.

"I'll take care of all of this. Hurry!"

Neroma and Nevander hastened back in the direction of the woods. Kelgan turned back to the pile of purchases, now an untidy heap on the ground. Scanning the market in a circle, he bespied an urchin of indeterminate age, who watched him with undisguised curiosity. Beckoning the boy over, he held up a silver scutto.

"Do you know what this is?"

The child nodded, a feral greed mingling with his interest in Kelgan's doings.

Kelgan reached toward the boy, who flinched as though in anticipation of a blow. Pretending not to notice, Kelgan continued his motion and produced a second coin from behind the boy's ear.

The child's eyes widened. Not, it seemed, in awe of Kelgan's sleight-of-hand, but at the sight of two silvers.

"These can both be yours," Kelgan announced, "if you will do me a service."

"What throat?" was the self-possessed query.

"What?"

"Does ya, or doesn't ya, want a throat slit?"

"Of course, I don't want a throat cut. I just want you to watch my belongings for a little while."

To Kelgan's carefully disguised amusement, the child looked immensely relieved, although he adopted a man-of-the-world air and drawled, "Me auntie's tea party."

"I assume that means the task is within your abilities?"

The boy bestowed a look of shriveling scorn on Kelgan.

"'Course," was the haughty reply.

He was tempted to pat the boy's head, but remembered how furious he always felt at that indignity when a child. Instead, he offered a hand to shake, which the child grasped with a grimy paw and shook with all the gravity of a gray-beard.

Stifling his amusement again, Kelgan asked, "What may I call you?"

"Piper," succinctly.

"That's it?"

"Yep."

"Very well, Piper. I will be back in one half of the hour. If by chance I do not return before the half strike—well, never mind. I *will* be back."

An uneasy expression flitted across the boy's face, "Trouble, huh," nodded the boy.

"No, *no,* no trouble. I just... Never mind. I'll be back, *with* the silver."

The boy gave a resigned nod, obviously considering how much he could get for the merchandise if Kelgan never returned.

Much haggling and sweating later, Kelgan showed up leading two mules. The child's face registered conflicting emotion, relief, disappointment, satisfaction, the last when he seized the two silvers from Kelgan's hands and melted like smoke into the crowd.

Afraid to use any of his power, Kelgan loaded the mules inexpertly but swiftly and set out on the road after the twins.

··· 33 ···

I'll See (Hear) You in My...

"I had another dream, Ez."

Ezrael kept his silent "Oh, no!" from registering on his face. "What were this 'un about, Bethie?"

She looked at him sharply, and he knew she read his thoughts. They plodded on for a while without a response from her. Then, just as Ezrael was cursing himself for not being more opaque, the story poured forth.

"I saw Pelly again, Ez, and our old nag, too; they wuz near that funny water like las' time. And they had others with 'um."

"Others? Who's that, Bethie?"

"Can't rightly say, Ez. They weren't clear like Pelly. Him... I know him, all right."

"But where, Bethne Anna?"

"We're goin' in the right direction, Ez. I feels it. You don't got no call to use my whole name."

Hands on hips, she rounded on him, face flushed with unexpected anger.

Ez stumbled, sorry anew to distress her, "Now, Bethie, don't get riled," he offered in a mollifying tone. "I jes' likes ta say your real name sometimes."

She continued to glare, so he added, "I allus thought it wuz almost as pretty as you."

Bethne shook her head, unable to stay angry. "Oh Ez, you're such a old fool."

The soft tone made the words a compliment.

Ezrael took her hand, as he had been wont to do in their courting days, and kissed her palm. Drier and more callused than when she was a maid, but still infinitely dear to him. He had loved her from the first moment; neither age nor illness could diminish his feelings a whit. He examined her face now with concern; along with the fading of her anger, her skin had paled, as well. He realized that she was proceeding purely on will.

"Bethie, we're goin' to find us another inn!"

"Oh no, Ez, let's keep going."

"No, I wants to buy you a good dinner and find us a decent bed.... I gots a kinda hankerin'."

"Why, Ez! You are an old fool." Bethne blushed and actually simpered.

Ez hated to deceive her and hoped fiercely that he could make his "hankerin'" come true. He knew it was the only way to get her to stop and rest, if only for a night.

A few more miles, during which Bethne wilted visibly, brought them to a small, but reasonably clean inn. The proprietress was a rotund, voluble woman in an amazing collection of garments—the number and combination of clashing colors gave her the appearance of an animated crazy quilt draped around a wine cask. Her good nature, however, spilled over on them, making even Bethne smile.

The food she served them, accompanied by an endless flow of chatter, was plentiful and well-seasoned, though plain. A chicken stewed with vegetables, a good cheese and fresh bread filled their bellies, as the ale warmed their souls. Ez had Bethne's cup filled several times, happily watching a little pink return to her cheeks.

The kindly prattle of their hostess—Merelia, as she introduced herself—who seemed all too glad to enjoy what must have been rare custom, prompted a response from Bethne. Soon the two were exchanging recipes, methods for removing stains, and the best time to plant snap beans. A little gentle gossip about neighbors they didn't know interposed itself among the recipes.

"We had some excitement last week. You know we don't see many strangers around here. We're not a big place, not like the port;

not many strangers want to come here. That is, I mean, *travelers* do stop sometimes. I mean, here *you* are, ain't you? I just meant *real* strangers, passing through.... Where was I? Oh, yes. We had a little excitement. A young man, a very good-looking young man came riding into the village, looking for the port, he said. He was so polite...." Her voice trailed off, and she sat staring vaguely for a moment.

Bethne's face, to Ezrael's distress, had gone deathly pale again. She sat bolt upright on the edge of the bench.

"Go on," she whispered.

Merelia jumped slightly, looking confused.

"Well, that's about it. Except the horse was all sweaty and its legs were shaking like he'd been riding her hard for hours...." Her voice trailed off again.

Gathering herself, she added, "He scared the dogs."

Bethne squeaked.

Ez laid his hand on her arm. "What's that mean?"

"The dogs all ran, and the cats, too, all their hair standing straight up. When babies saw him, they screamed, fit to bust."

Ez cleared his throat, about to speak.

Merelia went on, "It's so funny, he had such nice manners. I think maybe he'd been sick, though."

"Why's that?"

"Well, he looked kinda stiff, like he'd been lying in bed for a while."

"We gots to go, Ez." Bethie stood, grasping the table for support.

Kind as she had been, Ezrael wanted to take their too-talkative hostess by the throat to force her silence.

She curiously eyed Bethne. Ezrael attempted mollification.

"Now Bethie, it's dark out."

"We gots to go," she repeated stubbornly.

"No!" Ezrael's voice boomed. A voice he had rarely used toward Pellerin—never toward Bethne.

Merelia and Bethne both squeaked this time.

"It's frakking dark out thar, an' we're goin' to bed."

"Ez," Bethne began.

"Naow!" he drawled, grabbing Bethne's hand. "Thank'ee, Merelia, that were real nice. We'll be sayin' good night now."

He rushed a protesting Bethne from the room and up the stairs.

Once inside their spare, but clean and comfortable room, he turned on her. She flinched back from him—this was not an Ez she knew.

"Bethie, what the Darkness aire you thinkin'? You wuz jes' about to set out, at night, to nowhere. An' you wuz jes' about to tell that woman that were *our* boy, besides."

Bethne sank to the bed and covered her face with her hands. Between sobs she managed to mumble, "It were Pelly. It were Pelly."

"I know it," confirmed Ez.

She peeked at him through her fingers, then dropped her hands to glare at him.

For the first time in their marriage, her glare had no effect. Ezrael stared back, stone-faced, arms folded.

"Our boy's already dead, Bethie. No use yer killin' yourself, too. Wherever he's got to, we'll catch up. Ain't gonna matter... nor sooner nor later."

Bethne wasn't sure which astonished her more—Ez accepting the fact that Pelly was dead but still wandering around somewhere, someway, or Ez laying down the law to her so firmly. Paying her glares and tears no heed. A little prick of conscience assailed her; after all, she knew Ez so well, she used them rather frequently to get her way.

Only when I wuz right, was her silent rationale.

Ezrael proclaimed, "Now, we're gonna go to bed, and we're *both* gonna sleep. In the morning, we're gonna eat breakfast and we're gonna buy some food from that there Merelia to take with us. *Then,* we'll see if we kin find out which way Pelly went and follow him."

"I reckon you right, Ez. I feel awful tired, but it ain't easy to settle down, jes' knowin' he's out there."

She threw him a quick look. "I'll do my best, anyways; Lumen knows I needs it."

Ezrael smiled and dropped to his knees in front of her. "Atta girl, Bethie, I knowed you allus had good sense."

He clutched her convulsively in his arms, then gave her the kind of kiss he had when she was a girl. "Oh, Bethie, I duz love you, so."

A little later, Bethie found she had no trouble sleeping at all.

··· 34 ···

Here We Are Again

Cal's day was still going downhill rapidly. Unhappy clients, unhappy boss, unhappy ex—call from *her* attorney making more demands—and horrible buzzing in his head, where the slowly fading echoes of stranger voices still whispered. *"Kill, Cal." "No, no. Fill, Cal."*

"Somebody slipped me something, never had a hangover last this long," he told the men's room mirror. Splashing his face with cold water only increased his headache.

"Buddy boy, you look like shit," informed a gloating voice behind him.

Cal whirled to face his fat tormentor. "Yeah, looks like the flu, all right. Hope you don't catch it."

He leaned into the other's face, exhaling noisily. Pip the Drip backed off hastily and scuttled into a stall, throwing the lock.

Cal grinned; somehow that minor contretemps made him feel marginally better.

Stepping out of the men's room, he stopped himself just in time to avoid colliding with his supervising partner. Pete Hobbs eyed him with disapproval at first, then with genuine concern after further study.

"Cal, you look really bad. What's up?"

"Feels like stomach flu, although I did have some snapper last night."

"It could be salmonella. Get to your doctor, ASAP."

"Well, I've been working on the Lincoln case. Don't want to put that off."

"Bull, it can wait 'til tomorrow. Don't fool around, you look really sick."

"If you say so."

"I do. Get going."

By this time, Phillip had come out of the men's room and heard the last. Eagerly he offered, "I'll be glad to take over."

Hobbs appeared to consider the offer. Cal held his breath. Giving Cal an enigmatic stare, Hobbs shook his head. "No, I'm *sure* Cal will be up to it tomorrow."

As he started to turn away, Hobbs glanced back at Cal. "Come into my office for a minute, Cal. I have a couple of suggestions."

Cal followed the partner into his office where Hobbs shut the door behind them.

"A word to the wise, Cal, it wouldn't do to get the "flu" too often. Your work has been slipping steadily over the last eight months. The slip stops here, *if* you get my drift."

Cal's mouth felt so dry he could barely form the words. "Sure, Pete, I get your drift. I'll be right as rain, tomorrow."

Right as rain, he thought, *I'm beginning to talk like Pete.*

Pete Hobbs was known as a sharp, hip, and rather ruthless corporate defense lawyer, but in conversation he sounded like a relic of the Fifties.

Giving a sketch of a salute, Cal left the office and returned to his own. He was careful to gather up every scrap of paper concerning his case. Packing two large accordion files, plus his briefcase, he headed for the elevator.

"Hey, Cal, I'll take one of those files off your hands."

Gritting his teeth, Cal pretended not to hear. He jabbed the down button ferociously. Fortunately, the door slid open and he threw himself inside. The elevator was empty, for which he was thankful; no one else was going down, either, so the elevator dropped smoothly to the underground garage.

Cal heaved a sigh of relief as he approached his car. The files were heavy, his briefcase was loaded as well, his headache pounded at his temples like tiny construction workers with miniature nail guns, and his stomach roiled.

Sliding into the seat, he felt a bit of relief at laying down his burden. He rested his face for a moment on the steering wheel, then feeling a sudden anxious urge to be quit of the building, he started the car.

··· 35 ···

A Useful Talent, Seldom in Use

"Tell us all," demanded T'Jules.

Both normally open and forthright Mel'hachim faces closed, giving the appearance of naughty children caught sneaking sweets.

Daliane remonstrated with them. "You know all our secrets. Why are you keeping something from us?"

"It is not a thing we speak of, little sister," Jorgo's *basso profundo* was even deeper than usual. On anyone less kindly, Daliane would have called it a growl.

Surprised at the obvious discomfiture of their new friends, the Baron and Baroness stared in silence. A silence which grew until Nadi gave a short, explosive bark of laughter.

"You have the right of it, my sister. Our 'secret' is not as strange as yours."

"Because we are employed as warriors, and only that, we hesitate to proclaim other, well, abilities," Jorgo inserted.

"Not all are comfortable knowing we are more," contributed Nadi.

"Just as we do not speak of our mated status."

"Some are even less comfortable with women who fight," Nadi twinkled.

"Their distress is only increased when they *see* her fight," a rumble from Jorgo.

Daliane and T'Jules only looked bewildered.

"What talents?" a brook-no-nonsense voice from T'Jules.

"We are lookers," Nadi responded flatly.

"Lookers!" exclaimed Daliane. "Seers, you're seers?"

"Um, not exactly," Nadi searched for words to explain. "We do not receive images of the future. It's more... more an impression of the now."

"It is hard to put into your words," added Jorgo. "We look at the moment; judge the vibrations of the now, from there we can...."

"Feel a little way ahead. Thus, my sister, we could see the shadows gathering tonight. Not a time for you to be vulnerable."

T'Jules frowned. "I am still not comprehending. You see, but you don't see."

"I understand," Daliane smiled triumphantly. "It's not like pictures, it's like chills up your spine."

Jorgo's grin was fondly amused. "As you say, my Baroness."

She stuck out her tongue at him in a most un-aristocratic manner.

"My wife has a way with words," mocked T'Jules.

She stuck out her tongue at him as well.

"Am I to be ignored?" Nadi inquired in a tone of mock dismay.

Enjoying herself thoroughly, Daliane was unable to include Nadi in the group. Controlling herself, she became once more the Baroness—well, almost.

"What do we do now?" With her huge eyes and frail-seeming physique she reminded them of a small child wanting to know what they would play next.

Jorgo interpreted her question literally. "I think the time has come to think seriously of action, my sister. The forces of Darkness are gathering too closely to you for us to trifle with them longer."

"I am of one mind with my mate," agreed Nadi. "We have discussed this—at the time we were 'looking,'" she explained apologetically, "we feel the castle is no longer a safe place for you to remain."

··· 36 ···

Another Useful Talent, Put to Use

K elgan's experience with the vagaries of mules made returning to the shore where Terencia and the boy (and, he presumed, the twins) awaited, made the return journey both frustrating and slow.

The mules, intelligent animals, were well aware that they had the upper hoof and delighted, from Kelgan's viewpoint, in indulging every caprice of mulish behavior.

They wandered erratically off onto the shoulders of the road, forcing Kelgan to yank their bridles for long minutes to get them back on the straight and narrow path. They nipped everything—the plants, the grass, him, and each other—one such episode resulting in a frenzy of kicks from the smaller mule that threatened the destruction of all he carried. And they then stood together, gazing at him in malicious conspiracy as he sweated and swore while he attempted to repack the load more securely.

Kelgan surprised himself at the depth and breadth of his profane vocabulary. This, in time, made him feel smugly pleased with himself. By Lumen he was a real man—swearing, loading mules....

The skin between his shoulder blades prickled. He whirled, uneasily scanning the roadside verdure and the trees for signs of the someone, or something, spying on him. This feeling had come to him several times since quitting the outskirts of the town, but he had seen and heard nothing. To be sure, he made so much noise with the mules that an entire herd of oxen could have plowed through the trees and he would not have heard.

I couldn't have heard the herd, he thought foolishly.

Giving a little snort, he shrugged and dismissed his feelings as fantasies. Yanking the bridles once again, he actually succeeded in getting the mules moving smoothly behind him—actually on the road—for a short stretch.

The prickles only strengthened. With infuriating *sang froid,* the mules halted every few feet to crop the grass, or simply stood, affecting utter stupidity. Kelgan pulled, tugged, yanked, hauled, inch by inch, foot by foot, until it suddenly occurred to him that he was a wizard. Plopping into the dirt, he allowed himself a moment of self-pitying sobs, before he pulled himself together and set about conjuring up a spell of compliance. He pronounced the word softly but carefully, almost whispering into the pricked ears of the mules.

At the completion of the spell, he pulled, gently this time, on the reins; the mules fell into step and moved out smoothly. Kelgan realized he had never seen consternation on the faces of an animal before, but it was obvious the mules were patently both puzzled and dismayed at their sudden urge to obedience; nonetheless, constrained to comply, they stepped out smartly. Their newly-realized master, however, spent a good bit of the next mile mentally kicking himself for having forgotten his true occupation, Mage, not muleteer.

Finally reaching the shore clearing, he beheld a strange tableau. Nevander and Neroma stood in postures of uncertainty over the stretched-out bodies of both the boy and Terencia. Neroma's hair caressed Terencia's head. The old mare stood protectively close beside them.

Dropping the reins of the spelled mules, Kelgan ran the rest of the short way to their sides.

"What happened? What happened? Are they...?"

"Dead?" finished Nevander, a slight quirk curling one side of his mouth, "we don't know what happened yet, but yes, they still... live."

The boy's horse raised its head to Kelgan and whickered softly, engaging his eyes with an oddly meaningful stare. Unable to decipher horse, and feeling exceedingly foolish for thinking the horse was sending him a message, Kelgan stared back baffled. He broke the horse's gaze to find Neroma regarding him curiously. At the same moment, the prickles sounded a warning between his shoulder blades, and he spun quickly to catch a glimpse of something disappearing back behind the tress. With a shout, he took off in pursuit; flailing through the undergrowth like a man possessed. His long strides quickly caught up with the "something", which did its best to evade him, dodging this way and that. Catching, at last, a vanishing shirttail, Kelgan drew the intruder back to him. He stared in shock at the child from the marketplace.

"What are you doing here, and why are you spying on me?" he demanded furiously. "Speak the truth, or I'll cane you."

Kelgan had never caned so much as a mouse, but the boy could not know it was a threat with no teeth.

"I ain't spying. I'm... You're goin' somewhere, and I want to go, too."

Struck dumb for a long moment, Kelgan finally brought out, "Your parents."

"Don't have any."

"You uncles, aunts, cousins."

"Don't have those neither. I'm 'prenticed to the butcher," as if that explained all.

"Why do you want to go with me... us?" Kelgan knew it was the wrong question, but couldn't contain his curiosity.

"I saw *them.*" The boy jerked his head in the direction of Neroma and Nevander. "They was fat, and they got skinny."

Slapping his forehead, Kelgan realized that, as soon as the twins had gotten out of range of his influence, the illusion he had constructed had simply melted away, exposing the twins for what they really were. Then another thought struck him.

"Wait a moment; that must have been before I even hired you."

The boy nodded. "Yeah, I hung around so you'd notice me. I was hoping you'd want somebody to carry stuff or somethin' like that."

The boy gets a high mark for enterprise, thought Kelgan. Aloud he said, "It's impossible, you can't come."

"You can send me back, but I'll just follow you again. And this time I won't never let you see me, 'til it's too late to send me back. 'Sides, you need somebody like me—*you're* pretty dumb, and *they're* hopeless."

Kelgan began a guffaw, bethought himself of the situation behind him, and sobered in mid-whoop. At that moment a stir from the rear attracted his attention. The child's eyes went wide. Kelgan turned to see Terencia sitting up, dazedly rubbing her forehead. The strange young man had regained his feet—still in that stiff awkward manner of his—and had reclaimed the horse's reins. Peculiarly, the horse, which had seemed terrified of its enigmatic rider, gave a triumphant neigh, then promptly laid its ears back and displayed the whites of its eyes.

Releasing his hold on the child, Kelgan ran to rejoin the group. Looking back, he uttered an expletive, which drew a crooked eyebrow from Nevander. The child was nowhere to be seen.

Kelgan dropped to his knees in front of Terencia. "Can you tell us what happened?"

She shook her head as if to clear it; then raised a troubled face to Kelgan. "He," nodding at the young man, "started to shout. He yelled something like, 'Bad, bad! No voices, no voices!' He looked like he was pushing something away; and all the time he kept screaming 'NO!'"

Terencia stopped, obviously agitated at the memory. "For a minute," she began again, "he was perfectly still, the next minute, he made a lunge for me. I had my sword at his throat instantly. It touched him, and... and... that's all I remember." She dropped her head forward on her knees, muttering, "It burned."

"What burned? What are you talking about?"

Terencia kept her head pressed to her knees. "The sword. When I touched him... it burned me."

She looked up again, haggard. "That's the last thing I felt."

"You've been unconscious for hours," declared Nevander, "three, at the very least."

"So long," murmured Terencia, head on knees once more.

A sudden thought brought it up again. "What about...?"

She thrust her chin in the young man's direction. Pellerin had shrunk into himself, as before. Although his hand grasped the reins, there was neither strength nor purpose there.

"He was as tho... stretched full length. If he possesses consciousness as we know it, it had flown."

Terencia gave a convulsive shudder. "He may not possess it, but it possesses him."

Nevander regarded her shrewdly. "Thou hast the right of it, methinks."

Kelgan felt the same old annoyance that hit him whenever Nevander put on his airs. It made Kelgan's teeth ache from gritting, and he thought he would probably end up with serious arthritis, as well, from keeping his fists clenched at his sides.

Nevander evidently realized Kelgan was getting testy, because he dropped alongside Kelgan and reached gravely for Terencia's wrists.

"Let me see your hands."

Terencia obediently opened them, palms up, for Nevander's inspection. Outside of some workman-like calluses, they were unmarked.

"Psychical, but not physical," observed Nevander, "a powerful jolt, nonetheless."

Terencia seemed to have regained her wits. "He was right, you know." A wry smile flitted briefly across her face.

"Who?" "Right?" Kelgan and Nevander spoke together.

"The lad, our, um, guest. He was right about the voices. They *are* bad—really, really bad—they changed him... horribly." She shuddered again.

"You really think it was a change?" Kelgan peered doubtfully over his shoulder at the young man.

"Yes?" She hesitated, looking somewhat embarrassed. "I, well... I touched him with my sword earlier. Nothing happened then."

Kelgan and Nevander sat back on their heels, pondering Terencia's words. Kelgan remembered the something that had pushed briefly out of the young man's eyes. It had frightened him, because he seemed to know it, and it him, but that had not felt evil. Something else, far worse, far deadlier, had taken hold of the youth, albeit for only a short while.

Neroma had been standing silently, all the while, her eyes on the youth. Her hair roved this way and that, uncertain of what it sought. Then, as if in decision, several questing tendrils wrapped the young man's shoulders. Others turned his chin, softly, in Neroma's direction. As they had, for an instant, met Kelgan's, the boy's eyes locked momentarily with the fathomless ebony depths of Neroma's. She drew a breath, but evidently understanding, or at least accepting, what she saw there, she released him. He reverted to apathy; she to introspection, her hair mantling her like a cloak of midnight.

A faint rustling told Kelgan that the other boy was still concealed in the brush, looking on. Magic, of itself, obviously did not disconcert him, since he had taken a particular interest only after seeing the twins emerge from the illusion Kelgan had cast. *Not one of my better castings.*

Kelgan wondered if the child realized the significance of the older youth with them. Darkness! *He* didn't know it himself.

Terencia began to struggle to her feet. She started to brush aside the men's helping hands, then clutched gratefully as the scenery spun.

"Whoo! Better than Tinker's ale," she joked.

Kelgan had trouble believing his ears. Terencia's attempts at humor were rarer even than his own. *And no one could accuse her of good-nature.*

Once on her feet, Terencia sheathed her sword, a major concession for one accustomed to thinking with weapons. Being flat on her back, vulnerable to everyone and everything for hours, had pounded home the message that swords didn't solve every problem.

Kelgan, reminded of his own sword, doffed the long tunic he had donned to conceal it. Unstrapping it from his leg, he heaved a sigh of relief. He had had to swing his leg stiff-kneed, which had added discomfort to his frustration with the mules. As Kelgan adjusted his yet unbaptized blade, the motionless youth by the horse raised his head and trapped Kelgan's gaze with his own. For a fleeting second, the flash of something Kelgan had seen earlier looked out of the formerly vacant eyes; then it was subsumed back into the previous vacancy. Kelgan echoed Terencia's shudder.

"Come, my Mage, we must prepare. In the morning, we must begin our journey."

"Begin?" repeated Kelgan incredulously. "Haven't we arrived?"

Both Nevander and Neroma sniffed scornfully. "We have scarcely started. We are but two hundred miles from the Keep, as you well know. Is your world so small, my Mage?"

His cheeks burned. Would he never learn to at least conceal his naivete so that infernal Nevander wouldn't always have the better of him?

"But of course, the Academy keeps its very best close to itself until the time is right. Once introduced to the world, their extraordinary talent enables them to become Cosmopolitans very quickly. I am afraid we have acted *in loco Academis* in this regard, my Mage. We, too, have kept you grievously sequestered."

Kelgan favored his Lordship with a suspicious stare, which was returned blandly. Unsure whether to be mollified or not, he finally said, "Well, if we're going in the morning, I'd better unpack the mules and settle them for the night."

"I would not let you work alone, my Mage. You have done a splendid job of procuring the necessities and fetching them hither. I will do my best to be of assistance."

Still feeling there was some obscure joke in the air, of which he was the butt, Kelgan acquiesced with rather bad grace.

Neroma broke in with asperity. "The two of you are ridiculous; the only part of a mule either of you is acquainted with is the part which goes away from you. Unload the mules. Terencia and I will ready the packs for morning. Try to arise as adults."

The men stared for an instant in disbelief, then Nevander bent double, slapping his thigh in profound glee.

"Skewered, by Phosphene! She has run us through!" More seriously, he turned to Kelgan. "And she is right, my good friend, I have been a posturing cock and you a sullen schoolboy; let us try to be more like intelligent men."

Kelgan started to protest, "I haven't...."

The women watched, Neroma's hair pointing skyward in exasperation.

"Yes, you're right," he admitted, "I've been whining, at least to myself, the entire time I've been with you. And," he tacked on wickedly, "*you* really have postured."

A snort from the bushes made them all turn. Kelgan strode to the scrubby underbrush and dragged the urchin out once more.

"This rascal wants to come along," he announced. "Absurd."

"What do you think you could do to earn your keep, my lad?" inquired Nevander.

"I can do lots of things, tend mules, carry stuff, I can even steal stuff. I bet you folk don't even know how to cook."

"He *has* a point," opined Nevander.

"Nonsense," protested Kelgan. "He's too young."

"I am not. I'm twelve years old. So there!"

"Twelve, that much," mused Nevander.

"Ten," guessed Kelgan, "*and* small for your age."

The boy glared at him.

"Well, I'm almost eleven. I want to come; I don't have anybody else and the butcher beats me. Yes, he does," was the boy's defiant response to Kelgan's obvious disbelief.

The child pulled up his shirt to reveal dreadful red marks across his back.

There was an indignant gasp from Neroma. She poured her smooth alto over the child, like honey over his wounds. "We will take you, little one, at least until we can find you a home."

The boy's face shone with adoration. She had made this conquest, at least.

"All in favor, then," twinkled Nevander, "say aye."

Before any of the others could speak, a single flat voice said, "Aye."

An extraordinary silence followed before Nevander's weak, "Well that settles that."

··· 37 ···

I'd Like, to Be Beside...

"**P**lease, my sweet, leave off and sit," T'Jules implored Daliane, who had paced restlessly since the sunset. "Or is it the voices?"

"No. Yes. I don't know." Daliane wrung her hands in frustrated distraction. "Tee Jee, we must take some action. Jorgo is right, we can't just let things happen."

T'Jules stood and joined her. Taking her arm, he paced with her for some moments without speaking. After several turns around the chamber, he shook himself and agreed with a resigned sigh.

"We do not know whither, nor against what," he reminded her.

She buried her head in his chest for a little, encircling his waist with her slender arms that scarcely met behind him.

Her voice sounded muffled by his shirt. "I saw a sea, Tee Jee."

For a split second he thought she was making a joke. "A what?"

"A sea." She drew back her head and looked at him squarely. "It had two colors."

"Eh?"

"It was black and bright blue; the colors never mixed."

"Ebonspear."

"You know it?"

"Yes." No expression.

Daliane was curious, but well knew her Tee Jee. The explanation would be forthcoming, without prompting on her part when, and only when, he was ready.

As though he had read her mind, he chuckled and assured her,

"Oh, nothing bad, my dear, just an unfortunate relative. Unfortunately, a relative, I mean."

She raised an eyebrow.

"We speak of him as little as possible," he answered her unspoken question. "He's not *really* bad. Actually, he's not strong enough to be *really* bad, just a petty little criminal dictator who requires straightening out, now and then. Sad to say, I am the straightener."

"What is his connection with the two-toned sea?"

"His lands include the town of Callett, a port town on the Magnus Aurea bay—the area just around the docks is called Rivermouth. Ebonspear is an underground river which falls from one of the cliffs ringing the town."

"How can it do that if it's underground?"

A sharp glance told him she was not serious.

"Ahem," he continued. "The bay is really just a bit of the Sea of Forever."

Daliane winced. "I hate that name."

"Of course, it isn't actually forever, my darling. It just seemed so to the early seafarers in their tiny vessels, before galleons, my love."

"I know that, Tee Jee," she interrupted. "You needn't condescend. It's not that... I can't explain... it's just something."

"I'm a pompous ass."

Dally laughed. "I do love an introspective man."

He swept her up and kissed her. "Shall I tell you what I love?" he asked as he leered.

For a while, they played, "What I Like Best," and forgot all else. Around midnight, Daliane whispered in his ear, "Wake the others."

The Mel'hachim slept outside the door, awaiting a summons. In a bound, T'Jules was at the door, hissing at the warriors. No rubbing of eyes, no stretching, no fumbling. Instantly alert, they observed the situation and made a shrewd assessment.

"The Baroness has decided."

T'Jules did an almost comical double-take. How had they known she was contemplating a decision? Perhaps the tread of the Baroness' small feet earlier had communicated some of her turmoil. Perhaps she had hinted before they had separated in the evening. Perhaps....

"No, no, my brother," grinned Jorgo, seeing T'Jules' obvious confusion. "You are, um, informally disposed."

In horror, T'Jules looked down to realize he was totally starkers. Nadi's lower lip was fixed firmly between her teeth, just as her eyes remained firmly fixed on the floor. Only a slight quivering of her shoulders betrayed her. Aghast, he turned to Daliane, to be greeted to the spectacle of his Baroness, sheets over her head, beating the mattress with her small fists. Peals of laughter emerged from the sheets.

Mustering what dignity he could, T'Jules commanded loftily, "Be ready. We will call you momentarily."

Shutting the door firmly, T'Jules moved to the bed, wondering half-seriously if he would have to throttle his bride, who showed no signs of containing her merriment.

"You could have reminded me," he accused her.

Daliane peered over the top of the sheet. Her eyes danced. "Now they will know what a stalwart steed I ride," she responded demurely.

"Hmph," T'Jules was not entirely displeased.

He dressed quickly in practice clothing, as did Daliane. Grasping his arm with one hand, she pulled his head down to hers as though for a kiss. Instead, she whispered in his ear under the pretense of nibbling the lobe.

"Tee Jee, I'm afraid they can see and hear us all the time—at least, at night."

Aghast at the implications, T'Jules almost pulled away in shock. Daliane, however, anticipated his move and held him fast.

"Don't, Tee Jee, you must look normal."

Nuzzling her neck, he whispered in return, "By the Bright Lady, how am I supposed to look normal?"

"You must," she pressed the words against his ear, then backing away, she whirled and purred coquettishly. "Well, your Nudeship, shall we join the others?"

She dodged a bottom swat and made for the door. As soon as she opened it, two carefully controlled faces appeared around the jamb.

"Ah, you are ready for our, um, practice session?" Jorgo's bland inquiry revealed nothing, either of his former amusement or of his certainly present curiosity.

"Yes, however, I think we should have a short meditation in the chapel, if you don't mind, before we start." The notion had just struck Daliane. If they were safe from surveillance anywhere, surely the domain of the Bright Lady would be it.

Jorgo and Nadi looked slightly uncomfortable, unsure whether the Two would countenance such a "meditation," but acquiesced at Daliane's meaningful gaze.

"Ah, indeed, my sister, those who practice the contemplation of faith along with the more, um, active skills, frequently find their sword arms strengthened," agreed Jorgo smoothly, as though there had been no hesitation. He and Nadi stood at attention, allowing the Bervaines to proceed them, then fell smartly into step behind, neither even stealing a look at the other.

Daliane led the way to the private Bervaine chapel, dedicated to Phosphene in her guise of the Bright Lady. The Mel'hachim sucked in their breaths as they took in the scene. Directly opposite the door, at the far end of the chapel, stood a twice-life-size image of the goddess, gilded rays of light streaming from her ivory hands. Torches, unlit at the moment, lined the walls, and a dozen chandeliers, marching in two rows, hung suspended from the ceiling, the lofty vault of which was gilded as well.

Ringing a bell near the door to summon a servant, Daliane announced, "We will light all the lights."

This proceeding took the better part of half an hour, and was carried out by four young men, who did their deliberate best to appear incurious. Nadi and Jorgo simply gaped. As more and more of the chapel was illuminated, it became obvious that the walls were mirrored, reflecting and multiplying the flames until the whole dissolved into shards of dizzying brilliance. The rectangular contours of the chapel simply melted away, giving the impression that one walked at the heart of the sun.

Daliane drew the Mel'hachim forward toward the Lady's image; a spot the warriors were rather reluctant to assume. To their surprise, they felt a distinct lighting of spirit as they approached; the feeling that some inexpressible oppression had been lifted from their souls. Daliane whispered, "It is the same every time. I don't know why I did not think of this until now."

"Perhaps you were not meant to," Nadi suggested.

"Hmmm," murmured Daliane, "I hadn't thought of *that*, either."

In spite of the brilliant light, T'Jules had been standing rapt in a brown study. He roused himself now to affirm Nadi's surmise.

"I've been thinking along the same lines. You were becoming increasingly weaker, sleep-deprived, and nearly starved. I think the voices wanted it that way as a prelude to, well, taking command of your soul. When you began resisting them, and especially after Jorgo and Nadi arrived, you frustrated their plans by regaining your strength and thinking rationally again." He clasped her hands. "I almost aided them with our experiments." His face convulsed for a moment in an agony of memory.

"No, no, Tee Jee," she soothed. "I agreed, we all did, it was necessary."

"Yes, yes," chorused the warriors.

Jorgo grasped T'Jules' forearm. "We underestimated the power of the enemy, my brother," he declared. "That will not happen again." He turned to Daliane. "And now my small but strong Baroness," he twinkled," you wish to speak of... something."

Words tumbled from Daliane. "I told you I saw a body of water, a sea or lake, I don't know... but it was different! There was dark water... I think we should go there."

"A fine idea, my sister, do you know where "there" is?"

"I think so," Daliane's voice was tiny.

"I do," T'Jules reminded her.

··· 38 ···

The Third Useful Talent, Grudgingly Accepted

"I seem to be outvoted," Kelgan commented wryly.

Nevander agreed. "Will we, or nil we, it would appear."

Kelgan gave the boy a little shake of the collar. "It looks as though you win, urchin."

The boy permitted himself a small smirk. "I'll get my stuff."

"Stuff?"

"Sure, I knew I'd be comin'."

Piper dashed off to the bushes, returning swiftly in case they changed their minds while he was gone, with a neat bedroll and a stout staff. Nevander appreciatively eyed the staff, but made no comment.

"Let's go," the boy trebled.

"Stay, my boy. We will remain here until morning. The sun is nearly down."

Neroma's alto poured molasses into the discussion, washing over her twin's objections. "He is right, Nevander. We will move on for a bit, an hour or two from here, no more."

Kelgan knew she only spoke aloud for the boy's benefit—and for his own, he admitted. He had seen the sharp look Nevander had sent her immediately after he had spoken.

After a minute pause, in which he was sure the exchange between brother and sister had continued, Nevander voiced his agreement.

"My Mage, do you believe the mule-packs will hold a bit longer?"

Affronted, Kelgan assured Nevander there was no problem. Piper added his opinion.

"He didn't pack 'em *real* good, but they'll go for an hour or two."

Kelgan humphed, and Terencia snickered.

Quelling a rude impulse, he returned to the mules to reinforce his spell to compel. He could see the mules were just awaiting the opportunity to revenge themselves on their reluctant driver. He untied their leads and gathered them up. With virtually human sighs, they stepped behind him, his sigh of relief matching theirs. Their deceptive, but forced, docility somehow touched him, and he gave each a comradely pat on the nose, which widened their eyes.

"C'mon" urged Piper, bounding ahead of them eagerly.

The strange young man pulled his horse after the mules; his lack of interest in where he put his feet kept both women busy guiding him along the road. Nevander clucked impatiently but brought up the rear without further comment.

Uneasiness assailed Terencia. "I think we should get off the road. I think we attracted some attention we don't want."

"Thieves?"

"Very probably. I hear *someone* coming, any road."

"We trust your instincts and your ears."

As quietly as they could, the little band moved into the underbrush and waited with held breath. Soon four mounted men appeared, riding hard, their clothing proclaiming them mercenaries.

"Shoulda caught up with 'em by now."

"Aah, they hadda good head start."

The horses thundered on past, raising a storm cloud of dust on their way. Five hands were slapped over five noses—only Pellerin remained motionless.

"Could it be this easy?" whispered Kelgan.

A voice behind them answered, "I think not," as a fifth member of the group stepped out of the concealing foliage.

Whirling, Kelgan was astonished to find himself holding his sword in his hand with no memory of drawing it. Out of the corner of his eye, he knew Terencia was at the ready, as well. *As well, indeed! What am I ready for?*

The other riders had returned by this time and circled the party.

"Just drop the swords and hand over the mules and whatever else you're carrying."

Obviously the leader, the man who had spoken smiled at them with great charm and executed an elegant bow. Kelgan felt the prick of a blade in the middle of his back. Without warning, particularly to himself, he spun on his heel. Swinging his sword low, he cut the legs out from under the man behind him. Taking advantage of the surprise, Terencia lunged to the side, dropped to one knee and swung backward over her shoulder at the man behind her, cleaving his head neatly. Nevander held a dagger to the throat of a third man, the fourth having gained the side of the leader, who regarded the party with shock. Kelgan's sword arm stood stiffly out in front of him, and he felt himself impelled forward on his toes. Struggling to control his urge, he took two involuntary steps forward, at which the remaining would-be highwaymen broke and crashed thunderously through the brush into the gathering night. Nevander released his hold on the third robber, who lost no time in joining his fellows in their brush rush.

Piper swung down out of the tree from which he had been pelting the invaders with cones, "Wow! That was *great!*"

Kelgan's arm dropped heavily to his side, nearly slicing a piece off his thigh as it did so. Surveying the scene coolly, he then fell sideways in a dead faint. His next conscious thought was of Terencia slapping him heartily and exclaiming, "Get up, my hero."

Rising groggily to his knees, he noticed he still clutched the now quiescent sword. "In a death grip," he shrilled aloud, and threw up his last meal into an obliging hawthorn.

Nevander knelt beside him, his face creased with worry. "My Mage," he quavered. "Ahem, my Mage," he went on more firmly, "you evidently haven't told us everything about your, um, early training."

"If you mean as a man-at-arms, you knew everything I know. The sword's the one that's trained."

"I feared as much," muttered Nevander, rising and walking off to stand alone, turning his back to the rest of them.

Terencia sat back on her heels and stared steadily at Kelgan, "Always pick a well-trained sword," she commented wryly.

They all jumped as Pellerin intoned, "And a good man."

Their heads swiveled in unison to look at him, standing inert as ever. Even Piper did a double-take and whispered to Kelgan, "He don't talk much, does he?"

Nodding his agreement, Kelgan rose on unsteady legs, using the sword as a staff. On deciding he could actually stand unaided, he replaced it with exaggerated care in its sheath.

"What do we do with...?" He gestured at the two bodies.

"Leave 'em," Piper said authoritatively. "Wolves'll get 'em first, then the crows."

A sick look passed over every face but Pellerin's—death does not disturb the dead, after all—but they had to agree that was best.

Nevander turned back to the group. "Rather well-dressed for highwaymen, would you not say?"

Kelgan, feeling more in possession of his stomach, surveyed the two bodies. While attired in what could pass for the everyday wear of tunic and hose, a careful look told him something interesting. Both wore variants of the same combinations of black-and-red, unrelieved by any other color.

"The others were as these."

"Not just anybody, then."

Nevander nodded. "I had a little more opportunity to observe."

They gazed at each other for a moment more, then Kelgan shrugged. "Evidently a well-organized band."

Nevander continued to look troubled, but returned the shrug.

They gathered themselves together once more and stumbled back to the road. By now night had fallen fully, and they were in more danger of injury among the trees, at least they fondly hoped so. The mules appeared as anxious to move on as they. One gave Kelgan a brotherly nuzzle, as though in congratulation, and followed him with alacrity. In silence, they strode along at a brisk pace, wishing to put as much distance between themselves and the scene of their attack as possible.

Piper seemed to have the night vision of an owl, constantly nudging them around ruts, rocks, and potholes. Their pace slackened after a while with the realization that they were hungry, footsore, and really unaccustomed to a forced march. As they staggered into the second hour, Piper announced, "Okay, we're going to stop here."

Wondering when an "almost" 11-year-old had been elected leader, Kelgan was nonetheless glad that someone was in charge. He, himself, felt utterly incapable of either thought or volition. It vaguely occurred to him that they had carefully avoided the subject of the fight and the business with the sword. He felt too exhausted to give it much attention.

"We're gonna rest for two hours and then we're gonna go some more." Piper's emphatic tone brooked no argument. It was a measure of the party's fatigue that no one even thought of it.

Terencia and Neroma huddled together under one of the blankets and slept immediately. Nevander glanced briefly at Pellerin, shrugged and settled with a swirl of cloak.

Piper dropped beside Kelgan. "I'll take the first watch, you take the second," he ordered.

"Piper...."

"Go to sleep... sir."

Compliantly, Kelgan lay on his side and shut his eyes. As sleep claimed him, a tiny voice in the back of his mind said, *"Why?"* while a second tittered, *"Why not?"* Seconds later, it seemed, Piper shook him awake. Blurrily, he sat up, then snapped his eyes wide as he noticed Nevander, Terencia and Neroma standing silently watching him, as well.

"We couldn't wake you up 'til now," complained Piper. "The sun's about to come up."

Wide awake now, he leaped to his feet. "I've been asleep all night?"

A chill shook him and his teeth chattered. Waving his hands and gazing wildly about, he squealed, "Did anyone...?"

"No, no, no one," Nevander reassured him.

Neroma interrupted. "Let us move on before the sun rises; we have, at the most, one hour. We must hasten as we feel the breath of Doom."

"Don't we already? I certainly feel the breath of something." Kelgan couldn't keep a quaver out of his voice, although he attempted a jocular air.

Neroma gave a slight sniff, which demonstrated her opinion of his attempt, and moved to fold her cloak. The others followed her example, picking up their blankets and preparing to move on. They stumbled back out on the road, not exactly "hastening," but at least plodding steadily. Kelgan moved up to walk abreast of Nevander, leaving the mules in Piper's charge.

"Uh, Nevander, about the sword...."

"The what? Oh, yes, good work, my Mage. Excellent swordsmanship."

"Come off it, Your Lordship, you know I've never handled anything more lethal than a beginner's wand in my entire life before tonight." The tone was deliberately sarcastic and disrespectful.

Nevander started to bristle then sagged. "Aye, my Mage. This awareness has not been spared us."

Kelgan could not suppress a grin. Nevander was ever Nevander, declaiming even the shortest utterances. He found he could not resist gently patting his Lordship on the back, which evoked a self-deprecating grin in return. Worry shone, nevertheless, from the depths of those limitless black eyes—so like Neroma's.

"It would seem, my Mage, that someone or something besides ourselves is involved in our affairs."

"Oh, really!" an exasperated Kelgan stopped dead in the road, hands on hips. "Did this news just arrive by messenger?"

Becoming aware the others were not following, Neroma looked behind to see the two stalled on the road. "At it again," she murmured to Terencia and strode back to ascertain the problem.

"He," with a nod to Nevander, "thinks *something's* interfering in our affairs," Kelgan threw at Neroma.

Neroma rolled her eyes to the night sky, every ebony tress reaching upwards to implore the heavens. As she opened her mouth to speak, a commotion arose from the rear.

Pellerin, who had lagged somewhat behind, caught up, failed to stop, and walked his old mare squarely into one of the halted mules.

Both animals, having taken exception, engaged in a nipping, kicking contest. The other mule, simply feeling its fellow was having all the fun, joined the fray. Pellerin stood oblivious, while Piper did his best to control all three equines.

Kelgan rushed to intercede, forgetting Nevander for the moment, and shouted, *"Levanah!"* The animals instantly quieted to his considerable pleasure. The mules pricked their ears forward, giving Kelgan a show of teeth. Grins, he was sure of it. Pellerin's mare assumed a haughty old dowager expression, casting off any share of the blame.

Torn between real respect for Kelgan's magical ability, and disgust at the inability of the party in general to move more than a few yards without difficulty, Piper urged the mules forward and said, "I'm goin' first. You folks are the...." He checked himself before finishing. Kelgan's mind supplied *"dumbest,"* although he wasn't positive that's what Piper meant.

The light bloomed, the trees on either side showing black against an increasing pinky-gray. Conscious of a rising feeling, Kelgan decided it was simply hunger rather than anything more profound. He suggested a meal, which even their miniature slave-driver seemed to think a good idea.

Hunkered down in the leaves to enjoy their repast of dried meat, fruit and cheese, Nevander heaved a sigh which threatened his ribs. "All right, my Mage, we must discuss your performance."

Terencia agreed. "Yes! Suddenly Signeur Magus became the greatest swordsman Bellermond has seen, when yesterday he couldn't walk without tripping over his scabbard."

Kelgan wanted to be outraged, but could only acknowledge the truth of her statement.

"It appears, my Mage, that someone... something... wishes to protect you."

"The good are their own protection." Delivered in Pellerin's hollow tones, this second unexpected statement sent chills up the other five spines.

Piper nudged Kelgan. "I'm just as glad when he don't talk."

Kelgan made no reply, feeling somehow that giving voice to his agreement would be a mistake. Fortunately, Pellerin decided not to assume a sort of ghastly garrulousness, so they were spared further discomfort.

Surveying the drawn faces of his companions, who had not slept as well as he presumably had, Kelgan wondered how much farther into the day they could totter. Reaching their goal looked to be a slow process. Musing on this possibility, he realized he had no idea of their goal. Nevander had only hinted at a destination, and Kelgan felt some misgivings that Nevander knew its identity or location.

The four of them, on the road to Nowhere, accompanied by No One, plus a child. This last conceit rather tickled him, and he grinned to himself.

Kelgan shared his thoughts, editing out his doubts concerning Nevander, of course. Rather than smiles, he elicited serious nods and uneasy looks.

"It is true, my Mage. We venture into the murkiest of unknowns."

Without commenting on the redundancy, Kelgan voiced his first fear, "We *are* going in the right direction, aren't we?" The second he kept to himself, *What in Darkness are we supposed to do when we get there?*

··· 39 ···

Only a Mother Would Know

B ethne was up even before Phosphene began to spread a gray cloak over the hills.

"C'mon, Ez, we gots to be on the road. Pelly's expectin' us."

"Ezrael sat straight up, bewildered. "How'd you know that, Bethie?"

"I had another dream, Ez. He were with those folks, they was havin' breakfast."

"Havin' breakfast!" Ez fell back on the pillows with a groan. "Bethie, Pelly don't need breakfast no more."

"I reckon that's so, Ez, but them other folk wuz eatin'."

"Who aire these other folk, Bethie?" While he didn't entirely give credence to Bethne's dreams, he didn't entirely discount them, either.

"It's like I said afore, Ez; I knows they're there, but I can't 'zactly make 'em out. They ain't by the sea no more," she added.

"Well, how's we goin' ta find 'em then?"

"Don't worry, Ez. I knows we will."

They finished dressing, and went downstairs. To their surprise, their hostess was already up and laying out bread, cheese, milk and jam, as well as plates, cups and utensils. She wore another baroque mix of brightly-colored garments, different from the previous evening, but equally eye-catching. She bustled in the same energetic fashion, humming and trilling to herself, all the while.

"Oh, there you are," she broke off from her tune to greet them gaily. "I just knew you'd want to be going early." Sniffing at a cream pitcher, she shook her head and tsked.

"Old Freddo's cow needs to be retired—or maybe I should say Freddo's old cow...." She laughed heartily at her own joke. "Her cream's getting thin as water, I declare."

Surveying the table with a critical eye, she urged, "Sit down, sit down."

Bethne made an abortive move for the door, but Ez pulled her firmly toward the table. She turned a piteous face toward him, but acquiesced and plumped down on a stool.

"Sit, eat, eat," ordered Merelia, "you need to put roses back in those cheeks."

Bethne spread a piece of bread with jam, and sniffed a morsel of cheese. Astonishing herself, she discovered she was actually hungry and polished off both the cheese and the bread. Merelia poured her a steaming mug of tea, adding sugar and cream before Bethne could protest.

"Drink up."

A docile Bethne did as she was told, spreading another slice of bread with the thick, fruity jam and holding out her mug for more tea. Ez smiled behind his hand; Merelia certainly had a way with her.

"Good, good," Merelia chuckled as she refilled Bethne's mug. "You'll need this on the road... you've got a ways to go."

Both Ezrael and Bethne froze, staring at their hostess.

"Well, you aire going after the boy, ain't you? I saw the way Bethne looked when I mentioned him. He's been sick, hasn't he, and wandered off; that's the way those brain fevers takes them sometimes. They forget everything they knew, just like a baby. My cousin Jewel's boy was just like that. They thought he was going to die, but he didn't. When the fever wore off, he'd forgot his name and his folks and where he came from...."

Merelia prattled on without stopping as she cleared the table. Ez felt himself breathless from the rush of words, but Merelia evidently felt no such discomfort. The monologue continued to flow from her even as she trotted back and forth with the used dishes, scraps of the leftovers, and cloths to mop up with. Realizing at last that her guests were motionless and silent, she stopped and cocked an inquiring head at them.

Ez nodded and Bethne followed suit, assuring her that—yes, that was right, it was their boy. And yes, he'd been sick and didn't seem to remember things. It seemed safe enough to admit that much. Flushed with pleasure that she had so shrewdly guessed Bethne and Ezrael's purpose, Merelia kindly offered to put up a lunch for them at no extra charge.

"I know how worried you must be. I remember how Jewel felt, poor soul, I could hardly get her to eat, either."

Ez smiled to himself, again. It was obvious from her little round figure that Merelia felt food solved every problem. Although, he admitted inwardly, it certainly helped Bethne. Two good meals and a night's fair rest had made a noticeable improvement in both her look and outlook.

As if echoing his thought, Bethne squared her shoulders and thanked their hostess.

"We're much obliged, Merelia and we'll accept your offer kindly. We gots to get after our boy, 'cuz he's liable to have another spell, and we wants to see him safe home afore it happens."

Bethne's lies poured out so smoothly, Ez would have thought she'd had lots of practice. He chided himself for even the shadow of that thought, knowing Bethne was as honest as the sunflowers which stood by their door.

"Needs do as needs must," he muttered.

"What's that, Ez?" inquired Bethne, puzzled.

"Oh, nothin', ladies," answered Ezrael hastily, "I wuz thinkin' on somethin' else."

"Ez, if you'll jes' bring the cart around and hitch up the goat."

Ezrael hastened to comply. When he had left the room, the women faced each other.

"It's lots worse than that, isn't it, Bethie?" Merelia's words were not a question, but a quiet statement.

Bethne sighed. "Yes, it is, Merelia, but I can't tell you how much worse, 'cuz I don't rightly know."

"I could tell, Bethie... mothers always know. I had two boys... once."

Shocked, Bethne regarded Merelia with wide eyes. In scarcely more than a whisper, she asked, "What happened?"

"The stopping fever took them both, in one day." She obviously felt reluctant to say more. Unusual, from what they had seen of Merelia.

"Oh, Merelia, how could you stand it? I only gots the one... but *two!*"

"Well, you stand it because you have to," Merelia retorted with a snap; then she softened. "You already know that, Bethie, you're standing it right now."

Bethne acknowledged the truth.

"My Lights, your lunch!" Merelia hustled off, leaving Bethne contemplating the air where she had stood.

The stopping fever... Bethne had never heard of 'stopping fever,' and yet she sensed it made Merelia uncomfortable to discuss it for more reasons than the obvious.

Merelia came bustling back, her colorful costume swirling around her, carrying a tray piled with provisions.

"My Lady, Merelia, we'll never eat all that!"

"You'll see," Merelia assured her, "I'm only giving you enough for two days. Think you want to move as fast as you can, don't you?" Bethne nodded. "Well, if you have lots to eat, Ezrael will be a darn sight more cooperative."

Ezrael came stomping back in then, shaking the dirt from his boots before walking on Merelia's pristine floor. "We're all set, Bethie, the goat's ready to go."

The ladies exchanged embraces. Bethne, in spite of her eagerness to be on the road to Pellerin, felt a sharp pang of regret at leaving the first friend she had made in many years. Loneliness suddenly smote her—she loved Ezrael dearly, but they had lived an isolated life on their little croft. Neither had family in the immediate area, so any reunion meant a long trip, leaving their plot untended, their home unguarded. The same applied to any extended trip into the nearest town, therefore those were seldom undertaken. A second thought struck her. Ez had dropped everything without a word, or even a regretful backward glance, where she wanted to follow Pelly. Not once had he reminded her that all they had, except the goat, lay behind them with no one to look after it.

The pang melted in a warm glow. She threw her arms around Ezrael, exclaiming, "Oh, Ez, yer good as gold."

Ezrael, amazed and embarrassed and flushing scarlet, muttered, "Wal now, Bethie."

Merelia laughed again, patting Bethne's back, and winking at Ez over her head. "That'll set him up right for the day, Bethie."

They embraced again. Ezrael, still scarlet, managed a peck on the cheek for Merelia, and an unintentionally gruff, "Take care." Then they were gone, leaving a pensive Merelia staring at the closed door for many heartbeats, before she murmured, "My Lights," and turned to face the gauntleted figure in dull brown, who had stepped in from the back room.

··· 40 ···

Hi, Ho, Livers, Away!

Daliane, T'Jules and their stalwart Mel'hachim swirled like
dervishes throughout the day. Gathering the essentials for what
looked to be a long trek, and then hiding them carefully, consumed
them in frantic, but purposeful, haste. Even so, the shadows lengthened
too quickly to suit Daliane, who gave vent to her frustration by
swacking one recalcitrant bundle with the flat of her sword.

Before she could follow up with further heedless blows, thereby
undoing a goodly portion of what had been done, she was swung
gently in the air and deposited in a safe spot while Jorgo neatly
finished knotting the ropes which had confounded her.

T'Jules paused for a moment in his own efforts, watching with
interest Daliane's anticipated reaction. He grinned to himself as
Daliane burst into laughter, patted Jorgo on the back, and turned
her efforts elsewhere.

"We will need only the rest of the day, my Sister," rumbled Jorgo.
"This is not a bad thing, we feel."

"I bow to your superior feelings," retorted Daliane pertly. "After
all, we don't know where we're going, how long it will take, or what
we'll do if we get there, so why not leave immediately."

Jorgo's teeth flashed, but T'Jules felt it was more snarl than
grin. "It is so, my Sister," then he did grin, genuinely, "but not 'if,'
when."

Daliane 'humphed' happily.

The day was filled with equally frantic activity, as they all attempted to appear "normal," and tried to think of everything but their plans for departure.

They made swift estimates of how far they could ride the first night, how they would camp and what possible precautions they could take after the first day.

"What we need is a good Magician," T'Jules opined.

Jorgo and Nadi shifted uneasily in the water.

"I think I am getting cold," Nadi shivered to cover her discomfort at the mention of real magic.

They dispersed for a nap.

After the two, too short hours ended, they rose again, preparing and, they hoped, successfully covering their preparations.

"We're going to be in fine condition to begin a trek," groused T'Jules, "especially if we plan to travel through both the night and the day and then again the day, after who knows what kind of a night."

Daliane dashed a hand futilely at the sweat beading her upper lip. She nodded in rueful agreement. Even the ordinarily sleek, glossy skins of the Mel'hachim looked gray. Although, Daliane acknowledged, it was probably a result of the dust which coated them all rather than any Mel'hachi weakness.

"I think, my Sister," intoned Jorgo sententiously.

Nadi kicked him and quickly said, "We should leave at last light—it is best."

It was a measure of Daliane's exhaustion that she offered neither surprise nor objection, merely nodded thoughtfully. "Tee Jee, do you think we should leave together or separately?"

"Together," chorused three voices.

Daliane was startled into a giggle. "Well, *that* was definite." Diffidently, she addressed the warriors, "Can we, that is, if you don't mind...."

Nadi smiled, grasping Daliane's difficulty intuitively, "You wish to visit the chapel before."

With a grateful sigh, Daliane breathed, "Oh, yes, if you wouldn't be uncomfortable."

Leading them in, she turned with a question in her eyes to Nadi. "Will you...?

"We feel the Two are with us wherever we are, my Sister. Surely a holy place for you can be no less so for us."

Jorgo rumbled affirmation. "The same Light shines on us all, little Baroness. You who are filled with it must be a special daughter of the Two...."

"And must make them very proud," finished Nadi.

Daliane blushed to the roots of her hair and hid her face in T'Jules' shirt like a toddler, eliciting chuckles from her companions.

"Oh, isn't it a shy thing," twittered T'Jules, poking her ribs.

Daliane withdrew her head in mock disapproval. "Tee Jee, this is the Lady chapel."

She noticed, with some amusement, that Jorgo and Nadi were instantly abashed. She felt a glow of love for them, their goodness, their kindness, their sincerity. Pulling away from T'Jules, on sudden impulse she pushed out the chapel door into the corridor.

For a moment, no one else took notice. Then Jorgo, glancing over T'Jules' shoulder, gave a shout of alarm and leapt for the door, buffeting T'Jules out of the way as he did so. Hauling the Baroness back inside, he nearly threw her at T'Jules. Aghast at what he saw, T'Jules shook her at first gently, then more roughly. Nadi stepped in with her familiar slap.

Daliane drew breath in a great gasp, her eyes showing white. In another instant, she surveyed them coolly and remarked with sarcasm, "Well, it's 'Ow!' as usual. We're really going to need more soft foods on this expedition."

Brief exhaled breaths answered her and then a long silence.

Daliane slumped. "They were waiting for me, Tee Jee. They *wanted* me to look outside. All they needed was my head."

T'Jules fell back against the wall, "*We* don't know *where* we're going; we don't know *why* we're going; but *they* know it all!"

"My brother," Jorgo's hand descended heavily on T'Jules' shoulder—more heavily than absolutely necessary—"it does not matter what we know, ours is the Light."

"Light makes might; might makes right," muttered T'Jules a little crazily.

"My brother," Jorgo repeated, this time with a warning note in his voice.

T'Jules gathered himself and shook off Jorgo's hand, clasping it, however, before it fell too far. "It's all right, Jorgo, I'm all right."

Jorgo raised one eyebrow, but otherwise remained silent.

··· 41 ···

To See the Sea

"**I** sees it, Ez! I sees it!" Bethne's excited screech roused Ezrael, who had been plodding at the side of the goat in a sort of walking trance.

"Eh? Wha...." He jerked on the goat's bridle, eliciting a reproachful, "Maaa!"

"Sorry, Capriola." Ezrael pacified the goat with a pat and part of a carrot from his pocket. "What wuz you sayin', Bethie?"

"I sees the water, Ez. It's right ahead of you, Ezrael," she added impatiently. "I declare, where aire yore eyes?"

Shading his eyes with his hand, Ezrael detected a faint, possible glimmer of sun bouncing off what might have been water, but still too far to discern clearly.

"Hmph, you musta got yoreself a new pair of spectacles, Bethie, if you kin see that there's water. An' how do you know what water anyhow?"

"Well," Bethne conceded, "it is kinda a ways off, but I knows it's that funny water. I just knows it, Ez." Bethne looked up at him without a trace of doubt in her eyes. Ez knew she had to be right.

"I guess it'll take about an hour, Bethie." He said no more about not believing her. "Capriola gettin' kinda tired. She ain't never been driven for such a spell, 'afore."

Bethne eyed the goat with compassion and concern. "We ant none of us been driven for such a spell, Ez, not even our old mare."

Reminded of Pellerin, Ez grimaced. "He's got kinda a head start on us, Bethie. I ain't sure we kin catch him."

"Oh, yes, we will. We will, you'll see." Bethne's jaw jutted forward stubbornly, and she picked up the pace of her stride. The goat 'maaed' again in dismay, but broke into a resigned little trot, as though in sympathy. Bethne gave a little giggle. "See, Ez, Capriola knows, too."

··· 42 ···

A Little Child Shall Lead Them

The rag-tag, far-from-rested, and in-a-decidedly-grumpy-mood group stumbled on at an ever-slowing pace.

The mules, realizing that the geas compelling their obedience was weakening with every dragging step their nominal master took, flicked their ears at each other and wandered pointedly off the path to graze. Futilely grasping at their bridles, Kelgan attempted a shout. What emerged was more a broken croak, which fueled the glee evident in the eyes of his obstreperous duo; digging in their hooves, they refused to stir an inch.

Piper threw up his hands in disgust. "Oh, fer...." running back to where Kelgan swore and yanked, he stooped to grab up a broken branch. Swatting both astonished beasts a couple of good ones across the flanks, he yelled, "Get on, you glue buckets, or we'll roast you for tonight's supper."

Nevander, puzzlement written large on his face, grasped Kelgan's arm. "Uh, my Mage, I believe you were...."

Breaking in crossly, Kelgan confessed, "I was, I know. I did. I've forgotten the words."

Nevander stepped back aghast. "Forgotten... you mean... the spell?"

"That's exactly what I mean. That one and all the others I ever knew. I've been trying to manufacture a light; I can't even get a glow. I can't remember a single word!"

On hearing him, Piper dropped into the dust of the road, and to everyone's singular astonishment, burst into tears. "Y'mean, I've gotta do it all!" he wailed.

Carefully concealing both his laughter *and* dismay, Kelgan squatted and put his arm around the small shoulder, while the others busied themselves at suddenly important tasks. "You've been doing a splendid job; we are immensely grateful, but we are learning, thanks to you. I think we'll be able to hold up our ends... *soon.*"

Piper blinked swimming blue eyes. "You really think I'm helpin' you out?"

"Absolutely."

"An' you really are grateful?"

"Absolutely."

"An' you really think you're gettin' the hang of it?"

"Absolutely."

"Well, then, I guess I can hold us together a little bit longer," the boy stood, cheeks flushed with pride.

Kelgan bit his lip, torn between amusement and admiration. The boy, small as he was, had shown them a few things, after all. He didn't depend on magic, either, just determination and elbow grease. At the thought of magic, his heart thudded again, somewhere to the level of his ankles. Elbow grease was all very well, but.... He tried futilely to raise another witchlight, not so much as a twinkle in his palm.

"*Nameth lumen,*" sounded a hollow voice.

Kelgan's hair rose on his head very like Neroma's.

"*Nameth lumen,*" whispered Kelgan, then louder and more firmly, "*Nameth lumen.*" He stared at the ball of witchlight growing on his palm.

"*Nameth lumen, nameth lumen, nameth lumen,*" he repeated deliriously, tossing balls of light upward and catching them while the others, attention now caught, stared at him as at a madman.

"Stop!" Neroma's molasses tones held an edge of flint.

"Oh, er, I'm sorry. I just... I was just glad. Something, er, someone, er...."

"Yes, we *heard.*"

Jerking his head toward Pellerin, a now thoroughly sober Kelgan felt the hair stir on his head again.

"I... I think *he* reminded me."

"I think so, too."

Honey, strongly tinged with sarcasm, poured from Neroma's lips. Her hair stood straight out in all directions like a disc of midnight, expressing a multitude of emotions. Kelgan suddenly felt he could fall into it and drop forever, like a hole in space where the universe failed to intrude. He swayed toward her.

Catching himself self-consciously, he attempted a logical explanation. "He's heard me say it a dozen times at least. He doesn't seem to forget anything."

Terencia gave a short hiccup of tight laughter. "Anything, except that he's dead."

It was the first time anyone had actually stated what all knew. Heads, including Pellerin's, swung accusingly in her direction.

Finding herself the center of unwelcome attention, she queried defiantly, "Well?"

The answering silence was broken only by a little sigh as Piper slid down Kelgan's leg and back into the dirt.

··· 43 ···

The Ghost of a Chance

B ethne and Ezrael broke into the same trot put on by the goat as
they crested the hill, stopping short at the sight of the town
sweeping downwards away from them, out to the shore of the eerie,
parti-colored waters.

Bethne shivered and rubbed her arms, puckered with gooseflesh,
"It's jes' like my dreams, Ez."

Ez nodded, while Capriola gave a short bleat, as though in
agreement.

Somewhat reluctant, now they were in sight of their presumed
goal, they passed just a few scattered cottages at first, where grimy
children gave them incurious stares, then resumed their activities,
work or play. Used to a more or less constant stream of strangers,
they found little in two old people with a goat worthy of note.

"Ask 'em, Ez," Bethne prodded.

"Ask 'em? What?" countered Ezrael.

Why, if they's seen Pelly, o'course."

"Hmph, Bethie. They's kids, they won't know."

"Ask 'em anyhow, Ez."

Ezrael sighed, but searched the nearest group for a likely
prospect. A slightly older girl with a baby strapped to her back
caught his eye.

"Excuse me, little missy. You 'ant seen a boy on an old mare...."
He described Pelly as best he could, the clothes he'd been wearing
when he left, and the looks of the mare.

The girl stared at him, round-eyed.

"Your boy. That was your boy!"

Then she turned tail and ran as fast as possible while burdened with a chubby sibling, screaming, "Ma, Ma!"

A red-faced, plump woman, whose resemblance to the chubby baby was unmistakable, burst from the cottage, wiping her hands on a towel as she came.

"Lan' sakes, Saree, what's all the fuss?" she exclaimed.

"Ma," Saree clutched her mother, whispering urgently to her while Bethne and Ez looked on in stupefaction.

Saree's mother assessed them shrewdly, taking in their age, the state of their clothing, the probable value of their scrawny goat and rickety cart. Deciding they were harmless and no better off than she, the mother started to turn away, but another urgent "Ma," stopped her.

Saree began whispering again and pulling her mother toward the pair. Her mother came reluctantly with her, but then nodded and moved willingly with Saree, who sighed with relief.

"I'm Armina, an' this here's my Saree—an' my Jebey." She nodded in the direction of Saree's burden. Jebey, in turn, gave a gurgle at hearing his name, beating his fat, little fists on his sister's shoulders.

"Bethne."

"Ezrael."

"Saree tells me yer lookin' fer a boy."

Bethne could not restrain herself. "Have you seen him? Oh, please, please, say you've seen him."

Armina glanced at Bethne with new sympathy. Her obvious real distress, as well as her patent ordinariness, awoke her natural kindness, which she generally tried to keep hidden. Her neighbor's problems, not to mention her own, were many and varied. In order to cope, she had developed a defensive skill. Loss of a child, however, something she knew well, melted her defenses. Then she thought of the boy she had seen. She shifted her shoulders uncomfortably, resetting her shawl as though a chill wind had blown through.

Bethne had a shrewd idea of the reason for Armina's discomfort.

"He wuz awful sick, wuz Pelly," she asserted helpfully. "He wuz runnin' a fearsome fever, and he weren't rightly set in his head."

Armina seized on the subterfuge. "Yes, I knew suthin' ailed him," she agreed.

"Ma's a healer," Saree stated proudly.

The look that passed between the two women acknowledged that Pellerin needed more healing than Armina could administer.

"He 'ant alone no more, you know."

Bethne gasped in alarm. "Oh! Who...?"

"They looked like nice folk—two married couples, I think. Brother and sister, most like, with their handfasts. They had a little boy, too."

Oh, Ma," sniffed Saree scornfully, "he weren't their boy."

"Maybe he were a nephew, or little brother, or suthin'." Armina smoothly overrode her daughter. "He was happy to be with 'em."

"Yes, and yer, uh, Pelly," put in Saree, "he wuz glad to see 'em, too. Seems like he knew 'em."

Baffled—after all, who could Pellerin know that they didn't—Bethne and Ezrael gratefully accepted the offer of a cup of tea and some rough brown bread. For a short while they pretended to be ordinary folks. Bethne bounced little Jebey on her knee, while Ezrael entertained Saree with a piece of string and his repertoire of knots. Waving away their thanks and any offer of repayment, Armina gave Bethne a small bag of simple herb remedies, especially one for peaceful sleep, and bid them goodbye. She watched them down the road until they were out of sight and a brown-clad figure came trotting up behind her.

··· 44 ···

In Dampened Spirits

Kelgan sat, head on knees, arms trailing limply at his sides, feeling as soggy as the dew-laden branches dripping uncomfortably down his neck, wishing with all his heart he had been contracted to some nice normal patron. He could have been eating good food (on a regular basis), wearing dry clothes, and casting nice, safe horoscopes, or nice, safe abundant harvest spells—but no! He had to be singled out by a madman and his equally mad sister. Well, maybe not a *mad* sister—his heart gave a painful lurch as he thought of her ivory skin, her restless hair. He brought his wayward thoughts back to his self-pity, *not mad, but definitely different.*

Off on a wild-goose chase. *I think you've used that phrase before,* said the little voice-in-his-head. *Well, it is,* he thought, *and we're not getting to wherever it is, and we don't know where we're going very fast; and I killed somebody, and....*

"Kelgan, my friend, you are getting soaked," Nevander said, sounding surprisingly tentative, as well as, almost apologetic.

Oddly, the hesitant note in Nevander's voice somehow restored his spirits, at least as far as they could be restored. He looked up with a near smile at Nevander, lying diplomatically, "Just a meditation exercise I learned at the Academy. I guess I picked my spot, unwisely."

Nevander regarded him silently, but with a droll quirk of his mouth said with assumed gravity, "No wonder the Academy has such a formidable reputation."

Terencia overhearing, chuckled, but without derision.

Nevander's shrewd eye passed over him from head to toe; leaving him feeling as though he stood stripped bare. Starting to turn away, Nevander spun back smartly on his heel and commanded, "Let us have the whole of it, Mage."

Kelgan began to demur, but at Nevander's gimlet glare he checked. "All right, here it is. I don't know where we're going, I don't know why, and I don't know what you expect *me* to do when we get to wherever it is I don't know we're going."

"Ah, we come to the heart of the matter—what *you* are going to do. The other grumbles I have heard before."

Feeling that familiar, *yes, indeed,* sense of diminishment, he was both pleased, and scared out of his wits, to hear Nevander say, "I cannot tell you, my most favorite of Mages, I am counting on your skill and good sense when the time arises. As to where we are going, do you not feel the pull of our destination?"

Taking stock of himself, he was forced to admit that, yes, it seemed they were traveling in the right direction to somewhere. The *why* revealed itself to him, as well. Because out there was something inimical; because they knew about it and *somebody* had to oppose it; and because—his scalp crawled at the thought—it knew about *them.* It called to them, and led them, in cold fact. He gave a great shudder and his teeth chattered.

"Yes, my dearest Mage, you are correct."

Neroma's alto poured molasses-smooth over him. She had never called him *her* mage before, or indeed very little of anything. Did she actually pick up his thought, or did she merely read the language his body could not suppress? She had spoken behind him, close at his shoulder. He turned to find her standing a good ten feet from him, ringlets pointing like antennae in his direction.

··· 45 ···

The Three R's—Righteous, Reckless, Recalcitrant

Not reassured by Nevander's assertion that the equivalent of divine revelation would show them the way, Kelgan mulled over the recent past. So far, the trek had been *somewhat* uneventful.

Of course, there *was* that eerie rush through the ebon river, and those things in the water. Then, too, they were traveling with a dead boy given to sepulchral utterances, not to mention a horse that didn't look much better. On top of that, they *had* been set upon by presumed robbers. And he—Kelgan's scalp crawled and his mouth dried—*had* killed someone.

Resolving firmly to think of something else, he turned his mind to his capricious charges, the mules. One of them appeared to be limping, and turned an expression of pain on him.

"What's up, old friend?" he heard himself say to the sufferer. *Old friend, indeed!*

The mule smiled. Yes he did. Stopping, he held up the offending hoof. Embedded under the shoe was what looked, for all the world, like a jagged tooth. He pried it loose and muttering a healing cantrip, studied the offending object. A caltrop! Kelgan stared hard at the grisly reminder of their encounter with the robber band; the relationship between the name of his healing spell and the name of the vicious object in his hand struck him with its black humor. The mule regarded him placidly and fluttered its eyelashes in mulish thanks.

Determined once more to think about something else, Kelgan cast his eyes about him for some neutral topic of thought. His gaze alighted on Piper, who whistled under his breath and idly lashed with a stick.

"Piper," he burst out louder than he intended.

The boy jumped, stating sullenly, "I wasn't hurting the trees."

"I'm sorry," Kelgan apologized sincerely, "I wasn't about to scold you." He patted the child's thin shoulder. *Very* thin, he thought. "I just wanted to ask you a question. Have you ever gone to school?"

Piper stared in horror, "School!" His voice rose an octave. "Me?"

Kelgan chuckled. "It's usually not that bad."

Suspicion darkened the boy's face. "Say, you ain't plannin'!!!"

Kelgan hastened to allay his fears, "Of course not, at least, not now." At the boy's returned look of doubt, he went on seriously, "However, you are an exceptionally enterprising and talented young man," Piper brightened, "and you might want to add to your talents. For example, you can't read, and reading gives you an advantage."

"What advantage?" Piper countered.

Kelgan thought a little desperately, knowing Piper thought him a bit of an idiot, thus not wanting to hold himself up as an example. Looking to Neroma, he grinned to himself. He had seen Piper shooting sidelong glances at the dark lady and suspected the boy was both in awe of her and in the throes of a giant crush. His mind stopped for a moment there; his feet stumbling on the path. Catching himself, he continued with, "Well, take Lady di Nerrill."

"Yeah," said Piper, his face assuming a worshipful expression.

"Um, well, she has a lot of natural talent, um, er, yes, but she also has studied a great deal and added formal education to that natural ability."

Kelgan felt he had fallen over the edge into pomposity, but the boy didn't seem to notice in the contemplation of Neroma.

"Yeah," he whispered again.

"Maybe she would be willing to teach you to read."

He wasn't too sure what Neroma's attitude toward being volunteered as a primary teacher would be. Crossing his fingers in a rush of reversion to childhood superstition, Kelgan hoped he hadn't done something irrevocably stupid and destroyed the boy's trust in adults forever.

"Oh, I couldn' ask *her*," Piper declared. "She's... maybe *you* would? Then I could, maybe, surprise her."

A flood of feeling enveloped him. Sweeping the boy up, to the astonishment of both, he placed him on his shoulders. "We'll do it," he announced to the trees, creating some puzzled backward glances from the three in front.

Only Pellerin, who trudged behind, gave a hollow chuckle of appreciation, setting Kelgan's teeth on edge as he did.

No explanation from Kelgan being forthcoming, the others shrugged and continued.

Piper gave every evidence of childish delight with his high perch on Kelgan's shoulders. The boy's obvious pleasure both tickled and shamed him, as he was struck by the realization of how seldom the child allowed himself to be one.

The mules gave companionable snorts and nuzzled the boy's legs; evoking a genuine giggle from Piper and another horrible semblance of such from Pellerin. Neroma was moved to bestow one of her rare radiant smiles on Piper, catching Kelgan, as well, in the afterglow. Heartened and uplifted, the small, rather pathetic, band of would-be world-savers stepped on almost merrily to Not-at-all-shire.

Kelgan was as good as his word. After making their somewhat disorganized camp for the night—although Kelgan thought they were actually getting rather good at it, at least Piper had stopped rolling his eyes all the time—he sat Piper down with the only book he had available, a battered grimoire. Lacking proper equipment, he had provided the both of them with sharp sticks.

Opening the book to the section titled "Attractions and Repulsions," Kelgan announced, "That's an 'A'. Watch me." Scratching in the dirt with the point of his stick, Kelgan formed the letter with three quick strokes, then twice more very slowly.

Piper beamed in rapture. "An 'A'," he breathed, "that's an A." A second thought struck him. "What do you do with it, anyway?"

Kelgan stifled his laugh with difficulty; not wanting to mortally wound the child. Coughing and clearing his throat, he swallowed hard before explaining.

"An 'A' is the first letter of the alphabet. The alphabet...."

"What's going on here, My Mage?" a jovial voice interrupted them.

"I'm just apprising Piper of the benefits of magic," Kelgan temporized, rubbing his foot over the betraying glyphs.

Nevander snorted. "Little has he seen of those, so far."

Piper covered his mouth with both hands and rocked backward with laughter. "That's the truth," came the muffled response.

Kelgan looked pained, but in fairness could not dispute. With dignity, he reminded them, "Well there *is* the sword...."

He had the satisfaction of seeing Piper's eyes widen in remembrance.

"Ahem," coughed Nevander," I referred to *your* magic!"

Kelgan threw up his hands in disgust. From somewhere nearby, a mule whiffled in amusement.

··· 46 ···

Going Nowhere, Just as Fast

B ethne and Ezrael moved just as quickly, but alas, less merrily, along the same vague trail.

"We knows they went this way," Bethie repeated like a mantra, but with increasing anxiety as time went on.

Ezrael, frazzled, finally had had enough. "Bethie, we don't know nuthin' at all, so's you don't need to say that again. We only hope they went this way."

Lanced to the heart by the thought that they might actually be going the wrong way, Bethie staggered, nearly falling into the road bank. "Oh, Ez," she cried in agony, "You don't think...?"

Seeing Bethie's pain made Ez ashamed to have lost his temper. Although his anxiety nearly matched hers, he was less open with his emotions. Nevertheless, he knew his Bethie well enough to realize she needed to tell her feelings aloud in order to deal with them. He hugged her now, and reassured her as best as he could. "I'm sorry, Bethie. I was jes' worryin', too."

Bethie drew a long, shaky breath, responding differently than Ezrael expected, "You wuz right, Ez, an' you wuz right to say so, too. I'm an old fool who don't know where she's going."

For a moment, Ezrael stared blankly, not sure what to say next, then he laughed. "Well, we're a pair of old fools, Bethie. An' we've come this far, so's we might as well go on; 'sides we knowed they wuz a good ways ahead o' us."

Bethie's face didn't quite light up, but it smoothed out a little.

"Yore right, again, Ez. Let's keep goin', until we knows fer sure."

··· 47 ···

Whither Thou Goest...

As soon as the slightest hint of pink touched the Eastern sky, the Bervaines and their Mel'hachim friends assembled their packed goods for departure. The night in the chapel proved relatively successful, only their nerves caused them to startle awake on frequent occasions. Nevertheless, the four felt somewhat rested—if not at their best, then at least not at their worst.

They traveled swiftly the rest of the day, the horses and pack animals fresh and covering the ground more quickly than anticipated. As the shadows grew longer, however, apprehension assailed them. At the far too rapid descent of the sun, Daliane announced as she rummaged through her saddlebag, "I have brought something."

Triumphantly, she withdrew a small statue of the Lady. Jorgo and Nadi stared for a moment, then laughed simultaneously.

"We, too, have brought something." Carefully, Nadi unwrapped a small package which had been resting on the pommel of her saddle, revealing a portable shrine containing images of the Two.

Heads swung in T'Jules direction. Smirking self-consciously, he reached beneath his tunic to pull out a large, golden medal bearing the sun image. "It was my great-grandfather's." he offered sheepishly.

After a moment's pause, Jorgo observed, "It would seem we stand in the Light."

"Oh Lady, I hope so," muttered Daliane fervently.

"The horses must rest, and so must we," said Nadi. "It will be the first test."

Daliane clutched the Lady statue to her chest.

"You will ride with me, now, little Sister," growled Jorgo.

T'Jules started to protest, but was stopped by a rapier glance by Nadi. The wisdom of the arrangement came to him belatedly. Daliane's aura might (just might) be overlaid with Jorgo's, to be hoped it would cause some confusion.

They moved slowly now, searching for a sheltered haven to stop a bit. Not that shelter would of be any help against the unknown they pursued, but it would offer a psychological barrier and that might be as useful as a physical one. A large fallen tree provided what they looked for. The branches formed a natural grotto in which to tether the animals, while the brush provided a back wall that gave the illusion of security.

Jorgo swung to the ground first, easily carrying Daliane's slight body with him. Keeping her close to him, he settled warily until his back met the back of a tree-trunk and slowly sat, pulling Daliane along with him.

Following suit, hand on sword the entire time, Nadi dropped to Daliane's other side, leaving T'Jules in charge of the animals. Bemused and mildly resentful, T'Jules tried to decide how he would handle four horses and two pack animals without losing any or all. Something told him the Mel'hachim were enjoying the situation *in spite of* the situation.

Alighting, he grasped the reins of his own horse in his teeth, and seized the bridles of the pack animals before they wandered witlessly away. Tethering them to a handy branch, he turned to discover that the Mel'hachim steeds, trained to a fault, had followed him to the spot and waited quietly behind him, leaving only Daliane's horse free. Since Dally's mount was of uncertain temper, allowing only the Baroness to approach without a nip or kick, the problem was by no means solved, but at least T'Jules could devote his whole mind to it.

His audience watched with disconcerting interest as he set about it. Taking one slow step at a time, he spoke reassuringly to the animal in calm low tones. The horse, meanwhile, laying its ears back, took one slow step backwards for every step T'Jules took forward; causing the Baron's color to rise with every second the cursed animal eluded him.

The onlookers were by now in an advanced stage of poorly stifled amusement. Finally Daliane, unable to stand the sight of her helpless spouse, leaped to her feet—away from her guardian, the statue tumbling to the ground—and began to say, "Oh, Tee Jee, let me...."

The rest of her words flew out like birds unleashed from a cage, as, riveted to the spot, she was struck both dumb and paralyzed in an instant. Her eyes no longer saw him, but she obviously discerned a frightful vision unseen by her companions. Jorgo leapt only a second behind her. Pulling a stoppered bottle from his back, he dashed the entire content over the Baroness. At the same time, Nadi thrust the Lady statue into Daliane's hands, and roughly pulled her down to the ground again. Jorgo resumed his former position beside her.

After a heartbeat, Daliane's eyes began to clear. "Well, at least I'm not saying, 'Ow!' this time." She essayed a brave little joke. "Just Brr!"

The Mel'hachim acknowledged her effort with brief grimaces intended to pass as smiles. T'Jules on the other hand forgot Daliane's horse entirely and collapsed on his knees in the road. Teetering a moment, he gave an "unh!" as though the breath had been pushed out of him. He then continued to fall face forward into the ditch.

"Baron!" "Tee Jee!" "My Brother!" exclaimed the three onlookers, however, neither Jorgo nor Nadi relinquished their hold on Daliane, nor rose to assist the Baron.

Coming to himself after a bit, T'Jules discovered he was cropping the verge rather like the horses. Spitting grass, he rolled onto his back and surveyed the stars briefly before attempting to rise.

Noticing his companions had not stirred, he inquired crossly, "What happened?" Then as memory returned, the distinguished Baron crawled on his hands and knees to his small wife and laying his head in her lap, burst into loud sobs.

Daliane patted the back of her humbled spouse and made soothing noises, trying very hard not to break into uncontrollable giggles. The situation was not only serious, it was down-right dire. Nevertheless, the spectacle of the imperious Baron—hero to and ruler of his people—bested by a horse, her horse at that, was more than her gravity could withstand. Suspicious coughs and throat clearings emanating from the two Mel'hachim suggested a similar problem. The horse, in the meantime, joined the others with every impression of utmost cooperation, and was even now innocently cropping grass with a studied air of nonchalance.

Like an exhausted infant, T'Jules sobs had subsided to occasional hiccoughy breaths; his partially visible ears had reddened furiously. With extraordinary tact, Jorgo bent over him, although without releasing Daliane, and said firmly, "Ah, my brother, I knew you were a fine man, else our sister would not have chosen you; but you have proven yourself of true nobility. Only a man of the finest and deepest character could display the truth of his love without shame."

The deliberate manner with which Jorgo delivered these lines, and his obvious sincerity, robbed them of any hint of mockery. Still, T'Jules raised his head still red-faced, and regarded Jorgo with a touch of suspicion.

Nadi dispelled his misgivings by throwing her free arm around his neck—prompting an "Oof" from Daliane, who was somewhat crushed in the center—and exclaiming, "Tee Jee, we love you."

Her use of Daliane's nickname for him made him break into a wide grin. It was Nadi's turn to flush.

"Ahem, I mean, our brother."

Jorgo rumbled in his vision of laughter, and Daliane joined in with Nadi. The Light forefend that T'Jules should ever realize just why their laughter was so hearty.

The rest of the night was spent virtually in the same positions. A stiff and aching group rose painfully to their feet when dawn mercilessly unleashed them.

"Well, that taught us, we're not stirring a step after dark," remarked T'Jules, running a hand over his bristled chin and through his unkempt hair.

"Mmmm," agreed Daliane, "next time, let me get comfortable before you grab me, I sat on a rock all night. Tonight, *I'll* pick the spot."

Although they had taken turns dozing fitfully, all four were baggy-eyed and headachy, their limbs feeling as though they'd been drawn and quartered sometime during the dark hours. The Mel'hachim, whose splendid physical condition should have seen them through better, voiced a thought as uncomfortable as Daliane's rock.

"We think, my sister, that although we succeeded in keeping their thoughts from you, their psychic energy battered us heavily. We must find some better means of protection, else we will fail physically long before our goal."

This discouraging idea plunged both Daliane and T'Jules into instant gloom. The appalling prospect of being worn away simply by an invisible agency, without ever striking a retaliatory blow was more awful than the thought of perishing in combat, no matter how fiendish the enemy.

"We will find a way, my sister, never fear." Jorgo clapped Daliane's shoulder, making her stagger.

"I'll believe you, if you promise not to reassure me anymore."

Jorgo's thunderous laugh billowed forth again, lifting their spirits on waves of sound. Repacking the horses, they set out feeling relatively optimistic. Munching cold food as they rode, in order not to waste a moment of daylight, they regaled each other with outrageous stories of themselves and others.

··· 48 ···

If Needs Must

B ethne and Ezrael came upon the strange parti-colored bay, but
they lingered not even a night on finding that Pellerin had
passed that way with an odd party. Bethie insisted they double their
efforts to catch up, necessitating almost forcible restraint on Ez's
part.

"Bethie, this old goat cain't go no faster. We'll sleep on the trail,
but we *gots* to sleep and eat."

"You're right as usual, Ez, but I kin just *feel* Pelly now. I knows
he's close, and I jes' cain't keep my feet still 'tils I find him."

Ez felt some of Bethne's urgency. Until then, he had been
peculiarly reluctant to find Pellerin. He knew it was his boy; but yet
it wasn't. What it was (he didn't think of Pelly as *him*) he didn't
want to find out. But now, he discovered Bethie's need had become
his. Somewhere along the way, the same desire to reach his son, no
matter *what* Pellerin had been transformed into, had seized him.
Although he cautioned Bethie of the need to go easily and not
overtax themselves, or Capriola, for that matter, he now felt the
same itch in his feet that she did. Furthermore, an odd foreboding
had assailed him; under ordinary circumstances he would have cast
it off. *He* wasn't given to "feelings" like Bethie, however, this time it
wasn't so much a feeling as a certainty. They *needed* to reach Pelly
and why he didn't know, but he did know it was somehow essential—
something *bad.*

He glanced at Bethie, whose face had started to shine with the knowledge that they might find their boy any minute, and his heart gave a lurch that dizzied him.

"This is the way they went, Ez," asserted Bethne, "I kin feel Pelly jes' as plain as if I touched him." Ez looked doubtful. "It's true, Ez. I knows you don't allus believe my feelings, but I *know*. They ant that far ahead, neither. We're ketchin' up to 'em."

Capriola looked up from her grazing and bleated a firm "Maaa," making them both laugh.

"Well, Bethie, it don't look as if Capriola thinks all that much a yore feelin's."

"I jes' think she hates to hurry, Ez," chuckled Bethne, "she allus wuz lazy as a goat kin git."

"Well, Bethie," drawled Ezrael, "I cain't say as I blame her. I wouldn't mind settin' a spell." Catching Bethne's baleful look, he added, "If it warn't we needed to find Pelly fast. Come on, Cappy, let's go."

They set off at a faster pace, over Capriola's objections.

··· 49 ···

Looks Like They Must

Cal beat his fist against his steering wheel in frustrated rage. Of course, he really didn't need to be anywhere at any particular time, now that he had sloughed off his work burden for the day, but an unaccountable impatience seized him to be anywhere, fast. Going home... hah! home!... filled him with revulsion. Visions of the unmade bed, the dishes piling up in the sink, and his scattered clothing from the night before, rose before him to obscure the long, inching traffic ahead. A bar? His stomach roiled at the idea. Besides, there was a disturbing memory of those now half-lost nightmares.

"Voices," he said aloud, "something about voices."

He tried to forget the slow crawl of traffic and focus on remembering the frightening whispers in the darkness. At least it was something to think about, but they eluded him, slipping away like water over stones.

"Questions," he muttered, "crazy questions." No use, they didn't come any clearer.

Boy, oh boy, me boy, he thought wryly, and with a bit of pride, *did you ever tie one on.*

A slight heave in his gut answered him.

The traffic had begun to open up a bit now; he realized he had unconsciously headed his car toward the beach. *Well, why not? Might clear my head.*

Increasing his speed, he leaned back and began to relax. Humming along with the radio, he let a smile, more of a smirk, actually, creep around his face. He had managed to out-fox his jerk of a boss, and that whining toady of his, as well. By virtue of his supposed "illness", he had a long weekend to look forward to; and he just might spend it at the sea-shore. Lots of women there, after all, and good-looking, too. If his boss checked, he'd make a trip to the emergency room, when his "illness" had gotten unexpectedly worse. He chuckled at the thought of just how sick he might get.

Can always hope, me boy, can always hope.

With some surprise he noticed he was virtually alone on the road. Two cars, which had been following him, turned off at the next off-ramp, leaving him a solitary traveler on an otherwise empty freeway. Up ahead, a fog was rolling across the lanes, blanking them from view as though cut off by a knife.

"Hmmm, some of that 'night and early morning low clouds,' I guess," he muttered aloud. "Where is everybody? Never been *alone* before, here."

Man, that fog was thick! Probably why he couldn't see anything. He slowed his pace and turned on his lights; he thought of his boss' Lexus where the lights came on automatically. One of his customary waves of self-pity swept over him as the fog closed in around him. He was just as good as anybody at the office; just had more bad luck that's all. Slowed now to a snail's pace, he peered futilely into the fog. The lines of the pavement below him vanished, leaving him unsure whether he was actually in a lane or not. Still, he encountered no other cars, either coming toward or accompanying him in the same direction.

"Maybe the cops made everyone get off of the road," he reassured himself. "I ought to do the same thing. Next off-ramp, I will."

Sick dread began to settle like a lump in the pit of his stomach. *Damnit! Where was everybody?*

Rolling up the windows of his car, he carefully locked the doors in a feeble attempt to feel secure. Was someone whispering? Maybe the radio was still on, although he had a vague memory of switching it off when the fog closed in, the better to hear approaching vehicles.

Did those whispers sound like questions? *"Where to?" "There to."* Did the road, which should have been smooth freeway, feel more like a rutted track? Could he have somehow gotten off-road?

Gripped by sudden unreasoning panic; Cal slammed his foot on the accelerator pedal. The car surged forward.

··· 50 ···

Whither Thou Goest...

Kelgan became aware of a creeping uneasiness. The hairs at his nape began to emulate Neroma's wandering tresses, standing up with a life of their own. Glancing behind him he noticed that Pellerin, who usually trudged in an automaton's gait, was now questing the air like a restless stallion. Not really expecting an answer—or more probably, not wanting one—he found himself actually directing a question to the youth.

"Er, what's up, Pelly?"

His neck hairs nearly lifted him from the ground when the young man turned his empty eyes on him and responded simply, "Coming." With that short utterance, Pellerin pulled his horse to the side of the trail and stood stock-still.

Not knowing why he did so, Kelgan jerked the bridles of the mules in desperate haste; yelling to the others at the same time, "Get off the path."

To his relief, no one, including Piper, questioned him for a moment. Scattering like chickens before a fox, they leaped this way and that, just as a *machine* shot from between two trees, skidded across the road into the verge and came to a halt against the trunk of another tree on the far side with the sound of the clap of doom.

Frozen with shock, the small band did nothing at first. However, the sound of moaning which now trailed off into sobs, coming from inside the machine, sent them all with the exception of Pellerin, surging forward to surround the contraption. Kelgan was first to reach the side of the cart? Carriage? Where were the horses? Glimpsing Cal through the glass, slumped over the wheel, his shoulders heaving, Kelgan grasped what surely had to be a handle and gave a yank. Nothing. Trying again, he pushed up, down, outward, inward—still no result.

Remembering himself, he muttered, "Oh, for Light's sake," and shouted, "*Oporta*" at the offending handle. Instantly, all four doors popped open, nearly sweeping him off his feet, and eliciting a shrill scream from the now bolt-upright Cal.

"Are you all right?" "What manner of conveyance is this?" "Where have you come from?"

The questions, coming as they did from Kelgan, Nevander, and Neroma simultaneously, resulted in nothing more than a wild-eyed stare and a resumption of the moaning.

Terencia, more practical, said, "He's hit his head and probably scrambled his wits. Let's get him out of this... thing... and let Kelgan tend him."

The others agreed and moved back a bit, making room for Kelgan and Terencia to remove the terrified stranger. Cal's eyes were starting from his head and his mouth was a black "O" in the middle of his face, from which incessant keening was emerging. Kelgan held Terencia's arm when she would have reached for Cal and whispered, "I'm going to put him to sleep first." Terencia nodded, and Kelgan crooned "*Dormissinah.*"

Mouth snapping shut and eyelids drooping over his staring eyes, calm settled over Cal's face.

The staring eyes and "O" mouths seemed comically transferred to Kelgan and Terencia.

"Kelgan, he's...." Terencia sputtered to a halt.

"Holy Ones of Light, what Darkness is this?" Kelgan could hear the squeak in his voice, but was helpless to control it.

Puzzled, the others moved forward again. Kelgan emitted a shriek nearly as shrill as Cal's when Neroma's hair settled around his shoulders like a shawl, or a pall, he wasn't sure which. Her alto purred in his ear. "So, you are two. How fortunate we are."

Wondering how she could accept it so calmly, Kelgan turned his eyes upon her. Something in their troubled depths seemed to touch her, for her hair tightened in a reassuring squeeze as she explained, "We have encountered this phenomenon before, Nevander and I. We did not know of it where you are concerned; but we have seen it in our scrying."

Her eyes dropped to the vehicle. "He comes from far; farther than we have ever scryed. For good or ill, this will change all that we do."

So, Shall *He* Go

A deep sigh escaped Kelgan. "I don't think I want another me around," he only half joked. "I'm having enough trouble just with myself."

Nevander sighed, as well. "I... we... er, perhaps the resemblance is only superficial, my Mage." Then a realization struck the Lord. "Where is the child?"

Taller by far than the others, Kelgan swung his head around until he espied Piper sitting, if his eyes told him true, on the back of Pellerin's old mare. The child had shrunken so far in on himself, he was no more than a minute hump in the saddle. Forgetting Cal for the moment in his dismay at the child's appearance, Kelgan hurried to the horse's side.

Piper gazed at him in desperate appeal. "*He* put me up here and said to sit."

"He! You mean...?"

"Uh huh."

Pellerin, as usual, stood blind and deaf to events around him. It was nearly impossible to believe he had ever moved or spoken; and the thought of that cold touch raising the child to the horse's back. Kelgan gulped and distractedly patted Piper. "Uh, I'm sure he didn't want you to get hurt."

"Him," snorted Piper, displaying a little of his usual bravado, "how would he know?"

At a loss to answer the child's question, Kelgan held out his arms and the boy slid into them gratefully. He clung fiercely to Kelgan's neck when Kelgan would have put him down. A slight lump formed in Kelgan's throat at the thought that the child had turned to him for protection. He patted Piper's back again, this time with purposeful affection. The thought of the shock Piper would get when he saw the stranger sent him back into dismay. He started to fumblingly explain to Piper when a cry of "My Mage!" recalled him. With Piper still stuck to his shirt front like a burr, Kelgan returned hastily to the group gathered by the machine.

When he saw the inert figure, now lying on the ground beside the alien conveyance, Piper's eyes widened. "Oh, Light and Dark, he's one of them doubly things. The cook's gran told me about them." Rearing back, he peered into Kelgan's face. "He looks dumber, though."

A little chuckle, including Kelgan's, went around the group as they remembered Piper's not-so-long-ago opinion of the lot of them, most especially Kelgan. Neroma held her hands out to Piper. "Come," she coaxed, "Kelgan must tend to our visitor. Sit with me whilst he does so."

Utterly tongue-tied, and going beet red even in the dark, the child allowed himself to be led to one side. The others ringed him to sit in the leaves, while Kelgan tried to decide how best to help the sleeper without causing him heart failure when he awoke. The color of his patient was poor and his breathing shallow and irregular. There were no signs of wounds; nor did blood bedabble his clothing—that at least was a good sign.

Nevertheless, Kelgan did not feel reassured. Too many shocks, both mental and physical, in too short a time could kill as effectively as a sword thrust. Passing his hands over Cal's chest, he could feel the areas of chill; feel the thready, faltering of the heartbeat. If the stranger perished, still a stranger, what of himself? Were they entwined in any physical manner? Did he need to keep his "doubly thing" in perfect health from now on to ensure his own? Kelgan shuddered.

To his consternation, Nevander seemed to have at last read his mind, for he placed a comforting hand on Kelgan's wrist, murmuring,

"It will be well, my Mage, no matter the outcome of your efforts."

Devoutly hoping this was true, Kelgan muttered words of a waking spell mixed with those of a calming variety; feeling relief that the stranger's heartbeat steadied and beat with a stronger rhythm. "*Diminis noctor, serenimus loctor,*" Kelgan pressed his hands to the stranger's chest, then to his eyes. "*Optica, abreimus,*" he commanded.

The intruder moaned once, and then his eyes flew open. Recoiling in hysterical terror, his mouth resumed the same tunnel shape it had borne before and the moan rose to a shriek.

"Oh, Darkness!" Kelgan swore. "*Dormimus.*"

Cal's head drooped again; a mild snore escaped his now-shut lips.

Frustrated by the failure of his efforts, Kelgan looked to Nevander for some suggestions. Nevander, in turn, swiveled his head to his twin. Neroma responded with a baffled shake of her head and raising of her tresses.

It was Terencia's turn to swear. "Darkness!" Pulling her sword impatiently from its scabbard, she stood over the sleeping man, "Wake him!" she ordered Kelgan.

"What are you...?"

"Wake him, I said," she repeated. "Do it now!"

After a considering look into her face, Kelgan decided to accede to her demand. Repeating his formula of minutes before, he once again revived the stranger.

When Cal's mouth opened to resume its shrieking, she stepped forward and placed the point of her sword under his chin. "Shut up," she hissed menacingly. Her tone conveyed instantly to Cal what her words did not, and his mouth clapped immediately closed.

"There," Terencia proclaimed triumphantly, "now he's quiet."

Kelgan was forced to admit the effectiveness of her tactics; Cal was stiff as the sword blade under his chin, silent as the surrounding forest. *How come so still?* wondered Kelgan. No trees sighed, no bushes rustled, no chirrs, no whistles, creaks, snaps, nothing; only Cal's eyes continued to scream. Kelgan bent over him, trying to drive the panic from those oh-so-familiar eyes.

"We are... friends. We pulled you from your... machine... and only want to help."

Once again, the speaker's tone, soothing this time, penetrated and seemed to evoke a response—bafflement partially replacing the terror.

"Can you tell us your name," prodded Kelgan, "and perhaps how you came here?" Blankness met his query. "Do you suppose his wits have failed?" Kelgan threw over his shoulder at the others.

Piper piped up in disgust, "Double moons, you bunch are real mullets sometimes. He don't understand a word you say."

Kelgan slapped his forehead at this revelation. Turning to the others, he surprised hastily suppressed grins on the faces of the ebon-haired di Nerrills, along with a raised eyebrow from Terencia. "You knew that all along," he accused.

"We suspected, my Mage, but we really wanted to see how you handled it. While we may have been a bit unkind not to have pointed out the possibility to you, we were sure that as soon as you gave a little thought to the matter, you would realize. After all, the, er, conveyance which bore this unfortunate individual hither is not one we have ever encountered on this world. However, we also knew that meeting, uh, one's self, can be, um, overwhelming for even the best of magicians."

Neroma stepped to Kelgan's side. "Do not feel foolish, dear Kelgan," she began. At the sound of her voice, like a rush of velvet, Cal's eyes shifted to her for the first time, widening with a different kind of shock.

I know just how you feel, Kelgan thought with wry sympathy, *you never get used to it either.*

Neroma continued to pour the dark honey of her voice over the two of them. "It is as my brother says, you are seeing a sight infinitely more disturbing than what he and I see when we look at each other—this creature is not only your twin, he is, in his essence—you!" Her hair caressed Kelgan, wrapped around his chin and turned his face squarely toward her, widening Cal's eyes even further. "However, be assured, I... we... will always know the difference."

Her brief and rare smile dizzied him. An errant thought began to grow somewhere in the very back of his brain. Hastily he suppressed it, turning back to Cal almost brusquely. "Well, should I try again with a translation spell, or just let Terencia keep him quiet with her sword the rest of the night?"

Terencia darted a contemptuous glare at him from the corners of her eyes and dropped her sword. A tiny drop of Cal's blood welled from the spot where it had rested. To no one's surprise, their visitor forbore from resuming his monotonous caterwauling, and raised a markedly shaky hand to feel gingerly under his chin. He looked at the blood on his fingers and gulped audibly.

In spite of the stranger's resemblance to himself (all right, not resemblance, exact replication), or perhaps because of it, Kelgan found himself feeling an irrational antipathy to his double. With reluctance, he began to speak the words of the complicated ritual intended to bridge the gap between the visitor's speech and their own. He didn't feel it necessary to admit to the twin aristocrats that he had never actually done this particular bit of magic before. *Of course, he had covered the theory,* he told himself; *it was only a matter of putting it into practice.* Cal, he noticed, had gone even paler at the sight of Kelgan speaking what was, even to one who had never seen such a thing, obviously an incantation.

Any whiter, and we'll be able to use him for writing dispatches. Of course, it might be hard to fold him up to fit the mail pouch.

The amusement he felt at his private joke nearly ruined the spell. Catching himself in time before he laughed aloud, he completed the pronouncement of the words with rather more solemnity than necessary. After waiting for the space of three or four heartbeats, he carefully enunciated to the stranger, "Can you understand my words now, my friend?"

Cal's response was not reassuring. "Friend! Oh sure, right, why wouldn't I be *your* friend?" Then a prolonged bout of hysterical laughter shook him.

Terencia, rolling her eyes, made a motion as though to redraw her sword, effectively cutting Cal off in mid-guffaw.

Kelgan sighed. Was this the way *he* would act in a similar situation?

He felt himself flushing at the thought, just as though it had actually been himself.

He tried again. "Please understand that we mean you no harm. We... I... we're just as surprised as you are, and just as confused. We don't know how you got here, but you obviously came from...." Kelgan let the sentence trail off as he realized it wasn't at all obvious where the stranger had come from... another world... another plane... another cosmos? And Darkness, why did this inconvenient intruder have to be a perfect likeness of himself?

To his relief, the stranger seemed to be trying to get a grasp on his frazzled nerves, and actually give some reasonable thought to his situation. "I'm sorry, I really feel like a [jerk] (an untranslatable word, but the meaning was clear), but I was driving on the [freeway] (another untranslatable) one minute and the next I was dodging trees—big ones!—and you folks.... No offense, but you don't look like the people where I come from." He broke off and stared at Kelgan. "Except you, you're... *me!*"

"Yes, that is the crux of the matter." The dark velvet of Neroma's voice interrupted them; her hair pointed at each. "We have long speculated, my sibling and I, on the existence of parallel planes, each containing many worlds, each duplicated with all its beings an infinite number of times. We had not proof that such did, or could, exist—until now. You have been drawn here, we know not the reason, but the fact that you are here would seem to make you an essential character in our little drama. Of course, so far, we have only gotten a glimpse of our own roles, as well as the words we must speak when the rehearsal is complete and the time to proceed to the stage has arrived."

Silence followed her words, the longest speech Kelgan had heard her make, stretching out so long that Piper finally felt compelled to end it. "Ask him his name," he prodded Kelgan.

"Oh, my apologies." Kelgan began introductions, belatedly realizing that he had expected the stranger to be called the same thing he was. He named all of the group members, with a short explanation of who each was. Cal shook his head in disbelief when Kelgan referred to himself as a Mage, but made no comment. It was only when he got to Pellerin that the introductions faltered a bit. Since Pellerin had never vouchsafed his name but once, or precious little else, there wasn't much Kelgan could say. *Furthermore, the little detail that Pellerin was really dead,* he thought, *went better unmentioned.*

"He's, um, a traveler, who, uh, joined us, uh, a while back." Derisive snorts from the mules accompanied this lame description.

Calvin introduced himself, in turn, saying by way of a biography, "I'm a lawyer, if you guys have lawyers."

"Speakers of the law," intoned Nevander. "Indeed, we do." The grimace on his face left no doubt about his feelings.

Surprisingly, Cal laughed. "I guess we're just as popular here as we are at home. There's a slew of lawyer [jokes] making fun of us."

"Jokes?" inquired Nevander.

"Yeah, you know, funny stories at our expense. Like the one that asks 'What's seven...' uh, I'll tell you some other time. Maybe." Cal blushed furiously.

"Ummm, yes, perhaps that would be best." Nevander's eyes twinkled, even though his voice gave nothing away.

Serious again, Calvin turned the conversation back to Neroma's discomfiting statement. "You've told me who you are, but haven't told me why you're all together or what you're doing out in the woods, except what *she* said. What's this 'little drama?' Looks like you don't have [guns] here, but you wouldn't be carrying swords if you didn't expect trouble. And..." he paused for emphasis, "you wouldn't have said I was 'drawn' here to be an 'essential character' if it wasn't *big* trouble."

Neroma sat herself beside Cal and took his hand in hers, an action which did not escape Kelgan. Her wandering tresses settled around Cal's shoulder, causing him to shy like a skittish mare. The tendrils patted him soothingly, which appeared to have rather the opposite effect, however he made no further movement.

"It is a long and complicated story. We had thought, no, we had hoped we were the only world involved. Your presence here would indicate the contrary. We are sorry." She stopped for a moment to gather her narrative into a brief and cohesive whole. She outlined their purpose and the reasons behind it as simply and tersely as possible, leaving an aghast Calvin gaping at her in horror.

"You think this 'disappearing' act is affecting—infecting—my world, too? Or maybe it's jumping from world to world so that it's gobbling up every world in the same, er, plane? And maybe you think I'm here because I'm... because he's... because we're... But I'm not a magician!"

"Neither am I," said Kelgan dejectedly. "I'm just an under-Mage, really." He slid to the ground, hugging his knees as an unaccountable wave of depression swept over him. Well, maybe not unaccountable, but unrelated to their present circumstance. After all, he hadn't even graduated from the Academy. Besides, he hadn't even been called upon to perform more than a few minor, very minor, spells. Worse than that, he had forgotten even those until a dead man reminded him. Of course, the translation incantation had worked, but that was just luck. It was a wonder that Cal hadn't started speaking Iskval, one of the yet-undeciphered tongues of the old ones. The uselessness of it all, his training, his life, threatened to swamp him. Drawing his breath to sob, he was instead nearly swamped by the overwhelming perfume of dozens of roses. He seemed to have been dropped suddenly in the center of the Autarch's gardens.

Sneezing ferociously, Kelgan clambered to his feet, started to say, "What in Light?!" when he realized the others, even Calvin, were staring at him in mingled dismay and relief. A second realization hit him. He no longer felt hopeless or despairing, just a bit wheezy, since roses had always given him fits of sneezes whenever he forgot his Allergus spell.

"My sincerest apologies, my dear Mage," Nevander said earnestly. "We grew lax and let the wards weaken. Oh, uh, sorry about the roses, a strong aroma was needed."

Eyes watering, Kelgan expressed his appreciation, but was slightly baffled. "I heard no voices."

"No, my Mage, while we had been inattentive to the wards, still they were sufficient to keep the voices at bay, but yet weakened enough for them to slide in a suggestion of despair."

Kelgan was profoundly grateful that the plunging hopelessness, which had doused him like sea water, had had an external cause, rather than an internal. Along with gratitude that it wasn't an aspect of his own character, he hoped the excessive fear and hysteria shown by his counterpart could also be blamed in large part on suggestion. Looking at Cal, he wasn't so sure. Cal seemed to embody all the worst aspects of his own personality, which he hoped he had managed to successfully hide, and only agonized over in the middle of the night. He noted that Cal had pricked up his ears at the mention of voices and was listening intently to the exchange between himself and Nevander.

Nevander had noticed this as well. Addressing Cal with his head cocked to one side, he inquired in the mildest of tones, as though Cal were deficient in either wits or maturity, "Do you also hear things, perchance?"

Grimacing at this painful memory, Cal admitted it was possible that he had, but added, "I thought it was... uh, I'd been, well, I was a bit...."

"Drunk," Terencia chimed in with sympathetic laughter. "He was having a tinker's holiday. I've nearly heard voices, myself, at one time or another."

This unexpected confession from the usually sober and prim guardsman, although Kelgan cast his mind back to their earlier acquaintance and remembered some anomalous moments, caused heads to turn her way with interest, forgetting Cal for a moment.

Blushing at their regard, Terencia stammered, "Well, I was younger."

Piper tittered. "I'm younger, but I ain't been laid out with the tinkers... yet."

Kelgan shushed Piper and turned back to Cal, urging him to tell the whole story. Their obvious personal interest, as well as belief, gave Cal heart. He related his evening of drinking and depression and the resultant night of "dreams."

"I thought it was the drinks. They asked questions, I remember that, but I can't remember what the questions were. They laughed a lot, too, that was the worst part—I knew they were laughing at what a [friggin' wimp] I was."

Kelgan needed no translation. At the Academy, only the celerity of his learning had gained him the respect of his peers. However, his stay with the di Nerrills, and the discovery of their talents, had returned him to his earlier inadequate years. He was only just now feeling like an equal of theirs. Now, if he could just convince Piper....

Remembering the look of awe on Cal's face as he pronounced the spell of translation, Kelgan thought wryly, *great, I can really impress myself.*

Nevander had been pondering as Cal related the events leading to his appearance. "I like this little, my Mage," he stated aloud, giving voice to what all felt. "The net of darkness has been cast far wider than even we anticipated. Calvin's world has diverged well along a road we have not traveled. Our little earthen spheres do not lie cheek by jowl, it would seem."

Glancing from his battered car to the mules, Cal muttered, "Yeah." He gave a half chuckle, "I guess we call *our* magicians, engineers."

Kelgan thought about it. "We, too, have engineers. However, they are mainly concerned with the business of war." Realizing he sounded very like Nevander, he added, "Although it's not too big a jump from what yours create to what I create. I guess you could say a cart that pulls itself is a manifestation of magic; it's certainly power."

Calvin grinned. "Never thought of it that way. We call it science."

"So do we. All spells are based on sound scientific principles." Kelgan grinned back.

"Ahem." Nevander's slight cough sobered them both.

"What's my role in all this?" demanded Cal. "If our 'little earthen spheres' are so far apart, how did I get pulled in? I'm not a magician, I'm not even an engineer. I'm just a hack lawyer."

"The voices called you," mused Neroma. "We can only hope they do not feel they can easily use you."

Calvin bristled, while the others regarded him uncomfortably.

"Maybe the voices *didn't* call him," Kelgan demurred. "I think maybe *I* did."

Incredulous stares greeted this statement. Even the mules laid their ears back in frank disbelief.

"I said I wished there were two of me, it was just a joke, but maybe I got my wish, somehow." This bit of conjecture sounded lame, even to him. "Well, it was just a thought."

Cal's expression registered both remembrance and relief. "Maybe you did get your wish, even if it was a joke. I just remembered something one of the voices said. He... it... whatever... giggled in this horrible way most of the time. Well, he gave one of those giggles and said, '*If one is fun, will two be true?*' I had completely forgotten—I didn't understand what the hell it meant, anyway."

"Mmmmm, yes, I might interpret the couplet in that manner. What say you, Mage? Good or ill, the voices might have found it amusing to pluck one of your counterparts from his distant home and drop him in our midst. If so, even they cannot tell how the wild card will tip the hand. Hast thou an ace up thy sleeve?"

Piper performed his usual eyeball-rolling maneuver at Nevander's posturing. Kelgan, for his part, resisted the urge to say, "Oh, get off the stage." He simply shrugged. Owlishly, Calvin blinked slowly once or twice, but not before Kelgan detected the amusement in his eyes.

"There must be a commonality of which we are as yet unaware."

Hair fluttering chaotically, Neroma sat again by Calvin. He, in turn, managed not to wince as errant tresses wrapped around his neck, turning his face toward her. They sat in silence for a time, then he finally said after staring fixedly first in her eyes and then at Terencia's sword, "Well, I was on the fencing team at college. Kept it up through law school, too... and the archery team," he added as an afterthought.

It was his electrified audience's turn to blink. Terencia broke the stunned silence first. "Fencing... with swords?"

"Of course, with swords," exasperation colored Cal's tone. "What else, embroidery needles?"

Terencia doubled up. "Hoo hoo, hee, hee, what else, what else?" The mules joined in with gleeful brays.

"What is it with those damned mules?" Calvin inquired of the air.

Kelgan had oft asked himself the same question, but felt duty-bound to defend them. "They're, well, unusually intelligent."

This out-of-character defense caused the mules to halt in mid-bray and stare at him with exaggerated open mouths. Whispering, "*Levanah,*" out of the corner of his own mouth, Kelgan reduced the mules to docile grass croppers. Under the weight of his suspicious gaze, one of them looked up and gave him a wink, then resumed its cropping.

··· 52 ···

We're Movin' on Up

"**B**ethie, we gots to stop. It's too dark in these woods an' Capriola's goin' to break a leg." Ezrael could barely make out Bethne's face in the gloom, a white moon against the living darkness formed by the trees.

"I know, Ez. I wuz just goin' to say stop," Bethne lied.

"Bain't no inns out here, Bethie; we gots to bed down in the dirt."

"I knows that, too, Ez. We'll manage; I reckon it'll be a mite hard here, but the leaves'll help some."

Ezrael marveled anew at Bethne's resilience and single-mindedness. So intent on finding Pelly, she could completely forget her own fragile health and almost cheerfully roll up for the night in leaves. He thought wistfully of Bethne's hand-stuffed down mattresses she had been so proud of. Filled to a satisfying plumpness with down and feathers she had patiently gathered over a period of years, as well as bartered for with the neighbors, he remembered the shine of pride on her face when she could, at last, substitute them for their old straw ticks. He heaved a sigh.

No use, he told himself for the umpteenth time, *no use to dwell on what was—what is, that's what's important to Bethie and me. Yes, me, too,* he prodded himself firmly.

Unhitching Capriola, he left her to wander at will. He was not surprised to see her pick a likely spot and drop in a heap. Seeing the wisdom of her choice, Ez and Bethie followed suit, snuggling against Capriola's wooly sides for warmth and a measure of comfort.

As they huddled uncomfortably on the verge, Bethie voiced her fears once again, "Ez, duz you think he'll know us? Pelly, duz you think he'll...."

"Bethie, you've ast me and ast me. I don't *know*."

Even the sight of Bethne's quivering lip failed to quench Ezrael's annoyance. Softening just a little, he added, "He knew us the las' time we saw him, even tho' he warn't, well, jes' like allus."

"Oh, Ez, you're right. I keep sayin' the same thing over and over; I just cain't help myself. My mind jes' keeps goin' round and round—I knows he warn't himself. Oh, Ez, he warn't anybody *we* know."

"Yeah, tha's right, Bethie; I cain't get my mind around that. I don't know jes' who he wuz, but it warn't our Pelly."

Shaking its head, the brown-clad figure which crouched in the nearby foliage eavesdropped with a chill sympathy. Wrapping a cloak tightly around itself, the figure stretched full-length, preparing to keep a silent vigil until the sad little party of three journeyed on again, as it had for the many nights since the beginning of the pathetic quest.

"You know, Ez," Bethne remarked sleepily, "we been real lucky on this trip. We run into some nice people, and we ant met up with no bad folk."

Ez quickly made the sign of the horned moon before he answered Bethne, "Yep, Bethie, I 'spect we've got the Mother to thank for that. Now go to sleep; even Capriola is snoring."

The brown-clad figure smiled tightly and prepared to fall into a state of meditation—neither sleeping nor waking—but alert to every crackle of the underbrush, whisper of the trees, as well as sighs, snorts, and rustles from the vulnerable threesome. Twice, the figure sat up with sword at the ready, senses keenly testing the night, then settled back again satisfied that all was well. At the third alert, it drew quickly into a ball, silently drew its feet under itself and readied for a confrontation. The two brigands who crept through the undergrowth, certain of their quarry, were dead before they even thought to fall. So soundlessly had this been accomplished, only Capriola pricked her ears, as she had on many nights, and gave a muffled bleat. Returning her bleat softly, the brown one returned to its meditative posture; Capriola dropped her head again and dozed.

··· 53 ···

Slowly We Turn, Step by Step

"Oh, Tee Jee," moaned Daliane, "I've never been so *tired.*" She bent forward, laying her head on her horse's neck. "I've forgotten where we're going—if I ever knew—and worse, I can't remember *why.*"

Alarmed, since Daliane scarcely uttered a complaint, T'Jules reined up beside her and hauled her unceremoniously from her mount onto the saddle in front of him. A light sweat beaded her body, although it felt chilled to his hands. Alarmed even more, he rolled his eyes frantically over his shoulder at Nadi, who spurred forward to join him. Under the guise of patting Daliane's shoulder, Nadi's fingers made a quick and surreptitious check of the pulse beating at Daliane's throat and the clammy condition of her skin.

"I think it's time for a nap," she announced loudly for Jorgo, whose turn it was to lead, to hear her.

Without a word, he halted, slid from his mount, and waited for the others. "I'm in need of sustenance," he rumbled, "I've been listening to the growlings of my stomach for at least this past hour."

Over Daliane's drooping head, his eyes questioned T'Jules, holding out his arms to receive the little Baroness. Reluctantly allowing her to slide limply from his grasp into Jorgo's embrace, T'Jules dismounted with gratitude behind her. For the first time, he noted the gray tinge underlying the usually elegant dark faces of his companions—a gray tinge echoed on Daliane's cheeks and, he was sure, on his own. They had been traveling as fast as the Lady allowed during the day, and scarcely nodding off at night, only to rise at dawn to begin again.

He could barely recall their mission. *Where* were they going? What did they hope to find? How? His head whirled, obliging him to lower it between his knees until the ground stopped heaving beneath his feet. It was a measure of his weakness that he felt no shame at displaying it.

In the meantime, Jorgo busied himself making a show of noisily eating and exclaiming how good it was to finally get a bite; a charade which fooled no one, especially Daliane who had dropped instantly into a near coma. When T'Jules would have wakened her out of sheer anxiety, Nadi stayed his hand.

"Let her be," she admonished, "it is sleep only. She is in great need."

"And you are not?" grinned T'Jules.

She returned his grin with a brief flash of teeth before rolling up in her cloak and dropping into instant slumber.

"I will watch," stated Jorgo firmly.

Where he once would have argued, out of pride if nothing else, T'Jules simply nodded, sleep overtaking him before he could quite complete the gesture. It seemed only moments before he woke to Nadi's repeated shakings. Muzzy and confused, he realized Jorgo was cocooned beside him and that he had slept through two watches, rather than the one he had anticipated. Rolling over, he drew Daliane into his arms, giving her still-unresponsive form a gentle hug. Depositing a light kiss on her forehead, he turned back to Nadi to acknowledge his turn at watch, only to discover she had fallen like a cat back into sleep.

With a slight stab of panic, he noted that the shadows had gathered more deeply than he liked, seeming to wait for a lessening of guard. What if he couldn't wake Daliane? If she continued in this helpless state, she would be lost. They might have her body, but the voices would possess her mind. Without her... no, he wouldn't think of that.

Cuddling her tenderly, he began to whisper her name in her ear, hoping to arouse her as gently as possible. Evoking no response, he added a little mild shaking to his whispers. Still without a response, he began to shake her harder, and in desperation, threw in a good slap.

Daliane's eyes flew open and she yelled, "Darkness!" at the top of her voice.

Both Mel'hachim were on their feet with drawn weapons, even before the echoes of Daliane's shout had died away.

"You know," began Daliane wryly while rubbing her cheek, "with friends like these...."

The Mel'hachim sheathed their weapons with good-natured chortles. T'Jules kissed Dally's cheek repeatedly as they settled in for another night of wakeful discomfort, Daliane between the Mel'hach warriors, and T'Jules at her back. From time to time, one or the other would doze briefly, but never did the two Mel'hachim relax their hold on Daliane, or allow themselves to fade out of consciousness at the same time. Those awake sang, discussed philosophy, played word games, or told old war stories—anything to keep from surrendering their vigilance, until dawn began to lift the shadows from around them.

"We're going to have to stop at midday from now on to rest." T'Jules made his remark as close to an order as he could.

Somewhat to his surprise, no one raised an objection, but simply stared at him dully before making ready to venture forth again.

"We're getting close to *something!*" offered Daliane hesitantly. "It's not... I'm not sure *what*... It's important, I know that."

Only a two hour ride into the morning revealed, at least partially, that she was correct. They stood at the top of a hill gazing down on a settlement sloping to a parti-colored sea. Nearby, a waterfall the color of the bottom of a well burst from the rock, spilling its inky fluid into the sea's blue-green embrace. T'Jules shook his head to clear it. For a minute he thought he saw....

"That's it! That's the one!" Daliane exclaimed both triumphantly and fearfully.

"Yes, my dears, and that is the town of which I spoke... governed by my most unworthy relative. I would prefer to avoid a meeting, if possible. What I don't know at the moment, I do not have to deal with. It would only delay us, and put you in more danger."

"But Tee Jee," objected Daliane, "if he's a criminal?"

"He is, indeed, my darling, but as I told you, too stupid to do real harm. Most of the townspeople are way ahead of him when it comes to smuggling, petty thievery, and the like."

Jorgo snorted, prompting Nadi to belt him stiffly in the ribs as though reading his mind. "An unnecessary memory, my husband."

T'Jules raised an eyebrow, but made no comment. "We'll have to find a less obvious way around. My face is, um, well known to the soldiers."

"And we are not unnoticeable," added Nadi with a touch of smugness.

Daliane giggled. "I guess."

The four cast about in as many directions for a way to avoid actually descending through the town. Short of throwing themselves over the falls and swimming to the spot where the forest took up again, there seemed to be no possible means of avoiding the habitation. The path led in, the path led out, the town stood as a block in between.

"A suggestion, my brother," offered Jorgo, "These folk do not associate us with the house of Wysach. Furthermore, we are, as Nadi has attested, not unnoticeable."

The formality of his speech caused T'Jules to regard him suspiciously, "And...?" he prompted.

"A slight disguise for you and our sister—a little dirt, a little mussing—and Nadi and I will venture in full Mel'hachim regalia, directly through the center of town. I think we can draw most of the eyes." His own touch of smugness made Daliane giggle again.

T'Jules echoed her in his turn. Thinking of the Mel'hachim in "full regalia," he was sure that "most eyes" was a singular understatement on Jorgo's part.

"We will lead your horses, my brother, after we remove the saddles and conceal them as part of the packs. I am afraid you will have to walk in as beggarly a manner as possible, until we can safely rejoin our company with yours."

Daliane bent double with mirth at Jorgo's throwaway line. The thought of the Baron minging along in a beggarly manner was delicious. Nadi's face remained inscrutable, but laughter crinkled the corners of her eyes. Even T'Jules couldn't resist a "heh, heh" before he caught himself. With proper gravity he declared, "An excellent plan."

The Baron and his Lady immediately set about turning themselves into riff-raff with Nadi's enthusiastic assistance. She took a childlike delight in games of dress-up and proceeded to disguise the Baroness so effectively as a dirty waif that T'Jules could only gape. Daliane's fragility lent itself to the street gamine impersonation, while smears of dirt across her cheeks and rubbed into her usually immaculate hair altered her entirely.

"Now you," commanded Nadi firmly.

The same treatment was afforded his hair and face, along with an oversize tunic, rent in strategic places, which was forced unceremoniously over his head.

"My sister," admonished Jorgo at Daliane's fresh bout of mirth, "you must contain your good spirits."

"I know, but...." She stifled her laughter as best she could.

T'Jules looked at her in an almost painful paroxysm of love. How could anyone, who was enduring what she had had to endure for so many weary months, take such joy in living. A lesson to us all, he mused.

Disguises complete, the small Bervaine saddles were stored in their packs, which were rearranged to be carried mainly on the backs of the bewildered Bervaine horses. It took all of Daliane's coaxing to convince her recalcitrant steed to accept a much-enlarged parcel, rather than her own small self. Once this was accomplished, the Baron and Baroness stood by in admiration while the warriors displayed their full equipage.

T'Jules gave a whistle. "Yes, indeed, *that* should garner some attention." The final product dazzled the eyes of their audience, even accustomed as they were to the Mel'hachim's everyday rather gaudy plumage. Daliane clapped her hands in delight as the warriors strutted and bowed, conscious of their resplendence.

After a suitable period of admiration, the Mel'hachim prepared to cut a swath through the town, drawing the regard of any onlookers away from the (hopefully) unrecognizable Bervaines. Nadi paused to bestow generous kisses on both of them before vaulting into her saddle and riding grandly away. Jorgo turned, winked, and then followed his spouse.

Neither Daliane nor T'Jules moved or uttered a word until their companions had disappeared from view, then, turning to each other, embraced fiercely. After a breathless moment, they set forth on the same path as the Mel'hachim, T'Jules hobbling in emulation of a beggar.

"Lame, in more ways than one," muttered Daliane with a snort. T'Jules responded with a soft cuff, which provoked a second snort.

··· 54 ···

Someday, I'll Find You

Following Cal's unexpected claim of swordsmanship, Kelgan felt a shocking rush of envy. He trod warily down that path of thought. He could perform magic, couldn't he? And Cal couldn't. Although, granted, Cal seemed to be familiar with certain, er, mechanical arts, which Kelgan acknowledged might be considered complementary. On the other hand, he possessed a sword, with which swordsmanship did not seem to be an issue. He swallowed hard, recalling the ease with which he dispatched the putative bandit. Not only no need for swordsmanship, but very little need for him.

He closely studied Cal. Yes, certainly the face the stranger wore was his own, but on close scrutiny subtle differences were manifest. Deeper lines around ears and mouth, slight sprinkling of gray in the sandy curls, a touch of softness at the belt line. Cal was *older*? Could an otherworldly twin have been born first? Who knew how time ran in other planes? Who *knew* there were other planes until now? Kelgan rested his head on his knees for a moment. When he raised his head, Cal eyed him with the same frank scrutiny.

Meeting Kelgan's eyes with a wry smile, Cal ventured, "Maybe we should get to know each other a bit better."

Neroma and her twin, conferring in low tones, broke off at Cal's words. Terencia had been oiling her sword. Assuring herself of its keen edge, she had made no further comments after Cal's confession of fencing ability. However, she, too, looked up expectantly in Kelgan's direction, although with a trace of malice in her glance.

Kelgan surprised himself, and his listeners, by answering simply but firmly, "Yes, it is important that we do."

Terencia flashed Kelgan a wicked grin and went back to her equipment maintenance. Neroma and Nevander nodded as one. They resumed their private conversation, needing, of course, only occasional words, since the mind of one spoke clearly to the mind of the other. Kelgan was sure even those few words were for the benefit of others, rather than springing from any need of the twins.

Cal watched them for a moment; then moved closer to Kelgan. He still seemed somewhat unsteady and unsure, but was adapting, since no other choice was offered.

"Okay," he said once he settled next to Kelgan.

Kelgan did not understand the word, but he assumed it was some sort of pause filler.

"Tell me something about *you*, and about *here*."

Kelgan set to work filling Cal in as best he could on their world, himself, their journey up to now, and the reasons for it (as though he knew). Cal listened without question, interruption, or comment. When Kelgan, his throat dry, finally paused, Cal murmured, "Ummmm." and got up to stand staring. He stood and stared into the forest. The mules, their attention captured, moved up to stand one on either side of him. They stared into the forest as well without a hint of mockery.

Not knowing exactly what prompted him, Kelgan stood and joined the group, drawing his arm through Cal's. "I know how hard it is to take in, harder for you than for me."

Cal turned. With their faces only inches apart, he studied Kelgan narrowly. "Yeah," he acknowledged. His eyes shifted to Neroma and her brother, still engrossed in each other. "So they're twins, huh?"

Kelgan caught the speculative gleam in Cal's eye, and he experienced another shaft of emotion he did not care to name. "Yes, twins," he confirmed, his voice flat and carefully neutral.

"And the brown one's a soldier?"

"Terencia is a member of the Autarchs Elite Guard," Kelgan corrected. "They're a little more... *specialized*... than regular troops."

"More dangerous, you mean." It was not a question.

"Essentially," Kelgan admitted and then grinned.

Cal did not return the grin, but looked grave. His eyes lost their air of speculation, and he frowned slightly. Touching Kelgan spontaneously for the first time, he put both hands on his shoulders. He asked, "What about us? Are we twins? Doubles? One and the same?"

A range of conflicting emotions played over Kelgan. Some of them, he realized, did not stem from his own psyche, but were seemingly engendered by Cal's touch, emanating from him, rather than Kelgan, himself. Cal appeared to notice simultaneously, for he dropped his hands as though burned and gaped foolishly. Prompted simply by intuition, Kelgan grasped one of the limp hands between his own and said simply, "Friends, I hope."

What Cal would have responded, or what Kelgan would have added, was lost. Kelgan felt the words freeze in his throat as did the breath in his chest. The hair rose on the nape of his neck with a creepy familiarity. He realized Pellerin stood just behind him, almost against his back. His voice the usual sepulchral whisper, tinged with the despair of the tomb, he breathed, "Coming," in Kelgan's ear.

Whirling, Kelgan collided with Cal, who had stepped forward in alarm just as Kelgan recoiled. "Oof," exclaimed Cal as the breath whistled out of him resulting from Kelgan's elbow planted squarely in his middle. Kelgan's growl of pain echoed him as Cal's forearm smacked into his jaw when Cal threw up a warding arm. The pair tottered in comical pain before Cal drew a deep breath and Kelgan's vision and hearing cleared enough for him to be aware of an approaching disturbance.

The other four had frozen in their spots, although Terencia's sword was out. However, Kelgan noted curiously, her face wore an expression of anticipation rather than anxiety.

Voices floated toward them, raised in emotion. The on-comers were certainly not approaching in anything like secrecy, and a steady clip-clop, clip-clop accompanied their excited exclamations. While he attempted to assess the situation, Kelgan noticed another curious fact. Pellerin had clasped his hands together in what

Kelgan was sure was a display of emotion; something he would have sworn was impossible under Pellerin's circumstances. Pellerin's head was pointed in the direction of the nearing sounds, and the barely discerning quivering made him appear to blur in Kelgan's sight.

Ears pricked, the mules gazed in the same direction, one over each of Cal's shoulders. Feeling Piper grasp his leg, Kelgan glanced down at the child's gleeful up-turned face. "Are you going to use the sword?" he whispered hopefully.

Kelgan shook his head, not in answer, but in bemusement at Piper's bloodthirsty anticipation.

"Wait," he cautioned just as a peculiar group of travelers burst into view.

"What did I tell you, Ez. I sees him!" Bethne's triumphant cry rebounded from the trees, undoubtedly alerting every malefactor from there to the borderlands. Her mother's eye picked Pellerin out even in the deepening, lit only by the feeble firelight.

Pellerin's old mare, almost forgotten since her silence was generally as profound as her owner's, gave a wild whinny and proceeded to execute the equine equivalent of a jig; jerking her halter loose from Pellerin's belt to which he had attached her, and rushing headlong to meet the strangers.

Goosebumps stood out on Kelgan's arms. Piper clutched him convulsively around the legs as Pellerin sketched a short bow and inquired with courtly courtesy, "Good evening, Mother, Father. How do you fare?" A strange spasm then passed over the young man's face, fading as fast as it came, leaving him as usual an empty-seeming husk.

Ignoring everyone and everything, including Ezrael's attempt to restrain her, Bethne rushed at Pellerin, weeping freely. She flung her arms around his neck, crying, "Pelly, oh Pelly!"

Whatever had briefly animated him had flown. He did not respond. Pellerin stared dully into the distance without blinking. The mare, as though ashamed of her desertion, ambled back to Pellerin's side, nuzzling Bethne in passing acknowledgment. The tableau had taken on the air of a child's game of statues, until

Bethne, having dropped her arms in shock, threw herself, dissolved in tears, into Kelgan's astonished arms.

That tableau dissolved, as well. Betaking herself unexplainedly to the center of the roadway, Terencia stared back the way the strangers had come, ignoring them entirely.

Neroma took charge of Bethne like an elderly mother hen, rather than a skillful sorceress. This was much to Kelgan's relief, but also regret as his mind was drawn back to his mother and sisters. Nevander went to pull Ezrael toward the small fire, demonstrating a rare gentle concern for the older man.

The old man spoke for the first time in a mellow baritone that surprised Kelgan, although he wasn't sure why. Somehow, the gangly old farmer's appearance had led him to expect a rasp. "You know Pelly's our boy?"

Nevander answered soothingly, "Yes, and we understand that he hasn't been, uh, hasn't been, uh, well."

"Ant no need to be polite, son. We knows what's what. Don't rightly know *how* or *why*, but *what* we got a handle on."

Kelgan glanced doubtfully at Bethne. Following the direction of his gaze, Ezrael added, "Bit o' problem with whom, seems like."

Kelgan looked into the old man's eyes, seeing more awareness there than he had expected. *Well, why not*, he scolded himself, *these are his parents. They know a stranger when they see one.*

The old man addressed Kelgan again. "By the way, I'm Ezrael, she's Bethne, and our boy is Pellerin.

Kelgan shook the old man's hand. "Pellerin, we thought that was a nice name. Uh, we sort of... knew it even though he didn't exactly make it clear to us."

"No," agreed Ez with irony, "I 'spects not."

"Yeah, he wasn't big on 'conversation'," piped Piper unexpectedly. Kelgan nudged him into silence.

"He does occasionally... well, say some..." he began, but was caught up short as Cal caught at his arm and pulled him backwards. "What's going on?" he demanded.

"I'm not quite sure," was the cautious reply. *But then I never am.* Aloud, he said, "Our quiet friend has family, it appears."

"Do you think they know...?"

"Yes, I think they know. I suspect they had hopes that weren't realized."

Cal glanced sideways at Pellerin, still motionless and staring, as always.

"Another thing I don't understand."

"Just one?"

Cal gave a grimace that wasn't exactly a smile, but more of a wince. "Yeah! I don't understand any of it, and I don't like any of it either, but how come I'm so calm about it?" A pause, "Well, maybe that's the wrong word, but I'm not screaming anymore. I'm not even surprised that our zombie friend can talk to his parents like Little Lord Fauntleroy."

Although ignorant of Cal's references to "zombie" and "Little Lord Something-or-Other," in the main Kelgan understood Cal's plaint. Of course, he understood, or more to the point, *didn't* understand, much more than Cal did. Therefore, he *did* understand. Hoping to clear the whirl of thought Cal's questions evoked, Kelgan shook his head.

Taking Kelgan's gesture as an answer, Cal bristled slightly.

"You mean, you're not going to explain?"

Kelgan flapped his hands. "I mean I *can't* explain any better than I already have. I gave you the story as I know it, but there are questions I can't answer. I don't think they," he gestured with his head, "can answer, either. I don't know why Pellerin speaks on occasion. I don't know why—or how—he's walking around. I don't know who the voices are, and I don't know what ails those Dark-blasted mules!"

The last *non sequitur* made Cal blink in surprise until he realized there was a persistent maaing and braying coming from the tethered animals. He followed Kelgan over for a closer look. Capriole, it seemed, finding herself the only nonequine in the group, had decided to assert "goatish" supremacy. Feeling that they could claim precedence, the mules disputed her right to a choice patch of verge, while the old mare stood undecided whether to side with members of a similar species or her old barn mate.

Doubling up in laughter, Cal wheezed out, "Welcome to Oz," before succumbing to another fit.

Hissing *"Levanah,"* through his teeth, Kelgan quieted all four animals at once, which pleasantly surprised him. One mule insouciantly winked at Cal, before edging Capriole to one side to crop the disputed patch. Cal stopped laughing and gazed thoughtfully at the impudent haunch of the mule, which had turned its back on him.

"You know, Kel..." he began, only to have the mule turn back to him to give him a meaningful stare and an indisputable shake of the head. Kelgan caught the motion from the corner of his eye and glanced inquiringly at Cal. With the hand farthest from the mule, Cal made a small warning gesture.

Barely pausing, Kelgan let his glance sweep over the entire assemblage. Turning back to the animals, he said, "That's better," putting a rather satisfied expression on his face.

Sauntering casually away, he felt unutterably foolish. Dissembling for the benefit of a mule! What next?

Neroma, still occupied with Bethne's comfort, urged her to eat something while she described her journey. Bethne did her best to comply, but her eyes kept straining to the figure of her son, motionless now as a bronze statue.

"Don't he never sit down?" she demanded of Neroma.

"We have not known him to, my dear," Nevander answered for Neroma.

Taking Bethne's cold hand in his, he chafed it gently, all the while gazing meltingly at her from his great black eyes. Not even a mother in distress could resist My Lord di Nerrill at his most charming. Bethne simpered a bit and actually managed a few bites of food Neroma had pressed on her, held as she was in that dark gaze.

Coming up behind Kelgan, Cal noted wryly, "I wish I could do that, better than mule control any day."

Sourly, Kelgan had to concede it was so. The thought of his lack of success with regard to any control at all settled like an undigested breakfast sausage in his belly. A sudden vision of Neroma's hair winding around his body like a thousand kisses made him gasp aloud. Cal cocked his head to one side in inquiry, but was otherwise silent.

Neroma's own head came up, and she stabbed Kelgan with a flinty regard. His face flushed uncontrollably. Cal's arm snaked out suddenly and thumped Kelgan's shoulder several times. Then Cal turned away to engage Ezrael in conversation, leaving Kelgan to contemplate either a returning buffet or a grateful thanks.

Neroma's head finally dropped, her attention centering once more on Bethne, eliciting a sigh from Kelgan. He then, in turn, could not help noticing that Terencia still seemed distracted, paying no heed to the various tableaus. She continually raked the deep gloom of the forest with anxious sweeps of her head, bending for short spells over her sword, which should have been worn away to a straight pin, so long had she pretended to polish and sharpen it. Within seconds each time, however, she dropped her rag and scanned the darkness behind the trunks again.

Kelgan strolled to her side, dropped down beside her, and pulled out his sword. "Maybe you could lend me your polishing cloth when you're done with it," he suggested with a show of innocence.

"Here, you can have it now." Getting to her feet, she thrust the rag at him, deliberately turned her back and stalked off.

So much for subtlety, thought Kelgan, turning up his nose at the smell of oil emanating from the scrap of cloth. Since he had his sword out anyway, he examined it for signs of wear or rust, knowing he had paid it no attention for the entire journey.

I'm not a swordsman," he told himself. *I'm a wizard... well, almost,* there came the gloom again, *I'm not much of that, either.* He pondered that thought at length. *I must be something, nevertheless,* he told himself, *because the di Nerrills had their eyes... their scries,* he gave a soft snort of amusement, *on me. And somebody gave me this sword....* His thoughts stumbled once more as he remembered how it used him as an extension of itself, rather than otherwise. *And now there's another one.* Kelgan raised his gaze over to where Cal sat, wrapped in a brown study of his own.

For his own part, Cal's thoughts ran just as bewilderedly in the same vein. *What the hell am I doing here? I've never been a hero and, by damn, I'm not a magician. Hell, I've never even liked to read those kinds of books. I drink too much, my ex can't stand me, and I'm a second-rate lawyer, barely managing to do my job. Now I'm on another world—yeah, swallow* that *one—and I'm a friggin' twin!* He locked stares with Kelgan before both sets of eyes fell. Cal was surprised to find he felt like more of a man than before—oddly satisfying to be two people.

Searching out Terencia, Kelgan noted that she had engaged the old man, Ezrael, in conversation. While she had given over watching the trees as if she had expected an invading host, the tension was manifest in every line of her back. Ezrael, true to form, was as laconic as ever, answering her queries with terse monosyllables, but some of her unease had been communicated to him since he shifted continually from foot to foot. Kelgan's nape prickled to see that Pellerin had assumed Terencia's position and now stared out into the trees. Although the space had not lost its same dull appearance, it somehow spoke of expectation. The soft clip-clop of several hooves reached them

Piper wailed, "Oh, Darkness, not more bandits!"

Kelgan instantly hushed him.

··· 55 ···

Together at Last

Their circuitous route around the town had actually saved time, T'Jules thought with satisfaction. Saved time for what? He contemplated the sense of desperate urgency that gripped all of them.

"Off to Nowhereatall as fast as we can." He didn't realize he had spoken aloud until Daliane's puzzled query reached him.

"Say that again, Tee Jee. I didn't understand."

Jorgo, riding behind T'Jules, laughed. "I think my brother has the same problem."

T'Jules ruefully acknowledged that truth. "I'm sorry, Dally, I was just going over again what we went over before; we don't know why we're in the Dark's own hurry to get nowhere."

Daliane sighed. "It *isn't* nowhere, Tee Jee. It's... *somewhere*. I've *seen* it. Well... at least... sort of."

T'Jules was instantly contrite. "Oh, my dearest, that's the problem. You're the one who's had to fight. I can't see it, or hear it, or feel it; I don't know where it is or how to combat it. I don't know what I'm combating.

"Oh, Tee Jee, I didn't mean to...."

Jorgo, who had dropped back discreetly, coughed and observed, "The shadows are lengthening; we shall have to choose our resting place soon."

Daliane attempted to lighten the mood with a sarcastic, "'Resting place'. Now there's a slight exaggeration."

Nadi looked over her shoulder and grinned. "Our 'sitting-with-discomfort' place, then."

Jorgo contributed, "Our 'rising-with-rheumatism' spot."

And T'Jules added, "Our 'battling the bugs' spot."

Silence fell following this spate of sallies; then Jorgo's head snapped up. "Listen," he ordered, sharply drawing up his horse. The distant murmur of voices fluttered back to them on the errant breezes.

They had met few fellow travelers since skirting the town, taking pains to step into the trees off the road when they detected anyone. This, however, sounded like a fair-sized party.

T'Jules looked to Jorgo, who made quick hand signals, raising his eyebrows for confirmation. T'Jules nodded in agreement. The group broke apart, Jorgo and the Baroness swinging one way off the path, T'Jules and Nadi the other.

They eased their mounts forward as quietly as possible, making their way slowly toward the voices, as far as they knew, unobserved. They were thus astonished to find themselves confronted by a tall young man brandishing a sword awkwardly and demanding, "All right, come out of there, whoever you are."

He was backed up, however, by a young woman in brown, whose grasp of her sword was much more professional, not to mention a dashingly handsome man in black, who had drawn a dagger. Each faced a different direction, so there was no chance any of the Baron's group was undetected. Heaving a huge sigh, T'Jules, followed by Nadi, urged his steed out of the trees and onto the road, as did Daliane and Jorgo. Conscious of the gathering nightfall, he dismounted and held out his hands, palms up, just as Daliane toppled from her saddle.

Neroma, with a speed far unlike her usual deliberate movements, was there before Daliane reached the ground. Jorgo had been nearly as fast. Together they supported the little Baroness, while Neroma ordered, "Put up your swords," in velvet-over-steel voice which brooked no argument.

In total bewilderment, T'Jules still stood with his hands outstretched, witnessing the flurry of action, without even time to go to Dally's rescue.

"Get over here," hissed Neroma in exasperation. He found himself hastening to obey, coughing from the sudden inexplicable scent of flowers which assailed him. Goggling with amazement, he beheld a smiling Jorgo and a wide-awake relaxed Daliane. He started when Nadi whispered in his ear, "We are well met."

Well met! T'Jules surveyed the motley lot arrayed in front of him—two old people, two sets of twins (?), a swaybacked old mare held by a *very* peculiar youth, a goat, a child.... He stopped counting and sank to the ground.

The child observed wryly, "He don't look so good. Pelly looks better."

Kelgan agreed. Reaching T'Jules' side, Kelgan crouched beside him, inquiring with what he hoped was a reassuring air, "May I help you? I'm a... er... healer." He wasn't sure exactly why he concealed his actual profession from the new arrival, but something told him to withhold this information until the stranger's intentions had revealed themselves.

T'Jules gave him a weak smile. "I'm really all right, thank you. My wife has been ill, you see, I'm afraid I was just a bit worried. By the way, what *is* going on with my wife and your friend?"

Kelgan smiled in return. "Neroma is also a... healer."

Slightly prior to the latest arrivals, Piper had plopped on the ground next to Kelgan, leaned with elaborate casualness against Kelgan's knee, and in an exaggerated stage whisper remarked, "Awful lot of people showin' up."

Kelgan regarded him thoughtfully. "And...?" he prompted.

"C'mon," was the scornful response. "You're the smartest one o' the bunch. You know what I mean."

Taken aback, Kelgan was silent for a time. Then, choosing his words carefully, he began, "It may be there is some meaning behind this fact...."

"May be!" Piper swiveled to look Kelgan in the face. "Your twin brother drops outta the air. His," with a shuddering nod toward Pellerin, mute in the gathering dusk, "Ma and Pa...."

Kelgan acknowledged the sense of Piper's assertion, "Yes, you have the right of it. There is a tapestry being woven here and the pattern begins to emerge."

Piper looked suitably impressed at being spoken to in such an adult and formal fashion, and a small self-satisfied smile dimpled his cheeks momentarily, then he lapsed back into his former slightly belligerent mode. "Well...."

"Well, I don't know what we're supposed to do about it. The pattern will have to get a lot clearer before I, or any one of us, can guess what's next."

"What's *she,*" another nod, this time in Terencia's direction, "expectin', then?"

So, Piper had noticed Terencia's silent scan of the underbrush as well. *Why not,* Kelgan thought, *he doesn't miss a trick.*

He shrugged an answer. Seeing Piper's dissatisfied expression, he elaborated. "I have been wondering that, myself, but have no explanation. She obviously hopes, or fears, to see someone, but whether friend or foe...."

"Yeah," said Piper.

Pellerin and his old mare had silently drawn near to Kelgan and Piper as they spoke. Kelgan now noticed that he loomed uncomfortably over them. Piper, at the same moment, glanced up and said, "Uh oh."

When Kelgan looked a question at him, Piper added, "Somethin' allus happens when he starts movin' around."

Kelgan grinned at Piper in agreement. They both expectantly regarded Pellerin.

"Almost all here," gusted Pellerin sepulchrally to the accompanying soft drum of approaching hoofbeats.

The party rose to its feet as one. *We're getting really synchronized*, thought Kelgan a little wildly. They stared down the road, only to see the party vanish into the underbrush.

At Kelgan's command to show themselves, four riders crept into view, only to pull up in surprise at the sight of the assembled, and obviously waiting, group. The two parties stared at each other for uncountable minutes in silence. T'Jules and his party, uncertain whether to draw swords, Kelgan and party uncertain whether to cast warding spells, until Kelgan heard the literal ghost of a whisper in his ear, reiterating, "Nearly all here."

At that, he broke the silence to everyone's astonishment with a broad smile as he exclaimed, "Welcome, we've been expecting you."

"We have?" "You have?" said more than one voice.

Piper giggled.

"Of course," Kelgan added, "we didn't know it until just now."

Piper rolled in the leaves, clutching his sides. His glee was interrupted by the dramatic spectacle of the Baroness toppling from her horse as the sequence played out.

At Nadi's surprising comment of, "Well met,' the Baron murmured, "Expect the unexpected," and prepared to receive it.

"Join us at the fire," Kelgan enthused, while the de Nerrills looked at him askance.

"It's Pellerin's idea," Kelgan muttered to Neroma out of the corner of his mouth.

Neroma's eyebrows disappeared into her wandering hair, and the tresses tumbled about in what Kelgan recognized as amusement. Her thoughts were evidently transmitted to her twin, because the same mixture of amusement and bemusement appeared on his face.

Neroma instantly became the gracious hostess. "Yes, do join us and share what we have."

Bethne and Ezrael looked bewildered.

"Who aire these folk, anyhow?" Bethie whispered to Cal.

"I have a feeling we're going to find out," rejoined Cal, "maybe we'll like it and, then again...."

Worry creased Bethne's face like a road map. Cal, feeling ashamed for scaring her, patted her hand and sought to undo the damage. "They look like friends," he stated reassuringly, "not only that, but they look like friends we could use."

Ez gave him a grateful smile as Bethne relaxed visibly. Kelgan noticed curiously that the two warriors grasped the small woman by both arms and bore her between them to the fire, where they continued to hold her even as they sat.

Daliane, from her protected venue between Jorgo and Nadi, who clung to her even more fiercely than usual, surveyed the motley group with the same critical eye as Piper.

Barely moving her mouth, she asked, "Who *are* these people, and how did they know we were coming?"

Jorgo gave a soft rumble of amusement. "Who, I am not sure. How, we can easily surmise."

"Not so easily, my mate," corrected Nadi. "The voices, yes, we can assume some are here in the same pursuit. Nevertheless, the voices only ask—they do not tell."

"You are right," conceded Jorgo, "but I feel a power here among these people, which we have not encountered before."

It was Nadi's turn to concede.

Daliane was baffled. "But I don't feel a thing. I don't even feel that *looming* that I usually feel."

Jorgo and Nadi exchanged glances.

"Is it possible...?"

Daliane looked baffled again. "Is *what* possible?"

"We think, little sister, that more than just we are guarding you. Or, I should say, more are guarding and you are protected as well because you are here."

As the words left his mouth, Neroma came to kneel in front of the three, saying with one of her rare smiles, "I think you can safely release her, now."

Jorgo snorted and Nadi grinned. Carefully, they gave up the holds they had on Daliane's arms, and moved slightly away from her. Daliane let out a whoosh of breath and rubbed, as unobtrusively as possible, her biceps.

Meeting Neroma's eyes, Jorgo sent a silent question through the tilt of his head and a raised eyebrow. Neroma nodded slightly, her eyes straying to both her brother and Kelgan. Jorgo nodded thoughtfully in return.

Quick to notice the exchange, silent though it had been, Daliane demanded peremptorily, "Tell me."

This time both the Mel'hachim chuckled. "Our Baroness (slight emphasis on the word) does not like to be left out."

Neroma's mouth quirked slightly, "Perhaps I should introduce myself formally. I am Lady Neroma di Nerrill, and my brother is Nevander. Our father was the fourth Earl of that name, however, my brother and I seldom use our proper titles."

Daliane blinked in surprise, then exclaimed gleefully, "Outdone, by the Lady."

Neroma settled back on her heels, and let another small smile warm her ivory features. Then, more soberly, she suggested, "Now, having met you, we feel you must know all we know; which is little enough, I'm afraid."

Daliane protested, immediately suspicious. "But you don't know us at all, why would you trust us?"

Neroma glanced over her shoulder at the immobile figure of Pellerin, her hair pointing with unmistakable emphasis at him. "You are not strangers to all of us."

Daliane's eyes went wide, and she sharply sucked in her breath at the implication of Neroma's pronouncement.

Satisfied with the impression her words had made, Neroma motioned Kelgan to her side. "Give the Baroness (slight emphasis on the word) your part of the story."

Kelgan cocked a side-long eye at Neroma, but said nothing for a moment, just regarded her silently. Before he looked away, he could have sworn a slight flush rose to Neroma's cheeks. *Nah,* he told himself.

Obeying her directive, however, he succinctly filled Daliane and the Mel'hachim in on the events leading up to his joining forces with the di Nerrills.

Neroma added her bit, explaining their interest in Kelgan, but acknowledged, "Some of the tales are less easily told and less easily understood."

As one, they looked at Pellerin, being fussed over by his mother, but disregarding her as one would a buzzing gnat.

"His presence and its meaning for our cause...." She shrugged.

"He, uh, does he...?" Daliane fumbled for words. "I'm not sure I want to ask what I want to ask."

Kelgan sighed, "We know, or at least we think, he died several weeks or months ago. We have not yet had the opportunity to *exactly* confirm the fact with his parents as yet." He offered a self-deprecating grin and went on, "You can see we don't have any easier time discussing it. Any road, he seems to *know* things, and sometimes he *says* things, which is how we knew you were coming, because *he* did."

Kelgan forestalled Daliane's next question. "No, we haven't the slightest idea how. Maybe, being dead, or at least not exactly alive as we think of it, puts you more or less out of the normal run of time. I don't know...." he finished helplessly.

"Are you an Earl, as well?" Daliane inquired mischievously.

Wha? thought Kelgan. Aloud, he demurred. "No, just a sorcerer."

Daliane's look was ironic. "Umm," she murmured.

"Although, *some* of us can lay claim to more than one title," Kelgan added offhandedly.

Daliane, somewhat to his surprise, rocked with laughter. "Oh, I'm *really* outdone," she wheezed.

To his even greater amazement, she threw her arms around Neroma's neck in an enthusiastic embrace. Neroma was even more astounded than Kelgan. Her hair stood straight up like exclamation marks, trembled there for a moment, and then fell to patting Daliane on the back, while her arms remained limply at her sides.

Kelgan choked back a guffaw; seeing the ordinarily composed and collected Lady di Nerrill completely nonplussed.

So, we are assembled, Kelgan thought.

Piper, of course, had put his finger on it—there was an obvious guiding force beyond the seeming coincidence of their meeting on the road. A rather ill-assorted party, but at least one of each group had heard the voices. Strangely, he felt little kinship with the other hearers, including his slightly older "twin." But then, they had had little time together; maybe they would find a common ground.

He rather liked T'Jules and the Mel'hachim, but the little Baroness he found off-putting for no reason he could discern. Pellerin's parents just looked like dithery old people, well, not Ezrael, necessarily, but Bethne! Furthermore, his alien counterpart was too much what Kelgan did not want to be but was afraid he was.

Piper still snuggled up against Kelgan's knees, had fallen asleep and was slipping sideways into the leaves. Kelgan caught him just before Piper's face hit the dirt. Feeling a rush of protectiveness, he laid the boy gently across his lap. Pellerin's mother noticed his action and came over to sit beside him.

"Yore boy, I can tell," she stated rather than asked. "I knows how you feel about him."

Kelgan stared, nonplussed for a moment; then struggled for an explanation. "Well, no, he's... we're actually...." His voice died. Then to his own amazement, he heard himself say, "Yes, he's my boy *now.*"

"I knew it," Bethne claimed triumphantly, evidently overlooking the "now" tacked onto Kelgan's response, "you can allus tell a good father."

Kelgan stared blankly. "A good father!" He wasn't even a good magician yet. Well, sort of good—just not a lot of experience. Well, maybe a little experience. Kelgan realized his mind was babbling while his mouth was hanging agape.

Bethne regarded him a little oddly as the silence grew.

"Oh, ah, yes, thank you for the compliment," he managed.

"Ant givin' you a compliment, jes' the simple truth."

"Well, I'm flattered just the same," Kelgan responded, all the while thinking Bethne, or maybe he, was confusing himself with someone else. He shifted Piper to his shoulder and pushed up to his feet.

"I guess I'll put him to bed," he announced, feeling like an imposter.

Now his eyes met Terencia's, whose agitated vigilance had only increased with the appearance of more strangers. She seemed on the edge of complete hysteria. Seeing his alarmed regard, she straightened her tunic and defiantly raised her head. Whirling on her heel, she stalked to the fire and dropped cross-legged to the ground, turning her back on the forest with obvious effort.

··· 56 ···

Getting to Know You

"It would seem," T'Jules pontificated, "that we are all brought together for a similar purpose—a mission, if you will...."

"Oh, Tee Jee," interrupted Daliane, "stop being a Baron. Of course we are, everybody already knows that."

The Baron grinned sheepishly, then said with self-deprecating charm, "Sorry, I didn't mean to sound stuffy."

"Perfectly all right," said Kelgan hastily as Nevander appeared ready to equal the Baron in pontification.

"That's the *only* thing we're clear on."

"I wasn't even clear on that," muttered Cal.

Kelgan elbowed him sharply.

"I think Pelly knows more'n that, if we could only get it outta him," Bethne added.

Nevander eyed her with appreciation. "Yes, you are undoubtedly correct, and based on more than a mother's intuition, I'll wager."

"Yep, I seen how he wuz, and heard what he said, when he wuz... well... real sick."

Piper made a restless movement. Kelgan hushed him with his knees.

"Er, yes," agreed Nevander. "Furthermore, he seems to have a destination in... um... mind."

Piper piped before Kelgan could stop him. "And he don't want to share it, neither."

Nevander afforded Piper's comment the same respect he had the others. "I think he is trying, but can only do so much, and only occasionally."

"Yeh... maybe." Piper subsided.

Kelgan noticed Terencia once again sweeping the forest with her eyes, her head held quite still.

If I weren't looking for it, I wouldn't have seen it at all. I'll bet Neroma hasn't missed it, though, he mused.

As though in response, Neroma lifted her head and looked directly at him. Her hair swayed just slightly in Terencia's direction. Kelgan gave the ghost of a nod.

"Maybe we're not *all* here," he suggested pointedly.

Terencia gave an almost imperceptible start.

"You mean, there might be even more of you?" Piper's disgusted tone elicited a chuckle from the group.

"We will go on, and see if anyone else catches up," purred Neroma, bestowing one of her smiles on Piper.

Piper, reduced to incoherence, fell back between Kelgan's knees in a fit of bashfulness. Cal regarded him with sympathy, and then glanced wryly at Kelgan, who shrugged and forced a halfway grin.

Got us all, thought Kelgan, *although maybe the warriors are immune.*

Glancing at them, he was embarrassed to discover them staring back. White teeth flashed. *Does everybody read me like a book?* he huffed to himself, *some mage—a real mystery man.*

Neroma giggled; there was no other word for it. Eyebrows raised and heads turned. She immediately resumed her impassive demeanor.

Kelgan sat pierced by shock. His thoughts had reached her! Torn between elation and dismay, he sat with whirling head. Just the touch of a smug expression crossed her face.

"We will increase the wards...." A fit of general coughing ensued as Neroma suited her action to the words. "... and try to rest for tomorrow."

Gasps and nods greeted Neroma's suggestion.

"Maybe you could back off just a bit," pleaded Kelgan, wiping his streaming eyes on his shirtsleeve, and desperately trying to wheeze out his Allergus spell.

The suffocating presence of a thousand roses faded just enough for the group to take a few grateful breaths, but remained strong enough to give Darkness, Himself, serious respiratory difficulty.

Resigning himself to a night of wheezing, but grateful to escape the threat of the Voices, Kelgan settled himself in his cloak, only to feel a small body thrust itself against his back. Somewhat bemused, he rolled to gather the child into the cloak with him and the two drifted off together.

··· 57 ···

Quarterly Exam (the First Test)

With the graying of the East, the motley band rose to eat a few hurried bites before assembling with an air of purpose. The least befuddled-appearing were the Mel'hachim. As warriors, they were accustomed to accompanying their patrons without question. In this case, where their loyalty was mingled with affection and a real sense of the peril involved, there was neither hesitation, nor uncertainty.

Surprisingly, the most uncertain was the Baron, T'Jules. Far more used to having an enemy he could see and challenge face-to-face, this unseen foe who threatened his small wife left him aimless and swinging at shadows. Meeting up with his new-found allies had done little to bolster his confidence. He ran over them again in his mind, as he had been doing from the moment of their meeting. Two fragile old people, a child, a mage who appeared, at best, barely able, the Mage's twin(?), who looked years older and even less able, two effete aristocrats, only one fighting woman, two mules, a sway-backed elderly mare, and a goat! He didn't even count the mare's apparent owner. What an army he had to lead! The concept that he was leading no one did not occur to him.

The Mel'hachim, on the other hand, knew exactly who was leading, no matter how incompetent and untried he seemed to the arrivals.

Jorgo addressed Kelgan with respect, in spite of inner misgiving. "In the same direction, Magician? You feel the same pull as before?"

Both T'Jules and Kelgan appeared equally startled. Kelgan, recovering, realized that he did, indeed, 'feel the pull.' It had been there all along, subtly growing.

As the day progressed, the forest, which had seemed endless, thinned, and crofts began to dot the landscape. The farmers, while looking on the whole prosperous, regarded the travelers sullenly and with suspicion. Few even neutral faces followed their progress, and voices muttered behind as they passed. Kelgan kept his hand hovering near his sword, noting that Terencia and the four new arrivals did the same. Feeling a bit amused at his pose of a man-at-arms, he nevertheless felt reassured by the press of the hilt under his palm. Remembering the encounter with the "thieves" made his scalp crawl a little, but he trusted the sword to know what to do, even if he didn't.

The habitations were thicker now, and a town soon hove into view. The houses were neat cottages, well-kept and with window boxes sprouting blooms. The villagers looked fairly prosperous, or at least not in rags, and there looked to be a respectable-sized population. More people, however, only meant more unfriendly faces turned on them; some with outright anger written there.

T'Jules pulled up his horse beside Kelgan. He and Daliane had been slowly riding their mounts at a walk in the forefront of the group, while the Mel'hachim occupied the rear. Sliding to the ground, he said in an undertone, "Looks like we may have trouble. These people have been harassed, very likely, and don't like strangers with swords."

A thunk punctuated his words; Daliane, glancing back, had in an instant dismounted and drawn her weapon. T'Jules, his face a shade paler, stared briefly at the arrow protruding from his saddle, before drawing his own sword and shouting, "Circle." The words were swept from his mouth as the next arrow found his shoulder. With a grunt, the Baron toppled over his mount's neck. Righting himself, he repeated the shout, "Circle."

Daliane was beside him. Knife out, she cut the feathered end off the arrow and pushed it through the Baron's shoulder. He made a slight sound through clenched teeth, but was otherwise silent. Jorgo had his shirt off and was tearing it into strips at impossible speed; handing them to Daliane, equally fast. She wadded the first and second up and used them to staunch the blood, then, with Jorgo's help, tightly bound the wound.

Kelgan, although no knight, had nevertheless instinctively faced outward at the Baron's command. A third arrow hit the ground between his feet, and a fourth the tree behind him. He was abstractly proud that he refrained from flinching.

"They're coming from the windows above us, and across the road," the Baron pointed out unnecessarily, since Kelgan had seen for himself the source of the problem. He opened his mouth to reply, when a fifth arrow tore part of his sleeve away, before embedding itself beside its brother in the tree.

Kelgan scarcely knew what hit him. One moment hand hovering nervously near his sword sheath, the next yelling like a demon from Darkness, he was charging *alone* up a flight of stairs to a second-story room. Bursting through the door—*I think it was locked!* a small part of his mind whimpered—he lay about him like the very fiend, himself. He barely noticed that Jorgo and Nadi had joined him, teeth gleaming wolfishly.

The five men in the room, armored and bearing a black and red crest, sprang to their feet to give fight. The sixth archer at the window had a mere second to turn toward the fury before Kelgan's sword lopped his bow-arm from its shoulder. The archer stared stupidly at the sanguine fountain that followed before collapsing.

Kelgan's mind went on whimpering as he whirled, parried a stroke aimed between his shoulder blades, and then dashed backhand across his opponent's neck, taking the head cleanly at the base of the helm.

The next thing Kelgan knew, Nadi was bending over him on the floor, patting his forehead with a wet and bloodied rag. "My hero," she murmured wickedly while Jorgo rumbled his amusement.

The familiar nausea threatened to choke him. Appraising the situation instantly, Nadi thrust one of the enemies' helms under his chin and raised him enough to use it efficiently.

With surprising gentleness, she wiped his face and mouth; and she and Jorgo helped him to his feet.

"Thanks," he whispered; then, more clearly, "Uh, you won't mention...."

"Never a word, my cousin," rumbled Jorgo. "We, too, have had our moments."

Eyeing the huge warrior, Kelgan doubted it, but weakly smiled his gratitude.

They let him totter down the stairs on his own, only offering an unobtrusive hand at his elbow when his knees threatened to betray him. When they emerged from the building, they faced a crowd of what seemed to be the entire village. To their amazement, a rousing cheer went up and several of the villagers crowded 'round to slap them on the back and excitedly express their appreciation.

Dazed, and still green, Kelgan tried to appear nonchalant and not stagger under the well-meant blows of the crowd. Catching T'Jules eye, he detected a twinkle there in spite of the Baron's obvious pain, but approbation, as well.

Daliane, ever kind-hearted, easily sensed Kelgan's conflicted emotions and threw her arm around his waist, being unable to reach higher, and exclaimed, careful not to overdo, "That was well done."

Neroma's eyebrows rose a millimeter and her hair stirred ever-so-slightly in the direction of the Baroness.

Feeling an unaccustomed weight on his leg as he strove to cut through the thronged villagers, Kelgan glanced down to find Piper clinging in adoration, his face flushed with unmistakable pride. Suddenly, the weakness and nausea fell away from him and he swept Piper up in his arms, unmindful of the blood spattered across his tunic. Piper was equally unaware, treating the victory as though one of his own.

Cal sidled up to Kelgan, speaking in a low tone intended for Kelgan's ear alone. "As soon as you went screaming up the stairs, everything changed. The whole village did a 180."

"A what?"

"Excuse me," Cal apologized, "I keep forgetting we don't speak the same language. I meant, they stopped being hostile and turned into our buddies."

"Buddies? Friends, allies?"

"Both."

Just then, the mules brayed in unison, for all the world like a trumpet fanfare.

"They want us to stay for a banquet in our honor. It seems those black and red guys are not exactly the most popular around here. From what I could gather, they are the minions of a rogue warlord, who's trying to become a real big shot all of a sudden. Seems he's showing an unusual amount of strength," Cal added meaningfully.

"You got all that in those few minutes?"

"Few minutes? Man, you were gone nearly an hour!"

Kelgan blinked stupidly.

Cal laughed and punched his arm. "Time flies when you're having fun, huh?"

"Fun." Kelgan continued to stand as if spellbound.

Cal squinted at him. "Not so great, this hero business," he opined shrewdly.

For a brief instant, Kelgan entertained the idea of putting his head down on his double's shoulder and weeping like a two-year-old. He conquered the impulse. "It has its drawbacks, especially when you don't know you're doing it."

Cal assessed him again and nodded slowly, obviously digesting Kelgan's words. He merely said, however, "So what about the big feast?"

"What, uh, Darkness, I don't know. What does everybody else think?"

"Well, the brown babe doesn't like the idea. Ma and Pa Kettle don't care, now that they've recovered the Zombie, and the Black and White twins are on the fence. Our warriors were with you so I don't know, but the royalty are looking stern."

Kelgan blinked stupidly a couple of more times, and then doubled up with laughter, causing Piper to cling like a monkey to avoid a nosedive. Kelgan managed to set him down safely, while still laughing until the tears ran.

"Ma and Pa who? Recovered the z-z-z!" Kelgan stuttered and sputtered; finally sitting with a plump on the ground, trying to compose himself, but only succeeding in setting off into another gale. He knew a large portion of his amusement was reaction, but it felt so good to release some of his pent-up emotions.

He gasped and choked as a great gout of cold water hit him. "Wha'?"

Terencia stood, empty canteen in hand and looking smug. "You were obviously hysterical."

Kelgan rose to his feet with dignity, glad his legs supported him. "I was merely amused."

"Yeah," agreed Cal, "I keep forgetting some things don't translate exactly, even *with* a spell." He winked at Kelgan over Terencia's shoulder. "Some of the things I say... well...." He shrugged.

Terencia looked dubious. "You were attracting too much attention, anyway," she asserted defensively.

"You're probably right. It's a warm day, and I needed cooling off." Kelgan looked ruefully down at his stained clothing. "And a bath."

T'Jules took the opportunity to draw away from the crowd of admiring villagers and approach Kelgan. "The townspeople are most insistent on feasting us; the festivities, however, will go on until well into the dark."

Admiring the Baron's ability to ignore what must have been severe pain, he needed no explanation of the T'Jules' concerns. "I think we must find pressing business down the road, which must be attended to before nightfall?"

"Those are my feelings, as well," T'Jules answered with a grim smile. "We must make every show of gratitude and appreciation, but tear ourselves away with great reluctance."

"Exactly," agreed Kelgan.

How did I get to play leader? he mused. *He's paying no attention to the di Nerrills; and I thought they were in charge.*

Neroma and Nevander pushed their way through the well-wishers, gently but persistently. Kelgan wondered how such a small village could muster such a horde, although there were probably no more than around fifty, he estimated. Such was their enthusiasm, however, they seemed more like hundreds.

T'Jules nudged Kelgan. "Speak to them."

"Me... uh... I?"

"Yes, you are the obvious choice." T'Jules ironic gaze did little to assure Kelgan on that point.

"You know..." he began.

"Speak to them." The Baron's voice remained mild, but the steel edge was unmistakable.

Kelgan swallowed, trying to push his Adam's apple back down to its proper place; thinking that if the sword could only make speeches, he would be in better shape.

He cleared his throat. "My friends," he squawked and started again, an octave lower. "My friends."

The crowd turned and rushed toward him. Wanting to flee, he held his ground as they all tried to touch him at once. "My friends," he repeated, "we are saddened to leave you in haste after your warm welcome." T'Jules covered a snort with a hasty cough. "However, we are on a sworn quest, and must not tarry... our oath forbids it. While its pursuit does not prevent us from offering service where we can, still it keeps us from remaining overlong. We leave you, nevertheless, with the best wishes of our hearts."

A cheer went up from many throats in the assemblage. Kelgan noticed, nonetheless, that some were taking in the motley group with some skepticism.

"Our vow has brought us together from all walks of life," he improvised, "some are warriors only in their souls, but all are one in the cause of justice," another muffled snort from behind him.

The mayor, or alderman, or whatever he was, leaped at the opportunity to regain the attention of his fellows and assured Kelgan that his words touched them all deeply. They understood perfectly, he insisted, unmistakable relief at the expense of a village-wide feast being lifted from his shoulders, lighting his face.

Back on the road, with the sincere good wishes and farewells of the village still echoing in their ears, T'Jules found irresistible the chance to rib Kelgan about his oratory. "Have I the honor of addressing a warrior of the soul?" he inquired mischievously.

Kelgan punched the Baron's good arm, harder than a jest required, and then blushed at his daring, "You wanted me to speechify."

T'Jules startled Kelgan by giving him a hearty one-armed hug. "And you did marvelously well for an impromptu effort. You told them what was mainly the truth—always best when lying—and made it sound a holy war, moreover."

Kelgan looked seriously at the Baron, but approached the subject with a roundabout question. "You heard about the warlord?"

T'Jules' eyebrows knitted as he considered the real meaning behind Kelgan's question. "That, too, crossed my mind, a sudden show of might, considerable organization, previously not much of anything. We haven't encountered much so far, resistance increasing, do you think?"

"Uh, I thought maybe."

"Kelgan, you are new to warfare," the first time the Baron had actually used his name, "but you are more than you think you are. You see much and clearly. Stop touching your forelock every time you render an opinion."

"I don't..." Kelgan began, then said, "Yes, I see what you mean."

"You are a Mage, which most of us are not, and you have a stout heart." He waved his hand as Kelgan started to protest. "You are doing it again."

"It's because I know I'm sailing under false colors." Kelgan sighed. "I never really became a Mage, and I'm certainly not a swordsman."

"Oh? I would have said you were exactly that—the sword's man."

"Rather obvious, then?"

"Not at all... ah, well... perhaps a little. However, you *can* wield it, because it *knows* you can."

T'Jules' calm acceptance of the relationship—*yes, I guess that's what it is,* Kelgan admitted to himself—between him and the sword took him aback.

"And, as to your *next* question, yes, we have discussed it, myself, my wife, and the Mel'hachim. You don't need our approval, since it is as it is, but we approve, nevertheless, the Mel'hachim, especially."

On hearing this, and without realizing, Kelgan straightened his shoulders, rising well above the Baron, who looked up with a grin.

With more confidence, Kelgan insisted, "Let me see to that shoulder."

T'Jules obediently complied with a grimace of pain he tried to conceal. Kelgan felt a pang of guilt that he had not immediately made the offer. He tried to say as much to the Baron, but T'Jules cut him off before he had gotten more than one or two words out.

"Wait a minute. Weren't you saving our lives?"

Nonplussed, Kelgan could think of no answer, except to blush.

He gently unwrapped the hasty bandage the little Baroness had concocted for her husband, admiring her work as he did so. Holding the arm straight out, he told the Baron, "This will hurt at first."

T'Jules gave a nod, the pallor of his face told Kelgan his words did not come as a surprise.

"Sanatio coireo nunctis."

The Baron gave a gasp, color draining, and then returning, to his face. The wound, while still obvious, no longer bled, and it had lost much of its angry, red color. "This will be sore for a while," Kelgan observed.

T'Jules looked at him with an enigmatic expression, somewhere between bemusement and amusement. Near them, Cal stared with a similar enigmatic gaze and slight frown. He shook his head and turned away.

The farmlands they had been traveling through once again gave way to increasing woods, and shadows once more crowded the roadway. Kelgan knew they should be on their way. Roses blew backwards toward him, and he knew Neroma was taking no chance at being caught unaware.

At this sign, the Baron mounted with one-handed haste and rode to the rear of the straggling column. Kelgan felt a nudge between his shoulder blades as one of the mules chose to remind him the dinner hour approached.

··· 58 ···

Goin' Thy Way

Capriola bleated and Bethne, who had taken to riding more and more, chucked at her, eliciting a second bleat with a distinctly stubborn tone to it. Kelgan increased his stride and laid a hand on Bethne's shoulder.

"Are you all right, Bethne?"

She turned a tired face up at him. "Nuthin' wrong that bein' twenty years younger wouldn't cure."

He smiled and patted her, thinking that she looked a bit old and fragile for a "sworn quest" and a holy war.

After consulting with Neroma, Ez joined them. "Lady di Nerrill sez we're thinkin' about stoppin' soon. We all be a mite hungry an' it's startin' to darken up."

Kelgan nodded and strode forward again to catch up to Neroma. "Bethne's not doing so well," he said.

"I know, and I would do what I could, but age is not something I can ameliorate," she responded like syrup on corn cakes.

Kelgan stared. "I wonder." He turned and rejoined Ez and Bethne.

"Bethne, do you trust me?" he inquired.

"Why, Kellie, that boy thinks the world o' you, and chillern allus knows. If he duz, then I duz, too."

Speechless for a moment, Kelgan cleared his throat and blinked away the moisture forming an unexpected film over his eyes. Taking Bethne's hand tightly in his, he ordered, "Then repeat exactly as I tell you, *'Juvenissah meah.'* Say it now."

Bethne struggled a bit with the unfamiliar syllables, but finally got the pronunciation to Kelgan's satisfaction. "I want you to say it five times before you go to sleep, and five times when you wake up." He crossed the fingers of his free hand. "This will make you feel a lot better." *I hope,* he thought.

"What duz it mean?"

"Uh, we mages cannot reveal our secrets." *And we don't want to say that we don't know exactly what we're doing.*

Was it just his hopeful imagination, or did she look just a tad less drawn? He decided that if it worked, it was still too early to make a difference. His "remedy" was constructed more on belief than reality, he feared, but if she trusted him to work real magic, then it just might *be* real magic.

Kelgan plodded along mindless of the path, musing on the strange sameness of the days, broken by outbursts of murder, of course, but otherwise get up, walk in an unexplained direction, for an unknown destination, eat, sleep, and then do it all over again the next day. Even the occasional killing seemed like part of the routine. If he really could do something for Bethne, he felt it might lift some of the horror he could not squelch at the thought of depriving even the most unworthy of life.

He thought uneasily of the sword, and its mysterious donor— friend or foe. Its power made the hairs of his arms stand up like Neroma's. Why a power like that had been entrusted to one least able to control it baffled him. He mentally gave himself a kick. T'Jules had warned him against underestimation; there had to be something of which he was unaware. He reviewed his actions against the black-and-red soldiers, although that was something of an exercise in futility, since most of it was just a blur. What he could remember made his stomach knot. He couldn't even imagine wanting to do that as an occupation, as did Jorgo and Nadi. The Mel'hachim treated hacking an opponent to bits as a matter of course.

He stopped short as a thought struck him, then moved hastily forward as one of the mules butted him from behind. Could it be? Did the donor of the blade realize he, Kelgan, would be squeamishly reluctant to wield it, thus providing a slight check on its deadly proclivities?

That can't be it, he told himself, *when it takes off, I have no control,* none *at all... although....*

One of the mules nudged him again, and whiffled softly in his ear. Brought back to himself, he glanced to see Pellerin's eyes fixed on him, that eerie occasional awareness manifest in their depths. His nape crawled. He looked around with foreboding, noticing the quiet, the utter lack of the usual twitters, snaps, rustles and croaks associated with light forest. Wisps of greasy looking fog snaked among the trunks, its oddly purposeful meanderings uncomfortably giving the appearance of following the party.

Seized by a near panic, he croaked out, "Wait."

T'Jules, at the front, and Jorgo, who had taken over the rear position, stopped instantly without a question. Capriola gave a rather querulous bleat as she was yanked up by Bethne, but the entire group stopped in its tracks as silently and speedily as a trained unit.

"You noticed the fog, too." It was not a question—from Cal.

"Well, actually, it was the mules," Kelgan was forced to admit.

"The mules!" Cal looked askance.

"They're really very bright," Kelgan asserted defensively.

"I'm sure."

The twins conferred anxiously with the Bervaines. The smell of roses grew stronger. Neroma nodded apologetically in his direction.

"We had just begun to feel apprehensive, my Mage, when you called out." Nevander patted his arm. "I congratulate you on your vigilance and perception."

"Uh, actually, it was the mules," Kelgan admitted for the second time.

"You have trained them exceedingly well, my Mage," was the dry response.

A low rumble from Jorgo set them all off; even Bethne laughed heartily. Was it just wishful thinking, or did the wisps of fog seem to wince and retreat? He felt Neroma's eyes; she swiveled several tresses in the direction of the trees with a nod of approval.

Terencia, however, continuously scanned their surroundings

with patent anxiety. "We need to find a clearing," she grated between her teeth, "so we can see." The unusually shrill tone of her voice caused them all to carefully regard her.

Nadi edged to her side. "There is something you are not telling us, woman of war," an edge as sharp as her sword tinged her statement.

"I... I can't...." Terencia faltered.

Nadi's hand dropped almost casually to her weapon, but her meaning rang as loud as crossed steel in the silence.

Kelgan's attention was caught, however, by the fog. Where it had seemed to shy away, earlier, it had thickened markedly, and eagerly hung just beyond arm's length. Terencia, meanwhile, stiffened and dropped her own hand to her sword hilt.

"Stop," interjected Kelgan, "it likes it. That's what it wants. Laugh... laugh... say something funny. Anything," he ordered.

He knew he was babbling, but Cal was the first to catch his meaning, "Hey, did you hear the one about the lawyer lost in the desert and even the vultures wouldn't have him?"

T'Jules threw back his head and guffawed, albeit with a slightly forced quality. "If you mean readers of the law, we, too, make up the same kind of stories for our amusement."

Cal reeled off a few more 'readers of the law' jests, which all endeavored to laugh at vigorously, although the meaning of much of it must have been obscure, at best. The Mel'hachim added a few humorous anecdotes of their mercenary adventures, and the Baron was emboldened to sing a slightly bawdy drinking song, which caused Daliane to exclaim, "Oh, Tee Jee," in mock dismay.

The fog whisked backward into the denser protection of the trees with preternatural haste. In spite of their relief, the party was in concord with Piper, who observed, "Kinda easy, wasn't it?"

They settled in. Kelgan felt he had perfected his Allergus spell, but feared overuse would wear it out. The wards were at their strongest, and Neroma had thrown a touch of lavender into the mix, to mask any suggestion of anger. It was obvious to Kelgan that Terencia had sagged with relief when he had stepped into the burgeoning quarrel between her and Nadi; putting off for a while longer the question he wished answered, as well. What did she hide?

The morning dawned warm and fair. Now that Kelgan thought about it, every morning had been much the same. The weather, with the exception of the menacing fog, had been surprisingly bland. Even though it was the tail-end of summer, best time for a quest in Kelgan's opinion, still, thunderstorms did kick up fairly often at this time of the year, drenching the ground and then rolling on swiftly. The continued dry mildness made Kelgan suspicious.

Easy, he thought, *too easy.*

He let the mules precede him and fell in with Jorgo, who slid from the saddle in response to Kelgan's questioning gaze.

"Is it just me, or does it seem that we're not encountering much in the way of difficulties."

Jorgo's eyes twinkled for a moment as he obviously recalled the skirmish with the black-and-red liveried opponents, then sobered. He didn't immediately answer Kelgan's query, but considered it fully.

Kelgan went on. "I know I had the help of the sword, not to mention you and Nadi, but don't you think even that was a little too smooth? They could have picked us, or at least the horses, off easily. How come nobody but the Baron even got a scratch? And we haven't even had a drop of rain. And...."

Jorgo laid a restraining hand on his arm, "The Baron and I have also asked these same questions of each other. The voices try to assail us when they can, but otherwise we have seen little resistance. Even the fog seemed too quickly forced to retreat. It would seem it is only there to remind us that *something* waits."

"Herding us, do you think?"

"That is my thought," growled the warrior.

"Do we just march on into the open jaws?"

"Yes, my Mage friend, I think we do."

Kelgan sighed, an action which felt absurdly inadequate. Jorgo appeared to catch his thought and chuckled.

"I only have the sword, you know," Kelgan pointed out.

Jorgo stared at him in astonishment. "You are a Mage!"

Kelgan bethought himself of what T'Jules had said, and flushed, embarrassed at being caught whining again.

"Of course, I am. Sometimes I forget that part."

Jorgo's amusement grew and he fetched Kelgan a buffet to the shoulder, which was only half playful.

"Keep it to the front of your mind, my friend."

Staggering, Kelgan assured him he would do his very best not to forget. He wobbled up to rejoin the mules.

··· 59 ···

Peek-a-Boo

They drew close to each other that evening to discuss the issue Kelgan had raised. Remembering that he actually was a mage, Kelgan manufactured a small breeze, which soughed lightly among the trees to cover their voices, without, he hoped, dispelling the scent ward.

Pellerin, of course, simply stood with his mare, and his parents settled protectively near him. Bethne sent him puzzled, although meant to be reassuring, glances never succeeding in eliciting a response either from her son or whatever animated him.

Piper, as had become his habit, leaned against Kelgan's knees. A little to Kelgan's surprise, the twins sat on either side of him as though declaring their solidarity, while facing them, Jorgo and Nadi squeezed Daliane tightly between them, still reluctant to trust anything but themselves. Terencia and the Baron flanked Bethne and Ezrael, clearly the most vulnerable. Cal sat just a little apart, still feeling a bit of a stranger.

Without knowing why, Kelgan found himself shooting the same glances at Pellerin as he and the others talked and ate. There was a key there, he was sure of it, that unlocked part of the mystery. As if in response, Pellerin's head swung in his direction and the hollow eyes met his for a long enough instant to cause Kelgan to choke on the morsel he was chewing.

Piper pounded him on the back and muttered, "Don't get his attention."

"Umph," strangled Kelgan in agreement.

The discussion resolved nothing. Everyone but Bethne and Ezrael, who had no frame of reference, had noticed the mild weather, the lack of obstacles, the only token difficulties, even the comparative ease with which they had all fallen in together.

"Well, I'm not so sure about that!" exclaimed Cal.

The others had a short laugh in sympathy, and Neroma, to Kelgan's unexpected rush of jealousy, patted the ground beside herself to draw Cal closer into the group.

"We're not getting anywhere," Kelgan proclaimed. "We just say the same things and ask the same questions for which we have no answers." *I'm starting to sound like Nevander,* he thought, *pedantically stating the obvious.*

T'Jules shifted his weight in disagreement. "No," he replied with decision, "we don't have the answers, but we are asking the *right* questions, and we are all much more aware, both of our common purpose, and of the fact of our being manipulated."

"Herded," Kelgan corrected.

Jorgo winked at him, humorously.

"Well, herded, if you like." The Baron grinned widely and wolfishly, "But it remains to be seen what type of herd we really are."

Kelgan felt strangely reassured. He also wondered if old Bethie and Ez had a trick or two up their faded sleeves. Certainly, they showed no fear, now that they were reunited with Pellerin, who bore the distinction of being the most fearful thing encountered thus far.

"My Mage," insisted Nevander, "you must try to keep negative thoughts at bay. Neroma and I can only do so much to keep the voices silent—*you* must believe. Remember, you were chosen."

Kelgan started to respond, "Yeah, as what, the weakest link?" In the face of the continual remonstrations from nearly everyone in the group, he pulled himself up lamely and stuttered, "Uh... yes... I guess... I mean, yes, I'll remember. We all have a purpose, here... uh... I think."

This characteristic utterance struck the assembly as thoroughly hilarious, and the meeting ended in explosive laughter.

As though an alarm had been triggered, the morning dawned cold and drizzly, with the fog much too knowingly close for comfort.

Kelgan gasped awake as a wet *something* touched his cheek. Bursting reflexively into a jolly tune he had heard at an inn, he was relieved to see it was not a deadly tendril of fog, but a dripping tendril of Neroma's. The tendril wrapped itself around his mouth and cut off his voice abruptly. She put a finger to her lips, then bent to whisper in scarcely more than an exhaled breath, "Come."

Obeying her command, he rolled away from Piper's slight form as carefully as he could. Seeing that the others had not yet stirred, he rose silently, and with some surprise at his ability, to follow her. The sun had not yet made an appearance, and the light was barely sufficient to make out her form in front of him. She pointed toward the trees, where the fog hung sullenly just out of reach of the wards. Kelgan followed her gesture to where a doubled gleam shone out of the fog. Somehow Kelgan felt certain the gleam was not caused by something normal and reassuring, such as ravening wolves, or man-eating Gilka bears. As he watched, it was joined by a second doubled gleam, before they both winked out of sight.

"They—or someone—watch," was her brief observation, before she returned silently to her bedroll. Kelgan stared unseeingly into the canopy of trees for the time remaining until morning.

Another day dawned, or rather lightened. The mild weather, which had seemed so suspicious, now, even more suspiciously, swung the other way. The temperature fell precipitously, and wetness dripped from every leaf, limb, and stem.

In spite of a dragging, albeit irrational, reluctance to call attention to either himself or the rest of the party, Kelgan resorted to a brief flash of firepower to muster a blaze from the now soggy wood available. He reminded himself that whomever they pursued was already fully aware of them, and that Neroma's wards certainly broadcasted their presence. Still, he could not shake off the unease which crept up and down his spine like so many tiny fleas.

Neroma, either reading his face or his mind, offered, "It hardly matters what we do. We are known and seen, so let us be comfortable."

Her words ignited a spark of defiance in Kelgan, who gestured extravagantly, shouting, "*Igneaus toto.*" He nearly set the forest aflame.

"Er, uh," he amended, "*Igneaus partialis.*"

One of Neroma's rare giggles (rare until Kelgan had come along) escaped her, joined by snorts from Cal and Terencia.

Kelgan's eyes roved over the group of now slightly warmer and drier compatriots, stopping with a shock when he regarded the tiny Baroness. As slight as she had been when they had first encountered her, she seemed to have melted away in the short time they had been together. The pallor of her elfin face gave her almost a glow in the dim surround of the trees.

Kelgan rushed to her side and grasped her hands, startling both T'Jules and her Mel'hachim protectors. "Wha'...?" began the Baron.

Jorgo, however, gave a Kelgan a sharper look. "He has seen something we do not."

To the consternation of all, and as though suddenly released, Daliane collapsed forward into Kelgan's arms, shaking as though with the ague. Kelgan, although caught off guard, scooped her up and then stood uncertain of what to do next. He felt, rather than saw, Cal at his elbow.

"She's not the only one. I've been watching Bethne."

Kelgan swung around, still clutching the trembling Baroness.

The Baron, by this time nearly hopping with anxiety, attempted to seize her from Kelgan's hold.

To his surprise, Jorgo restrained him. "Not yet, there is something very wrong here."

His eye lighting on Bethne, who was slumped at the base of an alder, Kelgan was shocked anew at her haggard appearance. Her plump frame had wasted to a frightening wisp. Baffled, he fought to understand how such a transformation could have occurred unnoticed. A nudge from behind sent him swinging around again. One of the mules stared fixedly at him; then deliberately pointed its ears away toward its partner, barely standing with heaving sides and shaking legs. Every rib on its sides stood out like a plowed field.

"No," declared Kelgan. "It can't be. I'm with them all the time. I'd know...."

His protest was cut short by an insistent Piper, who had been tending to Capriola, and giving Pellerin's old mare a short rub. "What's happening? Why're you carrying her Ladyship?" A slight ring of indignation at the impropriety edged his tone.

"Can't you see?" was Kelgan's exasperated response. "She's terribly ill; and so is Bethne; and just look at the mule, besides."

Piper surveyed the named individuals; an increasing look of incomprehension darkening his small face. "They looks all right to me," he pronounced. "Bethie's lookin' a mite tired, but the mule's as healthy as I am."

"No, they're not. You have to look harder and believe me," asserted Kelgan firmly.

Piper tried again, screwing up his eyes in what would have been a comical expression at any other time. "S'no use," he whimpered. "They looks just fine."

Pellerin's old mare gave a surprisingly full-throated whinny: followed by the hollow cadence of Pellerin's own voice. "Seeming is not believing," was the short announcement.

Bewilderment followed. then Kelgan had what he hoped was an inspiration. He knelt, still cradling Daliane in his arms.

"Tell me what you see," he gently bade Piper.

Piper caught on immediately. "I sees different from you folks!"

Kelgan nodded. "I think so."

Piper scrutinized Daliane as though he were marking the holder of a well-filled purse, in a crowd, "She don't look no worse than the rest of you do." He blushed, and added so low Kelgan was barely able to hear, "'Cept she's better-lookin' than *almost* everybody."

If Kelgan could have added Piper to the burden in his arms, he would have swept the boy up in an unrestrained embrace. He knew Piper would have objected fiercely, especially in front of everyone, but a rush of affection filled his chest to bursting.

He contented himself with just asking, "How about Bethne, and the mule?"

Piper gave them the same careful scrutiny. "Same thing. Bethie really is tired, though," he added earnestly.

Kelgan shut his eyes and repeated, "Seeming is not believing," like the words to a spell.

After a number of repetitions, Daliane interrupted him. "I think you can put me down now."

He opened his eyes, which met hers quite close to his face. He realized he had been squeezing her up to his chest as he had been muttering Pellerin's statement. Blushing, he set her on her feet, not all that surprised to find her looking, if not quite healthy, at least as well as she had been looking during their time together. He felt none of his original animosity, and he wondered why he ever had.

Bethne, too, had regained some semblance of vitality, although her wrinkled apple-doll face *was,* as Piper had said, *really* tired. The mules, which were conferring (Kelgan could not think of any other word) with snorts and grunts, looked back at Kelgan, ears pricked forward in identical poses of inquiry.

A wisp of memory returned to him. Piper had not been fooled by the Seeming he had constructed for the twins back at the marketplace (it seemed so long ago!). It appeared that Piper saw clearly, through the eyes of a child; straight to a person's reality, not the mask one wore.

"Henceforth," he announced to Piper, "you are our Assistant-Seer-in-Training."

The child's chest swelled with pride. "Humph," he said importantly to laughter and applause all around.

"I'm always the last to know," said the Baroness in mock exasperation. "What just happened?"

T'Jules had recaptured his small spouse, holding her as though she would evaporate if he let go. He regarded Kelgan with outward calm, but terror lurked in the depths of his eyes. "Yes, what *did* just happen?"

Neroma and Nevander added their grave looks to T'Jules, worry patent on their ivory visages.

"They penetrated the wards." Neroma's even deeper-than-usual contralto gave the words the weight of an organ funeral dirge.

Kelgan gulped and nodded, sickly aware of the truth.

"I will double them," asserted Neroma.

Kelgan, foreseeing a journey continuing through tear-blinded eyes and permanently snuffling nose, began to protest. Nevander interrupted him in the final stages of exasperation. "My Mage, must we remind you *every* day that you *are* a Mage? Surely there is *something* you can do for yourself, if not for the rest of us who may be sensitive."

Kelgan slapped his forehead. "I keep *forgetting.*"

Jorgo's basso rumble set them all off; even Piper chortled merrily at Kelgan's discomfiture.

To Kelgan's surprised gratitude, Terencia, of all people, sprang to his defense. "Of course, he forgets himself," she exclaimed hotly, "he has to think of *us* all of the time. And," she added, "I think he's proved he does a good job." Her spirited defense was rather marred by the addition of a low-voiced, "Most of the time."

The others good-naturedly agreed, and dispersed to break camp. Only Cal, who had been silently deliberating, said slowly, "So... what we saw was not what we got."

Kelgan nodded "Essentially."

Cal grasped Kelgan's elbow. "These guys sure like special effects, don't they? A lot of smoke and mirrors—a lot of smoke, anyhow, maybe the mirrors later."

Kelgan gave a gruff bark of laughter, understanding the reference perfectly well. He only hoped their as-yet-unseen foes were of the "hedge" magician variety, but queasily knowing they weren't.

"They seem to be holding off for reasons we can't even surmise," he answered Cal. "Small inconveniences, nothing of substance— playing with us, dragging us in...." He heard a slight whine beginning to edge his words.

Cal raised his brows. "I don't think I'd call the archers a 'small inconvenience.'"

"They could have picked us off easily, and you know it," Kelgan retorted with some heat the whine gone.

Cal grinned and slapped him on the shoulder. "Maybe so, but they only got off a couple of shots. You kept that from happening," he said dryly.

Kelgan, in spite of a slight *frisson* at the memory, could not help grinning back and saying with patently false humility, "Well, yes, but it really wasn't me."

Cal snorted. "The villagers didn't know that," He added soberly, "Did you think what just happened was intended to be another small inconvenience?"

The color drained from Kelgan's countenance, as he thought what might have resulted had Piper not been immune from the lethal illusion. "You think they're...?"

"Upping the ante? Yes."

Again, Kelgan caught the intended meaning, if not the exact translation. "And?"

"You've got to act like a big boy. Even the Baron knows you're in charge here. I don't know why, either," he said impatiently as Kelgan seemed about to speak. "You certainly keep your leadership qualities under wraps."

Being criticized for a lack of authority by, for all intents and purposes, himself struck Kelgan as not only absurd, but unfair. "You're a fine one to talk," he asserted, then wondered how he knew that.

Cal hesitated, then grimaced. "Yeah, you're right, but that's all the more reason for you, for us, to grow up. I'm not a mage, but I do have some abilities that might come in handy—a knowledge of the law, for example," then doubtfully, "maybe." Pausing for a moment, he added, "If I had a sword, or a bow, that might be something of a help."

He continued, "You've got the power, but you're afraid to exercise it. Maybe we were meant to be a team. There must be some reason I'm here as the only outsider. I've been giving *that* a lot of thought. For instance, why did I just abandon *my car* (very important vehicle, almost like a woman, was the sense Kelgan received) and come with you? How come I just accept everything you people say? Do you still have that calming spell operating on me?"

"No," Kelgan admitted, "not since you stopped screeching."

"Okay, then. Someone, or some whatever, has me going along for the ride. Maybe the same whatever that has Pelly going along for the ride, too. Whatever *it* is, it doesn't like the whatevers *they* are. We're being pushed from the back and pulled from the front, whether we like it or not. Since that's a given, we've got to muster up all the strength we have. It's obvious we were chosen for some quality we haven't figured out yet; it can't be random."

"Why not?" Kelgan demanded.

"Use your head," exasperation made Cal snarl, "because of *us*."

Kelgan stared, thoughts working furiously. Himself, doubled, but from another world? Dimension? Universe? Bringing a different perspective to... well, their situation, muddled as it was. Neroma and Nevander, also doubled—the Mel'hachim, as nearly doubles as mates could be Bethne and Ez, too. *No, he shook his head, that didn't work... well... maybe. What about Piper, Terencia,* and, with a shudder, *Pellerin?*

"I don't see how that makes a difference, or gives us an advantage, or whatever you're suggesting," he answered stubbornly and with a trace of petulance.

"Man, I thought I had personality problems," Cal responded with disgust. "What's with you? Why are you so determined to be down on everything, especially yourself? Were you always like this?"

Kelgan thought back to his halcyon days at the Academy, where he had been so sure, so confident, so arrogant—believing in his demonstrably superior talent. "No," he admitted, "but I've learned a few things."

"And forgotten everything else? I heard the Bobbseys went looking for you... deliberately."

"Bobbseys... The di Nerrills?"

"Yes."

"It's true," Kelgan answered thoughtfully, "but they were somewhat disappointed."

"At what?"

"Well," Kelgan started slowly, "I'm headblind, it seems."

Cal looked a question.

"I can't hear thoughts. However, they discovered I'm unusually resistant *to* them, except at certain times—just before falling asleep, for example, or just when waking up. I have to actually let my guard down, either deliberately or accidentally."

Cal slapped his forehead. "Did they complain about your other abilities?"

"Uh, no."

"Has it occurred to you that they think you're just fine, that that gives you legitimacy and that you're doing this to yourself? Incidentally, you're playing right into the hands of the voices. They don't even have to wait for you to let down your guard. You've decided you're inferior, and nobody's going to talk you out of it. I've watched them try, and you give them your mealy-mouthed promises, and go right back to feeling sorry for yourself. When are you going to wise up?"

For the second time in the conversation, Kelgan was struck by the absurdity of being chastised by himself; as though his mirror had suddenly talked back to him.

A grin quirked the corners of his mouth. "All right, I won't make any promises, but I'll try to live up to *us*," he said as he placed sly emphasis on the last word.

To his surprise, Cal did not laugh. Instead, he reached for Kelgan's hand, holding it tightly in both of his. Pressing it for a moment, he dropped it and turned on his heel without a word, pausing to give Bethne a hand into the goat cart.

Mid-Term—The Second Test

The fog swirled greasily just out of reach as the group prepared for another damp, monotonous day. Terencia's tension grew so palpably from hour to hour, Kelgan began to wonder if she would suddenly shatter into hundreds of small brown shards. As for himself, he wished for anything, no matter how dire, to break the sameness. He hastily squelched those thoughts in trepidation, afraid to be heard even though the twins thought his mind unreadable as long as he remained vigilant.

Have I been? He fretted, *did I let myself slip?*

"Doubting yourself again, my Hero?" Nadi slipped her arm through his companionably. "Ride with me on my horse and let the young one demonstrate how well he manages the pack animals. I wish to speak with you, and Piper would be very proud."

Kelgan assented, curious to know of what the warrior "wished to speak."

Accordingly, he detailed Piper to lead the mules—astride one of them if he wished—telling him he knew no one else could handle them as well, making the child's frail chest swell with pride. Kelgan sat the boy atop the pack on one beast and looked long in the animal's eye. The mule responded with a wink and a nudge. Satisfied that all was well, he mounted a little awkwardly behind Nadi.

They rode for a time in silence at the head of the party. The rest were equally silent, whether on foot or astride, the depressing effect of the fog numbing them all.

After a time, Nadi broke the quiet, startling Kelgan out of a semi-doze, even though her voice was little more than a whisper.

"Tell me all that you can about your double."

"We told you about his arrival when we met up with you," Kelgan protested.

"No, I want *you* to tell me all that *you* can."

"On the grounds that I would *know* myself?"

"No, that you might *observe* yourself."

For some curious reason, her response tickled Kelgan. He remained silent for a time, considering for a time whether he actually *had* observed himself. Slowly, he began to comply with her request.

"Well, I didn't like him at all at first."

Nadi made a noise somewhere between a chuckle and a snort. "Since you seem to have difficulty liking yourself, this does not come as a great revelation."

"You didn't know me before. I liked myself only too well. At least... I don't know... I thought I had superior ability and potential."

"Then you saw the world?"

"Exactly so."

"But you have let it discourage you too easily. I know that the voices have assisted you along this path, but you are easily led; therefore, they have exploited your weakness. However, go on with your observations."

"Now that I know him better, I can see that both of us are just as you have said, easy to discourage. But he's got a lot more gumption, and a lot more wisdom, too, than I thought."

Kelgan could not see Nadi's grin. Keeping her voice carefully neutral, she asked, "So, you have come to believe we can depend on him when the occasion arises?"

Kelgan chose his words carefully—Nadi's tactics had not escaped him. "I think you can rely on him just as much as you can on me."

Nadi swiveled in the saddle to look at him. Her white teeth flashed wide and incandescent. "That is all I need to know, my Hero."

Kelgan gave her a hug that would have threatened the ribs of a less stalwart warrior.

"Me, too," he chortled, sliding from the saddle and dropping a lot less awkwardly to the ground.

He hastened back to where Piper proudly drove the mules like a seasoned muleteer. The mules, in turn, seemed to be enjoying it to the hilt. Both of them nudging Kelgan and rolling their eyes back to the little figure sitting bolt upright and masterful on the packs. Their benign expressions spoke volumes of suppressed mirth.

When Kelgan inquired how things were going, the youngster replied haughtily, "Why, nothin' to it. I could do this all day."

Kelgan lifted Piper from the pack, and set him on the ground. As soon as he had, the mules seemed seized by the spirit of Darkness itself, and began nipping (Kelgan, themselves, the brambles on the verge), kicking, braying, and generally acting as though they had been 'laid out with the tinkers.'

As Kelgan stared, astonished, one of the mules nudged him again; he took the hint and assured Piper that he would leave him to it. He then dropped back to let the T'Jules, who was leading his mount, catch up. Behind him came Bethne and Ezrael with the goat cart. After them, the Baroness, slowly walking her steed with the twins at either side; and then, finally, Jorgo bringing up the rear. Cal and Terencia engaged in conversation next to him. A thrill of fear shot through Kelgan as he realized the party was one short.

He clutched spasmodically at the Baron's arm. "Where's Pellerin?" he gasped.

The Baron, quick to pick up Kelgan's alarm, cried "Halt!" in a stentorian shout that would have halted an avalanche (or possibly set one off).

Bethne had turned at the sound, understood instantly, and added her scream to the echoes of the Baron's. The small band condensed into a knot, all facing outward and scanning the road in both directions.

"Darkness to this fog," T'Jules growled. "He might be ten feet away and we'd miss him."

Kelgan agreed. "But what could happen to him? I mean, that hasn't... I mean, he's...."

Thinking then of Bethne, Kelgan hurried to her side. She was lying back in the cart, completely inert. Ezrael turned a face of piteous woe on him.

"I cain't rouse her." His tone sounded completely despondent.

"Don't worry, Ez," Kelgan said automatically, thinking, *No, let me do it.*

He didn't like the faint thready pulse he felt, nor the waxy texture of Bethne's skin, moon pale. He breathed a little easier as he recited his healing cantrip and saw her respond slightly. Her eyelids fluttered open, but the look in her eyes made his heart constrict. He wanted to tell her it would be all right, but knew she would only have contempt for a lie.

"We'll do our best to find him, Bethne. The Baron and I—we'll retrace our steps and leave Jorgo and Nadi and Terencia with you. The di Nerrills will try to feel for him." Kelgan realized he hadn't asked the others, just decided for himself.

Surreptitiously making the sign of Light, he laid out his idea to the rest.

"I'm coming with you," Cal asserted in a tone that brooked no argument. "Give me a spare sword."

Daliane offered her extra, favoring Cal with a smile of pure appreciation. The Baron took note with a little frown, then shrugged sheepishly.

"We are all glad of your company," he acknowledged.

Kelgan nodded vigorously, thinking that Cal would perhaps be proving the truth of his all-too-recent assurances to Nadi.

"We will take Daliane's horse and mine," said the Baron. "You had better ride double on mine, and I will manage on hers, I hope," he muttered under his breath, thinking ill-humoredly of his recent contretemps with Daliane's steed.

The other two agreed, although not without misgivings. The Baron's war stallion presented a daunting challenge to two inexperienced riders. Nevertheless, they mounted up, Kelgan at the reins, Cal with sword in hand.

"Just don't wave that with too much enthusiasm," Kelgan cautioned.

"When I wave it, it won't be with enthusiasm," Cal countered.

The three moved out slowly, back the way they had come. While the fog kept its distance from them in front, it closed quickly behind, blotting out all trace of their waiting companions. They could see no more than three feet in any direction, and it seemed to lie like a damp sheep's pelt over all sound, as well. Calvin's nervous gulp sounded preternaturally loud in the weighted stillness. T'Jules continually scanned the track below their feet for signs that Pellerin might have turned off into the trees. He shook his head, dismay written large on his countenance. "Ours are the only tracks. It's as though no one has passed this way in years."

Cal's gulp sounded even louder.

It occurred to Kelgan to wonder why there had been no question from any that, of course, they would search for Pelly, a young man all assumed had not been among the living for some time. Animated by some awful force they dared not explore too deeply, and yet... one of their own. They had become a unit with astonishing speed, and they would not easily yield one of their members.

Between one step and the next, the fog vanished, revealing a sight that took the three aback and stopped their breath. Pellerin, his old mare, a brown-clad figure, and nine armed men garbed in black and red stood before them.

The figure in brown faced away from the three, a drawn sword dangling limply from its fingers. Pelly sat his mare, his stare blank as always, directed nowhere, seeing no one.

"Oh, Darkness," Kelgan whispered.

One who appeared to be in command of the black and red number directed a scornful glance at the approaching threesome. Amusement tinged his query as he asked, "And who might you be?"

"We have come to secure our friend," T'Jules responded with assurance far exceeding the reality of the situation.

On hearing this, the leader guffawed loudly, prompting echoes from his cohorts. The brown-clad stranger, however, wheeled to face them with both obvious relief and gleeful anticipation.

Shock nailed the rescuers to the spot. Only the leader's cry of, "At them!" forced them into action. As the armed band moved to cut them down, the familiar tingle swept over Kelgan. He leapt from the horse as the sword leapt from its sheath into his hand. His arm hewed wildly right, left, front, rear. He scarcely noticed that Cal spurred the war horse straight into the parade, chopping with Dally's sword as with an ax. The remote part of Kelgan, which held his awareness of "selfhood", silently commented on the fact that the hewing and hacking didn't bother him nearly as much anymore. Good or bad? Who was to say?

He did retain enough awareness to realize the brown-clad stranger, whose face he had not marked before the fray began, was no stranger to warfare. Amazingly efficient with not only a sword, but a short dagger, the unknown ally more than made up for the lack of numbers on their side by moving as though partnered by someone invisible. As for Cal, he demonstrated a prowess that registered as a slight shock inside Kelgan's otherwise occupied brain. The Baron seemed to be having what looked like a rather enjoyable time, his berserker's grin never leaving his face.

Astonished by the furious response generated by the three arrivals—aided by the brown-clad figure—the remaining attackers still on their feet fled. The sword, seeming to know, turned instantly quiescent.

Panting, Kelgan realized belatedly that some of the blood which splattered his chest and legs was his own. The realization came from the fact that his side had begun to smart fiercely. Knees wobbling, he sank to the ground amidst the ghastly reminders of the battle.

The Baron dropped beside him, alarm making his movements jerky.

"It's just a flesh wound, I think," Kelgan halfway reassured the two of them. Holding his side, he muttered a healing spell, feeling the flow lessen and the smarting recede. "I'll be all right until we can get back and it can be properly bound," he added.

Then, recalling something impossible, he looked up at the figure in brown, who exhibited the same concern.

"Terencia!"

The woman, as it was to be seen, dropped to her knees before Kelgan. A slight, and sly, pout crossed her features. "Why, Kelgan," she murmured flirtatiously, "can't you tell us apart?"

Kelgan's head swam; he dropped it hastily between his knees. Another Dark-Begotten set of twins! He recalled the abrupt changes in behavior he had noted during the weeks of collaborative sessions; the alternation between seductive and brusque, between come-on and hold-off. Neither behavior seemed to affect their fighting ability, he thought wryly, an image of his present companion ferociously slashing beside him in his mind's eye.

Another murmur, this one of concern, "Are you sure you're all right? You may have lost more blood than you think."

Raising his head, and looking her full in the face, Kelgan reiterated that he would be almost fine until he rejoined the others. While he did so, he studied her face. No use, he couldn't see the differences. "I don't know your name... I guess."

She gave a surprisingly girlish titter. "Actually, I *am* Terencia. My sister is also. Yes, I know," she put in before Kelgan could speak, "our parents saw it as a simplification for themselves—although not for others." She chuckled.

"You are what she has been searching for."

"I would suppose. We are seldom separated, although we seldom appear together. It was a self-protective device which has become a habit."

Self-protective from what, Kelgan wondered.

T'Jules now offered a hand up, which Kelgan gratefully accepted. He found he could stand more or less firmly on both feet. His gaze sliding to Pellerin, he caught that momentary flash of awareness which vanished as soon as Kelgan looked squarely at him. The young man had stood, motionless, right in the thick of action, and yet neither he nor the mare had received a blow. Neither had they given any indication of their peril, although the old mare's coat bore a fine film of sweat, and her eyes showed white.

Giving her a pat, Kelgan whispered, "Nicely done, Madam." She whickered softly in return, bumping his chest gently with her nose.

T'Jules cleared his throat and suggested they return to the others.

Cal, silent until then, tentatively offered the Baron's mount to Terencia Number Two, seeking T'Jules' affirmation.

T'Jules, in return, assured him that the steed was capable of handling two riders without turning a hair.

Seeming embarrassed, Cal helped Number Two, who accepted his offer with amusement, onto the horse. He swung up behind her. Kelgan received the same treatment from T'Jules, who assisted him with as much care as he would have given his aged and infirm grandmother. Kelgan wasn't sure whether to be grateful or insulted, since he was beginning to feel very much like an aged infirm grandmother.

With Pellerin in tow, the group made its slow way back to the main party. The fog only seemed to have thickened, leaving no more than an arm's-length of path ahead of them. They moved at a crawl in the unnerving silence, only the jingle of the reins letting them know they still moved through the land of the living.

Hours felt as though they were slipping past, even though Kelgan knew it was illusion. Their nerves stretched further and further, before other low noises began to reach them.

"I hope this is a good sign," Kelgan said over the Baron's shoulder. He realized he had been leaning rather heavily on that same shoulder and struggled to sit upright.

"I, too," T'Jules rejoined, "and don't worry about your posture at the moment."

At that instant, they caught the first whiff of roses drifting out of the fog. Both inhaled deeply and with gratitude. Kelgan, of course, fell into a fit of coughing, which hurt his side unmercifully. Cursing himself for an idiot, he muzzily tried to combat both the pain *and* the reaction. In his next moment of awareness, he realized that T'Jules was lowering him to a blanket which had been spread out, and the horse was tethered to a tree.

"Oh, Darkness, I thought you wuz dead!" shrilled Piper.

Kelgan began a laugh, which changed quickly to an "ungh!" as his side smote him. "No such luck," he managed.

Senses returning, his gaze turned from Piper to the rest of the assemblage. Terencia One and Two stood with their arms around each other, bearing identical expressions of concern, relief, and pride. So alike they seemed reflections in a mirror, both smiled with real warmth as Kelgan came to himself. Looking further, he was inordinately pleased to see the di Nerrills looking somewhat dumbfounded.

Nyah, nyah, nyah, nyah, his mind thought childishly, *there* was *something you didn't know.*

He struggled to sit up. The Baron moved instantly to his side, offering an arm. Just as quickly, Cal was on his other side, careful not to elbow Kelgan's wound. A guilty rush of pleasure rushed over Kelgan. *I've been wounded in a battle,* he told himself. Still, he could not rid himself of the nagging feeling that it had been too easy.

Bethne, however, left no doubt in his mind that she, at least, regarded him as an out-and-out hero. Sobbing, she plunked beside him and gushed wildly about his courage, nobility, swordsmanship, etc., while Ez tugged at her, repeating, "Naow, Bethie."

Embarrassed, Kelgan disclaimed most (but not all) of the credit, pointing out that T'Jules, Cal, and Number Two were superior fighters.

"I just followed their example," he demurred. *And the sword's,* he thought privately.

His gaze locked with Pellerin's over Bethne's shoulder, catching one of those eerily aware moments—this one of amusement. It was gone so quickly it could have been imagination.

Cal and the Baron, meanwhile, assured everyone that Kelgan had been a true warrior—causing the Mel'hachim to grin gleefully at Kelgan's discomfiture. Their grins were speedily replaced with alarm as Kelgan's head swam and his face paled.

"Lie down," T'Jules ordered, pushing him gently backward. Slicing Kelgan's clothing open with his dagger, the Baron tsked as he surveyed the damage. Although not terribly deep, the wound still bled freely.

Sensing his difficulty, Kelgan strove to concentrate on slaking the flow. Dizziness hampered his efforts, but Neroma was already there with linen, Kelgan's medicinal kit, and a bottle of wine given by the villagers. She poured the wine directly onto the slash, causing teeth to snap together on a gasp. Sprinkling one of the unguents from the kit on the linen, she then bound his ribs tightly.

Kelgan lost all hope of concentration during this operation—

lost, as a matter of fact, all sense of anything, but her nearness. The gentle pats of her hair, gusting over his face and chest, awakened a surge of something he was powerless to describe, much less resist. He fell into her eyes as into the Ebon River of their early flight, and felt them close over his head while he sank unresisting.

Neroma had been too intent on her ministerial duties to notice the enraptured state of her patient. However, as she started to settle back on her heels to say, "There, that will help," realization dawned on her. Her cool ivory countenance, and cool ivory demeanor were suddenly confounded. The first color he had ever seen on her suffused not just her cheeks, but all areas not covered by her clothing. Anger? Chagrin? Embarrassment? Something else? Dared he hope? He didn't know, but she slapped him brusquely on the shoulder with one lock, stating just as brusquely, "You'll live."

Hiding her face in a veil of tumbling tresses, she hurriedly gathered up the remainder of the linen and remedies and retreated, followed by her brother's thoughtful gaze.

Aloud, Nevander announced, "We had best make this our stopping place until the morrow. We know not whether we need to haste, or where, so progress in terms of miles accrued need not press us."

He spoke to the air, but there was a general murmur of agreement. Only Daliane looked uncertain.

"What is it, Dally?" whispered T'Jules, snugging her in his arm.

"It's silly. At least, I think so... but... I really feel that we *must* hurry, that we *have* to go on if Kel can ride at all. I know he can't walk, but on *your* horse—or the cart—or *something.*"

Daliane's voice had risen, and she had begun to tremble. Heads swung at the shrill urgency of her tone, and Kelgan was once again pulled away from his attempts at self-healing.

Looking long and hard at her, what he saw seemed to force a decision. Nodding his agreement, he tried to rise with no success. Frustrated, he demanded, "Somebody help me up, and put me onto a horse, or a mule, or a *goat,* if necessary."

Nevander looked surprised, but offered no argument. Neither did the Baron, nor the Mel'hachim, who knew the tiny Baroness was not prone to random hysterics.

Jorgo, who had been silent and watchful until then, said, "He rides with me. We can carry him in turn, but he will ride with me first."

Kelgan nodded his gratitude, then cautiously joined the combined laughter when Jorgo added, "I may have a spare tunic, as well."

As good as his word, he dropped a lavishly embroidered garment carefully over Kelgan's head. When Kelgan protested that it would suffer from blood stains, he was rewarded with a feral grin.

"It has seen *those* before."

Gulping a little, Kelgan expressed his thanks. Jorgo offered his hand, but Cal was quicker. With a rather proprietary air and a surprising show of strength, he hauled Kelgan to his feet, while Kelgan tried not to wince or scream. The depth of the pain surprised him—surely it wasn't much more than a scratch. Was he really that much of a weakling?

Together, Jorgo and Cal maneuvered Kelgan onto the still-saddled horse. Once on, Kelgan thought he might faint and disgrace himself by tumbling back into the arms of his helpers, but Jorgo leapt into the saddle and held him firmly.

Kelgan gritted his teeth and forced himself to concentrate on abating the fresh wave of pain. The difficulty amazed him. After some time, he muttered through his clenched jaw, "How do you manage?"

Understanding what Kelgan did not say, Jorgo gave one of his bass rumbles. Sobering, he voiced what had obviously been troubling him, "I think there is more to your wound than can be seen. It is, I think, fortunate that it has bled well."

Kelgan's hair rose on his nape. "Poison?" he whispered.

Jorgo replied in the affirmative, "Even so."

"I thought I was just... weak," Kelgan admitted. "It didn't look nearly that bad. Even to me."

"Nor to me," affirmed Jorgo, "however, I looked beyond. Your color was not just the pale of blood loss, and your eyes... I have seen their like before."

"That's why you wanted to double up with me first."

"Indeed. What is your thought?"

"My thought?"

"Yes. You are *our* antidote—do you not realize? *We* can combat what we meet with a sword. Lord and Lady di Nerrill have... other talents. *You,* and only you, can heal. And yet," he went on thoughtfully, "you are meant, it is clear, to *fight*. The warp and the weft of our tapestry are complex, indeed. Who works the loom?" he tacked on after a pause.

Jorgo continued, "I am distracting you, I meant to speak of this in a bit."

Kelgan realized with some satisfaction that he had been able to divide his attention fairly successfully. "I'm getting a little better at this. It doesn't hurt as Dark-frakking much."

Jorgo rumbled again, this time at the unexpected use of an obscenity from the generally mild-speaking Mage.

Even as he spoke, nevertheless, Kelgan realized that his hold over his injury was weakening. Pulling his thoughts together, he forced his concentration back to his side. He drove his thoughts downward. He could almost see the bane, like tiny black tendrils of Neroma's hair.... He shook off the image with a shudder, which caused Jorgo to start with alarm; however, when he peered around at Kelgan's face, he forbore to speak.

Kelgan sent his thoughts deeper. Never having been up against this particular problem, he was having to make it up as he went along. Imagining silvery beams of light, he pushed at the tendrils, which recoiled at his advance. Encouraged, he allowed his imagination to expand, summoning up a rotating ball of light, which threw rays everywhere as it whirled. Realizing he needed to direct his efforts more precisely, he slowed the orb, sending its shafts of brilliance along the blood vessels to their destination in his side.

He was suffused with exultation at each small victory. With each successful encounter between his silvered shafts and the loathsome tendrils, he sent up a mental shout. So rapt was he, he failed to realize that the horse had stopped and that Jorgo had summoned the di Nerrills to his side.

Comprehending the situation instantly, the Dark Twins were at once fiercely attempting to add their abilities to his. Kelgan saw none of this, but felt a surge of power which reduced the last of the swirling bits to simple motes of darkness which popped out of existence with a faint scream.

Regaining himself, he looked around in bewilderment to see the entire party gathered around him, staring. Piper, secured in the Baron's arms, dropped his head on T'Jules' shoulder and began to cry the first tears Kelgan has ever seen him shed. The Baron, unfamiliar with the fatherly role, patted his back in a kindly, but a bit awkward, manner.

"I, uh... I've been... Jorgo said... that is...." Kelgan stammered.

"How are you feeling, my Mage?" Nevander inquired with an anticlimactic mildness.

"Uh..." Kelgan assessed himself with care. "I'm feeling..." He broke off, realizing he felt exhausted, but totally without pain.

"By the light," he breathed, and joined Piper in tears.

··· 61 ···

Hallelujah! I'm a Mage!

"**T**his is a good place to stop," announced Daliane.

Several expressed their disbelief. The party had scarcely traveled on from the point of Kelgan's epiphany.

Daliane made a self-conscious moue. "I know, I know, I said we had to hurry. I can't explain it clearly. I felt a terrible urgency to keep moving. It simply evaporated a while back. I'm guessing, but I think that maybe it was because Kel would have gone to sleep... and then...."

Kelgan was mildly tickled at her diminution of his name. He had heard her call the Baron "Tee Jee", and he was pleased to be included among her intimates. The import of her surmise was more chilling, however. Kelgan felt sure he knew what would have occurred. *It would have been a long sleep,* was his dry thought. Ice trickled down his spine, then the full impact of what had just happened burst over him. He had actually performed a *real* healing, not just a theoretical one. Of course, it was on himself, but he wasn't at all sure that he knew himself any better than he knew his companions. Nevertheless, he had seen! Down into his body's inner life—the tiny structures that would perform their generally invisible duties while his outer self moved through its day, unthinking, unheeding.

Jorgo interrupted his dazzled thoughts. "Well, Master Mage?"

Startled, Kelgan hastily brought himself back to the present. "Oh, er... yes, I think Dally, uh, the Baroness, is right." A furious blush rose to his cheeks as he realized he had reciprocated the diminutive. Daliane seemed not to notice and turned her lovely smile full on him.

"There, I'm sure Kel would know; if anyone would."

T'Jules humphed, then appealed to the others, "Do we agree?"

Nevander, not always perceptive, was this time quick to detect the slight ruffling of the Baron's feathers. Smoothly, he suggested, as if weighing possibilities, "All along it has appeared that both our lovely Baroness, as well as our talented Mage, are more sensitive to the malign unknowns we seek. Although some others of us, as well, have heard the voices; the baneful influence, it would seem, falls most heavily on them. It is probable, therefore, that both are equally sensitive to the lessening of these influences and can be trusted to discern the differences."

Cal shot Kelgan a glance full of laughter. The Baron did not miss this by-play, nor Nevander's rather supercilious assessment of the obvious. He grinned in good-natured capitulation. "Stop, it is."

Bethne, Kelgan could see, was much relieved by this decision. She was trying gamely, but every day of travel, no matter how uneventful, etched more lines into her elderly face—this day most of all. Her reserves seemed nearly depleted.

How about some of his own? Not today, of course. He had used his up on himself, but in a day or two? He mulled over the idea while he watched Cal tending to the mules. Terencias Number One and Number Two ruefully parceled out what was left of their food supplies to the Baroness, who had volunteered for the cook's position that evening.

"I have all the domestic graces," she asserted cheerfully, "I just don't use them often." She looked a trifle daunted nonetheless at the paucity of choice. "Well, my friends, the situation looks a bit bleak. Breakfast will be the last, and we haven't seen so much as a sparrow for some time. Actually, we need more than a baker's dozen sparrows...." she broke off, realizing that at least one of their number needed no supplies.

"Four and twenty blackbirds, baked in a pie," sang Cal as he dropped beside Kelgan.

Kelgan stared at him in wonder. "And when the pie was open the birds began to sing?"

"The very same! Don't tell me...."

They simultaneously whooped with laughter. The fog retreated as though touched by a flaming torch.

"By the Lady," breathed Daliane, "we forgot! We forgot to laugh."

Smiles touched all the faces. Number One and Number Two turned to each other with a decisive nod. "We're going to laugh up a little game."

"How are you going to do that without scaring it away?" inquired Cal practically. "Besides, we haven't heard or seen *any*."

"Well, we're going out there to look, chuckling quietly, of course, and then we're going to laugh it this direction," replied Number One.

Bemused expressions flitted across the faces of the listeners. "Oh, of course," Cal responded. "So simple."

"You'll see," Number Two said airily. Both turned smug grins his way. Without further word, the two melted into the trees, low chortles clearing a narrow path for them.

Neroma distributed the few bits of remaining food among the group; Kelgan doing his best to make it look as ample as he could, and they settled quietly to wait. As time passed, uneasiness spread. At one point, T'Jules jumped to his feet, only to be pulled back down by Daliane, who shook her head at him. Just when they felt they must take some action a raucous burst of sound began to swell from the woods.

To their astonishment, not one, but a pair of deer, burst from the trees and charged in their direction. Without pausing a heartbeat, the Mel'hachim were on their feet, swords at the ready. As the stampeding game bounded their way, they stepped simultaneously to either side and dispatched both with one powerful neck stroke apiece. One deer staggered a short distance and fell, nearly on Kelgan's feet.

"Oh, Darkness," whispered Piper, "that were a sight."

Kelgan agreed. He looked beyond the dead deer and saw the Mel'hachim and the Terencias congratulating each other. The four drew daggers and advanced on Kelgan to skin and gut their prizes. Kelgan, still weak from the effort he had made to dispel the poison, felt his stomach lurch.

"I'll just move over there to give you more room," he offered lamely, suiting action to words.

Knowing expressions followed him, but no one said anything. Kelgan sat down a little apart from the rest of the group, and gave thought to the events of the day. At first, it was with some satisfaction. They had dispatched several fighting men; he had successfully overcome a poisoned wound—he dwelt on *that* one for a while with pleasure. He was becoming a real healer! As he considered, however, he grew increasingly less satisfied and increasingly more disturbed. It was easy—and it should not have been.

Gooseflesh crawled across his arms. Maybe *easy* was the wrong word... what if he hadn't discovered the right method? Was it a test? What if he had failed? Did the voices intend that—his thoughts whirled. *But I* didn't *fail*, he thought with triumph.

Cal sidled up to Kelgan, dropped beside him, and spoke from the side of his mouth. "I don't mean to minimize your performance, but did it strike you that we mowed down those guys rather easily considering how many there were? And," he added, "They were carrying poisoned swords on top of it."

"That thought visited my brain, as well," Kelgan admitted. "The tests have been getting more difficult by increments, but nevertheless we prevail. Nor do I wish to minimize *your* performance," he grinned wickedly, "but I doubt you have seen *real* battle with a sword, previously.

Cal grinned back. "Quite the superstars, aren't we?"

Kelgan gave an explosion of laughter. "Oww!" His side, while much improved, nevertheless remained a wound.

Cal frowned a little at the reminder. Just at that moment, Jorgo and the Baron joined them. Nadi, Daliane, and the Terencias were in conference with Neroma, leaving Kelgan somewhat puzzled by the gender split. Ezrael fussed over Bethne, who manifested more spunk now that Pellerin had been returned.

"Naow, Ez," he could hear her say, "I'm feelin' right pert."

He gave a small smile at her adjective, before looking inquiringly at T'Jules.

"Actually, the women chased us away," the Baron responded uneasily to Kelgan's look.

"We are rather lacking in numbers," rumbled Jorgo.

Kelgan started to ask, "Where is Nevander?" just as Lord di Nerrill popped out from behind the nearby foliage, looking a bit guilty. The look deepened as the other males regarded him questioningly.

"I'm afraid I was eavesdropping," Lord di Nerrill confessed shamefacedly. "I couldn't imagine what...." He broke off as his sibling raised her head and gave him a hard stare.

"Wouldn't...? How could...?" Kelgan began several questions, all the while thinking, *But they can hear each other's thoughts. Wouldn't he know what she intended? Wouldn't she know he was spying?*

Nevander, seeming to read Kelgan's thoughts, grinned self-deprecatingly and acknowledged, "I probably wasn't the best choice for such an action."

Just then, Ezrael joined them. "Waal, looks like a hen-fest over there. What's a-goin' on?"

"Haven't a clue," responded Cal jovially, throwing an arm around the elder man's shoulders. "How's Bethne?" he asked more seriously.

"She sez," Ez began slowly, "she sez she's doing just fine." Worry creased his features, revealing just how elderly he actually was.

Cal hugged the old man in sympathy while the others stood silent for the same reason.

"Looks like the party's breakin' up," observed Piper, causing several starts among the men, since all but Kelgan had completely forgotten him.

Indeed, the women were coming their way with purposeful looks on their faces. "We have some news which Number Two has chosen to share with us," announced Neroma.

"Why not to all of us?" inquired the Baron testily. "After all, *we* had a hand in the rescue."

Kelgan was surprised. He had not heard the Baron descend into pettishness before this; whatever else, Kelgan felt certain the Baron was not a small man. Nor was he the only one taken aback. The Baroness let her mouth drop, and Jorgo gave a grunt which said much.

Neroma, however, seemed to understand better than the others. "Yes," she said, taking his hand in hers, "we realize the extra worry you have been trying to hide."

T'Jules blushed. "I'm... well, I guess I fail as an actor."

Cal snorted. "Not from where I stand. What's this *extra* worry we're all unaware of?"

"Without Kelgan, we are blind," he responded simply.

Kelgan stood riveted in shock. *There's an* extra *worry, all right,* said a detached portion of his mind, while his conscious thoughts whirled in confusion, even as another small, detached portion of his mind said smugly, *I'm important."* He batted this thought away, stammering, "Wha'... what do you mean?"

"You are our focal point. You, for reasons unclear to us," the dry tone did not escape Kelgan, "are what has drawn all of us together. What has caused the voices to center on you...." He shrugged expressively.

Neroma began slowly. "This is, in part, what Number Two has...." She broke off in exasperation. "We cannot continue referring to them thusly. They must have names." She beckoned to the twin guardswomen. Peremptorily, as they approached, she ordered, "Choose names!"

The twins looked startled for a moment, then began to laugh. Number One offered, "You can call me Terri." Number Two suggested "And I will be Cenci." Number One explained, "Those were our childhood names for each other."

Cal said with some annoyance, "Guard ladies, I can't tell you apart."

Terry smiled. "We are mirror twins. I am left-handed, and Cenci is right-handed."

Kelgan smote himself on the forehead. "I saw that. I just thought you were ambidextrous."

Amusement greeted his announcement.

A brief smile touched Neroma's lips, but vanished immediately. "While Teri has been with us, Cenci has been following Bethne and Ezrael," she announced with some badly concealed asperity.

Kelgan heard Ez take a quick in-drawn breath. "Why?" he demanded.

Deadly serious now, Cenci sought to explain. "Kelgan was not the only one to appear repeatedly in Neroma's scryings."

Ez seemed to understand instantly. "Pelly."

Cenci nodded. "We decided on our own to see if we could come up with a reason; but except for what we all know, we were unsuccessful."

Neroma broke in. "We have no idea what forms the link, or why, but link there is."

"Between Pelly and him," Ez motioned with his head toward Kelgan.

"Yes," Teri confirmed, "there is a focus here which has us somewhat puzzled, because we..." She broke off, uncertain of how to continue.

Cenci took up the sentence. "We just can't figure out *who* Pellerin is."

"*Now,* is whatcha mean," Ez put in with surprising comprehension."

Identical heads nodded identically.

"There is more than meets the eye." Cenci glanced at Kelgan with a grin.

Teri went on to explain at greater length. "We, the rest of us that is, are somewhat peripheral, but necessary in ways we have yet to determine, to whatever scheme is unfolding. However, *they are the focal point*. Cal makes a third point of a triangle, perhaps, or perhaps only the same point from a different angle. Again we," a gesture of her head encompassed Neroma and Nevander, "don't know the why, but they are our special hope."

Cenci put in, "Daliane has been marked as well, but whether she is a focal point by herself, or if Kelgan and Cal are the other two legs and Pellerin is an outside force?" She shrugged.

From where? Of what? Kelgan shook his head to clear it. *The focal point of evil—the focal point of anything! I! The great savior of the world—no, worlds—this was nonsense!* And... somehow linked to Pellerin. A cold finger traced his spine. Pelly was, for all practical purposes, not exactly among the living, but was he, *exactly,* among the dead? *Some* force animated him—Kelgan shuddered to think *what* force—and kept him moving along with the rest of them. Kelgan knew he had glimpsed those occasional flashes of a dreadful awareness. He shuddered again.

Teri was still speaking, and her voice brought Kelgan back to the present. He noticed that most looked expectantly at him, rather than at her.

"I can't be... I can't be the most important," he protested. "I'm not even a full magician. I'm still learning what I *can* do."

Several eyes rolled.

Jorgo cleared his throat. "How is your sword arm?" he inquired mildly.

"Well, it's...."

"And your self-healing—was it successful?" he went on, still mildly.

"Uh... yes... I guess so. Er... yes... it was."

"From poison, I believe?" still in gentle inquiry.

Grins began to spread across several faces.

'Well... yes, but...."

The grins widened. Kelgan felt his cheeks burn; he began to demur again, when he felt a sharp pain in his ankle.

"Ow!" He halted in mid-protest with a squeal. Looking down, he discovered Piper had bestowed a swift kick.

"What's the matter with you all the time?" the boy asked indignantly. "Ain't you been a big enough hero? What's it gonna take?"

Cal chose this moment to break in. "Unaccustomed as he is to public salvation, he accepts the hero position."

Tension fell away in gales of laughter, including Ezrael's. "Not 'zactly whatcha expected when ya got up this mornin', eh, son?" He jovially buffeted Kelgan's shoulder.

"I... uh... guess I need to sleep on it," Kelgan jested weakly, "maybe I'll expect it *tomorrow* morning,"

Another round of laughter greeted this minor sally, and the group dispersed to ready the camp for bedtime. Kelgan's eyes strayed to Bethne, who, as usual, was trying to hide her increasing weakness under a veneer of false cheer. Not wishing to draw attention to the failure of her pretense, Kelgan checked the mules, admonished Piper to wash, gave Capriola the once-over, and casually dropped down beside Bethne to wish her a good-night.

Under the guise of checking her pulse and respiration, Kelgan poured a touch of newly discovered healing power into Bethne. Just a touch, since he as yet could not afford to deplete himself; and he didn't want her suddenly leaping around like a young colt. Capriola, tethered nearby, maaed in what looked to be approval, and the mules joined her in cacophony.

"My sakes," declared Bethne, "them animals is sure noisy this evening. Them mules gots the ear-splittin'est brays I ever heard."

Chuckling, Kelgan agreed. "They do like to put in their two coppers."

"I think this little rest done me good," Bethne went on. "I'm feelin' a bit o' pep comin' back."

Kelgan clasped both her hands. "I hope so," he said simply.

··· 62 ···

Tests of a Different Sort

They settled for the night. The scent of roses filled the air. Kelgan, of course, warded himself against the wards. *A double bubble,* he thought sleepily.

Piper claimed his usual spot against Kelgan's back. In spite of the wards, the Mel'hachim still flanked the Baroness. *Much to the Baron's annoyance, I'm sure,* another sleepy thought flitted through Kelgan's relaxed mind. He made a slight amused noise. The next thing he knew, Pellerin's icy hand gripped his forearm.

"Come." His empty eyes glittered in the dying firelight.

Compelled to rise, Kelgan stumbled to his feet, to find himself in a vast hall ringed with doorways. The ceiling rose to height so measureless it vanished in the mist which hung above them. The walls between the doorways were covered in tapestries—some so ancient that shreds hung from them like the tracks of tears, others as bright and fresh as though just hung.

Pellerin's grasp turned Kelgan toward the seeming oldest. "Regard."

As Kelgan watched, the ragged rivulets wound up, back into the places they had fallen from. The colors, faded and dusty, brightened; and the pictured scenes regained their former splendor. Kelgan, enough of a Mage not to be surprised, nevertheless felt his scalp prickling as he watched with wary interest.

A king sat on a splendid throne. His robes spoke of the distant past. A ring of courtiers in stiffly formal stances stood posed below him. To one side, on his left hand, was a figure garbed in the ages-long traditional robe of the Mage. *Nothing unusual* about *this,* thought Kelgan. *Well....*

He was pulled to the next. Again, the hanging shreds rejoined their fellows; again, the colors resumed their original hues. This scene was virtually identical to the first. For a moment, Kelgan saw no difference; then he realized the Mage figure had become subtly larger than the King, who was now a bit smaller than his throne. The stances of the courtiers had altered slightly, turning them in just a barely discernible shift to the left.

Again, Kelgan was forced on. Again, the pattern repeated. The King had shrunk to an obvious degree in the third tapestry, and the Mage had been joined by another in apprentice's garments. Kelgan felt a foreknowledge steal over him. He glanced reluctantly at Pellerin. "Continue," he demanded in his toneless voice.

The next tapestry followed on the first two, as did several after that. Each depicted the rise of the Mage, and his "assistant", who ran through the colors until he assumed his full status. The King continued his inevitable diminishment.

"You are not seeing?" A long statement from his usually monosyllabic companion.

Especially long for a dead man, Kelgan thought before he could stop himself. The grip on his forearm relaxed ever so slightly, then resumed its painful vise.

Kelgan turned his attention back to the tapestry they faced. What was he missing? The courtiers definitely faced the two Mages. Something odd about those courtiers, as well.... They seemed less... something. Kelgan couldn't quite come up with a description. He looked harder; then his breath caught in his throat. He had ignored the coat of arms displayed above the King, who was now barely bigger than a child. In fact, it was displayed all over—on the King's robes, on some of the shields, on banners. How could he have missed it?

After his first shock, he accepted what he saw with weary resignation. Of course, what else? He wore those same symbols himself, right at that very moment. He noticed another detail he had overlooked, so gradual was its progression. The robes of the Mages had darkened, little by little, until they were now black. *Yes, yes,* thought Kelgan, *also, what else?*

The next set of tapestries were less damaged but more ominous. A new king sat on a new throne. The weaver managed to capture a surprisingly life-like image, one that made icy sweat run down Kelgan's sides. It was a look of profound evil. The same mage stood to the side and a similar ring of courtiers below. Now they faced outward, weapons drawn and at the ready, faces eager for destruction. As they moved from arras to arras, Kelgan grew more and more sickened. The scenes depicted brutality without measure. Fields laid waste, towns burned, their inhabitants slaughtered to the last man, woman, and child. The manner of their deaths grotesque and horrible in the extreme—no detail spared. Each drop of blood glittered like a gemstone.

Kelgan attempted to swallow his rising bile. He looked to Pellerin. Silent this time, the wraith simply drew him forward.

The final set suggested the present time. The clothes caught up to contemporary fashion. Once again, a new ruler occupied a throne. The same Mages inhabited the scene, however, this time flanking him. Once more, the weaver captured personality. A weak man, Kelgan noted, and terrified; stained, nevertheless, with incipient evil. The ring of warriors now wore the familiar black and red.

What followed did astound him, although he might have foreseen what was coming. He saw the Black Mages reach out to other worlds, which first blackened like soot motes then were gradually enveloped in a devouring cloud. *The mist,* thought Kelgan.

A disheartening number of those worlds succumbed like grain gobbled by hens. Now and then, there seemed to be pockets of resistance, since bright spots glowed in one tapestry only to be subsumed in the next. Kelgan felt his knees begin to buckle, but the relentless grip held him upright.

"What does it mean?" Kelgan gasped out, then choked in horror as *other* voices answered him.

"You really want to know, pretty boy?" An obscene giggle. "We're just *thrilled* to show you. We know you'll be *dying* to know." A deeper, but no less repellent chuckle.

Kelgan woke with a yell that rebounded from the encircling trees. Every member of the party surged instantly to their feet. Bemused, Kelgan noted that not only the Terencias and the Baron, but Cal, as well, stood with drawn swords. Only the Mel'hachim protecting Daliane with their fierce hold remained sheathed. Looking down, he realized Piper had grasped Kelgan's sword and now offered it hilt-first.

He didn't even try to pretend it was just a nightmare. He knew that, somehow, it was all too real, and he knew his chattering teeth betrayed him.

Pellerin stood, as always, vacantly by his horse, but Kelgan felt certain of Pelly's awareness.

He strove for a semblance of calm, at least enough to control his jaws. When he thought he could speak, he only managed one word. "Vision."

Neroma, understanding the difficulty instantly, came to his side and grasped his hand. "Let me try something," her velvet voice soothed him, but the touch of her hand and the gentle embrace of her hair had a distinctly opposite effect. He swallowed convulsively, and nodded.

Drawing him over to where Pellerin stood, she astonished him by taking Pelly's hand, as well. With detached amusement, Kelgan thought for an instant that he also saw surprise flit across Pelly's face.

"Be still, now," Neroma admonished, as though Pellerin was anything but still. Closing her eyes, she became lost in concentration.

Kelgan felt a fluttering in his brain, like the feathery touch of her hair, then a grayness, as though a shawl had been dropped over him. He had no idea how long they stood like figures of marble. He returned to himself when Neroma gave a low moan and dropped to the ground. She waved him away as he sought to assist her. Feeling helpless, he met Pellerin's eyes in time to see that millisecond flicker of awareness come and go.

After a time, Neroma allowed Kelgan to help her to her feet. Impossible to believe, but her face contained even less color than usual. It became obvious the little Baroness wished to attempt some form of assistance, but the Mel'hachim refused to relinquish their hold.

T'Jules, gathering his authority around him, boomed, "Well?"

Neroma, fluttering her hair like so many waving hands, failed to respond, but looked with wide eyes at her twin. Kelgan realized just then that Nevander had not moved a muscle from the first moment. *Of course!* Everything she knew, he knew. Kelgan's stinging wave of jealousy astonished him. He looked at himself in the mirror of his mind's eye. *Fine time to fall in love,* he excoriated himself.

No, it wasn't "fall." He'd been falling from the start; he'd just hit bottom. *Okay, he's her twin. Go easy with the irrationality.* He had to admit however, it was the *communication* that woke the demons. If he could just do *that*—even with Cal!

He realized that T'Jules was growling. "Talk." Fast losing patience, the Baron reached the red-faced stage, shortly to be followed by violent action of some sort.

Kelgan, for whatever reason, wordlessly accepted the sword, which Piper still held. He felt amazingly better with it in his hand. Clearing his throat, he commenced, as best he could, the "explanation."

At its conclusion, there was silence, finally broken by T'Jules, who said, "Harumph," so decidedly, and so much the way it was written, Kelgan hid a smile with another throat-clearing.

As though timed by clockwork, all turned simultaneously toward Pelly, whose vacant posture was unaltered. Just as simultaneously, they swung back toward Kelgan. This time Bethne gasped, "Merciful Lady."

"It's undoubtedly a true seeing," Nevander said for the first time, "and, I suspect, more than simply a metaphor, as well."

Kelgan nodded, still dry-throated. "It didn't look very metaphorical to me. It looked only too real, just in some speeded-up time frame outside of ours."

Neroma nodded. "Yes." Her syrupy contralto was scarcely more than a whisper. "Corruption and evil, starting small; then reaching far—and through—the dimensions?" Her voice rose questioningly at the end.

"Starting on this world?" queried Cal.

"It would seem," said Nevander, then, "No, it cannot be. We are affected, but not as yet consumed."

"Certainly reaching my home," persisted Cal, "how many others?"

Nevander shrugged.

Kelgan reached back into memory. "I saw... I saw... a *lot* of them, but I don't know if that was what *had* happened or what *would* happen."

Nevander stated the obvious in a voice that was almost a moan. "We can only hope it hasn't happened yet."

"Well, I know I drove into a fog," Cal said unsteadily, "so it'd started where I came from."

Kelgan reached out to him, forgetting he held the sword. "Oops," he exclaimed, then stood transfixed.

"Hey, I'm on your side," Cal admonished. When Kelgan still stood like a wooden soldier, he added, "You in there, Old Buddy?"

"You moved!" Kelgan said idiotically.

"Well, I do tend to back away from sharp objects," Cal joked.

"No! You moved before I did!"

Cal chuckled. "I don't think so. I saw you starting to gesture, and guessed that point was coming my way."

Kelgan was unconvinced, but let it go. *I guess I just talked myself into what I saw, because I wanted it,* he told himself, remembering his earlier wishful thinking.

Feeling his neck prickle, he caught Neroma eyeing him speculatively. She raised one eyebrow, and then turned away.

T'Jules harrumphed again. "Well, since we're all up, we might as well have breakfast. I'll cook."

General laughter followed this offer, since there was precious little to cook, dried venison, and a nice, hot cup of some incredibly bitter herbal concoction Neroma had gathered in the woods.

"Oh, yummy," whispered Piper.

Kelgan resheathed his sword as a thought struck him. He didn't know how (yet) to transmute the basic elements, but he sure as Darkness could make them taste better.

He went over and knelt beside T'Jules, who busied himself with the fire. "I've got an idea." He blew on the fire, whispering *"Lignis,"* and created a nice blaze. "Let me have the herbs."

"It's about time," muttered the Baron; then they both laughed.

"Somehow, it's the small things that escape me."

"Uh, huh," agreed T'Jules ironically.

"Well, all right, the big ones, too."

"You're learning, my friend—and quickly, too."

"But not quickly enough," Kelgan countered.

The Baron sat back on his heels, brow furrowed. "You're too used to doing what you're told. You haven't gotten out of the habit of being a schoolboy, and you're not in the classroom anymore. These lessons are for real. I'm afraid you're going to have to think ahead—and try *everything*."

"A lot of what I know is illusion."

"That's a start; and we just might need a few good illusions. However, you're going to have to dig deeper, the way you did with the poison. You're only scratching the surface. Forget what you were told in school! Forget you didn't graduate from the Academy! You graduated when you swung that sword the first time!"

That was the longest speech Kelgan had heard from the Baron, to date.

"Gotcha," he agreed. At the Baron's quizzical look, he stuttered, "I, uh, got that from Cal." T'Jules shook his head and snorted.

The Baron remained squatting beside the fire while Kelgan busied himself with the herb drink. Finally, he gestured for Kelgan to sit beside him. When Kelgan obeyed, he began, "Look, Kel, you're a leader—I've told you that before and I believe it—but *you've* got to believe it. You continually focus on your weaknesses; how about your strengths?" The last ended in a question mark.

Slowly, Kelgan considered it. "Well, I'm really good at seemings." T'Jules nodded. "And I've always been a pretty good healer. I just couldn't do what... I did... to myself... before." T'Jules nodded again. "And, I'm *really* good at enlarging and diminishing." T'Jules raised an eyebrow. "Well, any mage can do that," Kelgan admitted, "but I'm *really* good. His eyebrow remained raised.

"Doesn't sound like much, does it?" Kelgan said, sounding discouraged.

The Baron shook his head. "How about the brew?"

Kelgan hastily set about making the noxious (but nourishing, Neroma assured them) mixture palatable. Then he applied a little of his enlarging talent to the venison. What had been barely enough to go around managed to at least look like a more satisfying portion for each.

T'Jules tapped Kelgan on the shoulder, "Not much, huh?" Chuckling, the Baron got up to wander over to check on the horses, and then wander on to his wife, leaving Kelgan looking after him in some confusion.

His spot was immediately filled by Neroma, who loomed over him. "You are frightened." Not a question.

"Well, yes, that's not hard to figure out." Kelgan squinted up at Neroma. His gaze slid behind her to Daliane, who ruefully grinned at him. Since it was now dawn, she was, as usual, tight in the grasp of Jorgo and Nadi. This, despite the ever-stronger wards, both Neroma's and his. T'Jules crouched protectively behind her on a grassy tuft, padded further by leaves.

What season is it? Kelgan wondered idly. *Fall? Is it Fall?*

Returning his attention to Neroma, he did something unexpected. Patting the ground beside him, he gestured with his head for her to sit down. She blinked for a second, and then dropped into the leaves, leaning against the same tree-trunk he now occupied. A tendril of hair slipped companionably around his neck.

Breathless and seeing stars (constellations, galaxies, he didn't know), he gulped and squeaked, "You said I was frightened."

Knowing exactly her effect, she regarded him from scarce inches away with amusement. "Um, yes," she purred.

I'm not very experienced, Kelgan thought, *well not at all, but....*

His thoughts broke off as she said seriously, "The tapestries— they have done this. Their message was of an unstoppable, age-old foe. Not a man to be defeated by a sword, not by several swords, almost beyond magic."

Her words were smothered into an "ulp" as Kelgan wrapped his arms around her and clamped his mouth fiercely on hers.

Darkness, this is easier than I thought, his mind told him from somewhere a long way off. He regained his senses to find himself the center of rapt attention as the entire group pondered this display with fascination.

Scattered applause broke out among the group. Neroma, white-faced, sprang to her feet and stalked away, hair tumbling in disarray. Kelgan continued to stare stupidly until Cal and the Baron strode forward, hauled him to his feet and walked him in the opposite direction.

"Way to go, Old Buddy," enthused Cal.

The Baron cast a wry glance in that direction, but could not repress what sounded surprisingly like, "Hee, hee."

Gazing quizzically at their retreating backs, Nevander shook his head. Giggles of a muted variety arose from the women. Kelgan was still in a state of advanced paralysis when a buffet between the shoulders sent him flying out of the grasp of his two supporters.

"Looks like ya gots red blood after all, son." Ezrael's mellow voice sounded to Kelgan a lot like the Last Trump, since it was only inches from his ear.

Spinning around, Kelgan drew himself up to give a withering retort—somewhat marred by a distinctly breathless quality. Forced to gasp a couple of times, he gave it up as a bad job and did a little withering himself.

"We've been wonderin' just how long it was goin' take you."

"You've... been wondering?"

"Yup, and bettin', too."

Panic spiraled in Kelgan, mingled with a sense of pride. A small voice within was whispering *Whee!* along with *What do I do now?* Recalling himself, he repeated with greater heat, "You were wondering!"

Cal wrapped an arm companionably around Kelgan's shoulders. "Don't take on. You're the only one who didn't see this coming?"

"Even Nevander?"

"Even Nevander," spoke the smooth voice behind him. "I will admit to some doubt, my Mage, until the poison episode."

"The poison...? But that was...."

"A while back, yes."

Stunned by the implications of what he was hearing, Kelgan

lapsed back into stupor, rousing himself to say, "You mean she...."

"Was just waiting, uh huh." Cal's glee seemed boundless.

"Why are you so happy?" Kelgan inquired petulantly.

"Oh, it's just, well, uh...." Blushing, he stuttered to a stop, then continued lamely, "Well, we're pals."

A rumbling snort from Jorgo, who had relinquished Daliane to Nadi long enough to join the group, showed what he thought of that idea.

Kelgan eyed Cal thoughtfully. Pals—the word didn't quite translate, but the meaning seemed clear—was that the way one referred to *oneself?*

Kelgan decided he needed some time alone, away from the smirks, winks and knowing looks of his companions. Still feeling rather lightheaded, he edged backward as casually as he could until shielded by the embrace of the trees. To his surprise he was not alone. There, huddled in a forlorn heap amid the roots of an ancient oak, he discovered Piper. The child refused to look up even when Kelgan dropped down beside him.

"Hey, what's going on?"

Raising a face streaked with dirt and tears, the boy wailed, "What about me?"

Kelgan stared blankly for a minute, completely without understanding, before light dawned.

Sweeping the child up in his arms, Kelgan declared, "You're my boy," on a gust of laughter.

Piper peered fearfully into his face. "Are you sure?"

Kelgan stared gravely and steadfastly back without speaking.

What he saw seemed to reassure him, because Piper heaved a sigh that threatened to crack his fragile ribs and he hid his face in Kelgan's shoulder. After a minute, he began, "Dad...."

Kelgan's start almost dislodged the child into the leaves. Piper drew away, the fearful look back on his face.

Seeing this, Kelgan said hastily," Sorry, hit my elbow on a root." He settled the boy comfortably again. "You were about to ask?"

"Are you going to marry Lady di Nerrill?'

Things were moving a little fast for Kelgan. From his first kiss (although he would have cut out his tongue before admitting it), to assumed fatherhood, and now a whole tidy little family.

"We, uh, that is, uh, I haven't, uh...." Kelgan gave it up and simply shrugged.

"She's *really* pretty," Piper said admiringly.

Kelgan could, at least, admit that. Looking into Piper's wide eyes, he was struck suddenly by how young, and fragile, the child actually was in spite of his bravado and pluck.

Not having any words of wisdom, Kelgan could only say, "Well, we'll figure it out, sooner or later. Come on, let's eat."

Bracing himself to rerun the gantlet, he hoisted Piper onto his shoulders and rejoined the group. Once back among the party, he couldn't help noticing with both embarrassment and exasperation, how studiously casual everyone behaved.

Only the little Baroness had the temerity (or honesty) to address the subject as he dished up some of their meager rations. With an elfin grin, she observed, "I think you should revisit the issue."

Kelgan pondered the unsatisfying result of a slightly less than full-on immersion in smooching. *One kiss, for Darkness' sake!* Although personally inexperienced, he did know the particulars of further involvement—physical, that is. *Not even one good grope,* he grumbled to himself, *if everything was going to go to the Dark, anyway, I could have at least been faster with my hands.*

He met Cal's eyes and whose smirk made Kelgan sure that his thoughts were obvious. "Short, but sweet," offered Cal nastily.

"Dark you," muttered Kelgan.

Jorgo's bass rumble of amusement told Kelgan he had been listening. One of Jorgo's tremendous wallops accompanied his laughter. "I was once in your shoes, my brother," the Mel'hachim warrior assured him jovially.

Kelgan stared for a moment, since Jorgo had never before included him in the "brother" ranks. He shook his head, however, and sullenly retorted, "I doubt it."

Jorgo laughed again and persisted. "Oh, yes, and I acted exactly the same way."

Curious, in spite of himself, Kelgan asked, "But why?"

"My beloved's father thought me an unworthy suitor—too poor, too weak."

"Weak!" uttered Cal and Kelgan simultaneously.

Jorgo ignored the interruption. "Nadi's father was something of a legend—a mountain of a man with the strength of a Mel'hach bull; no one had been able to stand against him in combat. Nadi and I used to meet in secret, but one day he discovered us and challenged me. He did not know I had been expecting his challenge. I knew it would come one day, and I wanted her more than anything I had ever wanted—before or since. I had been practicing every moment I could spare. I hoped that being younger and faster would be to my advantage, since I could not hope to best him in strength, only by outwitting him. I could not kill him—not Nadi's father—she would never have forgiven me, in spite of our love. I had to be not only quicker of body, but quicker of mind. I had to let him think I was as useless as he had made up his mind I was."

Jorgo paused, all amusement gone, and stared off into the distance. Neither listener interrupted him, realizing an old sadness had surfaced. After a second, he shook himself like a wet dog and went on.

"In our combat, I let him press me, over and over I backed away, avoiding his blows—we fought with club and sword—letting him strike more and more wildly as he grew more impatient. The crowd jeered at me... finally, I could see he tired, just a little. I knew I had to make my move; I could not avoid him forever. He made a particularly wild swing with his club, and I darted in under the swing and knocked his sword arm up. With my club I caught him just under the chin and knocked him out. When he awoke, I had possession of his sword and club and my sword was at this throat. The crowd cheered for me; I had won and shed no blood...."

Once again, Jorgo stopped, old anguish written bitterly on his face. "He gave me Nadi that night," he continued, "and cut his own throat."

His listeners gasped as one.

"She did not blame me, no," Jorgo guessed at the meaning of the gasps. "We did not know he was only strong on the outside, but weak within. I had shamed him...." Jorgo's voice trailed off. Then recapturing some of his usual spirit, he walloped Kelgan again on the back. "You, my brother, have strength inside, you will see."

Feeling somewhat cheered, as well as sympathetic, Kelgan decided to wallop back. Jorgo, laughing, pretending to be staggered. Kelgan and Cal joined the laughter, pleased to see that the fog cleared and lifted for some distance around.

Quicker of mind, thought Kelgan, *hope I can remember that one. I'm sure not going to best anybody with strength.*

Giving his surroundings a second look, since more could be seen, Kelgan was appalled to see that the landscape presented a horrifying sight. A few scattered dwellings with only one or two walls left standing; blighted trees, their bare limbs beckoning like the walking dead; barren ground, and not a bird, not a squirrel, not even a skulking rat visible, just devastation with melancholy clinging like lichen. Frowning, Kelgan surveyed the area of the camp—verdant forest, well-traveled road, green verge. *Which was real?* he wondered. *Did they bring their own world with them?*

Cal, again seeming to read his thoughts, voiced the obvious, "Kinda different, isn't it?"

Jorgo rumbled in agreement.

Feeling the hairs on his nape stand to attention, Kelgan glanced toward Pelly. Pelly, in turn, regarded him fixedly with no sign of awareness on his countenance. Kelgan, however, could feel *something* under the usual vacancy. Shuddering with the accustomed *frisson* Pelly always awoke in him, Kelgan knew the significance of what they were seeing, although how it was to work in their favor, he had yet to discern.

··· 63 ···

A Lesson in How-To

The aftermath of his impulsive act was not quite what Kelgan had hoped for. Neroma avoided him so pointedly, his cheeks remained in a permanent state of flush; while Nevander went out of his way to be solicitous and courteous, making Kelgan long to tuck his fist neatly into the aristocratic jaw of her twin. The Terencias dissolved into fits of laughter at his expense, with Teri batting her eyelashes and wagging her hips at every opportunity. Cal and the Baron clapped him on the back so often, he was sure his spine developed a concavity; and the Mel'hachim regaled him continually with old war stories he knew were intended to make him feel better, but only succeeded in making him feel the complete jester in cap and bells.

Only Daliane, with both her innate forthrightness and tact, spoke to him frankly. Catching him as he settled the mules, she went straight to the point. "She loved it, you know," Daliane whispered, "but she's never been kissed before, and she doesn't know what to do with it."

Kelgan goggled at her, capable of nothing but random stammers.

Daliane chuckled, not in mockery, but in compassionate understanding. "You two *are* a pair! Well, I was that way, too. Not so the Baron, however," she added dryly. "My suggestion is more practice—if you can get her to stand still."

Kelgan was still stammering, but one thought had managed to penetrate. "You said... you said... she liked it?"

Daliane made a sound of disgust. "I said she loved it! Try listening for a change." She grinned and walked away.

Kelgan slumped against the nearest mule, who for a change stood patiently as a wall. Piper poked his head from behind a tree. "I think she's right; you really need practice." He disappeared quickly after delivering that piece of wisdom.

Kelgan's first impulse was to rampage through the camp, pin Neroma to a sycamore and practice until his lips fell off. His second was to lay a Hypnos spell on everyone but Neroma, and then rampage through the camp. His third was to take several very deep breaths and think things through a little more clearly. After the deep breaths, he felt light-headed and giddy and less clear than ever.

Voices behind the mule made him freeze. Nevander and Neroma were strolling by, deep in conversation. Nevander was ostensibly discussing strategies against the unknown, his light tenor punctuated in occasional agreement by Neroma's liquid alto.

Nevander broke off in mid-sentence. "Wait here a moment while I get something to show you." He strode off, leaving Neroma standing obediently on the other side of the mule.

Kelgan wondered if this was a sign from the Light or a lure from the Darkness, then decided he didn't care either way. Springing around the mule, he clutched a seemingly astounded Neroma and gave practice his whole-hearted attention (not forgetting the hands this time).

Too whole-hearted it would appear. Daliane screamed, long and loud. Ez gave a shout of dismay as Bethne collapsed, and the nearest mule set up an ear-splitting braying. The Terencias were on their feet with swords out, followed instantly by T'Jules and the Mel'hachim. All faced in different directions, searching for imminent attack as Kelgan realized his own head echoed with mocking laughter.

Before he could recover, or make sense of what was happening, a suffocating blanket of attar of roses swept over him. He suffered several seconds of asthmatic angst before he managed to throw up his own wards and, belatedly, those of the camp.

The Mel'hachim, who, as always, held the Baroness firmly with one hand and swords in the other, sagged with relief as Daliane's eyes regained their focus.

Bethne sat up groggily, saying, "I musta had a spell."

Kelgan was suffused with guilt as Ez shot him a look of reproach. To his utter astonishment, however, he watched the Baron sink to the ground in a paroxysm of laughter. Clutching his sides, T'Jules managed to gasp out, "There's a man after my own heart," before doubling up again.

His laughter was infectious, and even Ez joined in. Bethne looked a little puzzled, but smiled at the general merriment. Kelgan was terrified to look at Neroma, who stood in silence behind him. He got a second jolt of astonishment as a rather cold hand clasped his, along with several rivulets of hair. She squeezed his hand, nearly causing the wards to drop again.

"We must have a general council meeting," she announced to the group, the molasses of her tone deeper than ever.

A consensual murmur of agreement ran through the assembly. The Baron was still wheezing somewhat from his hilarity, but managed to nod.

"It is obvious," Neroma purred, "that the Mage and I have developed a strong... attraction."

Obvious, my philtres, thought Kelgan, *not to me.*

"However," she continued, "we constitute a danger."

Kelgan was shocked back to reality by the ice-water jolt of her words.

"We are unable," she continued, "to allow our feelings to surface. We must avoid contact until...."

The Baron had sobered completely. Sending Kelgan a glance of sad understanding, he nodded. "Unfortunately true, we cannot allow ourselves any distractions." Looking at his wife, he went on, "No matter how pleasurable." Hearing a sigh, he stared Kelgan in the eyes. "*You* are the most important."

Nods from all emphasized a dreaded inevitability to this declaration.

Wait a minute, thought Kelgan, *don't I get a say? There must be some way to get around the problem.* He looked around the circle, sympathetic expressions on most, but a little sly amusement on the visages of the Terencias, worst of all, absolute agreement with both Neroma and the Baron.

Neroma gave his hand one more squeeze, then dropped it with finality, leaving Kelgan gaping helplessly at them all. Turning on his heel he marched off, feeling the old sense of not-measuring-up assailing him once more. He sought the shelter of the trees.

··· 64 ···

Going Bats

Kelgan was beginning to feel that he was becoming a Dryad—he seemed to spend much of his time lately hunkered down in tree roots, fighting depression, or panic, or both. Hugging his knees, he summoned every ounce of backbone he thought he possessed, as well as some he was sure he didn't, in order not to surrender to the waves of self-pity threatening to engulf him. Then, a small form plopped down beside him.

"Come on, Dad, it's not that bad. You and Mom'll git together when we git outa this."

Kelgan's eyeballs threatened to roll in the leaf-mold as they stretched to their fullest extent. *Dad?* Okay, he had started to get used to that one. *Mom?*

A snort of laughter, hastily covered, told him that Cal had not been far behind.

"Yeah, *Dad,* this is only a temporary set-back."

Piper glared, aware of the mockery in Cal's voice. However, he softened, when Cal squatted beside him and enveloped him in a one-arm hug—not too long or too short—just man to man.

Kelgan gathered the remnants of his tattered dignity around him and said as tendentiously as Nevander, "Yes, we must all look to the future."

Even Piper snorted.

Neroma, in the meantime, conferred urgently with her brother and the Mel'hachim. Oddly, they were not glued to the side of the

Baroness, who was unashamedly making kissy-face with her husband. The Terencias were raptly involved rolling dice with Ezrael and Bethne. Feeling the world had turned upside down, Kelgan took this all in with a glance as he attempted to rejoin the party with as much composure as possible. Knowing this was a total failure, he decided the better part of valor was self-deprecation.

"Well, my friends, I really feel like an idiot—but I'm an idiot who enjoyed it."

The tableaus dissolved in sympathetic agreement. T'Jules threw him a thumbs-up sign, and the others pulled him into the group with them; chattering about their reactions and joshing him gently.

Nevander, theatrical as usual, struck a pose, twinkled ostentatiously and said, "Well, my Mage, or perhaps not entirely mine, there's more magic to you than I had thought."

Automatically reacting to this sally with laughter, Kelgan, for some reason, felt compelled to turn his gaze to Pellerin, motionless by his horse. As had happened previously, Kelgan caught that brief flash of spectral awareness before Pelly's gaze resumed its usual vacancy. *Approval? Disapproval? Sympathy? Am I seeking the good opinion of a corpse?* wondered Kelgan, surprised to find that, since the night of the tapestries, he actually felt a sort of camaraderie with Pelly. His mind skittered away a bit from that idea, frightened by what it might mean.

"You know," mused the Baron thoughtfully, "even though our journey has been fraught with drama, it seems almost random—if there is a pattern, beyond the herding we have all felt, I cannot see it."

"And yet," put in the Baroness, "if we drop our guards for a moment...."

Kelgan blushed.

"And," added Teri, "we are all called upon to use our different strengths at different times."

"Testing," was her twin's contribution.

"Kel gets tested *every* time," stated Cal, "we get it off-and-on."

"To see how strong we are together, or separately?' Nadi's ironic tone amused her hearers.

"With you it's the same thing," rejoined Cal.

She fluttered her eyelashes at him, breaking up the group.

"Waal," drawled Ez, "'cept for bein' Pelly's Ma n' Pa, I don' rightly know what our talents is."

Another laugh, however, Nevander considered the statement seriously. "I think that's it exactly. You *are* Pellerin's parents *and* his link to... well, to *life*. You keep him here, and it would seem that is where he is meant to be."

Again, Kelgan's gaze swung to Pelly. Again, that infinitesimal flash.

"Yes, that's what Pelly thinks, too." All eyes shot to Kelgan. "Uh," stammered Kelgan. "That is, *I* think...." He trailed off, unsure why he *was* sure.

Nevander shrugged elaborately. "Ah well, I'm glad to be, um, supported in my opinion."

Ezrael chortled, but sent a shrewd look to Kelgan, and Bethne smiled broadly with the unmistakably proud smile of a mother hen with one extraordinary chick.

The strange thing, mused Kelgan, *is that neither of them really goes too near him most of the time nor has attempted to touch him since the first meeting.*

An uproar broke out amongst the animals. "*Levanah,*" shouted Kelgan automatically.

The neighing, bleating, braying cacophony quieted instantly. Detaching himself from the others, Kelgan went to determine the source of the problem. The mules stood at rigid attention, their ears far forward. Seeing him, they simultaneously pulled them back, then flicked them forward like arrows, rolling their eyes to suit the motion. Feeling that same old ice-water-down-the-spine, Kelgan followed the ears with his eyes. Seeing nothing, he was not reassured. He had learned to trust the awareness of the mules. If they said something was wrong, he believed it.

Returning to his friends, he said that very thing. "The mules think we're being watched."

No one gainsaid him. Hands went to swords and Neroma's wards intensified, catching Kelgan unawares for a sneezing, wheezing moment before his own defenses slammed into place.

"Sorry," he muttered, blowing his nose and wiping his eyes.

"Kel," scolded Cal impatiently, "you've got to do better than that. You can't let down *your* guard for a minute. You could have been taken out in the time you got your wards up."

Everyone's heads nodded in synchronization, and then burst into grins as Piper added disgustedly, "Yeah, and he wasn't even kissin' Mom."

It was Neroma's turn to shutter her popping eyeballs.

"Sort of an independent thinker, isn't he?" Kelgan elbowed Cal's ribs, urgently and not at all gently.

"It would be easier if we could travel all night and sleep during the day," opined Cal while clutching his side. "Then the Mel'hachim wouldn't have to be so uncomfortable hanging onto Daliane all night and...."

Kelgan cut him off. "They'd just clutch her all day, instead, and we would be blind as bats and totally vulnerable at night."

"I guess you're right," agreed Cal. "Of course, if we had a Mage who could make some light for the road, well...."

Kelgan groaned loudly enough to attract attention. "Does everybody have to keep reminding me that I can do magic?"

"It would seem so," responded Cal through pursed lips.

Discussing it with the others produced mutual agreement. When Cal told the Mel'hachim what Kelgan had said about "clutching Daliane," he elicited one of Jorgo's rumbling laughs. "He knows us well."

··· 65 ···

Laughter—the Best Medicine

K elgan lay on his back, gazing unseeingly at the green canopy above him. Since they had all agreed to switch their *modus operandi* to night travel rather than move by daylight, they were all feeling restless and uncomfortable in their first attempt. All that is, except Piper, who was curled beside Kelgan and fast asleep. Kelgan envied a child's ability to adapt—as long as Piper had his group (and his self-christened family), he fell instantly into the rhythm. Kelgan, on the other hand, found sleep less easily in his grasp. Too much light, for one thing. He could hear the others stirring and sighing as they, too, tried to will relaxation.

Too much light! Kelgan mentally slapped himself in the head. If he could *make* light at night, why couldn't he make, if not complete darkness, at least a twilight ambience. Leaping to his feet and startling everyone (with the requisite reaching for swords), he shouted, *"Ombrade!"* To as much his surprise as anyone else's, a brownish haze of shadows fell around the little camp, like the last ebbing light of sunset, shrouding the group in artificial night.

A restrained cheer went up as the companions shifted their mental attitudes to a more evening psychology. As Kelgan dropped back to the leafy undergrowth, Piper opened one eye and mumbled, "You're awful loud, Dad. Uh, how are we gonna know when it's night?"

Exasperated, but conceding the boy had a point, Kelgan answered, "Don't worry, I have it all figured out."

Reassured, Piper fell immediately back to sleep.

Kelgan, on the other hand, lay wide-awake and pondering Piper's question. *How the Darkness* were *they going to know when the time was right to leave?* Still pondering, he fell into a semi-doze which ended with a start of terror as a chill hand grasped his.

"Come," ordered Pellerin.

Feeling, actually, less apprehensive to see the cold hand was only Pelly's, Kelgan thought, *here we go again.*

Rising obediently, he was instantly transported back to the ruined castle with its melancholy Great Hall. The same tattered tapestries with their faded stitches lined the walls; and, as before, at the arrival of Kelgan and his dreadful guide, they began to renew themselves, rejoining and brightening. Kelgan expected to see the same story, and for much of it he was right. However, additions had been made.

This time a new chapter intruded into the previous. A princely-appearing young man rode across a drawbridge and into a courtyard. Waiting at the portal to the Keep stood a girl of astonishing plainness, although elegantly dressed, and an older man. The young man slid from his horse. Kelgan realized that they were not proceeding from tapestry to tapestry as they had the last time, but viewed just the one as though through a window onto a scene of real life—and, rushing up the stairs, seized the hands of the young lady and gave her father a rather perfunctory half-bow. The maiden broke into a smile of such joy, her plain, angular face transformed into one of great beauty. The Prince responded seemingly with the same joy.

Just as Kelgan started to step closer to the scene, it switched before his amazed eyes. Now, the view was of a bed chamber. The same plain woman, no longer a maiden, sat up against an army of pillows. She held a swaddled bundle in her arms.

The Prince sat on the edge of the bad, visibly swelling with pride.

Though no sound could be heard, the woman's words were easily understood. "Your son, My Lord."

The scene switched again. This time a boy about three or four stood beside his father at the same bedside. This time the plain-looking woman said, "Your daughter, My Lord." The Prince gazed on the tiny bundle with the same swelling pride as previously.

Another switch as a hill appeared, bright with wildflowers. A chubby toddler of around two years tumbled among them to the delighted laughter of her parents. The boy, now a sturdy six-year-old, held what was obviously a kite-string. Their happiness was palpable.

The next scene brought a cry of horror and a reflexive recoil from Kelgan. Pellerin grasped his arm tightly enough to cut off the circulation. Kelgan felt his hand grow numb under the remorseless pressure. The castle lay in ruins. Corpses littered the courtyard in postures of horrible grotesquerie. Smoke rose from the keep and in the most awful of the vignettes, the body of a still-young woman lay flung atop two small, pathetic, and most terribly still bodies.

Kelgan fought for breath, his free hand pressed to his chest to still his thundering heart. Looking to Pellerin, he understood all too well what animated the ostensible corpse to his right.

"*You* found them."

Kelgan discovered he was sobbing as though they had been his own. He did not know who the you *was*, but knew he did not speak to the departed son of farmers. Pellerin made no response, of course, but he gripped Kelgan's arm ever more tightly until Kelgan felt the very bones themselves must surely warp. The hollow eyes never left his own, but burned with the intensity of a madman. Kelgan felt sure there was no madness there, just unremitting pain.

He wants me to see something else, thought Kelgan, *but I don't know what it is.* Frowning, Kelgan turned his attention back to the tapestry. The same unbearably sad scene met his eyes. The grip tightened again, until agony shot up Kelgan's arm to his shoulder. *If I don't find it soon, I'm going to lose my arm,* was Kelgan's somewhat frantic thought. He looked closer, and then with a horrified intake of breath, he understood. *There's no blood. They're all dead—slaughtered—and there's no blood!*

Even in their grotesque, twisted postures, their gaping wounds obvious, there were no sanguineous pools drying around the fallen. As a matter of fact, they were strangely *pale,* realized Kelgan, *they don't have any blood!*

At this realization, the remorseless grip relaxed, allowing Kelgan to drop to the floor, the strength entirely gone from his legs.

Kelgan put his head between his knees, fighting nausea. The bodies had been drained completely. *After death? Before?* The thought of what could have done something so obscene—and so thorough—threatened Kelgan's dinner. Breathing deeply, Kelgan pushed himself to his feet, feeling the trembling of his thighs. Following a sudden unconscious impulse, he pulled Pelly into an embrace and simply stood there for a long minute.

"We'll get 'em, Pell," he promised.

The next minute, he felt his shoulder being shaken vigorously. "Dad, c'mon, Dad, wake up." The words were nearly a shout.

His eyes shooting open, Kelgan noted that he was the center of concerned attention. Piper was bending over him, his face white, his hand still on Kelgan's shoulder. Others peered down at him, expressions of worry on their faces.

"Boy, Dad, you must have been really tired," Piper observed shakily.

Only Nevander seemed to understand. "Another seeing."

Kelgan nodded. "And definitely no metaphor." Thinking about it threatened Kelgan's dinner a second time.

"The real deal," Cal said in a flat tone reminiscent of a death knell. "Piper's... we've... been trying to wake you for at least an hour."

Kelgan stumbled to his feet, shook off Cal's helping hand, and strode away, brushing rudely past Nevander, and deeper into the trees. Forgetting the state of things they had seen, he pulled up short as the "forest" gave way to the twisted tree-trunks, fire-blackened ruins of dwellings, and upheaved earth of the "real" world.

All right, he thought, *I'm not the only one existing in a dream world. We're all there—or somewhere.*

Cal followed Kelgan. Seeming to pull the thoughts from Kelgan's mind, he observed quietly, "I said it before. What you see isn't what we get, is it?"

Kelgan turned to him and made a helpless gesture. "What's real, Cal? Us? That?" He indicated the wasteland.

"I'm willing to bet that's real," Cal retorted grimly. "But I'd also bet *you're* what's keeping *us* real."

"Not just me," Kelgan demurred, "Neroma and Nevander, too."

Cal made a *faugh* of disgust. "They don't do this, Kel. When are you going to own up to being a Mage? How many times do we have to say 'grow up'? I'm getting really tired of the big whine."

Stung, Kelgan answered with some heat. "I wasn't whining. I'm just giving them some credit. If it weren't for Neroma's help with the wards...."

Cal interrupted with a grin. "Sorry, didn't mean to touch a nerve."

Kelgan grinned, too. "I'm just humble."

Cal snorted.

"Seriously, I probably am doing it, but I don't know how—it's not conscious—it just *is*."

"Hey, okay by me," said Cal.

"I actually can feel my power growing," Kelgan told him a little nervously. "I'm—well, frankly, it isn't exactly comfortable."

Cal soberly regarded him. "I think maybe I better tell *you* something."

Kelgan's eyes widened, he *knew* what was coming—hadn't he had that feeling himself?

"You—and it's because you're me—we're us—I mean...."

"Yeah," agreed Cal. "I think so."

"When did you notice?"

Sheepishly, Cal stared at the ground. "Uh... when we had that first fight with the black and reds on the road."

"When I got poisoned?" Kelgan was incredulous.

"Yeah," tersely.

"And you just failed to say anything?" Kelgan clenched his fists and considered Cal's nose.

"Well, I didn't know what it was. I thought when I was fighting, I just remembered my fencing really well, and that I was damn scared and that made me stronger...." Cal trailed off for a long minute. Resuming, he said, "But now I think it was your sword. When you swung, I swung—and connected."

"But I don't control the sword."

"Yeah, I know that; you know that; but the sword doesn't."

Kelgan gasped and black dots swam before his eyes.

"I think it's retroactive, Kel."

Kelgan gave him a bewildered stare.

"The sword knew you could use it before you did, Kel. The trees knew, the mules knew, everyone else knew what you could do. You're the only one who had to find out."

"And now *you* can do it, too?" Kelgan asked, still trying to comprehend.

Cal favored him with an impatient glare. "C'mon Kel, you just said you could feel your power growing. Some of it is spilling over into me. I seem to be your counterpoint on my world, just a little older and not even slightly special *there*. But here, there are two of us. Your unconscious knows that already, and it doubles a lot of things."

Kelgan considered the "lot of things" and felt a sudden stab of both pity and guilt. He remembered the look on Cal's face when he first encountered Neroma. Stuck for something to say, he fell back on, "So you feel power, as well?"

"I can't really do anything with it on my own. Uh, I did try a couple of things." Cal blushed furiously.

Kelgan giggled. He couldn't help it. The picture of Cal trying out a few spells when no one was looking was irresistible.

Instead of looking hurt, Cal chuckled, too. "I didn't set fire to the forest, and that's a good thing."

"But you think together... it amplifies the power?"

"I kinda get that idea." Cal's voice dropped. "I *saw* the last tapestries."

Kelgan gripped Cal's wrist with enough force to make Cal wince. Dropping his wrist, he impulsively he threw his arms around Cal's shoulders and hugged him tightly.

I'm doing this a lot lately.

Cal fervently returned the hug.

"I'm sorry," Kelgan whispered.

"Don't be," Cal retorted, "we're—I'm fine."

Mutually embarrassed, they backed away from each other.

Cal spoke first. "It's obvious that Pelly is an amp, too."

Puzzled for a moment, Kelgan realized Cal meant an amplifier. "Yes," he agreed dryly, "when you're dead, it helps to have amplification."

This struck the two of them as hilariously funny and they doubled over, holding each other up. The Baron's towering form interrupted them. "What mighty jest has seized you? In other words, what's the joke?"

"Actually," explained Kelgan, "it was in rather bad taste."

"At Pelly's expense," added Cal.

"Mmmn," murmured T'Jules. "I can think of one or two bad taste jokes in that regard, myself."

The other two blinked and grinned, then sobered.

"In reality, we're giving the landscape an eyeball," offered Cal.

"Mmmn," T'Jules repeated. "That's a vista to think about, all right. We seem to be dragging our world through here, by force."

"I think it's all Kel, here," offered Cal.

"I wouldn't be surprised," opined the Baron. "I'll wager he denied it, however."

Cal and Kelgan made identical faces. "There's a bet I wouldn't take," said Cal, "He actually admitted he just *might* be keeping us all in some comfort. Being generous, he tried to share the glory, of course."

A wide grin spread over the Baron's face. "Generous to a fault, I'd say."

"All right, all right, I'm the greatest Mage in at least five countries. I'm certainly the greatest Mage of the three of us. Happy now?"

Another wave of hilarity swept over them, catching the Baron as well. They doubled up, pounding each other on the back and wiping away the tears of laughter that rolled down their cheeks.

Kelgan was the first to regain some semblance of sobriety. As his guffaws subsided from gasps into mere giggles, then faded entirely, he regarded the other two with some concern. "Did it strike you we found that a little *too* funny? Cal and I had the same reaction to my really feeble jest."

T'Jules' laughter died instantly, followed in a beat by Cal's. "The camp—the wards...."

The Baron spun on his heel and set off at a run, followed by the other two. Rushing into the clearing, all three pulled up short at the serene vignette that awaited them. The others looked up in some alarm, as well as bafflement, at the precipitous arrival of the three.

"What transpires?" queried Nevander with a frown.

T'Jules stuttered in confusion, "I... that is, we... we... were...."

"Laughing," put in Neroma, with honeyed sarcasm, "we heard you from here."

"We were rather overdoing it," Kelgan explained, "it made us think that it was another form of attack through our minds to render us helpless."

"And to make Kelgan drop the wards," Cal continued. "Again," he added snidely.

Neroma and Nevander considered this idea in their silent communication. Kelgan felt his usual pang of jealousy at the sight, but firmly repressed it.

"Any reason why you just... possibly... needed to laugh?" Another feminine voice, as sarcastic as Cal's, joined in. Daliane, who had listened to the exchange, stood with folded arms and raised eyebrow, waiting for an answer.

"Them voices, they'z just waitin' for us to go all crazy, and see whut ain't there. Then they don't have to do nuthin' but wait for us to kill each other." Ezrael remained at Bethne's side, but his sonorous baritone carried clearly across the space separating them.

A chorus of voices from the rest of the party affirmed his opinion. "We know already that laughter tends to drive them away. Or at least drives something away," said a Terencia, "and we're pretty sure whatever it is comes from *them*, so why would they *want* us to laugh?"

Kelgan heaved a big sigh, admitting the sensibility of Terencia's words. "I'm sorry, I just got a little paranoid. We haven't laughed like that since... well, really, never."

"All the more reason you should," said the other Terencia. "All the more reason we all should make as many opportunities to laugh as possible. You told us that before, but we've been forgetting."

"I forgot," Kelgan sheepishly admitted.

There was general eye-rolling and a muttered, "Save us from the magicians," in the Baron's not-so-subtle whisper.

"Yes, yes, I know," Kelgan said grumpily. "I'm supposed to be the preternatural genius around here."

Nadi, in an unaccustomed show of girlishness, bumped his hip with hers and tittered, "I just love a man who knows his abilities—it's soooo masterful."

Kelgan could only laugh with the rest.

After a meal (Breakfast? Dinner? Who knew?), the group packed up and prepared to move out. The uneventful course of the next few hours on the road struck Kelgan as menacing rather than a respite.

··· 66 ···

The Day Was Made for Love—and Something Else

Kelgan arranged for the now accustomed twilight as the camp settled down for the day. Their night travel became a bit more familiar, and surprisingly more comfortable.

Phosphene knows it shouldn't be, thought Kelgan. *We ought to be terrified of the dark, since that's where the most danger should be lurking. Has it been too easy, or am I just having another bout of paranoia?*

His thoughts trailed off, and he smiled faintly as Piper huddled up against him. Just as he felt himself going under, a slight smack on the cheek brought him back to full awareness. It was a tress of Neroma's hair stiffly tapping him.

"A word," she demanded tersely.

Carefully arranging Piper against his cloak so the child would not notice his absence, he got to his feet as silently as he could manage and followed her deeper into the trees.

"What is it?"

"This," she replied simply as a bower of roses sprang up around them.

Kelgan's personal wards slammed into place to keep him from strangling, and then almost dropped completely as she pulled the shift, which was her only garment, over her head and let it fall to the ground. Winding her arms around his neck, and her hair tightly around his back, she pressed her mouth and her body to his. Kelgan didn't know whether he gasped from incipient asthma or an all too real and rather embarrassing arousal. He found himself envying the giant sea kraken he had once seen in a grimoire, since he didn't know where to put his hands first. She took care of part of the problem by lowering one of her own hands to the belt of his breeches, tugging them down. He helped her with one of his own, while the other tried to grasp both of her perfect breasts at the same time. Giving it up as an impossibility, he just sank to the ground after the shift, and pulled her down on top of him. *You don't even need lessons,* was his last coherent thought.

❋

"Now we know *how,*" Neroma giggled in amazingly girlish fashion. "Next time we won't have to hurry so much."

Feeling dizzy from the import of the phrase "next time," Kelgan could only mumble. The "next time," he was rather appalled to discover, was already an issue with certain parts of his anatomy.

Neroma giggled even more girlishly as she discovered it, too. "Well, maybe, not this "next time," but the one after," she stated, cocooning them in her hair again.

"I've been practicing," Neroma announced proudly afterwards.

Kelgan's baffled, "Whaa," made her flush.

"No, no, not *that,*" she said sharply, but with a hastily concealed smirk. "I mean the rose-bower. I knew there must be some way to split the wards, so that the camp was still guarded, but we...." She flushed again.

Kelgan was enchanted by the way her usual pale ivory coloring was washed by a rosy glow. *No wonder her skill with everything connected to roses,* he thought. His mind and eyes ranged over her with besotted pleasure. He tangled his fingers in the tresses that waved his way, and they curled around his fist.

"Are you listening?" she poured the melodic syrup of her contralto over him, but he caught a slight edge in its smooth flow.

He attempted to bring his mind to bear on what she was telling him. Although he knew something important had happened (something *else,* that is), concentrating on anything but her loveliness was causing his eyes to cross.

"Yes, yes... well, I'm trying." He grinned sheepishly.

She smiled back, enough of a girl underneath the sophisticated mage-woman to enjoy the consciousness of her power. "I have been trying since the day we decided we could not be together. In theory, I thought it would work, but I am ashamed to admit that I took a long chance, because I had no proof—until now. I managed to split my mind—half here with you, and half with them. You did it, too, without even realizing it."

"You have the right of that," Kelgan laughed ruefully. "I didn't even realize I had half a mind right here."

"There is more to you than meets the eye," she replied enigmatically. She pulled on her shift and walked away.

Certain that aeons had passed since they had left the sleeping group, Kelgan was astonished to find that everything and everyone was just as it had been. He slid down beside Piper as carefully as a sneak-thief.

Piper stirred and mumbled, "Where ya been, Dad?"

"Oh, er, call of nature," Kelgan offered lamely.

"Oh," affirmed Piper drowsily as he settled against Kelgan's back.

Kelgan, for his part, lay awake reliving the past couple of hours as religiously as a priest of The Two. Her eyes, her lips, her hair, the faint scent of roses; the rest of it, he drowned a dozen times in memory. For some unaccountable reason, in the midst of his musings, Kelgan found himself wondering what Pellerin thought of his relationship with Neroma. Shaking his head to clear it, he wondered why in the Lady's Name he was wondering. With a snort of self-deprecation, he thought, *well, the mules approve—but I haven't asked Capriola, yet.*

Pelly was dead and yet Kelgan remembered the unrelenting grip on his arm, and the fixity of Pelly's usually vacant eyes. *No, not even slightly dead!* At least not the *somebody* who animated Bethne and Ezrael's son.

Kelgan finally sank from his generally blissful daze into a doze. He was just beginning to dream of pursuing Neroma across fields of black and red uniforms—her hair continually beckoning him on—

when the now familiar steel-vise grip on his upper arm brought him wide-awake again.

No! he thought. Recognizing the futility of objecting, he rose as had become his habit for transport with Pellerin to the ruined castle.

The tapestries whirled into action with unprecedented speed, telling their stories of disaster over again, though the previous scenes flew past as blurs. Kelgan tried to ignore what had already been revealed. They were indelibly imprinted on his memory, most particularly the last set. The horror of the exsanguinated bodies was still fresh in his mind's eye. But try as he might, he could not keep his eyes from straying to the two tiny corpses covered by their mother. He could feel Pelly's eyes burning holes in his soul, although every time he looked in that direction, the vacant gaze seemed elsewhere. His attention, however, finally became riveted on the last, and newest, offering.

To his astonishment and despite the dire message of the tapestries, a smile flitted so quickly across Pelly's face, Kelgan would have thought it imagination had he not found himself enveloped in what he could only consider a brief but sincere bear hug. Then, once again he was turned to face the tapestries, to which a new one had been added.

This one needed no repair; it was bright; the colors gleaming like small gilded butterflies. The weave was crisp and even, the stitches precise, the small figures. The small figures! An icy fist clutched his chest as he realized it was a raptor's-eye-view of the camp! He saw his own figure stretched out, sleeping next to Piper, his cloak covering them both. Neroma nearby (nearer than usual, he noted with a slight glow of pleasure), and his other friends disposed in various postures of sleep. The only figure missing—his hackles rose as he noticed—was the silent watcher by his side. He looked at Pelly, whose attention was now fully focused on him, for a clue as to what he *should* be seeing in what he was seeing. Pellerin simply turned him back to the tapestry again.

"Yeah, I see it, Pelly," Kelgan acknowledged. "I'm there, but *we're* here!"

The tiny flash told Kelgan his answer to the unspoken question was correct.

The scene drew back, the figures grew smaller still—the forest, the dead-land, a stream where, free of restraint, tiny heads bobbed up and down, seemingly chortling in glee. The water, itself, was an ominously inky black. It seemed to Kelgan that the vista shook a little as it passed over this stream.

"The Obsidian Ophidian!" Kelgan exclaimed.

Another flash of acknowledgment from Pellerin.

The scene shifted again, flying over the blasted landscape as though on eagle's wings. A village hove into view, and the viewpoint dropped dizzyingly down to show the inhabitants—or rather what had been they—again the bodies, which lay everywhere, were completely bloodless.

"Why, Pelly? What's the point?" Kelgan gasped. Looking at Pellerin, he amended, "Oh, uh, I guess that *is* the point."

The perspective rose again, onward to a castle rising to an enormous height above the black and twisted plain. Inside they flew. Kelgan swallowed a lump of desperate fear as he took in floor after floor of heavily armed men, all garbed in red and black. *Thousands,* just in the castle alone. Kelgan knew without being told that this was only a minute sample.

The viewpoint swooped upward—a sickening lurch. Kelgan clutched Pellerin for support.

"Oh, uh, sorry," he mumbled, pulling away.

The point-of-view zoomed backward, becoming a globe which Kelgan assumed was the world on which they stood. Then the globe became only one of many displayed. They now stood within a room in which several men—no! To Kelgan's choking horror, these were not men, at least not as he knew them. Yes, they had all the normal accessories, two arms, two legs, a head on top with eyes, nose and mouth. But these eyes glittered like faceted emeralds, while four-fingered hands continued their enigmatic play among the even more enigmatic surroundings. On the occasions when they communicated with each other, teeth as sharp and long as those of a tigracelot flashed ominously.

The *beings* appeared to be busily engaged in viewing more than one world similar to his own. He watched, awestruck, as the creatures moved among the glowing orbs, which, he realized, actually were hanging, unsupported, *in front of the walls.* Occasionally, one or more of the globes would flash. On other occasions, the lights would flash around the room in dazzling patterns, drawing the attention of one or more of the beings. The creatures—he couldn't think of them as men such as himself—who watched moved to attend to the patterns almost too swiftly for the eye to follow. He had thought himself immune to more astonishment, but he reeled as he realized that the entire display, not just the orbs, but all the flashing, blinking lights in the room were not on the walls, but *hanging in air in front of them.*

Stunned by the inescapable confirmation of what Cal's presence suggested, Kelgan found himself clutching Pelly once again.

"Not our world, Pel! Not our time! Not even *us!" How can we prevail?* he wondered, sinking to the ground in despair.

The next thing he knew, it was genuine twilight and Cal was shaking him again. "Wake up, WAKE UP," he repeated fearfully.

"It was one of those damned seeings, again, wasn't it?" Cal frowned in concern.

Remembering only Neroma at that moment, Kelgan felt the blush rise to his cheeks. "No, just some dreams. I had trouble falling asleep."

Cal cocked his head, regarding Kelgan with suspicion. And certainty. "Hmmm," was all he said before rising and walking away. Belatedly, Kelgan realized Cal had told him he also saw when Kelgan did, and he knew he was lying.

Kelgan busied himself lighting the fire for the evening meal, then set out to tend to the mules. The mules regarded him in very much the same manner as Cal. Slowly, deliberately, one of them winked at him, while the other nudged him with a shoulder, nearly knocking him off his feet.

"Were you watching?" Kelgan demanded indignantly.

The mules, affronted, stepped back a pace and sternly eyed him.

"Oh, all right, I apologize."

The heads of both mules swung pointedly in the direction he and Neroma had taken.

"Obvious, was it?" he muttered. "I take it you still approve?"

The mules bared their teeth in identical equine grins.

Why am I discussing this with mules? His thoughts were interrupted by Piper yanking on his tunic.

"Dad, Aunt Teri says there's a stream. Maybe it has fish, and we can catch 'em before it gets too dark."

Aunt Teri! Mom! Dad! He certainly is getting a good-sized family. Wonder if he's going to call Pelly "Uncle."

Overwhelmed with love for everyone, Kelgan swept the child up in his arms and kissed him soundly on both cheeks.

"Aw, Dad! What was that for?" Piper scrubbed at his cheeks with his sleeve.

Setting Piper down with a chuckle, Kelgan noticed Bethne watching him with an indulgent smile.

"You takes good care of that boy of yourn," she observed, "just you and him. You lost your missus pretty young, din't you?"

Taken aback, Kelgan blurted, "I've never been married."

At Bethne's shocked look, he hastened to add, "He's an orphan... uh, he's adopted."

He didn't know how to explain to Bethne that he had picked Piper off the street and didn't know if he had family or not.

"Well, you love him like your own, thassut counts." Bethne smiled again and went off to join Ez at the goat cart, where Capriola favored him with the same knowing look he had received from the mules.

"You've been gossiping, haven't you?" he accused the nearest mule. Both of them instantly became interested in the merits of a promising clump of grass a ways away from Kelgan. *Why am I talking to mules?*

Thinking about Piper made him uncomfortable, however, as he realized he *didn't* know if the child really had family—and he had made no effort to find out.

Piper, who had run off to "Aunt" Teri, now came running back. "Goin' fishin'," he announced.

Kelgan caught him by the back of his tunic. "A question first. I want to know about your parents."

Piper looked puzzled. "Ain't got none. You know that."

"What happened to them"

"Dunno. Don't know nuthin' about 'em. I was promised to the traders 'fore I was born. Never saw 'em, least not so's I can remember."

The hair rose on Kelgan's neck. The traders! Everyone knew what that meant. Desert tribesmen, whose "trade" consisted of human flesh. Many stories circulated about abductions of the unwary—Kelgan's mother often threatened that the traders would catch him when he misbehaved—and everyone had heard that poverty-stricken parents with more mouths than they could feed sometimes sold inconvenient offspring. Kelgan had never actually known anyone who had. He stared at Piper in horror.

Piper, with an offhand shrug, said much too casually, "Didn't stay with 'em long."

"What do you mean?"

Obviously enjoying the effect of his revelation, Piper answered, "Soon's I could figure out how to, I left."

Kelgan took firm hold of the child's arm. *So small!* "Tell me," he commanded sternly.

Piper looked somewhat abashed, seeing that Kelgan was really acting like a father.

"Well... they put you to work as soon as you can walk really good. 'Fore that you're just with a bunch of other babies—I don't remember that too much, but I remember them coming to get me." He stopped for a minute, frowning, trying to recreate a past that for most children would have been only playtime. "I was sold... I guess... to a rich guy who needed kitchen help. I had to peel carrots and potatoes, and stuff like that, and they wanted them just so—I dunno why, they was just goin' to be cooked. If they had to throw any of them out after I was done, the cook smacked me in the mouth with a fist. I was a *real good* peeler. When I got big enough, four, maybe, I had to peel and wash the pots and pans. They had to be just so, like the veggies. I was a real good washer. I only got smacked a few times. They was goin' to give me more jobs when I was about six, but I didn't want no more, so I planned and planned how I was goin' to get out. When the time come, I had it all figured out. I'd been savin' bread and cheese for a couple of days—couldn't keep it longer than that—but I figured I'd find some more out there somewheres. So, I wrapped it up in a towel I used for the pots and pans, tied it around my waist, and stole the cook's apron for a coat. Wasn't too warm, but I folded it a couple of times and it wasn't bad. Then I followed the cat outta one of them little swinging doors they make for cats, and ran faster than I'd ever run. I hid for a long time; ran out of bread and cheese, too, but I didn't dare come out of my hole too soon, 'cuz they'd find me, and I'd get more than smacked. When I thought maybe they wasn't lookin' for me anymore, I lit out. Stole what I could, learned to eat just about anything (pride sounded in his voice). When I got to the town you found me in, I figured I was far enough away so's I could settle down for a while; get some odd jobs. That's it, till you came along."

Kelgan stood, speechless and stunned, still holding Piper's arm. *What was he, about five years old! On his own, traveling for miles alone, stealing his food!* Kelgan's head whirled, all he could think to say was, "How old are you now?"

Piper, remembering he had told Kelgan eleven, shuffled from foot to foot. Finally, he raised he chin and drew himself up as tall as possible. "About eight, I reckon. Maybe I'm nine," he added hopefully.

Releasing his grip on the child's arm, Kelgan put a fatherly hand on Piper's shoulder. "Let's go look at the stream before we fish."

As he said it, one of those Dark-induced *frissons* coursed through him. *A stream—with fish! If I'm keeping part of our world around us without even knowing how, how in Blackness can I have brought a well-stocked river as well?* He held Piper back when the child would have run enthusiastically down to the water's edge.

Both Terencias were standing there on the low bank quizzically regarding him. Noticing each held a hand over their sword hilts, he feigned a casualness he did not feel, and asked, "How does it look?"

"Just what we were going to ask you," replied Cenci pertly.

"Very smooth, very clear, very *familiar,* very, well... very *unexpected,*" added Teri.

Kelgan thought back to the last time they had loaded one of the mules with enough water for several days. He knew it was before they discovered the dual nature of the terrain through which they traversed. *Not that long ago,* he realized, *in spite of* some *of the....* His mind broke off at that point.

At a loss, he motioned the others back, and knelt at the stream's edge; peering into the crystal liquid. He paled. Staring back with saucy malice and instead of his own reflection, he beheld unpleasant visages. The little faces he had seen from the boat at the very beginning of their journey, their tiny, sharply pointed teeth bared in knowing grins. The memories struck him forcefully—the obsidian water, the strangely unmoving twins, the hurtling waterfall, *and* the tiny faces, all displaying cold glee. The entirety of the events of the night before struck him just as forcefully. *How could he have forgotten?*

"What?" demanded Cenci, shocked at his ashen look.

"I don't know," he replied. "I only know we're not going to fish—at least, not yet."

Teri afforded him a measuring glance. In this instance, as quick to know his mind as she knew her sword, she inquired, "Wouldn't have anything to do with some other water, would it?"

Giving an almost imperceptible nod of his head, Kelgan temporized. "Not sure the fish are good to eat. I might have seen something, uh, inedible, lurking, but I can't be sure."

The gathering shadows turned the water darker and darker as Kelgan watched. Teri joined him and her fingers found his. "More than meets the eye," she observed, echoing Neroma, "gives you something to think about."

Kelgan transferred his gaze to her. Was he getting so full of himself that he had gone from insecurity to complete arrogance? Had he also fallen into the habit of thinking of the Terencias as simply thick-headed soldiers, *and women to boot.* He admitted to himself a little of that had crept into his attitude. *Shame on me, when did I get so smart?*

"More than one thing," he agreed gently.

"Still waters aren't the only ones that run deep," Teri chuckled. Then she turned serious. "Kel, Cenci and I want you to know that we're behind you—all the way. We aren't sure what's going on here, but however it plays out—we're there."

Tears sprang to Kelgan's eyes, and he enveloped Teri in an awkward hug, somewhat to her dismay. She stepped back, muttering gruffly, "Just wanted you to know."

"I don't know what's going on, either," Kelgan assured her soberly, "every day, I know less. But I really appreciate the help in not knowing."

Remembrance held and bound them until Kelgan broke away and started for the camp; he ordered, "Stay here with your aunts, son."

Amused expressions flitted across the faces of the Terencias, but they made no comment.

Kelgan strode quickly back to the camp in search of Nevander. *The water was black, now it's clear, but the little somethings are still there. Nevander must know.*

He marched up to where His Lordship quietly chatted with the little Baroness. Without even a nod to Daliane, he seized Nevander's arm and demanded peremptorily, "Come with me."

Nevander's astonishment was palpable; Daliane cocked her head quizzically, but said nothing.

Hustling the astonished Nevander down to the stream-bank, Kelgan demanded curtly, "See?"

Nevander regarded the stream, regarded Kelgan and responded, "Oops!"

"Oops?" Kelgan echoed, turning a baffled face toward His Lordship.

"Well, we were hoping for a source of reliable water," Nevander gestured vaguely behind him, "what with the state of the land and all." He shrugged helplessly and apologetically.

"A source of water?" Kelgan echoed again, staring blankly.

"Yes, my Mage, we... well, we didn't mean to bring the whole river."

"How did you bring anything?"

Nevander grinned an obviously false, self-deprecating grin. "That's really my specialty, my Mage. It—water, that is—runs in the di Nerrill family."

Kelgan stared, then whooped with laughter at His Lordship's bad pun. Nevander looked quite tickled with himself. Once he sobered up, Kelgan asked, "What about the...." He made the same vague gesture in the direction of the water as Nevander had in the opposite direction.

Nevander became very still. "The...."

"Yes, the, well, 'inhabitants,' I guess you'd say."

"You're an even better Mage than I thought—and I have always thought more highly of you than you have of yourself—the inhabitants are not meant to be seen."

"I thought everyone saw them. That's why I kept Piper away from the edge. I don't know this for a certainty, but I think Teri sees them, too, or at least senses them in the water. You'll have to ask."

"I may be a *worse* Mage than *I* thought, and I *didn't* have too high an opinion of myself." Nevander chortled ruefully. "A little like you, I'm afraid."

"What do you mean?!" Kelgan exclaimed in disbelief. "You moved a river!"

"Yes, but I only meant to bring a small rill. I have to confess to you, My Mage, that even though the di Nerrills were known for water wizardry, I... well... I have always suffered with lack of exact control."

Kelgan turned to His Lordship with eyebrows raised. "Are you trying to tell me we might have had an ocean?"

"Or a mud puddle, yes," answered Nevander. "I actually only wanted to transfer a rivulet, so we had a bit for drinking and bathing. I seem to have gotten more," slight emphasis on the last word, "than I bargained for."

"How does the 'more' affect us?"

Nevander shifted uneasily. "I cannot really say, My Mage. We have servitors...." His voice trailed off.

"Servitors," echoed Kelgan. *The inhabitants,* he thought.

"As I was saying, My Mage, I have always suffered from a lack of control."

"The *servitors?*"

"Exactly."

Maliciously grinning faces with needle-sharp teeth rose vision-like in Kelgan's mind.

"So drinking and bathing?"

"Should be safe enough, if we scoop up buckets from close to the water's edge, where it is shallowest."

"What about the fish?"

"What fish?"

"Are there any in the river, or do the 'inhabitants' eat them all?"

"Oh, I hadn't given it any thought."

Kelgan rolled his eyes.

Nevander looked abashed. "We never ate anything from the Black River, it ran under the di Nerrill property for more aeons than anyone could remember. We aren't even entirely sure of its original purpose, but we occasionally make use of its... properties, you might say."

Not even bothering to reply, Kelgan wandered off in bemusement. The idea they might be facing a fatally dangerous enemy in front of them was depressing enough; but the thought that they might have deliberately brought one to chase them, as well, was more than he could easily wrap his mind around. He felt as though he had stepped off the edge of an abyss, free-falling and somersaulting into thin air.

His thoughts continued to whirl like eddies in the stream. He knew Neroma was more powerful than he had believed women to be but he had made the mistake of dismissing His Lordship as no better than a bush magician, differing only in position. Now, it seemed, Nevander possessed hidden talents which were, however uncontrolled, disturbing in their implications.

Piper's high voice interrupted him. "Gee, Dad, can't we ever fish?"

Kelgan squinted at the boy. "I don't know. We'll have to ask Lord di Nerrill."

"Him!" Piper's voice dripped scorn. "He don't never fish."

Kelgan smothered a smile. "No, but he has some expertise in, um, the composition of water."

"Ya mean, he can tell us if the fish are poison?"

Kelgan smothered another smile. "Something like that, yes."

Piper plumped down in the leaves. "Couldn't we jes' pretend?"

Kelgan felt a momentary thrill of homesickness so sharp, he became breathless. A vivid picture of his sister with her undeniable talent for magic rose before him. He thought of the many times he had heard the same words from her lips, and knew of a certainty she never "jes' pretended."

He swallowed the painful lump in his throat, then gave Piper that time-honored response of beleaguered parents, "We'll see."

Piper snorted and rolled his eyes in the time-honored response of children. To Kelgan's absolute astonishment, he stood and trotted off to the side of Nevander. From the expressions and gestures involved, he was obviously importuning His Lordship with vigor for an opportunity to catch something fresh. To Kelgan's further amazement, Nevander squatted down to Piper's size and continued the dialogue as gravely as though addressing a personage of rank. The outcome of the whole seemed to be favorable, since a wide grin spread over Piper's face, eliciting an answering grin on Nevander's. Skipping back to Kelgan, he announced triumphantly, jerking his head back toward Nevander, "He says he'll fix it."

Kelgan experienced a little chill at the word "fix," but managed a smile. "I think we'll have to wait until tomorrow morning. We have to get going now."

"Oh, that's all right," was the insouciant answer.

The camp broke up quickly after that. Kelgan was disturbed by Bethne, who had gone even quieter than usual, and appeared to be moving with difficulty. He was even more distressed when he actually caught Pellerin shooting her a glance of consternation before resuming his impassivity.

Kelgan hurried to her side. Grasping both her hands, he questioned, "Bethne, what is it?"

"Oh, shucks, it's jes' my bein' old," she replied, striving to pass off the problem.

"Bethne, tell me, what is it?" Kelgan repeated firmly.

"Well... I do have jes' a touch of discomfort."

"Bethne!"

"It hurts here." She indicated her chest.

Kelgan grasped her hands more tightly, careful not to hurt her, and for the second time, probed deeply into a human being. What he saw shocked and saddened him—Bethne's stout heart was failing her, beyond anything he could do to repair. Feeling helpless, he set about making her feel more comfortable, as well as ameliorating what damage he could. Ultimately, the power of life and death was beyond him, but he could forestall the inevitable for a while.

Releasing her hands, he asked with a reassuring smile, "There, is that better?"

She gave him a beautiful smile in response. "Oh, yes, I'm jes' as right as rain, now."

He kissed her cheek, and then reacted with shock when she asked innocently, "So what was all that commotion when you wuz wakin' up?"

"When I was...?" Kelgan broke off as realization flooded him. Spinning on his heel, he whirled to the others in an obvious panic; his frantic white-faced signaling drew everyone to him. Cal stepped instantly to his side, knowing, of course, that Kelgan had not told the whole story when queried earlier.

"I've seen more," he gasped. "They're not us—I mean they're not men—I...."

Cal seized his shoulder at the same moment as Neroma stepped to his side and grasped his wrist.

"Suppose you take it a little slower, Old Buddy," suggested Cal with a slight squeeze of Kelgan's shoulder.

Kelgan drew in a couple of deep, calming breaths. Beginning again, he attempted to explain his 'vision' as briefly as possible. "I was with Pelly again in the tapestry room. This time I saw us here at camp, as though I was an eagle flying over. Actually, I saw all of you, but Pelly wasn't there, uh, here. He was missing. Then we, I, we...."

Cal squeezed his shoulder, again.

With another breath, Kelgan continued. "I guess I should say the viewpoint altered. I seemed to span worlds in seconds, and I saw a room with creatures which resembled men, but were *different*. I really can't describe the difference, so don't even ask—eyes, teeth."

Kelgan shrugged in frustration. "They just weren't *right,* that's the best I can do. They also had *things, machines, something...* well, alright, they had pictures and charts which just hung in the air; and lights that blinked on and off in the air, as well."

At some of the incredulous murmurs, he simply went on. "I am aware of how it sounds," he said, "but I know *that* was not *any* kind of *metaphor.* I was seeing the here-and-now, and those creatures were *real.* And I know that's what Pelly has been working up to telling me. Those creatures are actually the ones seizing all the different worlds and controlling those who are stupid and greedy enough to fall under their dominion."

"ETs," observed Cal.

"What...?" began Kelgan.

"Extra-terrestrials. That's how we refer to them on my Earth. Of course, I guess all of you are technically ETs, too, since this *isn't* my Earth, but you're human. Kel seems to be telling us that those guys aren't—even slightly. *And,* they're a lot more advanced than anyone on this planet." He added slyly, "I don't have any trouble believing him, since we're a tad more technological than you are, and we've got some of that virtual stuff, too." What he didn't say was that he had probably shared most, if not all, of the vision.

Thinking of the machine in which Cal had arrived, the others had to agree, to general laughter.

"Of course, you have no magic," Nevander rather haughtily reminded him.

"Well, a guy from my world said something about a sufficiently advanced technological society being indistinguishable from magic, but you're right, I sure can't do what Kel can."

With good grace, Nevander acknowledged that he couldn't begin to understand Cal's machine ("automobile," inserted Cal), so Cal was undoubtedly right, it was just like magic to the rest of them.

··· 67 ···

Third Quarterly Exam—Other Fish to Fry

Although the night's trek was again uneventful—*too much so,* thought Kelgan—the entire company was obviously on edge as they wound their way through the trees until the lightening of the sky overhead announced the imminence of dawn.

As they prepared to settle down once more—*the Enemy must be trying to bore us to death,* thought Kelgan—his vision was the topic of conversation on everyone's lips. Only Piper seemed to have a different agenda.

"Gee, Dad, ain't we never goin' to fish?"

"Aren't we," Kelgan corrected automatically.

Piper rolled his eyes in exasperation. "*Aren't* we?" he echoed with scorn.

Kelgan started as Daliane's voice spoke at his elbow. "A little water problem, perhaps?"

Kelgan spun to look at the little Baroness. "What problem?" He tried to sound innocent.

"Oh, come on, Kelgan," Daliane answered with asperity, "we didn't have a stream near us when we stopped for the morning before yesterday. Then in the evening, poof, there it was. Did you think no one would notice?"

Kelgan acknowledged that, once again, he had underestimated everyone else. Of course, they would notice. Daliane never missed a thing; he blushed as he thought that, and certainly Jorgo and Nadi, whose business it was to maintain vigilance at all times, and the

Baron, and.... He thought maybe Bethne and Ez might have missed it, but Bethne had never shown any lack of wit, in spite of her age, and Ez would know anything Bethne knew.

"I'm an idiot," he moaned disconsolately.

"Yes," Daliane twinkled, "but you're our idiot; and we know you have *other* things on your mind."

Kelgan regarded her suspiciously.

"No, not just that," she seemed to read his mind. "We need to discuss the *other,* other things."

Kelgan nodded. Signaling to the others, he called one more council of war—at least he guessed it was war. They were pulled in a certain direction by something; he saw something, they heard something, they had a dead boy in the lead.... *Yes!* In the lead, Kelgan acknowledged. Pellerin had gotten them all together by dint of a power Kelgan didn't even want to examine. *Why this particular motley crew? Were we the only ones sensitive to his cry for help? We certainly don't seem to be exceptional, well, maybe Jorgo and Nadi, they're certainly warriors.* His head spun, but he managed to maintain a calm exterior as he suggested they spend time debating the issues they faced.

The Baron snorted. "Over and over," he sneered. "What else do we do? Chew on those meager scraps of information, that we have gummed all the flavor from."

Kelgan nodded in agreement. "Yes, but what else *can* we do? We don't know where we're going, we do know whom we face, we don't know why Pelly keeps showing me what he shows me, and WE DON'T KNOW WHO THOSE BLASTED ETs ARE." Kelgan's voice rose to a shout, startling everyone.

T'Jules, taken aback, nodded in his turn. "You have the right of it, Mage, let's have a parley."

Daliane stifled a giggle, causing T'Jules to glare at her. A couple of other stifled giggles arose in the direction of the Terencias.

Kelgan cleared his throat, but before he could speak, Piper asked, "Are we going to fish?"

The little party dissolved in laughter, which resulted, to everyone's delight, in a sudden bloom of flowers amongst the trees and a twittering of birdsong.

"Uh, I guess… I know," he amended, "you all saw the stream, I'm not… I didn't have anything to do with that. It was entirely Lord di Nerrill's magic."

Murmurs of appreciation arose among the group.

Nevander demurred. "Before my Mage gives me too much credit, it was more a matter of luck than skill. His is the only magic worth mentioning; I'm just an amateur."

Murmurs arose again, this time of denial. Kelgan was now the one having to stifle a giggle.

"His Lordship is too modest, but we do have a problem. The stream came complete with more than fish."

Heads swung expectantly toward Nevander. Looking uncomfortable, His Lordship admitted he wasn't sure how safe the water was. He repeated what he had told Kelgan. "As long as we keep close to the bank, I think we're perfectly safe. I also think that if we ventured out on the stream in a boat, we would have no problem, as long as we kept our limbs out of the water."

A chorus of 'hmmms,' this time.

Piper elicited another round of laughter when he demanded, "What about the *fish*?"

"We'll go down to the bank and take a look right now," Kelgan promised. We'll talk about other stuff when we get back."

"We'll *all go*," asserted Nadi, taking Piper's tiny hand in hers. The others indicated their agreement.

Even Bethne insisted, to Kelgan's concern. She shushed his arguments against it. "Now, son, I knows what you knows, you cain't hide it from me. I'm goin' to enjoy what's I kin enjoy."

Kelgan's answer was to sweep her up in his arms. "I'll take you; you'll be my date. Just don't let Ez know that I'm trying to steal you for myself."

Bethne smiled as flirtatiously as a girl, and fluttered her eyelashes at him. "Shucks, he'll never guess a thing. Might make somebody else jealous, though."

Kelgan caught a glimpse of the young woman who had stolen Ezrael's heart and hugged her tightly. "I don't care, you're worth it."

Bethne chortled, and hung on with both arms.

Reaching the stream, there was only a deafening silence.

Facing them, across the not-so-wide divide of water stretched a seemingly endless line of formidably armed, black and red clad soldiers; those formidable arms at the ready. A mounted officer walked his steed back and forth in front of the line. Seeing the small group standing frozen in horror on the other bank, he bared his teeth in a wolfish grin, then signaled his troops to prepare for attack. The muted, but daunting clank of armor floated over the intervening space as the soldiers leaned forward in anticipation. The officer's arm swung down, and the army surged forward into the shallow-appearing stream.

Kelgan, Nevander, and Neroma stood together; Daliane and T'Jules joined the Terencias and the Mel'hachim with swords drawn. Cal crept up behind Kelgan and nudged him, silently pointing at Kelgan's own sword. Mentally slapping his forehead, Kelgan drew it from its sheath, a small part of his mind astonished at the fact that he no longer questioned the sword's power. Cal drew the sword given him by the Baron, and assumed a fencer's stance. Kelgan was feverishly going through all the spells he thought *might* work in a situation like this, but had yet to fasten on any.

In the meantime, the eerily silent army reached the middle of the stream. The next moment, there *was* no army. As silently as the army advanced, the water began to thrash, erupting in a myriad of whirlpools both in front and behind the invaders. The soldiers frantically slashed at the water with their swords, as if at a fiercely encroaching foe; then they disappeared, the waters closing soundlessly over their heads. The officer, who had remained on the opposite bank, opened his mouth in what had to have been a scream of absolute terror, yet no sound struck the ears of the defenders. Frantically whirling his mount, he disappeared into the trees.

Immediately, sound returned, the stream water chuckled, fish leapt upward with a splash, the winds soughed in the forest canopy, and the heavy breathing and beating hearts of the brave little company seemed thunderous.

To Kelgan's consternation, Nevander made a small sound and sank to the ground unconscious. Neroma gasped and fell to her knees beside her brother, her hair patting him frantically. *First time for her, too,* thought Kelgan.

He bent and felt for Nevander's pulse, a little weak and a little fast, but not thready, Kelgan noted with relief. He chafed the hand he was holding, as Neroma was doing with His Lordship's other hand. Nevander moaned and opened his eyes, staring blankly at nothing.

Kelgan put his arm under Nevander's head and raised him to a sitting position. "I think the 'servitors' decided to be of service," he whispered in Nevander's ear.

Nevander's eyes took on more focus, and he turned to Kelgan, who still held his hand. "I'm not sure I have an appetite for fish after all," was his ironic rejoinder.

Over Nevander's head, a slight movement from Pelly caught Kelgan's attention. Looking up, for one of those flashing seconds he surprised a distinctly triumphant expression on Pelly's face; vacuity replaced it as always. Kelgan's chest jerked with his indrawn breath as he realized Pellerin was not standing with his horse, as he habitually did, but was one of the group surrounding Nevander. The others seemed to notice at the same moment, and there was a subtle, but definite, shift in their positions away from too much proximity with their silent companion.

Nevander rose to his feet and put an end to the awkwardness of the moment, as well as amusing and surprising Kelgan, by saying, "Piper, my boy, let us gather our equipment. I am sure we can easily find a worm or two for bait."

Piper, with the resilience of youth, agreed enthusiastically—the adults with somewhat less enthusiasm, the memory of the silent, horrifying disappearance of the enemy still too fresh in their imaginations.

Since Kelgan was positive that His Lordship had never put a line in the water—had never even considered the idea—he volunteered to accompany the duo, but he was countermanded by Cal and Jorgo. *A somewhat odd pairing,* Kelgan thought

"We will be the fishers," rumbled Jorgo, "you will be the chef when we return." He winked broadly at Kelgan and prepared to follow Nevander as he 'gathered up his equipment.'

Kelgan was not even a little astonished to see that both Jorgo and Nadi carried flexible poles, which would serve admirably for catching fish. He was more interested, however, when Jorgo affixed arrowheads rather than lines to the poles. Cal, too, cocked his head quizzically when Jorgo presented him with the improvised spear. Jorgo winked at Kelgan, again, and propelled Cal in the direction of the water.

"We must hurry, the darkness will make it impossible to secure the fish."

"That's not all that will make it impossible," Cal demurred, "I've never speared a hot dog, much less a fish."

"Hot dog?" was Jorgo's baffled inquiry.

"Forget it. Lead me to the fish."

Darkness shrouded the camp completely by the time the "fishermen" returned. Jorgo had speared three fine specimens, and Cal even managed one. His Lordship and the small accomplice obviously had a rollicking, as well as drenching, good time, but the fish had no worries from them.

"Light moons, Dad; that was *great*. You shoulda' seen Jorgo." Piper mimed stabbing motions. His enthusiasm lost its edge when Kelgan suggested he might have to scale and gut the fish.

Manfully, Piper rose to the occasion, and proclaimed, "Ain't nothin,' I done that before."

Kelgan, remembering Piper's story, scooped him up and sat him on his lap. "We'll do it together. Watch this."

Laying the four fish out before him, he held out his hand and drew just a touch of power. "*Accleanar*," he demanded. Turning to Piper, he said, "Now it's your turn."

"Huh?" exclaimed Piper.

"You say *Danfiletat*," Kelgan whispered.

"I do?"

"Just go ahead, say it nice and loud."

"*DANFILETAT*," was the response.

Fortunately, Piper's shout was not actually accompanied by a burst of power of the same magnitude. Kelgan shook his head while he waited for his ears to stop ringing. Nevander and Cal, who had witnessed the scene up close enough to be assaulted by the volume, convulsed with laughter, although Nevander looked a bit concerned. Kelgan shook his head, again, this time to reassure His Lordship that only Piper's voice could have attracted uninvited ears. Since the wards were in place, the bit of power he had actually applied was unlikely to leak out; the shout even less so.

"Dad! Look! They're all sliced!" Piper's tiny chest swelled with pride.

"Atta boy, Pipe," commended Cal, "good job. Now we'll cook them, they're pan ready."

Piper looked disappointed. "Can't we do more magic?"

Kelgan acknowledged that they could, but added, "They really taste better when we fry them the ordinary way. And besides, we don't want to waste our abilities on something too small, we might need that power some other time."

Cal grinned, "Yeah, Pipe, if you're going to be a Mage, you need to know when to hold 'em and when to fold 'em."

Kelgan whispered in Piper's ear just as the boy was going to get indignant "I don't know what he means half the time, either."

Cal held up one finger. "Just a minute, young fellas, I think it's time I gave a few lessons." Going to his pack, he produced a battered deck of cards.

"Aah," said Kelgan, in comprehension, "the Tarock."

Cal squatted down in front of Piper. "As soon as we eat, we're going to have lesson one."

Dinner, as it turned out, was less than a ringing success. While the fish were greeted with pleasure at first, when the filets actually turned up on the plates, a marked diminishment of enthusiasm ensued. Even Piper, who speared the first bite with alacrity, never got it as far as his mouth. It didn't take a Mage to guess what was on the minds of everyone in the party—the horrifyingly silent disappearance of an entire unit of armed and armored troops was an all-too-clear memory.

"I... I guess I'm not so hungry after all," was Piper's plaintive observation. Concurring murmurs followed.

Kelgan stood, walked a few feet away, and drilled a small hole in the leaf-mold with his sword. *I bet it's never been used as a digging stick,* he thought. "All right, everybody, toss it all in here."

The group obeyed with unusual alacrity, even Bethne. After the plates were emptied, Kelgan covered the dinner remnants carefully, obliterating all signs of the offending filets. The Terencias tossed their bows over their shoulders and stated flatly, "We're going for rabbits."

Kelgan stopped them briefly. "I've been thinking. We're not fooling anyone by night travel, and we don't seem to be any less vulnerable—or any more, for that matter—so I vote we stay here the rest of the day, and tonight, and start out again tomorrow morning.

"We're with you," Cenci agreed. Teri nodded.

"I'll put it to a general vote."

The others readily agreed.

"It will put us all in a more hopeful mood, my Mage," Nevander concurred. "Skulking by night has made us look—and feel—like scurrying rats."

Kelgan felt chastened. "I didn't realize."

Nevander hastened to reassure him. "No, no, my Mage, we all agreed with you. It seemed a necessary and wise precaution. As it develops, we are, as you say, neither better nor worse off, so the need is gone even if it existed. The arrival of the late unlamented army proved that. We are well noted, and closely followed."

Kelgan nodded with a frown.

"They know us, but why do they want us?" He thought of what he had seen in the waking dreams with Pellerin.

"That, of course, has always been the question. We have all been compelled from the first to embark on this journey and, at first, did not really question. More and more we cannot explain the reasons behind our compulsion, but now we cannot stop."

Kelgan thought again of what he had seen, and once again nodded in agreement. "Yes, we've said before that we were being herded. But why did they pick us? We don't look very formidable, and we would never have known about them."

Nevander stared owlishly at Kelgan. "Why do you think *they* picked us?"

Kelgan gulped. He whirled to locate Pellerin, meeting the young man's eyes full on. That lightning flash of awareness told him the answer to Nevander's dryly expressed question.

"Pelly," he whispered.

"Oh, yes," Nevander agreed in turn. "I suspected it as soon as the seeings began. Else, why would his mother and father, or at least his body's mother and father, be included, being that they are both old and not warriors?"

Kelgan looked his incomprehension.

Nevander expressed his impatience. "Think, my Mage! The 'hero' of your visions took Pellerin's body, because it was presumably the handiest vessel. However, he knew how painful the death of a child can be, therefore he arranged for them be reunited."

"But," Kelgan protested, "Bethne knows that isn't really Pelly."

"Her *head* knows, but her heart says something different. She need not mourn—yet."

Kelgan mulled that over. "Yesss," he said reluctantly, "I guess I see that. That still doesn't explain why the lot of us. At our best we're less than a double hand of swords, and I'm a Mage, but...." He broke off, seeing in his mind's eye the alien smiles of the Not-men in their incomprehensible workroom.

"I cannot even truly surmise, my Mage. *You* have an invincible sword, *and* you have uncovered your superb talent for healing, which was deep inside you all along. I am skilled with water, Neroma with scent, and Pellerin cannot be killed. The warriors are just that, and a bit more, I think, but even if not, they will fight to the death without ever giving up. You and Calvin are the dark horses, I believe; our bond across space has meaning we have yet to discern."

"What about Ezrael and Bethne?"

"They are all about love. It may be the most important element of all."

Kelgan thought about Neroma, and blushed furiously.

A tiny smile quirked the corner of Nevander's mouth, "Mmm, yes," was his only comment.

"But," Kelgan continued to protest, "we march along practically unhindered, every once in a while, we run into a fairly simple snag—simple is a relative term, I admit, but for Nadi and Jorgo, and the Terencias, it's practically like the nursery."

Nevander shrugged. "It is as you say, but you must remember there was nothing simple about your poisoning. Had you not found the power within yourself, we would have lost you. And," he mused, "you are somehow the catalyst."

Kelgan wrapped his arms around himself.

Nevander continued, "Today's army was not intended to be 'simple' either, I vow. The adversaries seemed not to know of the water's inhabitants—it was a bit of luck we shall not possess again." He paused. "At least not in the same way."

Shaking his head forcefully enough to cause a dizzy spell, Kelgan could not let it go. "Why? Why me? Why us?"

In a surprising show of compassion, Nevander pulled Kelgan to him in an embrace. "*We* know you are special, my Mage. *They* evidently know it, thus now it is time for you to know it, as well. We cannot supply the 'why' as yet, but the who is not a mystery." He nodded toward Pellerin. "Even the dead know."

Kelgan rested his head for a moment on Nevander's shoulder, and then pulled away. "Well, if I'm special, you must be, as well."

"We all must have a part to play," Nevander acknowledged, "but we are the supporting cast. You, and possibly Cal, I suspect, are in the starring roles. Pellerin, ah! His role is yet to be determined, we have not the entire playbook."

"Entire! As nearly as I can tell, I'm in a different play."

Nevander grabbed Kelgan's shoulders and shook him—not gently. "Stop it! Right this minute, my Mage! Let me not hear thus from you again!"

Shaken as he was, Kelgan could not help noting that His Lordship had reverted to being His Lordship. Just discussing role playing had set Nevander right back onto his imaginary stage and into his aristocratic role as Lord of the Manor. Kelgan couldn't repress an interior smile, even though he was aware that Nevander was serious, and besides, was absolutely right.

Seeing Kelgan's slight quirk at the corners of his mouth, Nevander slapped his forehead theatrically and responded with a grin of his own. "I seem to be less impressive than I had wished."

"No, I apologize, the Baron read me the same lecture, so did Cal, and I promised them to abstain from whining; now, here I am doing it again. Fine example for Piper, I must say. You're right, there is obviously some element that marks us as a problem for the... well, whoever we face. They want us together to keep an eye on us."

"I believe they want to keep an eye on us, but I think the possessor of Pellerin's body is the one who wants us together," Nevander reminded Kelgan patiently.

Kelgan was now the one to slap his forehead. "Of course, you said that, and I was too busy anguishing to pay attention."

"The goals of both have become the same, however."

"Keeping us together, and herding us in the same direction."

Nevander nodded.

Kelgan noticed that Pelly had been gazing at them fixedly throughout their conversation. *Strange,* he thought, *strange, that it doesn't seem strange, any more.*

Gesturing to Nevander to remain where he was, Kelgan strode over to Pelly and addressed him directly.

"Pelly, I feel things are shortly to come to a head. I think the 'easy' part is behind us and the really hard part is just about to begin. Any suggestions?"

Pellerin's hand fell heavily on Kelgan's arm. The most frequently vacant eyes held—could it be amusement? He didn't speak, but Kelgan sensed that another seeing was in store. Satisfied, he went back to Nevander.

"Speaking of keeping an eye on things, would you and Cal keep at least one on me tonight. I don't know exactly what to expect, but it's getting harder and harder to come back to myself after I've been with Pelly in the Great Hall. I don't want to get lost that way, either."

"And, you think, again tonight?"

"Yes, I'm sure."

The group was glad of the respite, and a return to a normal schedule, even though there was no guarantee Kelgan was correct in his assumption that they would be just as safe during the day as the night. It felt something like a holiday. Cal returned to explaining the mysteries of something he called 'draw poker' to Piper, Jorgo and Nadi attended to their somewhat neglected warrior exercises—T'Jules and Daliane joining in—while Kelgan performed a bit of healing on Bethne, as well as seeing to the comfort of the mules.

Still a muletender, was his wry thought, *I may be special to Nevander, but the mules know differently. They know I'm just here to keep them happy.*

As though catching his thought, one of the mules fluttered its eyelashes, and nuzzled his shirt in a mulish display of sarcasm, while its partner offered a rude noise.

"Thanks, I appreciate your gratitude."

A slight sound came from behind him. The mules instantly sprang back, and assumed an air of total respect and cooperation.

Kelgan turned to see Neroma watching with a definite smirk on her face, seeming like an ivory cameo that had developed sense of humor. "They have perfect faith in you," she observed. "They recognize a leader when they see one."

The mules brayed with enthusiasm, making Kelgan wish for a cattle prod, if for no reason than to at least look as though he had some authority.

"I wish I could—yes, yes, I know—I'm it."

"Have you thought that it is the very fact you do not see yourself as a hero, which actually makes you one. You have shown a remarkable talent for rising to the occasion."

Kelgan, embarrassed at the double meaning his imagination pictured, tried to pass her words off with jocularity. "The sword does the rising—I just hang on."

She gave him a look of exasperation and turned on her heel.

He discovered Cal watching the by-play with a look of sarcastic amusement. "Didn't have to be a mind reader to know what you were thinking."

Kelgan, furious at again being read as easily as a beginner's Grimoire, started for Cal, ready to plant a fist in his double's face, only to find himself standing foolishly with his fist raised and Cal several feet away.

"Whoa, hey, I have to keep reminding you we're on the same side," Cal began in a deceptively mild tone.

Kelgan cut him off. "You did it again—you moved! You moved before I started!"

Cal stared back blankly, mute with shock. Finally, he managed a lame, "Well, that has to mean something," and gave a forced laugh.

With asperity, Kelgan growled, "That means I'm going to have a hard time punching you in the nose." He lapsed into a baffled silence.

The two of them stared at each other witlessly until Nevander, attracted by their peculiarly rigid poses, joined them. "Does there seem to be a difficulty?"

As one, they turned their intense gazes on him.

"Why, no," answered Cal, completely without conviction. "We're thinking of going on the stage—as tent poles."

Kelgan waved his hand at Cal to keep him quiet, and tried to explain what had occurred to Nevander.

His Lordship, in an unconscious echo of Cal, commented, "Well, that has to mean something."

Not wishing to disturb the others right away with another mystery, Kelgan waved both hands this time, and abandoned the whole matter for the time being.

Swearing Nevander to silence, he joined the others as they settled for the night.

··· 68 ···

Prime Movers, and a Prime Movement

As Kelgan anticipated, he wakened to Pellerin's cold grasp on his arm.

"Hi, Pelly," he said, almost cheerfully, "I've been expecting you."

Pellerin's eyebrows lifted a fraction of a hair, but otherwise he offered no response. Kelgan felt the night's chill grow even chillier. Pelly didn't even command him to "come" this time, just grasped his arm tighter and they were away.

Not to the castle! An astonished Kelgan stood with Pelly above a windswept plain. Below, thousands of shaggy, horned beasts with heavy forequarters galloped clumsily but rapidly, raising huge dust clouds in their flight. Bare-chested warriors, riding spotted ponies, pursued the beasts, bringing down several with bows and lances.

As Kelgan watched, a machine of some sort, belching smoke, roared from the East across the plain. The scene shifted. No sooner had the machine disappeared than a fantastic city of giant buildings rose into view, dwarfing the tiny inhabitants who skittered like ants among them. Hundreds of self-propelled vehicles raced back and forth in a seeming endless stream.

Uncomprehending, Kelgan gaped until prompted by a painful squeeze from Pellerin. Pelly's intense gaze persuaded him to look closer. The scene zoomed closer to the bustling streets until Kelgan felt himself one of the scurrying crowd. He looked to the road and gasped in recognition.

"Cal's world! This is Cal's world!"

A brief shine of approval on Pellerin's blank visage told him he had guessed correctly.

Kelgan marveled at the scene spread before him; the height of the buildings, like so many gauntleted hands reaching for him, the speeding vehicles Cal called 'cars,' the sheer numbers of the population, all filled him with amazement and delight. A brief glimpse was all that was allowed him, however.

Without the aid of the tapestries, the scene shifted once more to the sad vignette Kelgan had seen before—the tiny bodies futilely covered by their selfless mother. As before, Pelly's grasp nearly crushed Kelgan's bicep. He made no protest, however, knowing the depths of Pelly's despair.

While he observed, the pitiful display faded—or more correctly, drifted to a new location. Rather than the ordinary, run-of-the-mill castle, a city of such stunning beauty, which brought tears to Kelgan's eyes, rose before him. Crystalline structures seemingly wrought from spun sugar twisted like acrobatic dancers into an equally crystalline sky. This time the message was unmistakable.

"Oh, Pelly," Kelgan whispered, "you're not from around here, or even around *here* there, are you?"

He began to laugh, which quickly grew into hysteria. He collapsed sobbing onto the dusty grass. Pelly waited, endlessly patient, until Kelgan sobbed himself out.

Surprisingly unembarrassed and renewed, Kelgan rose to his feet, dusting himself off.

"Four worlds, Pelly, four worlds—how many others before we knew and before we stop them?"

Pellerin's response was to clutch his chin and force his head down to his own. Placing his forehead to Kelgan's, he held the other captive for a long moment. Kelgan felt a rush of *something*, he could not have said what. It was like being a half-empty goblet of watered wine being mingled with another just slightly more powerful quaff. He squeezed shut his eyes. When they flew open, he stared into Piper's frightened blue ones.

"Yer doin' it again, Dad," said the child.

A puff of laughter behind him revealed Cal, covering a look of anxiety with forced humor.

Rolling to his side, Kelgan used the extra seconds to compose himself before he stood with a shrug.

"More of the same, I'm afraid," he said, attempting to dismiss the events of the vision.

To his amazement, it was still night, rather than morning, as it had been after the other seeings. Glancing around, he noted the armed members of the group were all awake and watchful; no swords drawn, but hands at the ready.

"What? Why?" he began.

Cal understood and answered, "I had a call of nature; you and Pelly were gone." Delivered with the solemnity of a judge, the implication struck Kelgan like a blow.

His eyebrows met his hairline.

Cal nodded affirmatively, "We saw you... materialize, for want of a better word."

"Ner... Nev," Kelgan stuttered.

"Still asleep." Cal nodded with even more significance.

"Oh, Darkness!"

"*I* think so," agreed Cal.

"No, wait, Pelly's definitely on our side."

"Or his own," said Cal laconically.

Thinking of the tiny bodies, Kelgan could not help but agree.

"And, this time," Cal went on, "I didn't see anything 'til you got back."

Stunned into silence, Kelgan sat and stared at nothing while Cal fidgeted. *Pelly! Pelly moved us—just MOVED US!*

"You know what this means, don't you?" demanded Cal.

"No," answered Kelgan.

"*He's* a Mage."

Giving Cal a look of disgust, Kelgan replied, "Well, of course, he is. How did you think he was doing the tapestry thing?" *The tapestry thing, I sound more like Cal every day.*

"I don't think you're getting it." Rising abruptly, Cal strode over to where Pellerin stood beside his ancient mount. He studied

Pellerin's face in the dying firelight. Pelly, in turn, gave the tiniest of nods, shocking both Cal and Kelgan.

Oh, Darkness! thought Kelgan.

For some unfathomable reason, this exchange appeared to perk up the little Duchess, who watched without offering any comment, but her sharp eyes caught Pellerin's slight movement. Prodding her husband, and signaling with her hand to the Mel'hachim, she lay down and prepared to go back to sleep. This, in turn, reassured the Terencias, who followed suit.

Kelgan, who thought he had missed a great deal, tendered Cal a helpless shrug and joined Piper, who was already fast asleep.

He awoke again, with the vague notion that something had disturbed him. Feeling a discomfort under his chin, he opened his eyes, expecting to see that a twig had somehow lodged itself under the collar of his cloak. His eyes flew open, and his blood gelled, as he realized that a figure bent over him, and that the discomfort came from the stranger's sword, the point of which was pointed directly at that spot.

The stranger was garbed in a black and red uniform, the heavy use of braid telling Kelgan that the intruder was of high rank. He met the enemy's eyes, which displayed a trace of amusement, as well as triumph. A careful rolling of his eyes to right and left, being very careful not to otherwise move, presented him with the disheartening knowledge that they were surrounded by an entire army of the black and reds.

More straining of his eyes told him that Neroma was awake and staring. Her tension brought her brother to full awareness, but neither moved nor spoke. Daliane, with her preternatural awareness, was barely an instant behind, only her slight motion alerted her protectors. The Terencias, Kelgan noted, had been awake the whole while.

We are joined, he exulted, then realized that would not help if the enemy decided to strike.

Moments passed with no change. The Commander still bent

over him, the sword tip still pressed under his chin, the unnaturally quiet army still stood in orderly files. Finally, with the somewhat bemused realization that he was growing bored, Kelgan decided to act. With exaggerated slowness, he began to inch out from under the sword point, making sure to pull his neck as far back as possible into the leaf-mold. Holding his breath, he moved at a painfully snail-like slither, until he was lying beside the enemy, rather than under. The intruder made no sign he noticed Kelgan's departure; remaining in the posture he had held from the beginning.

Seeking Neroma's eyes, he felt, rather than saw, her released breath. Recommencing his slither, he made his way in her direction. He finally reached her side, and began to rise to his feet. All awake echoed his endeavor.

As silently as the motionless army, arms were drawn as soon as they had found their feet. Kelgan proffered a hesitant motion toward the army, receiving soundless agreement from the entire band.

Two, four, six, eight, who do we appreciate? sounded in his head. His eyes flew wide as he recognized Cal's sardonic tones. He couldn't afford to make any unnecessary movements, so he ignored this latest of surprises. Just as an experiment, however, he shot back, *actually it's ten,* to catch a tiny nod from Cal.

As one, those with weapons began to move. Slowly, slowly, and oh, so, carefully, the little armed group edged toward the "warriors" from their various positions. Kelgan glanced in the direction of Neroma and Nevander, standing tensely, frozen to their spots, but nevertheless obviously muttering almost silently to each other.

Everything seemed preternaturally clear. Every person, every object stood out as though haloed in light despite the night gloom. The silence rang with—silence. Still the black and red army stood arrayed like chess-pieces on a board, the only disturbance the minute shuffle of the leaves as they inched.

The Commander still leaned forward sword tip pointed at the spot Kelgan had vacated. Kelgan heaved a silent sigh, unobtrusively touching the nick the sword had made; it was wet, telling him it still bled a bit. Catching his eye, Neroma favored him with the minutest of nods; acknowledging that she saw.

When the group, (*at last*, thought Kelgan) reached the serried ranks, the small band paused, then, as one, plunged forward with their weapons extended as far as possible. Row by row, the black and red opponents simply vanished. They now stood alone. Alone, that is, save the Commander, who retained his vigilant posture. Kelgan looked at the others and shrugged, eliciting shrugs in return.

Well, thought Kelgan, sensing it was up to him, *here goes.*

He shuffled silently backward until he stood beside the Commander. Swinging his sword, he thunked it off his opponent's breast plate, expecting the same disappearance. To his astonishment and horror, the Commander straightened, grinned evilly, and swung back. A cry of consternation escaped the watchers, waking Bethne and Ez, who sat up groggily, then froze as well.

Unprepared, Kelgan dodged backward awkwardly as the blade sliced through his tunic, effecting a similar, although shallow, slice to his chest.

His sword leapt instantly into action, Kelgan's shoulder pulled nearly from its socket as he tried to keep up with the blows.

The enemy's grin was replaced with surprise as he found himself desperately parrying. Even as he battled, Kelgan shook his head in wonderment at the undisturbed silence—no clang of steel, no gasping breaths from his opponent or himself, just his own heart laboring in his chest as he sought an opening.

Who am I fooling? he mused. *The sword is the one seeking.*

His attention faltered a moment at that thought. Sensing the minute advantage, the grin returned to the opponent's face, and he stepped forward to deliver the killing blow. Without hesitation, Kelgan skidded to his left, brought his left arm up under the other's sword arm. Deflecting the stroke, although it felt as though his forearm was broken, he slid his blade under the other's ribs and upward.

Surprise and chagrin fleetingly touched the Commander's face before it assumed the blankness of approaching death as his knees crumpled. Before touching the ground, he brought his arm up in what seemed to be the beginning of a salute, then fell face forward.

Immediately, the surrounding forest seemed to erupt with sound—

the whistle of wind, the creaking of boughs, small skitterings and scurryings amidst the undergrowth—all scarcely noticed before, but now creating a cacophony by comparison.

Kelgan remained motionless, stunned by the realization that *he,* not the sword, had dictated his final actions. As he pondered that fact, he became aware of the spreading agony emanating from not only his chest, but his left arm, where the other's weapon had caught it.

Oh, Darkness, he anguished, *poison again!*

His knees buckled. Fighting to keep from losing consciousness, which he was sure would be fatal, he found himself supported on each side by Jorgo and Cal.

"The same as before," Jorgo rumbled. "Concentrate, my good friend."

"Yeah, Kel," admonished Cal. "Think!"

Kelgan's vision blurred at an alarming rate. He became dimly aware that several loops of rope seemed to have been thrown around him. *Ropes?*

The slightest of snorts from Cal told him just what they were. Neroma's hair (!) was embracing him—patting anxiously at his chest and arm, holding him upright with the ferocious strength of her will.

Will! Drawing strength from her strength, Kelgan forced himself to begin the tortuous process of looking deep inside himself, down, down, to where the dark tendrils of dissolution were forming a hideous mass within.

Dark tendrils, he thought in a dreamy haze, *hers against theirs— no contest.* He found himself giggling weakly. Jorgo gave his arm a slight squeeze.

"Concentrate," he ordered sternly.

Kelgan refocused.

One by one, he followed each dark snaking wisp to its end and brought his power to bear. Not so easy this time. *Not that it was easy the first time,* he inwardly groaned.

The enemy had evidently stepped up the killing power, and he feared he was making no progress at all. After what seemed forever, he felt a slight loosening in his chest and a minor mitigation of the pain. Neroma sensed it, too, for her tresses tightened almost as painfully as his chest, causing him to gasp and lose concentration.

Sensing that just as quickly, she released just enough for him to catch his breath and return to his task. Surprisingly, it now felt easier; he realized. Although painful, she managed to impart new strength into his endeavors.

The mass unwound with all of the reluctance of a sleeping serpent, reminding him of the Obsidian Ophidian.

"*Water!*" he gasped suddenly.

Cal reached for his hip flask.

Kelgan shook his head as firmly as he could.

"River," he managed to choke out.

His friends looked at each other, baffled.

"River," he reiterated, trying to motion.

"You want to go to the river?" Neroma breathed in a syrupy cascade.

"Mmmhmm," Kelgan managed.

Jorgo, without further ado, swept Kelgan up like a child—Kelgan dangling ridiculously to either end—and strode off to the water. Reaching the shore, he awaited further instruction.

"Toss." Kelgan exhausted his ability to speak with that request.

Jorgo hesitated, appalled.

Cal grasped his elbow. "Do it, Jorgo. He knows what he wants—I hope," he added.

With an agonized expression, Jorgo did as he was bade. Tossing Kelgan out as far as he could, he and the other onlookers were horrified to see Kelgan sink out of sight without a bubble.

Kelgan went down, an astonishing ride into an unsuspected depth; even more astonishing was the realization he was not holding his breath. His breathing had been coming hard on shore; it was coming no harder under water.

Frightening little faces began to appear at the periphery of his vision. Forcing himself to regard them with what he hoped came across as serenity, but probably looked more like despair; he let himself continue to fall, arms and legs limp.

The faces had become a crowd before him; they surveyed him

with teeth bared in those terrible little grins. At last one swam forward to inspect him at close range—far closer than Kelgan wished. Rising before Kelgan's eyes, its grin widened, narrowed, widened, narrowed, then it backed off in what looked exactly like anticipation.

Kelgan stared as an idea hit him; he grinned back at the imp—widened, narrowed, widened, narrowed—then he, too, waited, hanging in the water.

The imp regarded him motionlessly for an instant; then did a backflip that made Kelgan start and recoil. The rest of the horde followed suit. They began to descend on Kelgan.

Frightened out of his wits, Kelgan nevertheless remained as still as possible. The leader, Kelgan assumed, swam close and fastened his teeth in Kelgan's arm. The front row of attendant imps imitated his actions. Soon Kelgan became a porcupine of attached imps. There was not the slightest vestige of pain, but Kelgan felt his heart pound as though he climbed a steep mountain. He felt no less terrified, but he made no attempt to throw off his clingers.

The leader made a movement with his tail, and as though at a shouted signal, all of those attached sank their teeth into his body all the way to his bones. There was a moment of exquisite agony; then he felt himself flying through the air and back to the shore, where he landed with a thump and a grunt. Those waiting ran to his side, expecting the worst. Cal turned him over and began to prod him rather painfully.

"Ouch! Quit it! Kelgan protested.

Cal sank back on his heels, jaw dropping. Taking a closer look at Kelgan, he exclaimed, "What's happened to you?"

Kelgan looked at his arms, the only things not covered by clothing, and saw that he was tattooed with tiny tooth marks. Tearing open his shirt, he saw they extended over his entire chest, but... there were no other marks at all, chest and arm bore no trace of the wounds he had received. Moreover, except for a slightly itchy feeling, he felt quite well.

To his chagrin, this discovery made the world spin, and he was forced to drop his head between his knees to keep from fainting like a... well... like a weakling. He stopped himself from thinking he would be fainting like a girl, before Neroma caught his thought.

"I think our accompanying river inhabitants have previously unplumbed depths, my Mage," said Nevander.

Cal snorted. "No pun intended."

Ignoring him with dignity, Nevander continued, "I have been overly dismissive of our 'friends,' thinking them merely unfortunate, and possibly malign, aspects of the water spell. Recent events have shown them to be no less dangerous than I thought, but perhaps much more helpful and aware than they have been given credit for."

"They called me," Kelgan replied shortly.

There were concerted indrawn breaths.

"Called you? How then?"

"No idea!" Equally short.

··· 69 ···

Pellygram

Kelgan woke with a start. Pelly? No, Pellerin was in his usual place beside his bony old mare, gazing vacantly into the forest.

Kelgan sighed, preparing to roll onto his other side when his scalp prickled. Gazing vacantly *into* the forest? Reversing course, he rose quietly to join Pellerin.

"Something's up, isn't it, Pel?" he whispered.

No response from Pellerin, who didn't even turn to look at Kelgan. Nevertheless, there was a heightened *something* he could feel in the air.

As he stood, puzzling, the forest melted away before and behind them, leaving the sleeping company lying exposed in a blasted landscape. The same bleak scene of utter destruction they had previously caught in glimpses. The only vestige of the illusion which remained was the ebony ribbon of Nevander's river to their backs.

Kelgan realized Nadi and Jorgo were already on their feet, the soft snick of drawn swords betraying them.

A hand grasped his; Neroma stood as silently as Pelly. Rapt as he was, he had heard nothing of her approach. He was aware, however, that Pelly's gaze had swung to him. No longer vacant, it bored like an auger into his cheek, although he dared not turn to engage it.

Still feeling the weight of Pelly's gaze on him, Kelgan gave a violent start as Cal spoke directly into his ear.

"Looks like it's showtime."

Kelgan swallowed hard and tried to quiet his racing heart. "Uh," was his brilliant retort.

The mules brayed sonorously with astonishing gentleness—a mere breath of a bray, but leaving no doubt of their concern.

"I don't know any more than you do," Kelgan said, prompting derisive noises from the listeners in spite of the seeming crisis.

Looking back over his shoulder, Kelgan noted with mingled dismay and pride that Bethne was sitting up and focused on him with a confident smile. He swallowed hard again, and finally answered Cal.

"Yes, I would say we are taking center stage."

Cal broke into song, making Kelgan blink.

"*What's it All About, Alfie?*" He winked at Kelgan.

The song might have been unfamiliar, but the sentiment seemed all too apt.

"Darkness if I know," Kelgan muttered.

"They dissolved the wards, just like that!" Neroma's great dark eyes sought Kelgan's.

"And the woods," added Cal.

"Yes!" Kelgan was only *too* aware of the implications of that. The power appalled him.

"Wait a minute," protested Cal. "Seems to me we were able to give tit for tat a few times."

"Mmmmn, possible," Kelgan grudgingly acknowledged.

"Damn straight," affirmed Cal.

"I think he's right, my Mage," put in Nevander. "Our interactions may have been only tests, but consider the encounter at the river, and your duel with the Commander of the last illusions. There was unmistakable surprise at both outcomes."

Yeah," agreed Cal, "especially that Commander; I don't think he expected to die."

Kelgan sighed. "No, but I did."

Neroma swiftly covered a titter with a cough.

Encouraged by her amusement and by the support of the others, Kelgan turned to Pellerin, whose blazing stare told Kelgan that Pelly's 'owner' was still in there.

"Onward and upward, eh, Pelly? Or maybe downward...."

Pellerin mounted his mare, and the light of his gaze went out.

"Guess so," said Cal.

Turning, Kelgan's glance swept over Jorgo and Nadi, the twins, and T'Jules and Daliane; all at the ready. He took in Bethne and Ez, gathering their things to move on, and finally Piper, who, childlike, had slept through it all.

Feeling a wash of paternity, Kelgan knelt and swept up the child. To his amazement, Piper said fuzzily, "Yeah, I know, Dad, but I figured you'd know what to do, so I went back to sleep."

Over Piper's shoulder, Cal's grin split his face like a jack-o-lantern.

"Yep, *Dad*, that's what we all figure."

Overwhelmed by both gratitude and responsibility, Kelgan could only nod, fearing that if he spoke, it would only be to scream, "No! No! No!"

Looking up, he caught the eye of the Baron, who also grinned, knowing exactly what was passing through Kelgan's mind.

Finally, one of the twins spoke with asperity. "Well, when are you going to put the forest back so we can have breakfast?"

Kelgan stared blankly.

"Aunt Cenci's right, Dad. I'm hungry."

Kelgan drew in a breath so deep, his stomach threatened his backbone. Blowing it out in a whoosh, he thundered, "*SYLVANAMA, BIOTIS!*"

He tumbled hastily aside, pulling the boy with him as a tree sprang up nearly in the spot where he had been crouching with Piper.

A cacophony of bird and animal sounds arose, sending the onlookers into gales of hysterical laughter.

Bent double, Ez rasped, "When ya duz it, son, ya reely duz it."

Rooted in shock, he only came to himself when Piper protested, "Dad, yer squeezin' me."

Cenci continued crisply, "All right, let's bag some birds."

The twins headed off.

Kelgan released Piper, but otherwise didn't move. Pellerin had turned his old horse's head back inwards, and Kelgan was conscious of a vast spectral amusement of more than just Pellerin's.

Worlds whirled before Kelgan, making him dizzy and nauseated. Jorgo's firm grasp on his upper arm as he hauled Kelgan to his feet restored him somewhat. As did Jorgo's sly, "That was a fair start, my brother."

Nadi doubled up again.

The Baron made his way to Kelgan's side. "Just a hint, Infallible Leader, never look surprised."

Kelgan snorted. "That's the way I *always* look, since I always am."

"We know," the Baron observed dryly, "more practice on inscrutable."

Kelgan was actually surprised again, by finding that funny.

"Well, I guess I've got trees down pretty well—I can move on to something else."

The Baron slugged Kelgan's shoulder with approval. "Good man."

Kelgan set about turning some of the ferns and flowers into nourishing edibles, while Cal built up the fire with the anticipation of roasting birds.

No one mentioned that, occasionally, the trees took on a rather transparent aspect, but opaqued quickly under Kelgan's glare and repeatedly muttered, '*Sylvanama perpetua.*'

After their meal, Cal inquired casually, "So... where are we off to today?'

Kelgan bestowed a look of profound exasperation on him.

"Just asking," Cal jauntily threw out.

"A good question, nevertheless, my Mage. Do we have a direction?"

Seemingly at odds with her brother, Neroma spoke, "You know we go where we are pulled."

Her voice was impatient, unlike her usual syrupy tones.

"I apologize, my Mage, I was not implying criticism. I should have stated that another way. We march, and are pulled, as my sister says, but at an infuriatingly slow pace...."

He was interrupted by T'Jules.

"I, for one, am not overly eager to meet our opponents without practice. This, it seems, we are getting more and more of as we go along." He made an almost imperceptible gesture of his head toward Bethne and Ezrael.

To his credit, Nevander grasped his meaning. "You have the right of it, Baron, although most of the practice has been Kelgan's." His answering nod was equally imperceptible. "Perhaps," he continued smoothly, "we should determine a way for all of us to enter in."

"Nevander is absolutely right," put in the Baroness. "We have been remiss. There has not been enough regular exercise among the rest of us, and Kelgan needs to work at it daily."

Kelgan groaned to himself.

Daliane went on. "A little every morning to keep all of us in the proper condition." She gave her own tiny nod. "Then a bit of rest."

"But maybe, not this morning," Kelgan suggested hopefully.

Daliane grinned, and acquiesced.

Although afraid to let the idea float to the forefront of his consciousness, Kelgan could not keep from feeling a warm sense of pride at his ability to restore the forest (and all it contained). If he wasn't sure he knew better. Darkness! There I go again! he thought. He would have bestowed on himself the title of full-fledged Mage.

Needs must, he thought again. *When I must, it looks like I do.*

He gathered up some of the things the mules would carry and staggered toward them under the heavy load.

At sight of him, both animals brayed loudly with the sound of a trumpet fanfare. Fluttering their long mulish eyelashes, they mimed overwhelming awe until he whacked each of them with the tail of his cloak, upon which they broke into brays that sounded surprisingly like guffaws.

As to Cal's question—Kelgan leaned his head on the shoulder of one mule, who turned its head and whuffled gently at him—where would they go today? This aimless march to the end of the world had lost its meaning. They were going to save what? How? From whom?

Kelgan brought himself up short as he realized he was being dangerously lulled into the despairing frame of mind which allowed the voices to enter.

Tugging his mind back to the present, he whirled and almost shouted, "Conference!"

Heads snapped up and a sly grin appeared on both Jorgo's and the Baron's faces.

They all, as one, moved toward him. The mules looked pleased at being included.

As they eyed him expectantly, he felt a moment's doubt which he thrust instantly away. Clearing his throat, and making sure the wards were extra tight, he addressed them with what he hoped sounded like confidence.

"All right, I've come to a decision. I'm going to collapse the forest... until we need it," he added hastily, "and we're going to travel through the... uh... Blasted Heath..." as he recalled Cal naming it.

"We're going to look like we have a direction and a purpose, and that we're going to carry it out. We have spoken—rather offhandedly—of a mission, a quest. Well, we're going to look like that's what we know, that we're dealing with non-men, who are trying to take our world and have already taken others." He glanced at Cal, who stared stoically back.

"As I see it," the Baron interposed, "we *have* a common purpose, which *has* brought us all together, and we seem to have a direction whether we want it or not. And you, my friend, have been leading us unerringly to where we need to go. Yes, some things remain a mystery, but much has been revealed to you, which you have generously shared. So, your decision to dispel the illusion, we must surely consider a wise one."

I think he's been in Nevander's company too long, Kelgan silently opined.

"Hear, hear," said Nevander, firmly.

"Hear, hear," echoed the entire party, Piper piping in a little late to everyone's amusement.

The Terencias drew their swords solemnly and gave formal salutes, which were copied by all those who bore arms.

To Kelgan's horror, he nearly lost his composure and burst into tears. Biting his tongue, he held on to his dignity with both mental hands and simply said, "Thank you, my friends, for your confidence."

A sarcastic nudge in the middle of his back from one of the mules nearly propelled him into the crowd.

"And now, Exalted Pooh-bah, where *are* we going?"

At Cal's question, the group broke up in laughter and dispersed to their various chores.

Having some experience with forests now, Kelgan decided to use a tad more caution when performing his dispelling dis-spell. Truth to tell, his caution made the others a bit restive, but they held their peace until he had first turned the full-growth trees into saplings, then reduced them to seeds before securing them in a burlap bag.

The birds and animals he had already transformed into a feather bed and a skin blanket, which he loaded into one of the mule's knapsacks.

He stared at the river for a very long time before snapping his fingers and unpacking a stoppered glass flask.

Repeatedly muttering, under his breath, the words of what he hoped to be a successful transformation, he finally spoke the words aloud with the proper gestures.

"*Aquae mimim; pisces minim; portabulla integri.*"

A great whoosh nearly caused him to lose his hold on the flask, but clutching it with both hands he was overjoyed to see it filled with swirling water—sometimes clear, sometimes dark, and inhabited with darting minnows, some of which swam up against the sides of the flask and grinned ferociously.

With the reduction of the trees into a bag of seeds as his final act, Kelgan drew in a breath so deep, he feared his lungs would be permanently attached his backbone. He let it out with a whoosh nearly as powerful as the one which had sucked up the river.

Exposed with the departure of their leafy canopy, the members of the party mimed dismay, bafflement, and confusion with more or less success.

Cal gave a snort behind Kelgan's back. "That'll fool 'em."

"Well, so we are not professional players," Kelgan protested with asperity. "Do you have a better idea?"

Cal threw up his hands in defeat, and turned away with a headshake. Then, turning back, he inquired, "Hey, Kel, what was that carry the blister bit all about?"

Kelgan goggled at him, uncomprehending. "What the Dark are you talking about?"

"That *was* Latin you were speaking. Really bad Latin, but Latin just the same. Although you don't use it all the time, that word you're always shouting at the mules, for example."

"Lateen? That was Rheemâni, the language of the first Mages who founded the Academy," asserted Kelgan with hauteur. "'Levanah,' if you must know, is my homeland language."

Cal cocked his head. "Well, we call it Latin, and you said 'carry the blister.'"

"I said nothing of the sort, at any time." Kelgan crossed his arms with finality.

"Yeah, you did, when you were waving that bottle around; 'portabulla,' I heard you."

"I was demanding the flask to bear the entire bubbling stream."

Daliane, standing nearby, convulsed with laughter. "One man's bubble is another man's blister," she managed.

"And we know who's got the blister," added Cal, joining the laughter.

The two laughed until Kelgan noted with alarm that green grass was starting to pop up from the barren ground, and small flower heads were similarly appearing.

"Stop, stop!" he cried, grabbing Cal's shoulder forcefully.

"Whaa?" Cal started to shake him off, thinking that Kelgan was annoyed at their mockery, until he saw the real concern on his face. He stopped mid-chortle as Kelgan nodded toward the burgeoning greenery.

Daliane, too, gave a gasp of realization. "We can laugh the ground into bloom," she said in wonder.

"Good to know," Cal observed.

Kelgan looked at him.

"We have a saying about laughter being the best medicine. We might need to remember that," he explained.

"You're absolutely right," agreed Daliane, "we already knew that gloom brought on those nasty shadows. This is a power we really need to keep a secret. You never know what will give us an advantage."

"And it sure looks like we need all the advantages we can muster."

Kelgan nodded his head thoughtfully at both of them. "We can only hope the wards were still sufficient to keep them from noticing what happened."

Daliane frowned worriedly. "You had dropped them, hadn't you?"

"Yes, enough for them to see us perform our act, but not entirely—that was also to not provoke suspicion. If there were no warding at all, we would have drawn immediate notice, I'm afraid."

"So, the slight hint of spring might have been so slight as to have gone unremarked?"

"I... think so...." Kelgan's hesitation failed to reassure.

"Well, we just have to keep thinking so," Cal put in firmly. "Keep calm and carry our blisters."

The other two suddenly developed frightful coughs.

Once on the road, Jorgo dropped back to Kelgan's side. Sliding easily from the saddle to walk his horse at Kelgan's pace, he inquired, "I have been meaning to ask for some time, my brother, the device you bear, it is some indication of ranking at the Academy?"

"It's Pelly's," Kelgan blurted without thought.

A grin split Jorgo's face, displaying white teeth. "So! Our friend from the middle world is not only more than meets the eye; but more than we could have guessed."

"The middle world?" Kelgan grinned in return.

"Neither within ours nor in the realm of The Two," replied Jorgo, looking serious for a moment.

Kelgan regarded the warrior just as soberly. "Not even then."

His ambiguous retort caused Jorgo's eyebrows to meet his hairline.

"Reveal," Jorgo ordered firmly.

Kelgan sighed. "I'm not sure Pelly would want me to tell; it's his life, after all."

Jorgo blinked at Kelgan's use of the word 'life,' but subsided.

Kelgan felt a nudge between his shoulder blades. Unbeknownst to him, and even more astonishingly, to Jorgo's, Pellerin's horse had somehow crept up behind them and was giving Kelgan gentle pushes.

Kelgan turned to glance up at Pellerin. "I guess you think it's all right, then, Pelly?"

The old mare whickered softly as Pellerin stared into the distance, then moved on.

"It would seem you have gained approval, my brother."

"Well, it's just that Pelly showed me *his* world, and it certainly *isn't* this one. I'm not even sure about his family's." He added, "Well, actually, I am pretty sure—he's from somewhere else entirely. And his device...." Kelgan remembered his first confrontation with the tapestries. "I think it's really his wife's, uh, that is, her father's."

Raising his eyebrows, Jorgo absorbed the information without further comment. His usually erect shoulders sagged a little. "So many," he finally observed. "He picked you from the start. 'A good man'... I remember...." He trailed off; then said, "And he has given you his sword and sigil, which means even more to him than his own."

Throwing his arm around Kelgan' shoulders, Jorgo gave him a short but fierce embrace. Remounting his steed, he rejoined his position with Nadi.

Kelgan was unsure what to make of Jorgo's response, as well as his use of the word 'sigil.' Device, yes, coat-of-arms, yes, but sigil? As though he'd been stamped and sealed. The implications of this froze his breath for a moment; then he shrugged. *Guess that's what we all are,* he thought to himself.

The next to pace alongside him was the tiny Baroness. She gave him a twinkling grin that took full advantage of her dimples.

Surveying her from at least a foot and a half above her, Kelgan well understood the Baron's devotion. The urge to sweep her up like a toddler and position her to ride piggy-back on his shoulders was almost irresistible.

Good thing she can't read my mind, he thought, *I'd be staunching my bloody nose right now.*

"Look's like you're the star of the play," she observed mischievously.

Kelgan grimaced. "Yes, if I'd only been given a copy of the playscript."

She patted his arm in sympathy. "None of us knows our role any better than you, Kel."

He acknowledged the truth of her statement. "We're marching blind to Nowhere, with no plan for when we get there—if we do...." he sang to her amusement.

She soberly answered, "We know we'll have to fight."

"Yes, but how? Against whom? With what?"

"Swords, magic, strategy, and whatever cheating we can devise," was Dally's pragmatic response.

"Cheating?" Kelgan arched an eyebrow.

"Of course! Do you think this is going to be a *fair* contest?"

Kelgan regarded her anew.

"Dally," he surprised himself with the familiar, "you have more sense than all the rest of us. Of course, cheating is the answer. Now if I can just figure out how!"

She hugged his arm, remounted her horse and rejoined T'Jules.

Cheating! Kelgan grinned fiercely to himself. *Yes! Love that Dally, love that idea! And Cal's going to love it even more.* Kelgan chuckled warmly as he thought of Cal's demonstration of poker playing to Piper. Sleight of hand, that was Cal's strength. *Well, maybe a* slightly *good sword hand, as well,* Kelgan admitted to himself. He could see it coming in handy. He congratulated himself for his double pun.

I don't know how we're going to use it, but we'll just have to break it out when the time seems right. It's got to look like real magic, so we seem to have more magicians than we really do. The problem is more warriors. They know we have just what we have, although I gave them a bit of a surprise.

He felt a sudden breeze on his neck. Pelly had crept up behind him again, and the old mare was blowing down his collar. Glancing up at Pellerin, he realized what was on Pelly's mind, if you could apply any terms which applied to the living dead.

"Of course, Pel, you're our biggest surprise, and you're a warrior if any of us is. That's one more and...." Kelgan stuttered off as he realized something else. No one could kill Pellerin, neither with weapons, nor with sorcery. In essence, Pelly wasn't even there.

Absently rubbing the old mare's nose, Kelgan stared blindly while Pellerin waited for Kelgan to absorb the unspoken information. Kelgan finally dropped his arms and stepped back, shrugging helplessly.

"You're our secret weapon, Pel. You've got more talent than the whole bunch of us... and more rank," he added.

A flash, and a slight bow, before Pellerin moved on.

T'Jules took his turn.

"Get up behind," he commanded, and Kelgan scrambled to obey. "Dally told me we were going to cheat," he threw over his shoulder as Kelgan settled himself.

"Looks like it," Kelgan retorted.

"Best idea yet. I always like the all's fair notion. Never give the bastards an even break's my motto.

Taken somewhat aback, Kelgan mumbled unintelligibly.

"Shocked, eh, my honest Mage?"

"Uh, well, yes. I thought maybe Barons were...."

"Above deceit, venality, lust? Come on, Kelgan, you're a bigger boy than that."

"I'm getting to be," Kelgan almost snarled.

The Baron reached backward and slapped Kelgan's knee. "You'll do." Then seriously, he said, "You'll cover all the facts as we know them, all the resources you can think of that we possess, and then extrapolate from that to at least some preliminary answers; you've already begun."

Startled into silence, Kelgan turned the Baron's word over and over in his mind. How had he gained the Baron's evidently complete confidence? Was whining about your deficiencies the answer? He gave a slight snort.

The Baron pulled up. "Get down, I'm going to go give my wife a kiss."

⋯ 70 ⋯

We need a long spoon

Kelgan trudged on, deep in thought. He pondered the memory of the various "armies" sent to harass them. The not-for-real highwaymen were comparatively easy pickings. The red and black soldiers in the town fracas had been all too real, but still ordinary, run-of-the-mill bully-boys. Fancy clothes, but, as he now realized, not possessing superior fighting skills. The more disciplined following group were also real, but succumbed quickly to the river denizens.

He shuddered to recall that silent disappearance. They looked much more menacingly competent, although their prowess had not been tested. Really skilled? Unknown; but it was safe to assume they constituted a greater threat.

Chalk one up to our secret weapon, he mused.

The last "army" had been illusion, with the exception of the Commander. How was that done?

Kelgan had never tried creating an illusion that large, containing so many people. Nor had he tried to hold the illusion while transporting a reality.

He mentally slapped himself twice—once for letting things slide and not anticipating their needs, and once more for underestimating himself and probably overestimating their opponent. I've been maintaining almost the same illusion all along! He berated himself with disgust. *Some leader!* He chided himself further. *Do I still have time to practice something bigger?* was his next panicky thought.

Yes, he told himself grimly, *I'd better.* He fell even deeper into a brown study as he studied the various possible options.

Pelly rode up beside him. Gazing at Kelgan, meaningfully rather than vacantly, he gave a slight nod. The old mare instantly began to limp on her left foreleg.

Kelgan's eyes widened. He quickly called a halt.

"It looks like Pelly's mare has picked up a stone. We'd better stop while I check. Maybe we'll have to call it a day."

A flash in Pellerin's eyes told Kelgan he'd made the right call.

Under the pretext of examining the old mare's hoof, Kelgan addressed whomever shared Pellerin's body.

"I think you want me to start practicing deceit right now."

Another flash, this time of almost admiration, before Pellerin's face resumed its empty stare.

The others stopped, awaiting Kelgan's word.

"It looks like we'll camp here," he announced. "Her hoof looks mighty sore. I've taken out the stone, but I don't think she should go on today."

Kelgan's eyes met Daliane's. She gave an almost imperceptible movement of her head.

No flies on that one, as my Gran would have said.

He felt somehow uplifted, to think she would place her trust in him, as perceptive as she was.

He performed a totally unnecessary healing spell over the mare's hoof; she whickered and gently nudged him as if in gratitude.

It occurred to him later that she might have been grateful. She was elderly and had been asked to keep up with the war mounts, which she had done with amazing fortitude. He rubbed her nose with affection and with his other hand sent a probe deep into her body. He was shocked to see how elderly she actually was.

Pelly! Pelly must be keeping not only his borrowed corpus alive but the mare's, as well.

"I'll take over now, Pel," Kelgan assured him, kicking himself for not thinking of it sooner.

To his complete befuddlement, a broad smile spread across

Pellerin's face, and a hand dropped from the reins for an instant to rest on Kelgan's shoulder.

All was so brief, Kelgan almost felt he had imagined all, but he sent another delicate healing spell into the mare with what he felt sure was Pelly's approval.

Next, he began the even more delicate task of warding them just enough so that they were comfortable but looked the opposite. Neroma added her cleverly disguised efforts to his, all the while trying to look completely powerless.

Another secret weapon, we hope, O Lightbringer, was his fervent thought.

While Kelgan unloaded the mules, Cal, with the ostensible excuse of helping, said *sotto voce,* "Okay, I saw through that ruse. What's up?"

Kelgan eyed him with exasperation. "I hope I'm not that transparent to the enemy—Daliane didn't miss it, either."

"I don't imagine she misses anything. The Baron's a swell guy and no dope, but she's the brains of the outfit. So again, what's up?"

Kelgan filled him in and related the Baroness' suggestions.

Cal snorted. "What did I say? The brains of the outfit. Cheating, hmmm... I'm pretty good at that." He grinned wolfishly at Kelgan. "We need to have a pow-wow."

The word didn't translate, but Kelgan took the meaning with no difficulty.

As he waited for the others to gather, Kelgan pondered the weeks spent on the road. Weeks, nay! More than two months now, he marveled. The people with whom he traveled had been strangers. Now they were welded to each other with ties deeper than blood. His oddly acquired, but true to the meaning of the word, extended family. He looked with pride at Piper—his son—his beautiful, talented, extraordinary wife... well in everything but the eyes of the law. His friends, his sisters....

Feeling his gaze, Teri and Cenci joined him with enigmatic expressions. They sat down to skin the hares they had procured for dinner.

He froze in place. What was the source of his well-being? From whence the familial benevolence—the patriarchal glow? While he would, and did, trust his life to these others, he certainly never felt they belonged to him. He had not ever in his wildest dreams felt himself the head of an admittedly diverse, but united clan.

T'Jules, about to settle himself near the twins, noted Kelgan's sudden stillness and the look of consternation which passed over his face. Alarmed, he hastened to drop down beside Kelgan.

"What is it, Kel?" he asked quietly so not to attract attention.

Kelgan unburdened himself, detailing his fears and finishing with, "Surely it can't be the voicer. They seem to thrive on fear and hatred...." He broke off after taking in the peculiar expression on the Baron's face. It looked to Kelgan as if his listener was doing all he could not to laugh.

"Something amuses you, my Lord Baron?" Kelgan inquired stiffly.

T'Jules placed both hands on Kelgan's shoulders. "Kelgan, we have told you repeatedly—and we're getting really tired of it, you *are* our head. We are your clan. Forget rank, age, background, sex. We follow *you*. The why is not yet revealed, but follow we do. If you feel pride, if you feel a familial bond, we are all the better for it. *This* time, try to remember for more than fifteen minutes."

The Baron spoke with exasperation mingled with amusement.

Kelgan struggled for an answer, *something,* but ended with a helpless shake of his head. "I should just enjoy it?" he inquired sheepishly.

This time the Baron did laugh. "Yes, but what did I say about the fifteen minutes? Do the best you can while you can." He administered a slap to Kelgan's shoulder.

By this time Nevander and Neroma, as well as the elderly couple, joined the group, along with Daliane, who plopped herself down beside her husband in a decidedly un-Baroness-like manner, shadowed of course by Jorgo and Nadi, the ever-watchful, who sat just behind her.

Nevander, giving Kelgan no time to say what was on his mind, seized the floor. "It's only too obvious that those we seek are Dark Mages," he began.

Kelgan shot him a look. Nevander might speak sententiously, but he never sounded like a lackwit. Something else was on his mind.

"Yeess," Kelgan responded cautiously.

Nevander shifted uncomfortably; not like him, either. "Can you fight them with Dark Magic?"

Kelgan looked at him askance. "I wouldn't know how, or where, to begin."

Nevander looked dubious.

Kelgan, exasperated, growled, "Okay." *Really starting to sound like Cal,* he thought. *Have no idea what it means, but Cal uses it all the time, and it sounds authoritative.*

"Let me go over this one more time. No, I'm not whining or underestimating myself, I'm stating facts. I was not an 'Under-Mage,' I was a Senior Apprentice. It's only at the *very* end of our *last* term that we—very cautiously—study *anything* about Dark Magic. Quite simply, I wasn't there yet and, as a consequence, know absolutely nothing. It's a bit more than, 'Ooh, I think I'll do something naughty.'"

Nevander looked abashed, and Kelgan realized he was standing belligerently with his hands on hips and chin stuck out in His Lordship's direction.

Daliane looked up at him with her virtually always laughing face. "I've never known anyone who was so determined to convince everyone he was less rather than more."

Kelgan smiled back at her. "Sorry, Dally, I put that badly."

T'Jules blinked once or twice at the familiarity, then his mouth quirked, but he said nothing as Kelgan continued, "What I meant was that I might be able to make some educated guesses, but it would take me some time, I'm afraid. I think perhaps time is what we have run out of." Pausing, he mused for a moment, then went on, "I did get a little hint when I was poisoned." He gave a slight shudder. "I'm not sure how that helps, because I'd have to use that knowledge the same way."

"You mean, you would have to get close enough to poison someone?"

"That's it."

"Your sword?"

Kelgan looked troubled. "I don't feel the sword would like that—and I know I wouldn't."

Daliane afforded him a little applause. "Of course, he can't do that. Swords are... well, they're like people. You don't force them to do something against their will and conscience."

"The sword doesn't seem to mind killing others."

"That's in a more or less fair fight," Daliane retorted stoutly. She continued with a self-deprecating smirk. "I did suggest cheating, however. That's perfectly white."

There was general laughter at her definition of 'white.'

Somewhat surprisingly, Cal unhesitatingly supported Kelgan's misgivings.

"That wouldn't be Kel. He has to... *we* have to do, whatever the heck it is we're supposed to do, as ourselves. If we try to be something—someone—else, we're sure to f..., uh, I mean, get it wrong."

A little more applause from Daliane, this time for him.

"'A rose by any other name,'" Cal quoted. Blank faces greeted him. Shrugging, he continued, "We don't call it Dark Magic. We call it cheating. Perfectly okay with me."

Kelgan, recalling again Piper's lessons in card, er, manipulation, gave Cal a knowing sidelong look. His face turned troubled, however, as he considered the fine line that had to be walked between the two definitions.

Like the garb of the Academy seniors, he thought, *gray, not black, but not white, either.*

Aloud, he demurred, "If only I had a better idea of how they were...." He broke off, realizing he had no idea where the rest of the sentence was going.

"Gotta just wing it, Kel," stated Cal.

"Wing it?" Kelgan repeated.

"Yes, make it up as you go along, and incorporate whatever seems promising in your repertoire, every time we have an, um, event. Think about every one of our encounters and see if there's any pattern at all that you can use."

"An excellent idea, Calvin-From-Another-World," cried Nevander more jovially than the occasion warranted.

T'Jules covered his mouth and cleared his throat. A chorus of throat-clearings echoed him.

Kelgan, on the other hand, his brow furrowed in concentration, took Cal's suggestion and desperately tried to put it to use.

"It's no good," he claimed. "They've all been different."

"No," contradicted Daliane, "I have noticed the enemy appears—always—in multiples of three. When you fought the Commander, there were six rows of fifteen soldiers, and when Pellerin was kidnapped, it was by nine men. This has been the pattern, every time. At least since we have joined you." Daliane nodded before anyone could answer her. "We here are governed by the light—that's why we are all of us *two*. I worship The Lady, but even she has a consort."

Nadi chimed in, "We Mel'hachim have a belief that The Two were once Three, but one, the brightest of all, turned to the ways of shadow and was cast from the Path of Light."

"What about Pelly," Piper piped. "He ain't got nuthin' but an old mare."

Unwilling to confess before Pellerin's parents that he knew Pelly was most definitely two, he dissembled. "Uh, well he *represents* two, uh, states of being, you might say. He sort of has a foot in two worlds." *At least two.* He kept that thought to himself.

Piper rolled his eyes, to everyone's amusement. "Only 'bout half a foot here, I'm thinkin.'"

There were chuckles, then Daliane asked urgently, "Can this possibly be of significance?"

"Well, every bit of information is good, but we'll have to wait and see how each bit can be used. It's quite possible," he said as Daliane looked somewhat crestfallen, "that even just the symbol of bonded pairs is significant; there is great power in symbols."

"But there are only two voices," objected the Baron.

"True, but they had to enlist the complicity of that king I saw in the tapestries. It may be they need a third on each world in order to have *enough* power." Kelgan rounded on Cal, "What about your world?"

Cal considered. "Well, we've had a couple—more than that

actually—in the last century, but they've all been defeated and killed. There is a *group,* at the moment, that definitely fills the bill, but we're not quite sure who the *real* leader is."

"But there *must* be one," put in Nevander.

"Yeah, unless they're a collective. They wear a lot of black; the *red,* well, that's something else." Cal's expression left no doubt of his meaning.

Kelgan took a deep breath, blew it out sharply as his eye met Pellerin's. The depths of pain that shone from the usually vacant visage made Kelgan's chest muscles constrict until it was almost an agony. The anguish was gone in an instant and the vacancy returned, but Kelgan could still feel its vestiges.

He gazed out over the desolate landscape they now stumbled through. *Okay,* he thought, echoing Cal again, *what have we got? Number one, and maybe most important, we have a dead alien. We have an insecure Under-Mage—good cover-up? We have a river full of somethings, that we hope they don't know about. And then, there's Neroma,* way *more powerful than she looks; and Nevander, good with water. Might come in handy. Six warriors—nine,* he amended, *Cal, Pelly, and me—another good cover-up?* He chilled as he remembered. *Pelly can move us! He moved me! Maybe it's only one at a time. Maybe moving me could be really useful. Ez and Bethie, they're all about love, and that's* real *power; Piper, he's the other part of me....* A sudden realization struck him, *He's also the other part of Pelly.... Death and Life, so we're even there, too. Even against odds,* I'm getting to be quite a punster, as Cal would say.

Cal interrupted. "I think that unfortunate Kelgan illusion is filtering through the wards, again. Bethne is looking really bad to me; and that old nag is about to collapse—at least it seems that way. Even Capriola is borderline peaked."

Kelgan surveyed the group. Even as he did, he could discern the illusion sweeping up the ranks, like a wind of ill-fortune. "Right, time for more play-acting." He called softly to the Baroness, "Dally, swoon, now!"

Without a moment's hesitation, Daliane clutched her chest and collapsed sideways off her mount. Cal, moving just as swiftly, caught her before her feet left the stirrups. She winked up at him, moaning all the while.

The momentarily startled Baron took in the supposedly alarming scene; and reacted just as quickly. "Daliane! Oh, Darkness!" he declared histrionically, which nearly undid Daliane. She covered with a fit of tubercular coughing.

Cal handed her off to the Baron, rolling his eyes.

Surprisingly, Bethne noticed and added her moans to Daliane's as her knees buckled. "Oh Ez, my heart... my heart."

Ezrael, stupefied, was not reassured to hear Bethne order, "C'mon Ez, get with it."

Cal and Kelgan had heard, however, and struggled to maintain sober expressions.

"'Get with it,'" Cal whispered to Kelgan.

"You're a bad influence on everyone."

Not to be outdone, Piper, fell to his knees and coughed up his lunch. Genuinely alarmed, Kelgan rushed to his side. Piper grinned behind his hand and confided, "Learned that in the kitchens."

By this time the rest of the party was in on the deception and crumpled in various poses of debility. Teri and Cenci covered a fit of the giggles behind their gauntlets, making Kelgan want to give them both a swift kick to make their debility more authentic.

Satisfied the group gave a reasonable imitation of disarray, he and Neroma conferred as to the best way to strengthen the wards slightly, without giving their knowledge away. Kelgan decided to give everyone a fake dose of one of his philtres, supposedly to get them moving again. Neroma was going to unobtrusively—at least it was hoped—add a little power to the wards to—again it was hoped—keep the enemy out. Not so much that they looked hale and hearty, but as though the philtres had had some temporary effect.

Starting up once more, they attempted to convey the idea that they were unaware and unprepared. *Well, we're certainly aware, but prepared? Just how prepared can you be for world-eaters?*

"They toy with us," Nevander murmured at his elbow.

"Not much longer," Kelgan responded, as, to his horror, the

landscape abruptly altered. Black rocks rose before them, jagged and treacherous. To each side, chasms fell away into an unfathomable darkness. Surmounting it all, a castle seemingly carved of onyx loomed to a ghastly height into the now deep gray, menacing sky.

Kelgan felt the hair stand on his arms and the back of his neck as he recognized the castle to be a twin of the one he had seen in the tapestries. Terror gripped him with an icy claw until he heard Cal say sarcastically, "Oh, come on, that's *really* overdoing it."

Kelgan couldn't restrain a brief shout of laughter, noticing as he did so that the rocks shrank just a millimeter. *Good to know.* He kept the thought quiet.

Regaining his sense of perspective, he realized Calvin was right. The whole vista was as theatrical as a stage's painted backdrop. Nevertheless, he replied with the now oh-so-familiar phrase, "I feel there's more than meets the eye."

"Of course, there is," Cal agreed, "but they want to soften us up for the real thing. If they think we're quaking in our boots, it's just that much easier to pick us off, one by one." He paused briefly. "So, now what? Do we march in like a victory party? With Bethne at the head in the goat cart?"

Kelgan gave another stifled breath of laughter. "Waving a shield made of Capriola's wool?"

Muffled snickering.

On a more somber note, he asked Cal, "Well, just what *do* we do with Bethne and Ez?"

Cal shrugged. "None of us knows what to do, or better, what we're *going* to do. I've never been a hero before. Have you?"

Kelgan grinned behind a masking hand. "Of course, I have. Didn't you see me 'port my bulla'?"

Cal nearly split all the seams of his tunic attempting to contain his laughter. Seeing a dandelion spring up at his feet, he hastily trod it into the muddy earth.

"Glad it wasn't an azalea," he muttered, which caused Kelgan in turn to desperately struggle for control.

This produced another dandelion, which was treated in the same manner.

A buffet from behind, which propelled Kelgan's breath out in a whoosh, announced Jorgo's presence behind them.

"You have the right of it, Calvin-From-Another-World," rumbled Jorgo. "We Mel'hachim have been heroes of a sort in the past, but this task will require a *different* sort from the kind we have been used to. None of us know how we will answer."

He and Nadi resheathed the swords they had drawn during the change. But in spite of Jorgo's sober words, they all tee-heed softly at Jorgo's use of Nevander's bombastic phrase.

By that time the rest of the group had gathered together. Wordlessly, the party continued to stare upward at the glowering towers.

Cenci broke the silence. "Well, so what *do* we do? Stand here and gawk? Burst into raucous guffaws and laugh it away? Dig in from below like raiding sappers?"

Kelgan pricked up his ears. "Dig in from below? That's a wonderful idea."

His response elicited a surprised "huh," from Cenci, who had not expected to be taken seriously.

"Yeah, good idea. Just how do we do that without anybody noticing?"

"I haven't quite figured that out yet," admitted Kelgan shamefacedly.

"Suppose we have lunch, just to show them how little we care, and talk it over?"

Kelgan gave Cal an appreciative glance, "Another good idea— see we're just full of them."

There were immediate grins, but everyone held their laughter severely in check.

Gathered in a tight circle with the wards at maximum—it was obvious it no longer mattered if they were discernible to the enemy or not—they considered suggestion after suggestion with none seeming adequate.

At last, Kelgan threw up his hands. "We're just going to have to explore the territory and see if anything looks promising."

There was a chorus of sighs, as all agreed.

"Should we split into groups?" inquired Teri.

"It would probably be more efficient, but I want us to stay together. I don't want to take the chance of us getting picked off little by little."

The Baron concurred. "I won't say there's safety in numbers, because we know there isn't, but I want us to stay together, too. As a matter of fact," he added impishly, "if we could all hold hands, it would be nice."

Smothered chuckles again.

Thoughtfully, Kelgan answered him, "You know, that's not a bad idea, either, but it would interfere with our sword arms."

Seeing that Kelgan was serious, the Baron suggested, "One hand on shoulder, drawing hand at the ready."

Ez's drawl broke in. "How about Bethie?"

"One of us leads Capriola; that way we have contact. We just need to explain it to both her and Bethie first. Same with the mules, although we probably don't have to explain. They should get it on their own."

It was a measure of their connection that no one even raised the issue of why they had to explain to Capriola, and needn't bother with the mules.

With a sort of unstated fatalism, they made a hearty meal. Kelgan doing his best to make the plain fare feel like a banquet. He knew they all felt as one; it might be their last meal of any sort.

Surveying his friends (His loved ones! His family!), he gulped, only too conscious of their small numbers, their inexperience at this sort of thing, and the fact they had all come to mean more than life to him. He glanced up at Pelly, who gave one of his enigmatic nods. He knew Pelly had read his thoughts. Who else knew the feeling more than Pellerin?

He noticed Bethne was staring at Pelly. Pellerin's gaze swung toward her, and to everyone's shock, the usually toneless voice intoned the single word, "Ma."

Bethne's beautiful smile broke over her face, transforming it into that of a young girl, but she replied simply, "Pel."

Kelgan's throat constricted. He felt tears threaten, although he knew they would be even more fatal than laughter in this bleak, harrowing land of no emotion except fear.

To Sup with the Devil

"I don't suppose we have to skulk," Cal said as he laid his hand on Kelgan's shoulder.

Kelgan grimaced. "I doubt it, since they've known where we were the entire time."

"We're going to look really silly, like the chain gang.'

"Uh?"

"Prisoners,"

Kelgan considered this. "Do you think...?"

"You pointed out they've known all about us, all the way,"

"Um, yesss." Kelgan thoughtfully drew out the words.

"Maybe we should act more like Joshua's army."

Kelgan looked blank.

"I guess that's not in your wheelhouse."

"My what?"

Cal scratched his head. "I guess not. Okay, here's the story—comes from a religious text of ours. Well, some of ours," he amended. "Anyway, it's about a warrior of God, who fought at a fortified place called Jericho. According to the text, he marched his army around and around, then blew on trumpets and the walls fell in. Maybe a miracle, maybe sympathetic vibration."

Kelgan gazed at him, rapt.

"Sympathetic vibration." His eyes lit up. "What else does this miraculous tome have to say?"

"Well, there are a lot of those miracles, like the parting of the

Red Sea, for instance.'

"Parting of the Red Sea." He glanced over his shoulder to the heaving, murky waters behind him. "Tell me more of this."

Cal filled him in on the particulars of Moses and Pharaoh, enjoying the absorption of his listener. He didn't forget to include Samson and the destruction of the Philistines, as well as the rod of Aaron. "That's just the Old Testament," he added, "you haven't heard about the New yet."

"Any more temple destructions or sea partings?"

"Well, no. Jesus only got angry once. He was more about love."

Kelgan's gaze strayed to Bethne and Ezrael. "Mmmm, yes."

"I thought there was no magic in your world."

Cal shifted his feet, "Well, some people think the stories got, uh, a little bigger in the telling... or maybe had a natural explanation."

"All magic has a natural explanation," Kelgan countered mischievously.

Cal grimaced. "So you say."

"Don't your machines have natural explanations?"

Cal considered Kelgan, remarking, "Ah. You're thinking that a few natural explanations are in order, aren't you?"

"They might come in handy."

"Well, we already know we could laugh a few things away."

"Yes, but big or small, that's the important question."

Cal nodded slowly in acknowledgment. "Yeah, if it were that easy, none of the worlds would have been lost."

"I am very afraid so."

Cal nodded again. "We also know we constitute some sort of danger, as motley a crew as we are."

Kelgan grimaced. "I think that's more Pelly's doing. He needed some warm bodies, besides his host. We just happened to be those bodies."

"Okay, how do you explain so many of us hearing the voices. Even me."

Kelgan stared so long, Cal shuffled his feet. "Even you," he whispered. "Only you, on your world?"

Comprehension dawned on Cal's face. "There were more." It

was not a question. "On every world, you think?"

Cal's suddenly wide-open eyes, as well as a nudge at his back, told Kelgan what he had already guessed. "You were waiting for us to realize, weren't you Pelly?" Kelgan addressed the air without turning around. "Took us a while." He turned then, to catch the aware flash of Pellerin's host.

Kelgan heaved a sigh that threatened his ribs and left him dizzy. "So now all we have to do is prevail here and then get in touch with everyone else—is that it?"

A barely perceptible nod answered him.

"Simplicity itself." Kelgan thought he would weep, both at Pelly's misplaced faith and the enormity of the task.

On the other hand, Cal astonished him by becoming instantly practical.

"Let's see, what have we got? We've got swords, but they've got swords. We've got magic, but they've got magic, and I'd be willing to bet they're no slouches...."

Kelgan broke in. "And I'm not...?"

"Shut up," Cal snarled ferociously.

Kelgan reared back, blinking.

"...either," finished Cal.

Amusement flashed in Pellerin's eyes.

"They expect us to fight fair," Cal continued, "but we don't mean to do that. Of course, they won't be doing it either, so we're even on that score. They've also got bows and we don't, but that can be a hindrance, actually. We plan to get in close."

Kelgan shook his head in wonder. *When did Cal become a general?*

"I think it's time for a little my-world technology—something simple—wouldn't you say?"

"Uh, uh," Kelgan stuttered.

"Molotov cocktails, is my thought."

"What?"

"Firebombs. I figure you and the Mages will be trying to incinerate each other with spells, but the soldiers need a *real* singeing."

"But I'll have to fight."

"Sure, but you just keep your *mind* on the spells, and let the sword do the fighting."

Sinking back against the stones, Kelgan stared unseeing into the distance. *Keep my mind on the spells—let the sword.... Why not? I'm only going to save the world—not like it's hard or anything!*

"Okay, we've got six really great warriors. You and me... well, I figure we're four more, since we act as two, each of us, so that's ten. The red-and-black guys look like a lot, but I think there's only about two-hundred garrisoned here. No! Wait! Threes—they like threes, so that's," he calculated, "probably two-hundred and seven. That's only around a twenty-to-one ratio."

Only twenty-to-one! Of course! Kelgan remembered Nevander exclaiming "mere bagatelles," on their first meeting. *Just more of those dark-fracking 'bagatelles.'*

"Piper's the one for the cocktails."

"Whaaa...?"

"Of course. He can stay hidden—well, more or less, since they seem to know where we are all the time—but at least behind something that will keep him for a while; he can fire off the Mollies whenever he wants. Uh, I guess Bethne and Ez should stay with him," Cal added.

"And if we win the castle?"

"I think maybe the next step might be a tad tougher."

Kelgan's look would have withered their opponents in their tracks.

"You think?"

"Won't be here, will it, Kel?"

Kelgan didn't bother to answer. He really didn't want to think of *where* they might end up. Sighing, he pulled out the sword and carefully looked it over. Naturally, it showed no trace of use—no discoloration, no wear, no blunted edge that he could see. He sighed again, returned the sword to its sheath, saying to Cal's amazement, "Well, let's get started. I'll make it up as I go along. What do you think, Pelly?"

Cal gave an enormous start; realizing Pellerin had made one of his silent approaches and was standing right at his back.

"Heroes need not ask," came the voice from the grave.

Cal's shudder made his teeth rattle.

Kelgan contemplated the lowering clouds, swirling like Neroma's hair around the black-fingers of the castle towers.

What if we did just walk in the front door with Bethne in the lead? She's not going to stay here, not with Pelly inside. And it's a sure thing he'll be inside. Oh, Darkness! Getting here was one thing... his thoughts trailed off as he froze with shock.

Teri stood close to him, eyes wide and blank; circling with her sword drawn. The others stood back, huddled like a herd of cows—also frozen.

Cenci! Cenci was gone!

Without stopping to think, Kelgan reached her in one great stride, took the sword from her with one hand, and drew her to him with the other. Her knees buckled, and he struggled to hold her up.

A collective gasp from the 'herd' made him turn. Where the Baron had stood, there was now a gap. Daliane implored him with the same blank, wide-eyed stare he had seen on Teri.

That does it! Fury smote him like a gauntleted fist. He began to bark orders as though he had spent his life in battle.

"Bethie and Ez in the cart with Piper. He, uh, he'll protect you." He saw Piper draw himself up to his, well, not exactly full four feet.

"Daliane and Teri behind them, Jorgo and Nadi, rear. Cal and I'll take the front; Pellerin...." he broke off. Pelly would do as he pleased.

"Nevander and Neroma...."

"We follow you, My Mage."

"Swords at the ready."

The sword leapt from its sheath into his hand. It thrummed like a struck harp and glistened a terrifying red. He barely noticed that his tunic had assumed the quality of fine steel armor, except that breathing became a bit more difficult as it shrank to a tight fit. Absently, he tapped his chest and it released him a fraction. His cloak had curved to flow around his sword arm, leaving it free to perform at will. The rational part of him was aware of these happenings, and quailed inside his brain. Strangely, it scarcely bothered him.

Although, as he ran his eye over his army, he felt a trace of humor. *Ragtag doesn't begin to describe it.*

"'Once more into....'" Cal's voice began, then cut off suddenly.

Kelgan whirled. For a moment, *his* knees buckled, then he caught himself, hoping the others had not seen. Cal had joined the ranks of the suddenly disappeared. He heard Jorgo swear an oath which should have split the ground asunder. Feeling as though his entire left side had vanished from his body, Kelgan faced the remainder of his army with desolation, written for all to see, on his face.

Gritting his teeth so hard his jaws sent whistles of pain to his skull, he growled, "NOW."

The entire band, including Capriola and Pellerin, broke into a maddened rush for the shadowed entrance.

Running like berserkers across the drawbridge, they were arrested in mid-stride just inside the walls. Kelgan, in the lead, teetered on the edge of a seemingly bottomless cavity in the floor of an enormous hall. Hanging over it by their outstretched arms were the disappeared, plus *Piper!*

Kelgan's rage grew to a fury of volcanic proportions. *My son!*

Facing him across the space of the declivity was the same Sorcerer he had seen in the tapestries. Smirking with the look of one who knows he is superior, the Sorcerer voiced his contempt.

Too rash. Followed by an insane giggle.

He was immediately joined by a younger man, who stated, *too immature,* and joined in the laughter.

Too, too unprepared!

The hair on Kelgan's nape rose as he felt the full force of the pair's contempt—that, and the full force of Pellerin's monumental hate on the back of his neck. He hadn't even known that Pelly had dismounted and now stood nearly against his own body. A slight rustling to his left and right told him, to his astonishment, that Bethne and Ezrael had moved up to join the stranger who had become their son. Goosebumps threatened as each of them, in unison, placed a hand on his shoulders. Bethne had to stretch on tiptoe to perform the action, and bore down a bit to keep from teetering.

Kelgan gulped. "Uh, Pelly, do I just keep making it up?" he whispered. A squeeze left him just as confused as ever. Hysterical laughter almost overcame him. Once for yes, twice for no?

He caught Piper's eye. Intending to send the child a reassuring look, his eyes widened in amazement as the small boy gave him a wink and a grin.

With an insouciance that made Kelgan hold his breath for myriad reasons, the child began to swing—slowly at first, but gradually faster.

Seeing this Daliane rushed to the edge, slightly off-center so the Sorcerers had to turn in her direction, and cried, "You'll never get away with this. We'll stop you."

Looking almost as tiny as Piper, she drew their derisive laughter and their cruel taunts. Jorgo and Nadi, catching on, joined her and drew their swords, which they brandished in the air. By this time, Piper had reached a fair speed and a fair arc. On his back swing, he slipped his arms from their supposed tight hold. On the forward leg of the arc, he released his grip, his momentum carrying him across the divide. He somersaulted in the air and landed beside his astonished father.

The next thing Kelgan knew, Piper slapped his cheeks and implored, "Dad, Dad, wake up!"

He raised his head to see Neroma and Nevander straining at the lip of the abyss, rays of baleful light bouncing in the air in front of them. Assessing the situation, Kelgan jumped to his feet to try to pit his will alongside theirs.

Gaining strength, he managed to help them push the rays a bit in the direction of the attackers, but he knew they could not hold them off for long. Once again, Pelly stepped behind him, and his mother and father resumed their positions on either side. Once again, they raised their arms to his shoulders, and with a force that chilled the marrow in his bones, directed their combined hate through him.

With an audible snap, the rays rebounded to their source. Alarmed, the Sorcerers vanished.

Unnoticed in the melee, Cenci and Cal followed Piper's example, Cenci easily slipping her bonds, Cal struggling. She let go and hit the edge of the chasm. Teri clasped her twin in her arms, and they fell backward onto the floor of the hall.

Cal was still fighting to get his wrists out of the shackles. Kelgan, heart still in his mouth, painfully formed the word, *Invenirtu!*

Cal's flying legs hit him in the chest, knocking them both to the ground with an *Oof!*

"Thanks, old Buddy," Cal said when he could speak.

Still attempting to get air back in his lungs, Kelgan waved him off. When he finally felt the danger of never breathing again was behind him, he turned to thank Daliane for her brave pretense, only to find his heroine weeping in despair. Astonished for a moment, he quickly understood. The Baron had not been among his hanging companions, and still remained among the missing.

So! A hostage. His heart ached for Dally, who would know exactly what that might mean.

Daliane, with the will he found so admirable, clamped her mouth shut, drew a deep breath, and banished the tell-tale tears. Turning to Kelgan, she said with exaggerated calm, "All right, what now?"

Unable to stop himself, Kelgan swept her into his arms and held her as tightly as manners would allow.

She gave a soft murmur of laughter as she submitted to his embrace, then pushed him gently away.

"Thank you, my dearest brother."

Tears sprang to Kelgan's eyes at the compliment.

Belatedly answering her question, he had to admit he had no idea.

A brief chuckle. "I do like a man who knows his mind."

Once again, he was tempted to clasp her in his arms, telling her that it would be all right, not to worry, they would get the Baron safely back for her. Her seemingly unquenchable spirit filled him with admiration, but.... He sighed, knowing she would never accept empty promises, she knew just how empty they were.

Feeling like a failure before he started, he simply said, "We'll do our best, Dally."

Startling him with her force, she grabbed his face in both her hands, exclaiming, "Of course, you will! Do you think I have ever doubted you? You would fight for us to the end! Don't you know how much we believe in you?" Releasing his face, she fetched him a box on the ear that made his head ring.

Dazed, he watched her walk away, mortified to discover that the entire exchange had been observed by both Neroma and Cal. Both wore identical expressions of mingled compassion and amusement. Kelgan felt his skin might just peel off from the radiant burn of his visage. On the other hand, he felt a perverse indignation that there was not even the slightest hint of jealousy on Neroma's countenance.

Awfully sure of herself.... He stopped thinking in shock. *Mind control!* "Raise the wards," he shouted.

Neroma's eyes flew wide. Instantly, roses overwhelmed him. Slamming his own wards into place before he disgraced himself as the Mighty-Warrior-with-Asthma-Attack, he quickly declared to Cal and Neroma, "They're trying to get inside us."

Immediate understanding, to his relief.

"I fear Neroma and I became a bit negligent, my Mage." He had not heard Nevander's silent approach.

Kelgan clasped Nevander by the shoulder, "I think perhaps you had other things on your minds." *Such as saving some of our lives, maybe? Making me look stronger than I am?* "I don't fault you in the least, we know magic has limits. *I seem to have mine—I didn't even hear behind me.*

"Not so stringent that we fail to maintain protection." Nevander gestured with his head toward Ez and Bethne.

Kelgan drooped a bit, then gave himself a mental slap. *Darkness bite me! Did I think this was going to be just me being a hero—with a little help from the less-abled? They're really going to be less-abled if we don't remember the wards.*

"I'm more to blame than you are. I let mine completely drop. We're lucky we weren't all hanging over a pit."

That elicited a rueful chuckle from Nevander. "Let us all accept guilt, hang our heads for a moment, and then regroup."

Teri and Cenci sauntered up with Piper in tow. Observing their seemingly careless attitudes, he was actually relieved to hear Teri say, "Keeping our nephew with us this time." The anger in her eyes belied her near flirtatious hand on hip and coyly cocked head.

Piper's face was red, but he obviously enjoyed being the center of their attention.

Cenci added, "Well, as conquering armies go, I'd say that was kind of a standoff, but not much of a victory."

Kelgan closed his eyes and nodded. "And we are still missing the Baron, with no idea where he has been taken?'

"It might be off-world," Cal reminded him.

"Uhh," Kelgan groaned as though punched in the stomach. He had, for a time, forgotten that this was a battle of worlds, not of rival states. "And they're not even men."

"Well, not as we know them, but maybe on one of those other worlds life has taken a slightly different path. Those guys had most of the things we've got—arms, legs, eyes, noses—just something a bit off about their heads, teeth mostly, but something else, too...."

Kelgan stared, mouth agape. "When... when...." He started over in a whisper, "When I go, you go."

"Told you that."

"I didn't... I didn't."

"You didn't think I meant it."

"I...." Kelgan gave up there. Somehow, Pelly managed to include more than just Kelgan and himself. Or... he and Cal were so tied to each other, they were nearly one body and one mind. Either concept left him breathless.

"Cenci's right. That last 'plan' was somewhat lacking. The fact that it sort of succeeded was mainly luck—and Piper's talent as a trapeze performer."

Kelgan acknowledged the truth in Cal's assessment, then inquired with puzzlement, "What's a 'trapeze performer?'"

Cal swallowed his amusement before an entire field of daisies popped up, and just answered mildly, "Tell you later. Let's try for another plan."

"You might as well tell me now. I don't have another one."

Ez had come up behind them as they spoke. "Ant no use in making one, anyways. We's jes' gots to play it like it's dealed. Ant no tellin' what them buggers goin' to do. When they throws somethin' up, we knocks it down."

Both men regarded him with admiration. Kelgan's first impulse was to throw his arms around Ez and give him a resounding kiss, something he was sure he shouldn't follow up on, however.

"That's the spirit," enthused Cal.

"Well, do we wait for the next 'throw-up,' or do we search the castle for the Baron?"

Ez gave a throaty chuckle. "Wa'al," he drawled, "we sure can do both," giving Kelgan another one of those spine-bending back slaps.

Marveling once more at the elderly man's strength, he coughed out, "Good idea."

He mustered his troops. Putting Piper again in the goat cart with Bethne, he gave him the charge to "take care of her." Piper grinned with confidence.

Kelgan then looked to Ezrael.

"Ez, have you ever used a weapon?"

The old man's eyes twinkled. Raising his pantleg, he motioned downward. To Kelgan's utter amazement, strapped to a hairy and muscular calf, was a *really* impressive knife.

"Pretty good with a pikestaff, too," Ez said laconically. "Jes' waitin' for you to ask."

Struck dumb, Kelgan just stared, rousing himself only slightly when Cal inquired, "How's this for a staff?'

While Kelgan gaped, Cal had noted the crossed spears hanging on the throne room walls, appropriated one, and struck off the spearhead.

Ez hefted the spear-pole, twirled it, tested the balance and took a couple of lunges.

"Think this'll do, Son."

Kelgan continued to stare stupidly.

Ez elbowed his ribs and offered, "Soldier, afore Bethie."

Kelgan shut his jaw with a snap. "Of course," he muttered,

wondering if Bethne was going to pull a breastplate out of her bundle and declare herself pledged to Phosphene's army of woman warriors.

Turning to the others, he called for a vote. "Split up or stick together?"

As one, "Together."

"If we stay together, My Mage," opined Nevander, "we will know instantly if someone goes missing. If we are separated, we will know neither when nor where... or even who, for that matter. Together, we might discern a clue as to the method of appropriation."

In spite of the circumstances, Kelgan had to smother a smile at Nevander being Nevander. Nevertheless, he had to admit the possibility of learning something, however remote.

Glancing around, he marked the exits from the throne room. All accessible, since the pit had obligingly closed with the abrupt withdrawal of the Black Mages.

Knowing that people usually turned to their right, he had an instinctual feel that a move to the left might confuse their opponents—at least briefly. Shrugging, he nodded just slightly to the leftmost door, saying softly, "Let's take that one." Over the heads of the others, he caught Pellerin's eyes, vacant, no sign of the inner Pelly, but the head nodded equally imperceptibly just once, but decisively.

Weapons drawn, the party surrounded Bethne, Piper and the cart. Then, as if their heels had been set aflame, they made a Berserker's rush for the door.

··· 72 ···

We're not in Kansas, Toto

O nly to stop short in a befuddled muddle.
The other side of the door was not another room, or a
hallway, or even an abrupt drop to the moat. A vast dusty plain,
punctuated by strange, dark-foliaged trees bearing equally dark
fruits, spread before them. The castle no longer stood, forbidding,
behind them, only more of the plain. Distant spires spoke of
civilization; heat spoke of the two red suns shining dimly above their
heads; the dimness spoke of twilight, although the suns rode high.

"Portal," said Cal, "another world shift."

Kelgan looked back once more over the heads of the party. "You
knew, didn't you, Pelly? It's home." Not a question.

The momentary flame of Pellerin's eyes tacitly answered him.

"Whither away, My Mage?" inquired Nevander, ignoring the
byplay.

"Well, we can't conquer the sand, so we find the people, I guess."

Cal narrowed his eyes. "I've got a funny feeling."

Pellerin's eye swung from Kelgan to Cal and back again.

"Oh, Darkness frak it! Please say we don't *have* to conquer the
sand," Kelgan moaned. Sinking to the ground, he dropped his head
to his knees.

Teri and Cenci immediately flanked him. "We're with you, Kel,
if it takes every grain."

He looked up, the grim sincerity on their faces told him there
was no mockery in that promise.

Rising from the ground to his full height, he announced with a lot more confidence than he felt. "All right, my friends, we're going to have a laugh contest. Best gets an extra piece of whatever we have an extra piece of."

Laughter—somewhat forced—followed on the heels of that sally.

All of the party felt a slight shift in their surroundings.

"We'll guarantee a rabbit leg," put in Cenci.

"Reminds me of an old story," drawled Ez, 'bout catching yer rabbit first."

Chuckles, all around.

"I guess none of you mighty hunters noticed the rabbit tracks over there." Teri pointed. "Good thing you have 'girls' to take care of it, for you." She smirked.

More laughter, more odd shifts in the ambiance.

"Looks like it's the 'grainy' season," remarked Cal, the observation causing Daliane to bend over in a fit of giggles.

A ground-wrenching rumble, eliciting more than a few "eeks," sent a storm cloud of sand into the air, borne on an unholy wind. As the group strove to keep the particles out of lungs and eyes, another forbidding edifice sprang into view, *complete,* this time, with a terrifying army of "Not-men." The edifice was not a castle this time, but resembled a huge, windowless, cube. The presumed floors were marked by ledges, which jutted a short distance from the otherwise featureless façade. The troops, who stood in serried rows that made them appear as impregnable as the fortress behind them, were dressed in the familiar color scheme of red and black, but rather than the also familiar tunic and hose, wore close-fitting one-piece garments covering them from neck to ankle. They also had weapons—at least, Kelgan assumed the strange tube-like objects pointed toward his group to be somethings which could prove to be fatal.

Piper shrank behind Kelgan. "Light, keep us," he whispered.

Kelgan silently echoed that sentiment. Then an idea formed in his mind.

Turning to his party, he said just loudly enough for their ears,

"Back up just a bit, I'm going to try something. You might add a few prayers while you're backing up."

Jorgo and Nadi stepped forward, followed by Cal, the Terencias and Daliane. They formed a solid row. Only a step behind them stood Neroma and Nevander, Piper, Bethne and Ezrael.

"Not goin' anywhere." Ez raised his chin and pressed his lips together.

Kelgan's mouth dropped as Pellerin led his old mare around the group and stood to Kelgan's right. The mare showed the whites of her eyes, but planted her hooves firmly in her spot. The mules, with haughty sidelong glances at Kelgan, planted themselves just as firmly on his left. He looked back at them, to catch the nearest mule giving him an eyelash-fluttering wink.

"Uh... maybe we'd *all* better back up. I think I'm going to need a touch of room."

The small crowd obediently took three paces to the rear, as did he.

Reaching into the pack decorating the nearest mule, he took out a water flask. He heard an "Uh" from Cal, who obviously recognized it.

"*Respui pulvis! Toto!*"

Cal's face was a study in conflicting emotions. "You just said 'spit in the dust, Baby'... well, at least, you kinda said that."

Exasperated, Kelgan retorted, "I am requesting the river to restore itself, entirely, and I said nothing about a child."

"Uh, Toto means baby in one of our Earth languages."

Kelgan gave him a look, then pulled the stopper from the flask, flinging the dark water outward.

The ebony fluid hit the sand of the plain. To the horror of the assembled army of aliens, the waters rapidly rose around the first rows of troops, which sank as quickly and quietly as had the previous army. However, those farther back took to their heels, instantly, at the sight of a black lake rising from nowhere; then they, too, disappeared, with a barely discernible flash of light.

"Teleporter," Cal observed.

"Huh?"

"Transports people by taking their atoms apart and reassembling them at their destination. We don't have them yet, but we're working on it; there's a lot of sci-fi about them."

"Sci-fi?" Kelgan felt out of his depth.

"Science fiction. Stories about stuff that hasn't been invented yet."

"Ah, we can actually *do* that with magic."

"Same difference," was Cal's laconic reply.

Kelgan busied himself reversing the water spell and restoring the stoppered flask to the mule's pack. The mule nudged in exaggerated admiration, and gave a throaty bray.

"Thanks, I think."

Jorgo's rumble interrupted him. "That was most well done, my brother, but we have lost the element of surprise. We must keep careful watch on the mules."

Struck with dismay, Kelgan found himself throwing his arms around the neck of the mule in question, who responded with a startled snort, echoed by his partner.

"I will carry the water," he told the mule, "and make a show of taking it from you. That way we will protect you."

For the first time, he saw a virtually human expression steal over the mule's face, and was amazed to see actual tears come to its eyes. It laid its head on his shoulder and whuffled softly, in obvious affection. Then, to his disbelief, it pushed him a short distance away, and turned its head as far as possible over the pack. If it had said aloud, "I'm keeping the water," it could not have spoken more clearly.

Their rapport was broken by Jorgo's basso tones.

"I, too, have a funny feeling."

"Too easy," Cal, flatly.

"That is it."

"Drawing us out. Seeing what we've got—like they've been doing all along."

"As you say," Jorgo said somberly.

"Now they know we have a magic lake, and at least three really good magicians." Cal glanced at Piper with a smile. "Not to mention a young man with several talents."

"But not I," Pellerin's sepulchral monotone contained just a touch of humor.

After the first moment of surprise, Cal regarded him steadily, "You're absolutely right, Pelly. You're our ace in the hole."

"And Kelgan has one up his sleeve." The blank eyes bored into Cal's. "Or up yours."

Cal blinked several times, not only at Pellerin's knowledge of poker, but also at the double entendre of the phrase.

"More to you than meets the guise, Pel."

A momentary gleam of appreciation shone in the vacuous gaze.

Kelgan found himself struggling for breath. No one, with the possible exception of himself, not even Pellerin's parents, really knew who Pelly was. Cal had a hint, but the opposition had no idea that their supposed victim had come home as an odd country boy with an aging, sway-backed farm horse.

"They can't kill you again, Pelly," stating the obvious.

Pellerin rolled his eyes, for all the world like the teenager he seemed to be.

Cal and Jorgo both snorted.

Neroma stepped to his side. Kelgan started, for a moment he had actually forgotten her *How could I? She fills my every thought, even when I'm fighting, she's there.* He felt a pang of guilt overlaid with fright. *Are they taking my mind?*

She stared at him for a very long minute, then tendrils of her hair wove together and tapped his heart. Firmly. Others pulled his head toward her, and she whispered in his ear, "We are one, you do not need to *think* of me, since we are never parted."

Releasing him, she turned away.

"Uh, I kinda feel maybe we need to decide something."

The "army" was back. This time they were more prepared.

A concerted gasp arose from the little group, since one row of troops blinked into view directly behind Cal and another row behind the rest of the party.

The sword flashed at the end of Kelgan's arm. It whirled him in a frenzy into the bunch behind Cal, who was scarcely a step slower. Flailing right and left, without conscious volition, he hacked and hewed like a warrior-born.

Taken a tad by surprise at his seeming insanity, the "Not-men" took a beat or two to respond.

When they did it was with fury. The odd tube-like fired projectiles with precision. Evidently, they had not considered that such primitive folk might be a step ahead with protection. The projectiles bounced harmlessly off the field erected by Neroma and Nevander.

Only then did Kelgan think to slam wards in place around both himself and Cal.

The army vanished in another faint flash.

Cal stood, panting. "We've gotta take it to them, Kel; we can't keep playing defense. They're going to keep at it until they have us all figured out."

Kelgan faced the nearly featureless cube.

How do we get in? Hopeless, helpless—then he mentally smacked himself with a cooking pot. *I'm a mage!* When was he going to stop thinking like his stepfather, who, kindly as he was, possessed not a shred of magic.

He turned back to the expectant group.

"It's going to be a little tough, since I don't know the interior. We don't want to materialize inside...."

He felt his arm gripped in Pellerin's remorseless grasp.

A vision arose in this head—the alien workroom with its flashing lights and floating charts. Cal's indrawn breath told him he was not alone in the seeing.

Concentrating on each detail, he took in the set-up with care, looking for a convenient spot to deposit a dozen intruders, some fair-sized equines, and a goat complete with cart. At the same time, he tried to make sense out of the marvels contained there. What had Cal called it? Technology! Yes, but the results looked very similar to magical illusion. He knew he didn't have time to understand the principles involved, but if he could produce a convincing seeming, that might distract the opposition for at least a heartbeat or two. They had the brief advantage of surprise—not much, but valuable. Long enough, perhaps, to dispatch a few of the inhabitants.

His heart constricted at the ease with which he now contemplated taking lives, even those who were surely deserving. These were, after all, humans of a sort. Differing, to be sure, but flesh and blood, and just as surely with families.

On the other hand, he thought of the tiny bloodless bodies Pelly had revealed to him. No! Not humans, but monsters!

And what of those who were so easily suborned? Those dark Masters who were responsible for the enslavement of world after world! Wait! They *couldn't* be on every world—could they? Yet he had seen them in the tapestries Pelly had shown him, over and over, on his world, Pelly's, the world of Pelly's family, here. He pondered that puzzle. A seeming? Was that it? What lay underneath? Did it offer a puzzle piece to assist them?

His mind whirled. Grasping his thoughts firmly in a mental hand, he filed that piece away, with the rather pitiful collection of others they had amassed.

Amassed! That was a laugh.

He returned to the thought, giving it more careful attention. The Not-men—were they a seeming, as well, hiding something possibly even more terrible? Or something even less powerful then they? They appeared to be from the future, but as he had already noted, Cal said they had some of the same mysterious technology on his world, and he wasn't from the future. Was he?

Kelgan steered himself back to near sanity and contemplated Cal's information. He had dismissed it at the time, but now wondered if it gave them another tiny edge. Did Cal know anything about the structure of this technology? If so, could he reproduce it? The enemy would be expecting magic, obviously, since they had tested it from the first. They wouldn't expect a complete departure from business as usual.

He came to himself with a start. The group had gathered around him and regarded him with silent concern.

"Earth to Kelgan," Cal began sarcastically, then asked, "What *do* you call any of these planets?'

"Heimterr," came Pelly's monotone.

Cal flashed a glance at Kelgan. "Homeland."

"We call where we, that is, most of us, came from, Domoterra," Daliane spoke for the majority.

"Homeland, of course." Cal sighed, "We call our home, Earth or Terra. Just means land, but it's the same idea—looks like everywhere."

"Is that significant?" Daliane inquired.

"Well… you never know."

"Cal's right," Cenci interjected. "Everything we can know about those 'others' could be important."

Kelgan nodded in agreement. "I was thinking the same… well, sort of the same. Cal, you said your Terra had some of the same, uh, *machines,* that the Not-men had. Could you duplicate any of it?"

Cal shook his head in frustration. "Not anything that elaborate. I was in the Army for a while, Ordnance, I could probably offer you some bombardment."

"Bombardment."

"Blow them up."

A grin crept over Kelgan's face. "Blow them up."

Cal grinned back. "I think I could handle some really good Molotov cocktails."

"Eh?"

"Bottle, fuse, alcohol—light, throw."

Kelgan slapped his thigh in glee. "That's almost as good as my fireballs."

"Well," Cal hesitated, then said, "More unexpected, at least." He grinned again, "It's my version of the fireball. I might be able to put together something bigger, but I need some stuff I don't think we've got—length of tubing, for example, and *lots* of alcohol." He grimaced in frustration. "We've also got drones."

"Drones.'

"Yeah, like my machine, only small and able to fly. They can get in close and destroy from the air."

"You *do* remember I'm a mage?"

"You can make a flyer?"

Kelgan gave him a look. "Now, what's the tubing for?"

"Flamethrower. Needs guy with pump, however, that's the disadvantage—you stand out on the field—big target."

"I know the feeling."

Cal slapped his forehead. "Yeah, I keep forgetting."

"Alcohol, and lots of it."

"Yeah, is that even possible?"

"If I'm not mistaken, there's a settlement over there." Kelgan gestured vaguely to his right. "Either they have vineyards or a brewery, if I know settlements."

"Even in really small towns?"

"Then they'll have a tavern, with casks and kegs in storage."

"How do we ask for everything they've got?"

"My guess is, they would really like to get rid of the same people we would—if this is anything like the other worlds."

"So—we just walk in and say, 'We're here to save the world,' and they're just going to hand it all over?"

Kelgan shifted his feet uncomfortably. "Well... I haven't quite got my speech ready."

To Cal's amazement, Kelgan virtually gave the exact speech that Cal had derided. "We're going to fight the Magicians, and their black-and-red soldiers."

Yes, people looked dubious, until Kelgan gave a demonstration of obliterating a small stool in the tavern without harming anything else (and a careless rat which made the mistake of running in front of the stool).

They staggered back to their makeshift camp with arms laden with possibly useful items, while the publican's two sons strode behind rolling kegs.

At the quizzical looks from the waiting group, Cal offered, "He wanted us to have something left over to drink, too."

Laughter all around, even from Bethne.

Some Like it Hot

The work went swiftly. Two flame-throwers—in spite of the concerned voices, Ezrael insisted on being one of the carriers. "Cain't do better, I jes' stand and let 'er rip."

And two drones. Cal looked far from satisfied, but Kelgan assured him they would work for recon, as well as something else. He refused to explain the something.

"Crows, you want to use *crows?*"

"They're smart, and I've placed a homing spell on them."

"What's the plan?"

"Don't have one."

Cal groaned. "It's going to be like the tavern owner. We just walk in and say, 'We're back to save the world.'"

"Yep."

❖

Cal shook his head in wonder. "They even shook our hands."

Kelgan repressed a giggle. "Just a touch of persuasion."

"You spelled them."

"As I said, just a touch."

"I keep forgetting you're not me."

Kelgan eyed him quizzically. "That was an 'interesting' thing to say."

Cal shifted his feet, looking uncomfortable. "Let's get busy."

Laden with their hastily assembled equipment, they rejoined the rest of the group, who paid them no attention. So busy with their toys, the two had completely missed the combined outward gaze of the others. Turning their heads, they followed the line of sight and drew in simultaneous breaths. The enemy, who had evidently watched all, was well ahead of them. The red-and-black army stood at the ready—seeming to number in the thousands. Knowing that could simply be illusion did not reassure them. At the forefront hovered the sorcerers, wearing robes that trailed off behind them into mist and gave them the appearance of black thunderclouds. Kelgan was sure *that* was no illusion.

"Uh," he said stupidly.

Only Neroma responded, swinging her head in their direction just a bit. "They wait."

The fur of her voice blanketed him for a moment, leaving him short of breath.

He shook his head to clear it, saying, "Well, let's not disappoint them."

Without another word, he directed a concentrated blast of energy to the first rows of the army. *Those* turned out to be real, at least, as they transmogrified into twinkling atoms, which then fell like raindrops onto the now-scorched earth.

A gasp arose from the facing soldiers. For a moment, they quailed visibly. The brief flash of triumph Kelgan allowed himself was cut short by the nearly instantaneous return blast from the younger sorcerer.

Even aided by Neroma and Nevander, Kelgan barely managed to divert the energy back onto the facing army, thereby taking out another two or three rows.

No time to be cocky, he thought, *that was nearly fatal.*

He fired off another blast. This time the opposition was ready—as one, the soldiers dropped to their knees, and the energy sailed over their heads to knock off a corner of the gloomy castle.

However, they failed to notice Cal, who was now in command of his deadly flamethrower. A low charge, directed just above the ground, caught the red-and-blackers by another unpleasant surprise. Closing his eyes to the charred corpses that now littered the ground, he paused only when he had to refuel.

Too easy, again, too easy, too easy, beat in Kelgan's head like a drum solo. He glanced behind him. Ez was slumped over the now empty goat-cart, and Teri was staring in horror at the now empty uniform of her sister, Cenci.

His eyes met Pelly's, and a scream of outrage erupted from his throat. Once again, the berserker overtook him and he whipped the sword out of its sheath, and took off. Pellerin followed, sweeping him onto his horse's back, the Mel'hachim after him, and Daliane following suit as she swept up Teri with astonishing strength.

Piper pounded Ezrael's back. "C'mon, c'mon, we gots to keep up."

Ez raised his head, one look and he had Piper and himself in the goat cart, and was prodding an amazed Capriola to gallop after them. The mules gave the cart a forceful push, and took off in the direction of the crazed bunch.

Kelgan forgot magic, slaughtering everyone he could reach with the sword, which had taken on a fierce, white light. The sorcerers, taken by surprise, forgot for a wide-eyed period that they, too, could do magic. They came to themselves, quickly, however, and unleashed a volley of fireballs at the on-comers.

Cal, in the meantime, had refueled and was searing the flanks of the opponents, as well as, to his delight, shooting down the fireballs. Then, suddenly, he vanished in a blaze of flames, which resulted in a pain so searing in Kelgan's chest, his sword arm faltered. Only Pelly's onward rush saved them. They reached the drawbridge to the castle, having charged all the way through the black-and-red ranks, and turned to confront. *Well,* thought Kelgan, *a rearguard action.* Thinking he had been hit, he examined his chest for the source of the pain—only then did he realize the enormity of his loss.

He whispered Cal's name, unable to speak it aloud. Again, the sword made his decisions for him, and the enemy realized where they were at risk. He hewed and hacked automatically, holding them at bay while he reached into himself for the greatest spell he hoped he could conjure. The castle behind him creaked and groaned, as pieces began to break off and fly toward his hated foe.

The sorcerers, made aware of what was happening to their edifice, were distracted by the flying masonry and kept busy deflecting the fragments from their army. In the confusion, Nevander and Neroma, with Piper in her arms, managed to sneak around the melee and come up on his side. They were silent, awareness in their eyes, but he felt the force of the twins' combined magic allied with his own. Even Piper's little brow furrowed in concentration. Kelgan's heart swelled with love at the sight.

The castle continued to explode outward as he relied on the twins' ability to keep the spell going, while he just had a little word with those fellows in the air. *Too easy, too easy,* the drumbeat continued in his head.

He knew why in short order. First Teri, then Jorgo, then Ez, vanished without a sound or a flash. One minute there, the next only a vacant space where they had stood. Heartsick, he dropped to his knees in near despair. They returned, including Cenci and Bethne. Just as Pelly's wife and children, they were white husks, drained of every drop of blood, as they lay before him.

An indescribable sound came from Daliane as the Baron was the last to join the dead. She stood her ground, however, her courage matching any hero of history. Kelgan turned to Pellerin, Pelly returned his gaze, and a wondrous thing occurred, Pelly walked to where his mother and father lay, and then his body dropped down beside them, while simultaneously the Baron rose from his spot, moved awkwardly to Daliane and kissed her forehead. Looking long and deeply into her eyes, he stared until she finally acknowledged him with a nod.

"I understand," she said simply, then she put her arms around him and gave him a fierce hug. Stepping back, she nodded again and turned away.

"Pelly... T'Jules..." Kelgan began. "Confound it, what *is* your name?"

The newly occupied Baron managed a rueful smile. Bending, he traced in the dirt, *I am Aswain—call me what you prefer, I hope it will be friend.*

"Aswain," Kelgan tested the name, "what now?" He heard his voice break, but was unable to control it.

The Baron/Aswain looked to the hovering sorcerers, still deflecting the aviating masonry, and back to Kelgan. Holding up his right hand, he captured Kelgan's attention. Forming a ball of lightning, he whirled and struck one of the magicians in the shoulder, tearing off his arm, and leaving the recipient gaping.

Not for long, however. The arm regrew, to Kelgan's horror, and the sorcerer let fly with a flaming orb of his own. Kelgan got the intended message, instantly. Seemings! Not there at all. He cocked his head in the direction of the not-yet completely derelict castle. Aswain bowed.

He turned to his decimated and devastated comrades. "One last rush, into the castle—uh, what's left. This is Aswain, by the way."

Tears came to his eyes as, one by one, they gravely shook what had been the Baron's hand, and expressed their pleasure at meeting him. He would have sworn he could see tears in the eyes of Aswain, as well.

"Let's go, Kel," said Daliane. No tears in her eyes.

Neroma was undoing her long belt. "You will be with me," she told Piper. "I am tying you to me. We will go together." Stooping, she waited for Piper to climb to her shoulders, then secured him with the belt.

"I'm ready, Mom," he responded.

She flashed Kelgan a look. "My son and I are prepared to follow his father." Her tone was sober, but her expression held amusement.

And then the world went white....

The sleepy chirping of the birds settling for the night woke him with a start as he realized the lateness of the evening hour. For a moment, he hated them....

Too clever! No, never! Too hard! Much, much, too easy! Too long! Never too long!!

Sitting up with a gasp that was nearly a scream, Kelgan rolled over the side of his cot and staggered to the small wash stand with its apologetic mirror. He surveyed his white-haired, lined reflection with horror. It regarded him in the same manner. Then the vision faded to the familiar snub-nosed, sandy-haired reflection to which he was accustomed.

Sinking to his knees, he buried his face in his hands to await the inexorable knock on the door.

NIGHTMASTERS

BOOK TWO ⋯ CHANGE OF ENGAGEMENT

The voices came, night after night. *"Too much." "Too little." "Too soon." "Too late." "Too few." "Too many."* Then came the laughter, one high and mocking, one low and scornful.

The voices faded with the dawn. An hour of blessed sleep ensued before he rose to begin another round of the day's obligations. This day, unable to keep his eyelids from drooping shut during his late afternoon tutoring session, he cut short his surprised pupil in the middle of an illusion. Muttering a feeble excuse, he hastened back to his room for an illicit nap. The sleepy chirping of birds settling in for the night startled him awake. He realized the lateness of the evening hour. For a moment he hated them, then he felt ashamed. They happily twittered, glad of every day. *So should I be. Am I not doing what I have always wished for?* So, *should* he be, but, of late, was not.

With a groan he rolled over the side of his cot and staggered to the small washstand with its apologetic mirror, Kelgan Defthand, Senior Apprentice Mage. Jokes about "SAMs" abounded among the lower classmen. He surveyed his hollow-eyed reflection with disfavor—*really, really, looking tired.* It soberly regarded him in return—a snub nose, a wiry crop of sandy curls, indeterminate hazel eyes. *Not exactly impressive.* Only his lanky height set him apart from the crowd....

Then, realization hit him. Sinking to the floor in an agony of despair, memory smote him like an icy blast from the East wind. Again! It happens again!

The knock came, as expected, sounding on the wood panels like the barking of a hound.

A bark from the Dark, Kelgan thought, remaining on the floor.

The lower classman, who had been most reluctant when pressed into summons service, must have decided that the renowned (or perhaps infamous) Kelgan Defthand wasn't within. Now, he could look as though he wasn't the least bit cowed by the Senior Apprentice and therefore pursued his errand assiduously. The knock sounded again, more confidently this time, not the hesitant tap as at first.

Wham! Wham! Wham!

Laughing sourly, Kelgan rose to answer. Regaining his feet from his kneeling position, he threw open the door. The resultant crash, as it rebounded from the jamb, plus Kelgan's glare as he confronted the boy, sent the astonished and terrified Junior to his knees.

"Ll—l—l—lost my eyeglasses." The Junior groped around the step. "Ah, th—th—there they are."

Grasping his dignity with shaking hands, the youngster gasped, "M—m—m—master Sargal c—c—c—c—called m—m—m—me to fetch you."

Kelgan cocked his head at the Junior. Feeling a pang of shame at the extreme discomfort exhibited by the boy, he temporized, "I crave your pardon. I stumbled over a carelessly placed object and hit the door with more force than necessary. I'm afraid you got caught in the annoyance of a stubbed toe."

The boy looked even more astonished, if possible. His stammer became even more pronounced. "Oh, n—n—n—no, m—m—m—my apologies, I disturbed y—y—y—y—you."

Kelgan gave the Junior a reassuring pat. "Nonsense—accompany me to the Master's apartments." All the while his heart was pounding in his chest faster than the boy's stutter. The words from the boy were different this time! What did that mean? Was there an alteration in the chain of events? Kelgan clutched at that hope like a drowning man clutches at a floating reed.

At Kelgan's invitation, the junior acquiesced with something like terror in his eyes.

Have I become so fearsome? Another pang.

He gave the boy a second pat. "Here we go," he exclaimed with forced joviality.

As they ventured forth into the driving rain (Driving! Again, a difference! Not the few threatening drops but a deluge), Kelgan threw his cloak around the Junior, who had instantly assumed the appearance of a drowned sparrow. At this action, the boy's knees buckled and Kelgan was forced to hurriedly drop the cloak and grab the Junior.

"You are going to catch your death. Better that you return to the dormitory, than going on with me through the wet."

The boy gave Kelgan a look of such relief that Kelgan searched his memory for any action of his that could account for the youngster's fear. *Surely, I wasn't THAT much of an ogre?*

Releasing the boy, Kelgan watched him scurry off for all the world like a field-mouse released from a trap.

Shaking his head, he continued on to Sargal's private lair.

Entering the cluttered apartment after Sargal's querulous summons to "Come in." Kelgan saw the usual (oh, so usual!) scene of a chaos of papers, books, mysterious vessels filled with equally mysterious substances, and the expected group of visitors. There was that same sense of shock at seeing armed retainers on the Academy grounds. The familiar (Kelgan's chest convulsed) mixture of feelings when he first laid eyes on Neroma di Nerrill, and the familiar feeling of mistrust where her brother, Nevander, was concerned.

Just then, that enigmatic brother, Nevander, turned toward him, with what Kelgan was sure was *his own* identical expression of despair and resignation, and gave just the barest of nods. Then he turned his back and resumed regarding the fireplace, as he had been when Kelgan made his entrance. Kelgan's heart gave another lurch. That too, was different! Seeing him standing with mouth agape, Sargal ordered, "Stop gawking," shaking Kelgan from his semi-trance.

What ensued, however, was the dismal repetition of the—how many other times? Kelgan had lost count. All, he was sure, would end with the same blazing whiteness that resolved itself into the whiteness of his sheets.

They rode out into the night and the still driving rain. The same group, Kelgan, the aristocratic di Nerrill twins, Nevander and Neroma, their handmaid (?), two armed retainers, and the same sense of futility.

They had almost reached the Keep, as always, when Kelgan gave the short laugh he had given every time when he had found himself dozing off. Nevander rode up beside him with the same sarcastic jab at his "ability to sleep anywhere," and Kelgan opened his mouth to make the same retort. "Sorry, milord, I was just hoping to get out of this pea soup and into some real pea soup." Struck by a thought mid-sentence, he revised his response to offer "potato soup," instead of the usual pea. Nevander's hand encircled Kelgan's forearm in a grip which threatened Kelgan's circulation, and responded, "A sense of humor is always welcome on nights like this."

The night then went as before—the trip up to Nevander's room, the scented, playing fountain which cloaked their words. Then! The sight of Neroma framed in the doorway, backlighted like a statue of the Goddess froze the words on his lips.

His heart shivering into a thousand pieces and not even knowing what he did, Kelgan held out his arms. She stood, poised in indecision, every tendril of her searching hair pointing toward him, and then she was in his embrace being crushed against him. He pressed kisses on her lips, eyes, throat, feeling the pounding of her heart against his.

Nevander gave a slight cough and turned away, busying himself with some activity near the fountain. Finally, he remarked firmly, "I think it best we go down to the Hall."

Kelgan gave a start, staring wildly. Neroma was still framed in the doorway, her hair rising like little questions marks haloing her head. Their reunion had been only illusion, not reality. Yet... Yet! This had never happened before!

Neroma stepped forward into the room. With a curious look at Kelgan, she agreed with her brother, in that velvety contralto that so matched the ebony of her hair. "Yes, that is what I came to say."

In silent answer to Kelgan's questioning gaze, Nevander again gave that bare hint of a nod. Whether an answer to his silent query, or an answer to something else, Kelgan did not know.

In the Great Hall, all went as before. Kelgan found himself compelled to repeat his every word and action, even though he strove with every fragment of his being to change just the slightest of them. Returning to the comfortable chamber provided by the Twins, discouraged and weary, he fell on the bed wrapped in a cloak of depression. Expecting to lie awake in misery, he remembered nothing until the cock woke him with the dawn.

In the morning, the well-remembered clothing was laid out for him, their gay turquoise and salmon colors bright. The remembered device was worked on the front of the tunic. And... The sword! It wasn't time for that! The sword stood jauntily upright next to the clothing with a note attached which read "No need for trying."

Kelgan fell to his knees and rested his head against the sheath. Cool beneath his forehead, it brought back a measure of sanity, which Kelgan felt was slipping away. Raising his head, he pondered the meaning of the changes, which seemed to come randomly, but only occasionally under his control. Or possibly, not even then. The alterations appeared to be dictated from without, sometimes allowing, sometimes refusing.

Would they, in the end, allow?

Acknowledgments

Writing is easy. You sit at the computer and your thoughts get translated into a story. *Then* you look for someone to appreciate your story. *If* you are lucky enough to find one, you are introduced to a whole new world of *publishing*. One can only hope to find a group of people as congenial, helpful, and welcoming as those at Acorn Publishing. My profound thanks go especially to Holly Youmans and Jessica Therrien for their guidance every step of the way; Laura Taylor for not only her excellent (and gentle) content editing, but also her kindness and belief in *Nightmasters,* and her glowing testimonial; Debra Kennedy, my careful line editor; and the talented cover artists at Damonza. My friend Laura Perkins, whose initial suggestions for Kelgan and his crew tightened the sprawling narrative into a readable one.

My gratitude to my husband, as well. He has been more than patient with the process of getting Kelgan and his companions launched into the world. and has been transformed into a sort of proud papa with a new baby.

My family, who have heard about Mom's writing until they're cross-eyed trying not to sigh in exasperation. And my friends, who are waiting to hear that it's *finally* done.

To you all, this is for you.

Loran Holt. 2020

www.ingramcontent.com/pod-product-compliance
Lightning Source LLC
Chambersburg PA
CBHW020504260626
47156CB00006B/1852